An Uncivil War

A sequel to *The 9th District*

An Uncivil War
GILLIAN LONG © 2026
All rights reserved.

This novel is a work of fiction. No part should imply that the events and characters occurring in this story are real people or actual events, other than that conceived in the author's imagination. Where real organisations, people, places, and events are referenced, their activities and interactions are imagined through a fictional lens for dramatization purposes.

This book has not drawn on Artificial Intelligence (A.I.) in any shape or form. Any portion of the text thereof may not be reproduced or used in any manner, including for training A.I., without the express written permission of the author.

First Published, 2026
Print ISBN: 978-1-7638041-2-8
Print ISBN: 978-1-7638041-4-2
Ebook ISBN: 978-1-7638041-3-5
Ebook ISBN: 978-1-7638041-6-6

Millaa House Publishing
PO Box 89
Millaa Millaa,
Queensland 4886

*"History repeats itself,
first as tragedy, second as farce"*
Karl Marx, The Eighteenth Brumaire of Louis Bonaparte.

Also, by Gillian Long

A Wilderness of Mirrors
The 9th District
(Book 1 in the Mark Anders series)
Greenwash
Becoming Helen
The Trouble with Maggie
Watershed
Dying Days

Contents

Author's Note

The Spanish Civil War (1936–1939) was fought between two main coalitions, the Republicans and the Nationalists, each composed of various political and social groups with often conflicting ideologies. (see table overleaf.)

In researching this novel I am indebted to multiple historical sources, most particularly Sir Paul Preston CBE, Hugh Thomas, Antony Beever, old newspapers, Warwick Digital Collections, and the British Hansard from the period.

The Republicans	The Nationalists
The Loyalists, affiliates and members of the legitimate Government, also called "the Reds," by their enemies, supported the democratically elected government of the Second Spanish Republic	The Rebels or Insurgents or Francoists also called "the Fascists," by their enemies, consisted of right-wing groups that launched the July 1936 coup attempt.
Political Groups:	
The Popular Front: A broad coalition of left-wing parties including the Spanish Socialist Workers' Party (PSOE) and the Communist Party of Spain (PCE).	The Military: Led by General Francisco Franco, after the death of General Molo. It included the elite Army of Africa.
Anarchists: Militants from the CNT (National Confederation of Labour) and FAI (Iberian Anarchist Federation) who sought social revolution alongside the war.	Falange: The Spanish fascist party, which became the sole legal party after the war. Monarchists: Split between "Alfonsists" (who wanted King Alfonso XIII back) and "Carlists" (ultra-traditionalist Catholics also called the red caps).
Regional groups: Basque and Catalan separatists who supported the Republic in exchange for greater autonomy. Anti-Stalinist Marxists: The POUM (Workers' Party of Marxist Unification), famously joined by author George Orwell.	The Catholic Church: Supported the Nationalists as a "crusade" against "godless" communism.

The Republicans	The Nationalists
International Support:	
The Soviet Union: Provided tanks, aircraft, and advisors in exchange for Spanish gold. Mexico: Offered moral support and limited military supplies. International Brigades: Roughly 40,000 volunteers from 50+ countries including the British Brigade.	Nazi Germany: Provided the Condor Legion (air support) and used Spain as a testing ground for WWII tactics. Fascist Italy: Sent roughly 75,000 troops and significant naval/air assistance. Portugal: Provided logistical support and thousands of "Viriatos" volunteers.
The Republicans lost the war with casualties estimated to be in the several hundreds of thousands.	The Nationalists won the war in 1939, leading to a nearly 40-year dictatorship under Franco.

Bilbao, Spain, 1937

The state of war is a state of enmity and destruction.

John Locke.

From his position on the side of a rocky outcrop, Javier pressed the field glasses to his eyes, squinted, adjusted the focus, and tried again. The usual fragrances of sea air and pines were swamped by the acrid smell of explosives and dust. His face was caked with the stuff.

The lenses magnified his view sixfold as he raked the valley running the length of the south-eastern flank. The cratered and burnt farmland between him and the line of hills to the northeast, came courtesy of the rebels' heavy artillery and bombing raids.

All yesterday, and the weeks before that, Italian and German planes had unleashed their destruction over the line of defence

1

fortifications the Basques called the Iron Ring, while Franco's troops let loose their Krupps guns.

The Iron Ring, a system of secret fortifications, began near the coastal town of Gorliz to the northeast. It tracked along the Bizkargi Range as far south as Galdacano and Miravelles before heading towards the coast west of Bilbao. Javier's commander boasted of the ring's impregnable power to hold the enemy at bay.

Bilbao's saviour, he'd claimed!

Behind the Iron Ring the Basque Army would keep the regional capital and its citizens safe. Although it seemed no one had counted on the rebel aircraft bombing with such uncanny accuracy. Uncanny, unless a traitor lurked in their midst.

Now, the iron defences were weak, and the Basque Army braced for an assault by the rebels' shock troops. They were sure to aim for the heights along Bilbao's eastern flank, but the Basque front-line defence stood at readiness.

Javier had a recurring premonition this battle would be his last, but he pushed it down to focus on the destroyed and silent valley. Other than a bewildered cow, only the broken shells of buildings remained. He felt a surge of kinship with the bovine, for like it, he'd been lucky up until now.

Most of his comrades, some of his cousins and many of his uncles were dead. He had no idea where his cousin Carmen was. She had been instrumental in his volunteering, and he'd last seen her when he had first arrived in Bilbao. Was that only January this year? It seemed like he'd been fighting this war for a lifetime.

Somewhere down there, Franco had positioned his rebel troops. Yet although Javier scrutinised the desiccated pine covered hills and valley for a sign, he saw nothing other than trees and rocky crags.

The familiar drone of planes flying in formation, sounded in the distance. He turned the field glasses to the southeast, and there they were, speckling the hazy sky. More than yesterday. Maybe two hundred.

Unlike the sporadic bombings of the weeks before, the latest wave of intensive, and systematic attacks had lasted for three days. It must mean this battle would be something more than the earlier skirmishes. Initially, the Basque air defences fought off the invaders, but the few biplanes they had left were no match for the sophisticated German fighters.

Two days earlier, the last of the heroic but suicidal attempts by Basque airmen were swatted down by a Messerschmitt Bf 109 as if they were annoying gnats. Today's assault would fly through undefended skies. The enemy might as well have left the Messerschmitt fighters at home. They would not be needed to guard the bombers' flanks today. Instead, Javier knew from bitter experience, those Messerschmitts would deploy their machine guns to mow down soldiers and fleeing civilians on the ground.

One by one the bombers unleashed their loads, a combination of missiles and drums of fuel. The lethal dominoes fell through the air with only seconds between each, landing in a line across the tinder-dry forest. The explosions resonated through the ground beneath his belly before a whoosh of flames leapt into the sky as the oil drums ignited and set off a conflagration.

Minutes later, a massive fire front raced south ahead of the prevailing winds. Soon, smoke obliterated the hillside. Those poor bastards at the front. The fire gobbled up the land, exploding pine trees and rocks, ripping across gullies as the northerly wind drove it southwest toward his position. He coughed and rubbed his stinging eyes.

A few minutes later a new bombardment began. It came from the rebels' heavy artillery across the valley. Their aim seemed to be focussed on the same section the planes had just bombed.

The air squadron veered off to the east. The field artillery fell silent, and the smoke began to clear. He trained his glasses on the area. This was where the shock troops would pass, not where they had anticipated. He moved his focus to the pall of smoke, which had shifted to show a clear patch beyond.

The fearsome Africa Army filled his vision.

He pointed. His sergeant nodded, called an order, and shifted his aim. The backup line would have to hold the advance.

Javier, checked his rifle as the rebels swarmed towards them, led by veterans of the Riffian Wars, more in number than he thought possible. Behind them rumbled tanks. He squinted against the smoke and took careful aim. Every bullet would have to count, but he had nothing to penetrate the tanks' armour.

Hendaye, France

Several months earlier...

The insurgents' planes rose above Spain's Jaizkibel Mountain Range. Their tumbling loads mere fly specs splattered against a cloudy pane. From this distance the sounds were muted, but still, Mark fancied he could feel the earth shaking as the evil slugs left tiny mushroom plumes in their wake.

Somewhere out there, Javier fought for the Republic—if he had survived amid all that carnage. But Javier had chosen his fate, and while it would be great to meet up again, Mark hadn't come all this way to rescue him.

In fact, he wasn't there to rescue anyone. Instead, he intended to expose the greed and corruption, in the pursuit of power, that inflicted war on its victims. Although how he might do that, stuck on the French side of the border, seemed a problem beyond his ability to solve.

He tightened his grip on the binoculars as he studied the hilly terrain across the river where the occupied Spanish town of Hondarribia lay. On this side of the river, only the distant shrieks of children playing, the slam of a taxi door, and the caustic wit traded between men and women of the press standing, like him alongside the shore, disturbed the peace.

A boat chugged past heading towards the Bidasoa River mouth, leaving in its wake the gentle slap of water against the boardwalk. A waft of the morning's catch filled Mark's senses as the breeze tugged at his jacket and threatened to lift the Fedora from his head. The hat had once belonged to a friend; the jacket, he'd bought second hand in a London market. Only the Leica camera, hanging from his shoulder by a canvas strap, was new.

Gulls dive-bombed the boat with a grace Mark could only envy. Oh, to have wings to fly like that. He swallowed a lump of unease. The pastries he'd eaten for breakfast or a sense of his own inadequacy, maybe guilt, he didn't know. Yet remaining safe in one place while, somewhere beyond your vision, terror and destruction rained from the sky, made for an eerie and uncomfortable reality.

He refocused his attention. The planes were too far away to see their markings, even through binoculars. Whether they wore the insignia of the Spanish military rebels, or the broken crosses of the German Condor Legion, or the Italian roundels, he couldn't tell. One thing he did know, they were killing innocent civilians, dropping bombs indiscriminately in a terror never before witnessed in the history of humanity's desire to wreak destruction on their enemies.

He had to find a way to make the world sit up and take notice—to stop the invasion of a democratic country and halt the slaughter of innocents. Surely, no one who witnessed such cruelty could remain impartial.

'Are you planning on hogging those glasses for the duration?'

Mark lowered the binoculars and turned to his companion. He'd met the man at breakfast when he'd walked, or rather swaggered, into the hotel's dining room dressed in, he had informed Mark later, a Lovat Green Glen Urquhart suit.

Mark didn't care; didn't know the names of fashion houses, but he had been interested in the man, who had made his way through the dining room, stopping to speak to several other journalists before sitting down at Mark's table, uninvited.

He demanded to know if Mark might be the newly arrived Australian reporter, and introduced himself as Charles West, a fellow Australian, working for *The Times*.

Mark had inhaled his coffee.

Charles had banged him on the back, making it all the more difficult to draw a breath and leaving him mortified by the undignified display.

After he had recovered, he merely introduced himself by name, saying nothing of knowing Charles's family.

Now, Mark held out the binoculars 'Can you make out the planes' markings?'

Instead of taking them, Charles lifted his Panama to a woman walking a small dog along the promenade. She nodded, and he ran his hand over short blond hair, slick with pomade, as he gazed after her. She crossed the road and soon disappeared from their sight.

Charles replaced his hat and took out a sleek gold cigarette case to offer it to Mark.'

Mark shook his head.

After Charles lit a cigarette, he inhaled deeply before blowing out a stream of smoke. Only then did he reach for the field glasses. 'Let's see about these planes then.'

The aircraft had all but disappeared, but then Charles seemed impervious to any sense of urgency. Earlier, he'd shown Mark the spot along the Boulevard de la Baie de Chingudy, where reporters came daily to track the progress of the Spanish civil war. Afterwards, he had suggested, they might try a spot of sea bathing, then lunch, followed by a siesta.

Even without the field glasses, Mark's keen eyes could see quite clearly across the bay, the Spanish town so close he could have swum across the estuary to reach it. But what could he do in a town crawling with Nationalist troops and him without a guide or a visa? That would be madness in the middle of a civil war. Yet remaining so far from the front line left him unable to capture a fraction of the terror on film.

Charles said, 'Tell me, have you heard what the hell is going on in Barcelona?'

Mark lifted the Leica and focussed on his fellow journalists. 'You mean the stoush over the control of the borders?'

'Is that what it is?'

Mark lowered the camera and frowned. 'I read the CNT union is calling for a general strike if the Republican government tries to take away their authority to control Catalonian borders. Why? What do you think is going on?'

Charles shrugged. 'I might head on down that way to find out. What do you say?'

Mark shook his head. 'Had my heart set on getting into the Basque country, but hell, it seems impossible.' The beguiling idea of photographing Javier with the Basque Army, stayed with him. The blokes at home would love it. One of their own, confronting the fascists.

Charles nodded. 'It's almost impossible now.'

'Didn't you say you did a tour?'

'Ah.' Charles sighed and gazed towards the river mouth. 'Last year, when this fracas blew up, I had a short stint in Bilbao. Then the press had some freedom. Now of course, with the blockade and the Nationalists occupation of the border towns in the north, it is trickier. You need a visa from the occupying army. They are not keen on the press... unless of course you have the right contacts. Without a visa, you won't get into their territory from here and you can't get in by sea.' Charles examined Mark. 'You're new to this game, aren't you?'

Mark shifted his feet, weighing up truth, lies and consequences before saying, 'This is my first reporting job.'

Charles chuckled. 'I guessed as much, but everyone must start somewhere. Look, Sir Henry is having some expatriates to lunch. Why don't you come along? You'll meet people who know about these things, and you can hear it firsthand. If Major Troncoso Sagredo is there, you might even wrangle a press pass into the Nationalist held territory.'

'Who's he?'

'The governor of Irún. But you'll need to show a commission from a paper they think suitable. As I said the press, particularly freelancers, aren't that welcome in the North.'

Mark waited, not willing to admit he didn't have a commission.

Charles seemed to read his silence. 'I take it you are freelance. In that case it's easier to get into Barcelona, more welcoming of the press so long as they reproduce the Red propaganda spewed out by the Republicans or at least pretend to.'

Mark scanned the far bank of the river as the image of Javier, posing in front of his comrades, fragmented. So much for getting into the north. Although perhaps if he could meet Major Troncoso, he might be persuaded to help with a visa. Or at least point Mark in the right direction. So long as the Irún governor didn't discern Mark's real agenda.

London

Beatrice stood in the entrance hall of the Pimlico house and buttoned her maroon leather gloves. Her low heels sunk into the Aubusson carpet covering the glossy walnut floor. Overhead a crystal chandelier lit the room and behind her a staircase swept upwards carrying the same pale-floral Aubusson design with it; her mother's latest efforts at modernising her grandfather's home.

Grandfather favoured the original wooden boards, yet, ever the diplomat, he kept his council. So now, most of the room bore her mother's compulsive upgrades although the plaster roses on the soaring ceilings and the stained-glass transoms still bore the marks of the Edwardian era of her grandparents' day.

Her mother, Lady Margaret, in Coco Chanel tweed, pearls, and twinset, stood arms held out either side of her body as if to bar her daughter's way. Beatrice turned away, to examine herself in a hall mirror lit by a deco styled lamp. The light globe, held aloft by a bronzed and turbaned child, reflected Margaret's nostalgia for empire.

Of course, Beatrice could say none of that, although she sometimes wondered if Margaret regretted the abolition of child labour. 'I'm going Mother, whether you agree or not.' She adjusted her maroon cloche hat. 'I would like your blessing but if not,' Beatrice shrugged, 'I'm still going. They need all the help they can get.'

'It's completely scandalous. My daughter hobnobbing with labourers and other riffraff. I thought you had learned your lesson after that awful debacle in Australia.' Lady Margaret clasped her bejewelled fingers. 'You shamed your uncle and aunt and mortified your father...'

Beatrice intervened before her mother could dredge up all her past misdemeanours. 'They are not labourers and riffraff Mother. They are Members of Parliament, publishers and writers.'

'What do you know about politics and publishing?'

'Oh mother, I explained. It's about fund raising. If you would consider it I could use your charity to raise...

'Absolutely not! I will not have my charity sullied by socialists.'

'They are not socialists, or at least not many of them. Mr Grenfell is Labour, Mr Roberts is Liberal, Eleanor Rathbone is Independent, and Mr Macnamara is a Conservative. They are a committee of humanitarian conviction. They simply coordinate all the work undertaken by different groups to help the Spanish people, mostly medical aid and evacuating women and children. Their mission is to help the refugees. And really, the children particularly, need help desperately. The committee is lobbying the government to allow them into Britain temporarily.'

Beatrice glanced once more into the mirror and straightened the nipped-in-the-waist, green velvet jacket. Did it jangle too violently with the maroon hat and skirt? 'If you will not let me join you in your charitable endeavours, I will just have to set up my own.'

'To fund-raise in a townhall! Mixing with the hoi polloi, trade unionist, anarchists and socialists and goodness knows what else... In your position, you simply cannot be seen in that company. I forbid it.'

Beatrice said in her most soothing manner. 'Dear Mother, I will be safe. Besides my independence allows...'

'That was a mistake.' Margaret placed one hand on her narrow hip and glowered.

'A mistake!'

'You have no experience and your trust will suffer without your father's extensive experience with financial matters.'

Beatrice imagined her mother still smarted from Granddad's decision to take the directorship off Father and give it into Beatrice's control.

'People will take advantage.'

'Fortune hunters, Mother?'

Margaret glanced at the floor. Clearly the remark had hit home. Her mother had read too many penny dreadfuls in her youth. Still, Beatrice should not engage with her distractions. 'I'll only be gone for a few hours...'

'Your father will be furious.'

She clamped down on the sarcasm, not wishing to part on bad terms with her mother. Not that Mother would suffer, but she'd drag the guilt behind her like a wet velvet train. 'It's only a short distance, and I will take a taxicab, so I will come to no harm.' She paused. 'You do know the Duchess of Atholl is involved.'

Lady Margaret pulled in her chin. 'Surely not.'

Beatrice couldn't help the flash of triumph in her eyes. 'She is co-president of *The National Joint Committee for Spanish Relief*. So, the whole enterprise is quite reputable, Mother.'

Lady Margaret pursed her lips in a way that told Beatrice that little titbit had impressed. She rammed home the advantage. 'I recall you dancing with the duke at the sugar ball?'

Margaret sighed. 'I wish your father were here. He wouldn't like it. He said the children should stay in Spain, not be brought over here.'

'Mummy!' Beatrice stared at her mother in genuine horror. 'They are bombed by German planes. How can Daddy say that? They're just innocent children.'

'Gracious Beatrice. I don't know what the right thing to do is. Besides, mixing with these people...Well, I am sure you will be exposed to diseases and lice.' Lady Margaret shuddered.

'I'll bathe when I come home.' This time Beatrice couldn't help the hard edge of irony creeping into her voice. Her mother's ignorance astounded her, but at the same time she didn't want to be mean. She knew her mother found the whole idea alien.

'Your father says the children will be little savages and thieves. There won't be any gratitude for bringing them here. You mark my words.'

Good grief, could Mother hear herself? Beatrice decided on a distraction of her own. She said, 'Would you rather I returned to Innisfail?'

Alarm drew deep creases in her mother's usually smooth face and Beatrice smiled. She had no idea that Mark had left Australia. She kissed her mother's cheek. 'I'll need to hurry, but I'll be back soon. Everything will be fine so please Mother, don't worry.'

As she left the house her smile faded. She had not recovered from the shock of Mark walking away. That first night after he had left for Spain, she'd cried herself to sleep. For weeks afterwards, she hadn't been able to extract herself from the depths of her own darkness until her friend, Gladys, had told her about the plight of the Spanish refugees.

Of course, as soon as she'd heard, she'd demanded that Dr Goodall, in charge of organising volunteers, included her name on his list. If she couldn't have Mark, then she could involve herself in the same mission, where at least she might enjoy the comradery of fighting for a common goal.

Port St. Jean de Luz

The British ambassador to Spain's residence at Port St. Jean de Luz overlooked a white-capped stretch of the Bay of Biscay, now grey green under a gathering storm. Mark suppressed a momentary tremor as Charles introduced him to Sir Henry Chilton and his wife Katherine. Would they call him out for the imposter he knew himself to be?

Chiltern had a pompousness about him, which probably rendered him the non-threatening everyman of diplomatic circles. Chilton's wife hailed from American money, judging by her accent and her jewellery. The two daughters remained aloof and scarcely acknowledged Charles and Mark before disappearing into the gloom of the house's nether regions.

Mark followed Charles out to the veranda where a small number of other guests were already grouped in conversation. Charles introduced him to the Governor of Irún, Major Julián Troncoso Sagredo, and his companion, a uniformed SS Captain von Graff. Mark had heard disturbing stories about the SS in Germany and hesitated a moment before shaking the man's hand. If von Graff noticed, he didn't show it.

Charles's eyes rolled and flicked sideways. It took Mark a moment of puzzlement before he realised the eye movement was not an affliction but meant to encourage him to approach the Governor of Irún. In turn Charles took the German's arm and walked a few paces away as if to give Mark space.

It seemed too soon to ask the man for a visa and with some reluctance Mark turned to talk to the governor, but too late. Troncoso had already engaged Chiltern.

His voice remained low as he said, 'Your Excellency, are you able to tell me whether you have yet received word from the committee about our request for recognition of belligerent rights?'

What the hell did that mean? Mark turned away. It was none of his business, and yet everything to do with these people remained newsworthy. To hell with the manners his mother had instilled. Eavesdropping had become part of his repertoire. He moved closer to listen to Chiltern's reply.

'My dear Major, if it were up to Britain we would oblige, but France is less keen. You know we need to assure the Non-Intervention Committee that all the German and Italian volunteers, fighting for the Nationalists, are removed from the country before such rights are considered.'

'What about the foreigners fighting for the Republic?'

'Hmm. We are speaking about what is within the Nationalist control.'

Mark looked around for Charles. He still spoke to von Graff with what appeared to be an urgency unusual for the man. He took a step closer, but Charles took another step away and turned his back, his voice muffled. All Mark could make out were occasional words. Mola...Franco... iron-ring... aerial map... Goicoechea's documents... mining concessions...'

When Charles finished speaking, Von Graff pursed his lips and nodded. As he turned away he said, 'I'll see what I can do.'

Mark cursed his lack of knowledge. Was Mola, General Mola, the mastermind behind the Spanish coup? He'd been José Sanjurjo's second in command, before Sanjurjo's plane went down in what seemed to be mysterious circumstances. What were Goicoechea's documents?

A distraction near the door into the living area interrupted his thoughts. A woman strode onto the veranda. She appeared to be about forty, on the bony side of slender, dressed in loose-fitting trousers and jacket. A long scarf, wrapped around her neck, fluttered in the salt breeze.

She thrust out her hand at the British ambassador. 'Apologies Sir Henry, Ambassador Bowers couldn't make it, so he sent me instead. Hope that's acceptable.'

The woman greeted the others, most of whom she seemed to know before she turned to Mark, 'Sylvia Boyle, Washington Post. I don't think we've met.'

Chiltern said. 'Miss Boyle, Mark Anders is an Australian journalist, newly arrived.'

'Australian you say. You are a long way from home. What has enticed you to this part of the world Mr Anders? The Spanish troubles.'

Before Mark could answer, Charles sauntered back and kissed Silvia on the cheek. 'Darling. It's been too long.' He turned to gaze at Mark, answering Sylvia's question for him. 'Can you believe he's on a mission to unearth the truth about this war?' He chortled and swung back to face Silvia.

Mark looked at his feet. He'd mentioned that at breakfast that first morning, and Charles had laughed, saying, you're a funny chap as if Mark had cracked a joke. At least Sylvia didn't join in the ridicule, just contemplated Charles with a level gaze.

A servant hovered next to Mark with a tray of drinks. Tall glasses contained pink juice with tiny salt crystals around the rim and a curl of fruit skin astride the lip.

Chiltern pointed at the glasses. 'Katherine is trying out some concoction called yea old salty dog—gin and pink grapefruit juice. You drink through the salt, which is supposed to refresh one in hot weather.'

Mark took a glass hesitantly, envying Sylvia's boldness when she refused and said to the servant, 'Bourbon Américain avec glace, s'il vous plaît.'

He took a small sip. It wasn't bad although he remained wary of drinking gin so early in the day.

Chiltern put his hands behind his back and expanded his chest. 'In answer to your question regarding the truth of this war, Mr Anders, the Republican government is Russia's puppet. The Nationalists simply feel honour bound to act and stop the Bolsheviks from seizing their country. Look at what is happening in Barcelona. The Republicans are powerless to control the revolutionary forces operating within the country.'

Revolutionary forces? Who did he mean? Mark stared at the man, his brain scrambling to catch up. Charles intervened.

'Which is why we will have to go to Barcelona, Sir Henry, and find out what's going on between the Republicans and the CNT unionists with this general strike. Mark and I were planning to leave as soon as we can get a visa. Do you think the Embassy might help in some way?'

Sylvia ignored Charles's interjection and responded to Chiltern's summary. 'Aren't you overlooking the fact that the people elected the Republican government. Spain is hardly a Soviet outpost. There are merely a couple of communist members within the popular front government, and President Azaña himself is a liberal? Army generals can't simply stage a coup because they don't agree with the people's choice.'

Major Troncoso joined the conversation. 'Yes, but was the election completely legitimate? There seems to be some question.'

'My dear Julián, I didn't see evidence of any ballot rigging when I visited Madrid last year, just jubilant people ecstatic they had won.' A light of pure devilment danced in her eyes.

Major Troncoso scowled but bowed towards Sylvia without saying more.

Aware his own ignorance left him clod-footed in this snappy discourse Mark attempted to learn more. Sylvia seemed not only well informed but also disarmingly frank. Mark wanted her opinion, without Charles foisting his point of view into the mix. He manoeuvred a step away from the others and closer to her before lowering his voice. 'You seem to have a good understanding of what's going on in Spain.'

'Is that a general observation or are you looking for information?'

'There are so many contradictory reports.'

'Not sure anyone really knows what's going on from one minute to the next, but I'll help if I can. What do you want to know?'

'Well... Who bombed Guernica?'

She regarded him with what looked like appraisal in her eyes. 'What do you think?'

'I'm certain they were German bombs, but I didn't witness the event. Charles is adamant that the Basque army blew up the place as they retreated.'

'Did you read George Steer's report?'

He nodded. 'I heard there is some doubt about its accuracy. Steer wasn't actually a witness.'

'Horseshit!' She patted his arm. 'Don't worry. Noel Monks told me it was most definitely German Heinkel's. The bastards strafed his vehicle as he drove towards Guernica. In this war it's who you want to believe, and that depends on whose side you're on. Although, I guess all wars are like that.' Her blue eyes crinkled at the corners.

He neutralised his features quickly although too late to hide his initial shock from her observant gaze. In his experience women of her class didn't usually swear like that. Clearly, he didn't know as much as he'd thought he did, about anything.

She added. 'I can see you're an idealist searching for what can only be described as an illusionary truth. You're new at this game, aren't you?'

He sighed. 'Is it so obvious?'

She tilted her head. 'So, what are you doing here, Mr Anders? This war will eat idealists for breakfast and spit out the bones. You should go home before you get killed.'

Stung by her summation, he said the first words that came to him. 'You're right, I am new at this, but perhaps idealism might be required as an antidote to the Nationalist propaganda and intolerance for democratic rule.'

Her laugh sounded like a short, startling bark. 'That's priceless. Idealism, the antidote for intolerance.'

The words had come out without thinking and he felt the hot flush of embarrassment creeping up his neck. He searched the group's reaction hoping no one else had heard before attempting to change the subject. 'What's Chiltern doing in France if he's the British ambassador to Spain?'

Amusement still lit her face. 'Madrid's a little uncomfortable right now, and as you might have guessed. Sir Henry Chilton's not a fan of the Republican government.'

'What else can you tell me about him?'

She glanced across at Chiltern. 'He loves us Yanks. Not only did he marry one, but he is especially fond of American companies that re-route oil, gasoline, and vehicles to Franco on credit. Actually, the Nationalists would have lost the war already if those supplies went to the Republicans, as intended. Claude... that is the American ambassador to Spain, Claude Bowers, begged our President to stop American companies supplying the Nationalists.'

'Because of the non-intervention pact?' Mark knew all about that fence-sitting ploy used by the British to avoid getting involved.

'Not just that, but also because if America doesn't act, Claude is worried this little Spanish coup will start a much wider European war. I must say I agree with him.'

📷

The next day, Mark returned to Paris to ask his contact, Rolin Leclerc, at *L'Humanité* newspaper, how he might get into Spain through Barcelona. He'd met Rolin through a letter of introduction his Australian friend, Jack Henry, had given him.

Jack Henry remained the Queensland state secretary for the Australian Communist Party. He and Mark had been in the Queensland cane fields together fighting injustice. Mark wasn't a member of the party, but he sympathised with their struggle and Jack had done a lot for him.

Rolin Leclerc, a rotund man with a serious demeanour and an impressive moustache, had helped Mark gain press credentials when he'd first arrived in France. Now, he directed Mark to the Spanish Embassy in the 8th arrondissement.

'Ask for Secretary Abaroa and tell him I sent you.'

Before Mark left the press offices, Rolin showed him through to a dark room, where he explained how to develop and print the photos he'd taken in Hendaye.

Still smarting from Charles's jibes, Mark asked how he could use a camera to represent truth.

Rolin nodded sympathetically. 'Truth is a subjective value. For the camera, emotion is the only truth. You have an eye,' he said holding up a print. 'But these photos are no use to us. They hold only what exists within the frame. Photos need meaning. If you come back from Barcelona with photos of Republican heroes or insurgent demons, we will buy them, but not these.'

Was this another request for raw political propaganda? It wasn't Mark's mission to add to a world already blinded by allegiances to either side. Still, if he got it right, he might be able to sell his photos to the paper.

Although it occurred to him that he should not link his name with a communist aligned organisation. Doing that could end his career before it began. Sympathising with the pursuit for greater equality and fairness seemed to bring out the worst of all prejudice and retribution. He'd learned that lesson in the Queensland cane fields.

If he thought prejudice against the communists remained rife at home, among the British establishment it was worse. The French and the Spanish were more accommodating with their popular front governments. Even so, Mark would not align himself again with the communists. The liberal democratic world wasn't ready to fit communism within its fold, and probably never would be.

Yet communists had given him support when no others were prepared to take the chance. Like Jack, they were decent blokes, simply wanting greater equality. Take Rolin for example. He gave his time and expertise without expectation of reward, merely to give a chap a leg up.

Mark thanked him for his help and made his way to the Spanish embassy, unconvinced that he would not find truth in war. Rolin's statement about the camera's truth arising from emotion matched Mark's understanding of art.

Wasn't that what he'd done back home with his political lampoons? Although sketching with pencil and paper felt infinitely more satisfying because you could highlight the points you were trying to make.

With the camera the world seemed too big. The proportions all wrong. The horror indistinct, grainy, and distant. He didn't know how to show the evil intent of those planes the way he could do with a drawing. For the next few days, questions about how he could convey truth without producing propaganda for one side or the other became an all-consuming conundrum that ricocheted around his skull.

Once the Spanish Republic had issued the coveted visa, Mark bought a train ticket to Perpignan, from where he would get another train across the Spanish border, which the French had briefly opened.

The month had tipped into May 1937 by the time he stood on the platform under the Meccano-like dome of the Gare d'Austerlitz. Two men with brown paper parcels under their arms stood nearby. The shorter of the two looked like he'd barely had a meal in weeks. His gaunt shoulders, pasty face, lank hair, and hollow eyes gave off an air of someone who had been hidden in a drawer all his life. The taller man looked healthier, albeit poorly dressed in collarless shirt and faded, fraying jacket. He had a ruddy face in the way of an outdoors man although with the appearance of a pugilist, a look that only a broken nose can provide.

Mark guessed the men were volunteers for the International Brigades, warned not to communicate with each other at least until they were on the train. This remained precautionary in case the gendarmes tried to stop one of the volunteers. The non-intervention pact precluded foreign volunteers heading off to fight in Spain. In this way, if they travelled individually and one was caught the others could still get through.

The man at the Spanish embassy had given Mark instructions he should not talk to any such volunteers until safely inside Spain, or he might blow their cover. He itched to speak with them, to find out what had motivated them to be here. But the train arrived, and they boarded a third-class carriage.

Mark climbed into a second-class carriage. He'd bought the ticket reluctantly because he guessed a journalist might not travel third but now, he wished hadn't. Still, it kept the temptation to speak to the men at bay and, as a bonus, he managed to find an empty compartment.

As the train left Paris behind, Mark distracted himself by watching the unfolding landscape. Beyond the city, the countryside opened onto a flat and forested plain on one side and farmlands on the other, all neatly arranged under a wide saucer of pale sky. The sun tracked to the right, indicating they were heading south.

A conductor rattled and then opened the door to his compartment. 'Billet s'il vous plait'

Mark handed him the ticket.

'Quelle est votre destination?' The conductor asked.

'Perpignan,' Mark replied.

The conductor examined Mark, his eyebrows slanting towards the peak of his cap, 'Vous êtes Italien?'

Mark's French accent wasn't perfect, and he realised he must speak it like an Italian. Not surprising given his background. He shrugged and said, 'Australian.'

'Quelle est votre entreprise à Perpignan?'

The conductor's prying began to irk Mark although perhaps he merely carried out his job.

Mark pointed at his camera. 'Photographié.'

'Ah, un journaliste?' the conductor nodded. 'Votre ami vous a demandé.'

Mark frowned. What friend could be looking for him? The conductor must have mistaken him for someone else, but before he could ask, the bloke had moved on to the next compartment.

A little while later Charles walked in. 'I thought you'd be here, but you might have waited for me.' He raised a sardonic eyebrow and looked around. 'You should come and sit in my compartment. It's much nicer than this.' He fell onto the seat opposite Mark and said, 'So, how did you manage to get a Spanish visa?'

Republican Spain

The day after Mark's arrival in Barcelona, gunfire rang in the streets. Guests were confined to their hotels, and a growing food shortage left drinking in the bar the only distraction. From morning to night gossip and intrigue swirled through the corridors.

Everyone he spoke to, journalists mostly, had different opinions about what had happened. He hankered to get out and see it for himself, but aside from it being forbidden, it didn't seem wise.

After a few days things quietened down, and an invitation arrived for the journalists to attend an official press briefing at the Generalitat de Catalunya.

The hotel receptionist explained that the Generalitat, or the Catalonian regional government, operated out of the Colon Hotel. A bus would arrive after breakfast the next morning to transport the journalists.

Mark boarded the bus with anticipation. The streets were silent now as if the city held its breath. Everything appeared so different from the day he'd arrived. Then, throngs of cheerful people owned those same streets. Vibrancy and cheer had coloured the revolutionary fervour.

Now, only the slogans and posters remained and even those were tarnished by bullet or artillery marks. The dark stains on pavements told an even sadder story.

Patrols were overt and ubiquitous.

The man sitting next to him, pointed at the patrols. 'Republican Assault Guard. Real professionals. They're the ones who quelled the uprising.'

Mark tilted his head in acknowledgement and stared out the window. Workers, under guard, removed barricades made from broken masonry, sandbags and what looked like cobble stones ripped from the streets. Sure enough, some of the labourers were returning the cobble stones to the roads from where they had been taken.

A journalist, sitting in the seat in front of him, turned and addressed the passengers generally. 'The Republic would be well advised to number the pavers in future, to make it easier to replace them.'

Several men laughed, privy to a story of which Mark remained ignorant.

Again, the man in the seat next to him explained, 'Same thing happened last year during the attempted coup.'

Mark nodded his thanks and extended his hand. 'Mark Anders.'

The man shook his hand. 'Sam Riding.'

The bus pulled up in the square outside a large and impressive building. A large banner hung between giant portraits of Lenin and Stalin. The banner proclaimed the hotel and therefore the Generalitat remained under the control of the PSUC or the Unified Socialist Party of Catalonia. This must be The Hotel Colón.

Once the journalists had disembarked, a soldier led them inside the building. They were taken to a large, high-ceilinged room, already packed with reporters sitting on chairs that would have been better placed in a grand salon. Round tables were piled haphazardly in one corner of the room.

The ubiquitous revolutionary posters, pinned to the walls, appeared incongruous against an intricate décor of barley sugar columns, and a mosaic ceiling. A chandelier with multiple glass globes lit up an atrium above a small stage or dais, probably once used for a string quartet or piano. The room perhaps had once been the dining room of the former hotel.

Mark took a vacant seat and waited.

After a few minutes a rather dapper, clean-shaven officer in khaki uniform, replete with Sam Browne belt and pistol, took his place behind a lectern. The room fell silent.

The officer cleared his throat, shuffled some papers and began to read from a memorandum. He spoke in English with a heavy Spanish accent. After he had read for a few minutes a noise, like drones readying themselves to swarm, filled the room.

A journalist from the *Daily Express* called out, 'Has the popular front government turned against its own people?'

The hum broke into a cacophony with questions flung at the press officer in a multitude of languages.

31

Beads of sweat broke out on the officer's forehead. He wiped a finger across his temple and appealed for silence to allow him to continue reading. The noise abated and the officer continued.

But the odour of propaganda oozed through the narrative like treacle through bread. Mark didn't need journalistic experience to discriminate between spin and what may have actually happened. He trusted his own instincts, which were usually sharp despite Charles jeering at his desire to find the truth.

Although he had to admit that even facts were not enough in this war because they didn't explain anything. It stood as fact that the Republican government tried to rein in the Catalonian anarchists' revolutionary fervour. They were in the process of trying to retake control of the borders when an incident occurred at the Barcelona telephone exchange.

The anarchists, it seemed, had no respect for generals and politicians claiming priority when attempting to run a war. A call from a grandmother to her daughter was as important as the politician's call to a general. Each must wait their turn. The government sent in the Assault Guard to forcibly wrest back control over the telephone exchange. The anarchist unions took up arms, and a serious brawl, amplified by the weapons of war, ensued.

Yet even these explanations left him with questions. For instance, why did the anarchists refuse the Republican government's directives, after they had agreed to participate in the popular front government? Could government unity be in jeopardy? Were the Catalonian anarchists only interested in their own revolution rather than supporting a united front to win the war? What about the anarchists in the rest of the country? Were they challenging government unity?

Knowing something has occurred, does not explain what led up to it. Neither does it explain the anger that motivates people to take the law into their own hands. Mark understood the anarchists were protecting their revolution from the Spanish Republic's need to gain control and focus on defeating the insurgent enemy. But to take to the street with guns...

He tried to imagine Australians on strike, coming out with guns, fighting pitched battles in the street. They might if they had the weapons, but surely not against your own political partners. In Spain, the enemy were supposed to be the Nationalist insurgents.

The press officer appealed for calm and once more continued reading. 'The Assault Guard were tasked with putting down a fascist rebellion, and I am pleased to inform you that they have succeeded...'

Bullshit. True, the Assault Guard had put down the rebellion, but the rebels in this instance were anarchist unions and political parties, the CNT and POUM. Anarchists would never side with fascists.

The facts were that the Assault Guard had arrived and put down a local Catalonian rebellion and had reestablished order. Although that still said nothing about why the fighting had started. Not for one minute did Mark believe the fascist bit. Whatever had started the street fight, it sounded increasingly like ideological rivalry between different factions within the popular front, rather than any sinister fascist conspiracy.

When ideological differences get in the way of a united front, winning remains unlikely. Bitter experience had convinced Mark that infighting remained the bane of any militant union action. He couldn't help noting the similarities to his time in the cane fields. Then unionists, communists, and anarchist had formed a united front to take on their own union, which was backed by the government. His own motivation for joining that united front battle had been to save men dying from Weil's disease. Although here such confrontations were more complicated, and in the middle of a civil war, where every man carried arms, it became deadly.

The Republican government clearly sought to present themselves to the world as a sophisticated and legitimate democracy, not one of infighting and chaos. From what he'd heard from the other journalists, the official press tours before he had arrived had been about Barcelona's culture. The city's beauty on display, as if the authorities were trying to convince the rest of Europe, they had nothing to fear.

In a nod to their liberal democracy, the Republican government, planned to return private property to the bourgeoisie. The anarchists had collectivised it at the beginning of the civil war. Now the government even allowed some churches to reopen after the anarchist had closed them, some with violence. Through these actions it seemed the Republicans had stirred up a jumping ants' nest, undoing the revolutionary gains made by the anarchists. And they were mad as hell.

He tapped his pencil against his notepad, remembering clearing the farm back home. The rainforest ants defending their territory in an attack frenzy that drove him into the river to escape bites like hot needles. The pain lasted for weeks. Consequently, like clearing an ants' nest, and with all the same level of empathy, the Republicans had cleared away their problems and the anarchist unions burred up.

Brutal.

Press briefings were useless if they only gave sanitised versions of events. He had to get out and talk to the people in the streets, and the soldiers fighting at the front. They would provide the real picture.

The briefing ended and the press officer announced busses would be leaving in one hour to take them to lunch. The hive cheered and, with a clatter of chairs, they began to filter out of the room. Mark remained seated.

Charles clambered across several rows and said, 'I've been looking for you. We're heading to the Continental for a snifter before the bus leaves. Why don't you join us?'

Mark shook his head. 'You go ahead. I'll call into the Continental later.'

He planned to escape the press officer and explore on his own. While reporters were welcome in Republican held territory, they were closely monitored, apparently for their own safety. Mark didn't want to go on bus tours to collect tourist photos.

He waited until the briefing room cleared, mulling over what he knew. Since the street battles had stopped, the boards had come off the windows. The early summer sun streamed through the glass panes. The weather forecast suggested a hot start to summer, but Barcelona wasn't as hot as home, or not yet anyway. Forecasts said it would get hotter, but he remained grateful for any sunshine after the feeble gloom he'd experienced during the London spring.

The room had cleared before he arose from his seat and walked toward the exit. Two women blocked the doorway; unaware he stood behind them. Mark felt no need to hurry and waited for them to move on.

One of the women, the dark-haired one, spoke in a low voice to her fair-haired companion.

When she finally noticed him, she said, 'Och, sorry,' and stepped aside, pulling her friend with her.

'Thanks.' Mark nodded and made a move to walk past them.

The dark-haired woman stopped him. 'I haven't seen you before. Where are you from?'

He paused. Did she want to know what country he hailed from, or what hotel he stayed at?

She screwed her face into what looked like disbelief, presumably at his frown. 'It's not a hard question, you know—which paper?'

His hand went immediately to his left breast, feeling the press pass in his jacket pocket for reassurance. '*L'Humanité.*' He said, feeling the blood of an imposter rise in his neck.

It wasn't too far from the truth for they had said they would buy his photos if they thought any were good enough.

'You don't sound French.' Her grey eyes narrowed.

'Australian.' He muttered; certain the woman could see straight through him—knew him for an amateur. 'I just arrived a few days ago.'

A softening flickered across her face. 'Well, what did you think of the press briefing?'

He smiled, but inside a warning went off. In this place, nothing felt like a casual question. He put out his hand. 'I'm Mark Anders.'

She took his hand and laughed. 'A canny one,' she said to her friend. 'I'm Ethel and this is my friend Sheena from *The Glasgow Herald*.'

Ethel's Scottish brogue sounded familiar.

'You're the one on the wireless.'

'Clever boy.' Ethel gave an exaggerated eye roll to her friend and shook her short, wavy dark hair away from her face.

Mark felt the heat of inexperience rising again. 'Excuse me.' He made a move to pass the women.

'Och...don't be in such a rush. Tell us all about you.' Ethel laid her hand on Mark's arm.

He hesitated. Yet this might be the answer. These women might provide a different perspective and perhaps introduce him to local people. Just what an outsider needed to gain acceptance, if not trust.

'What do you want to know?'

The woman glanced at her companion. 'We're going for a cup of tea; get out of this joint.' She raised her gaze to the vaulted ceilings. 'Find more friendly air. Would you like to join us?'

Eduardo Cardona

Mark followed Ethel and Sheena into a dingy canteen down an alleyway in El Raval area behind the university. The Café consisted of women mostly, although some men sat among them. Ethel and Sheena greeted several people before they both sat at a communal table, Sheena on one side, next to a powerfully built man who took her hand. Ethel sat opposite and patted the bench next to her.

Mark remained standing.

'Mr Anders, this is my friend Eddy.' She referred to the bloke holding Sheena's hand.

'Eddy, Mr Anders is an Australian reporter, just arrived in Barcelona.'

'Call me Mark.' He held out his hand.

Eddy glanced at the door before he stood to shake Mark's hand. 'My name is Eduardo Cardona. Only Ethel calls me Eddy.'

Mark grasped his firm, calloused hand, noting the man's broad shoulders and deep chest, with the accompanying shadow of aggressive stubble on his chin.

Mark sat down as Ethel folded her arms and said, 'So, Mr Anders tell us all about you. Why are you here?'

The café patrons' fell silent as their eyes rested on him, waiting.

How many spoke English? He might keep his limited Spanish under wraps until he knew the lay of the land. It remained a useful means of discovering stuff when people didn't know you could understand what they said. Although, most of the people here would speak Catalan, a language he was yet to learn.

'I'm just trying to find out what's going on.' He paused then took a gamble. 'I didn't buy the briefing this morning.'

Ethel gazed at him speculatively. 'That's because none of it is true.'

'What is the truth?'

'The truth is that the Communist Party have taken control of the Republican government and are calling the shots. They're the anti-revolutionaries supporting bourgeois democracy against the anarchist triumph of the proletarian revolution.'

'Ah, the stick that pokes the ant nest.'

'What?'

'Nothing. Sorry, you were saying...'

She glanced at him sideways but continued. 'They are trying to paint the anarchists as anti-revolutionaries, in league with the fascists. If you had been here a month ago, you would have understood. After the revolution, Catalonia became totally classless, with the land and factories collectivised, the workers in

39

control, women emancipated, and children fed and educated. We finally defeated centuries of oppression from the bourgeoise, and the church. All decisions were made in consultation and through consensus, even those of the war, and it worked. Now the bloody communists are trying to undo all our work, but they won't get away with it.'

Mark wondered if a classless society was possible. Australia called itself classless, yet they were clearly deluding themselves.

He said, 'Yes, I got that bit.'

Stories of the criminal gangs, which had quickly filled the law-and-order vacuum brought about by the anarchist revolution, particularly in the border regions of Catalonia, flitted through his mind. Some of the tales he'd heard about the coercive practices of forcing people to give up their land to the collective, were enough to make him wonder at the advisability of collectivisation.

But he wasn't there to argue, so he said, 'I don't get why, in the middle of a war.'

'It's simple. The revolution is more important than a bourgeoise war.' She looked around the room for confirmation.

Only Sheena moved, nodding her head in agreement.

Mark said, 'Nevertheless, the war is ongoing and if the Nationalists win, then the revolution and the Republic are both dead.'

Sheena sneered. 'Ha! But the Nationalists cannot win a war against the people if the people are armed. We showed that when they tried to take power last year in Barcelona. We beat them then, and if the Republic try to crush the revolution, we will beat them too.'

Ethel added, 'They want to give back the land and businesses we collectivised, to the bourgeoise. It is a ruse to demilitarise the revolutionaries and take back state control.'

Mark kept his voice low and moderate as he asked, 'You don't think that state control and organisation are needed to win the war first?'

Ethel pouched her cheeks and rolled her eyes. 'If they regain control, they will never relinquish it. It's Stalin who wants to control Spain, as he oppresses Russia.'

'That is what many in the British government say, but most of the Republican government is made up of liberals and socialists, isn't it? Not communists.'

'Perhaps in the beginning but the communists want control, and they are gaining the upper hand. If you are with *L'Humanité*, you're probably a member of the Communist Party, and a spy, so you'd know.'

Mark shook his head. 'Neither of those things. I'm freelance, but I'll take work where I can find it.'

Eduardo made a noise in his throat and glared at Mark. Then he stood up. 'Come, I show you what these communist bastards do.'

Mark had noted the weight of a pistol dragging at Edward's coat pocket, and said, 'Let's get this straight. I'm not anyone's spy. I'm only here to find out and report the truth.'

'We'll see.' Ethel added, 'Eddy's not going to kill you if that's what you're worried about. It's the bloody PCE, the communist union, who runs around killing people.'

Mark stood up. 'Aren't you coming?'

She shook her head. 'Bye bye Mr Australian war correspondent, if that's who you really are. Tell the truth of what you see for your newspaper, whichever one it is.'

Everyone wanted the press to report what accorded with their own beliefs. He wondered what his reports would show. Despite his views that a joint socialist/liberal democracy could work, he remained determined to report only what he found, not what he wanted to believe might be happening. Yet he had begun to realise that might not be possible. In any case, he couldn't say any of it to her. Instead, he said, 'Thanks for your help.'

He followed Eduardo out the café and down a back alley. Like many other parts of Barcelona, the walls on either side were chipped, pockmarked or shattered by bullets, grenades, and mortar shells.

After about ten minutes of walking through a maze of narrow lanes, Eduardo stopped and checked along the street both ways before he opened a door leading into a courtyard.

An old woman stepped out of a recessed doorway on the far side of the courtyard and beckoned to them. Dressed in black, with a headscarf or mantilla covering her head, the expression on her face arrested Mark, as if the crumpled mass of wretchedness were etched lines of sorrow.

Eduardo strode towards her and put his arms around her shoulders. The two remained enmeshed for a minute, while Mark stood to one side. Then Eduardo relinquished his hold on the woman and introduced Mark to his mother.

She turned back into the house and led the two men into a large room. In the centre, on a wooden table, a dead man lay with his head wrapped in fresh white bandages, his arms folded on his chest. His jacket appeared encrusted with what looked like dried blood.

Around the edges of the room, women and children sat on benches pushed against the walls. They stared at Mark, while Eduardo explained that the dead man was his younger brother, shot in the head by Assault Guards after the battle to take back the Telefonica.

Mark mumbled his condolences, paralysed by the unexpected situation. Recognising his inadequacy in the face of so much grief, he waited silently to one side of the room as Eduardo spoke with his family.

Eduardo hugged his mother again, and said to Mark, 'Come, we have not finished.'

They walked along more back alleys and passed the homes of Eduardo's comrades. Greetings and introduction took place, but they didn't stop long before moving on.

Eventually, they arrived at a tall building. Eduardo led Mark up several flights of stairs before he climbed out of a window onto a flat rooftop. He crouched behind a bulwark and motioned to Mark to do likewise.

Across the street, an enormous walled compound held numerous large buildings, which spoked out from a panopticon style central edifice. Civil Guards, in their distinctive three-cornered hats, strutted behind a gated entrance. Carts and lorries trundled back and forth. Soldiers milled about the pavement outside the gate. Women and children squatted within the wall's shade as they waited, presumably to get inside to see loved ones.

Eduardo said, 'The Checa.'

Mark scrutinised Eduardo then looked back at the prison. Checa was the Spanish term for an unofficial secret prison. This was clearly no secret, just a vast and forbidding prison complex from which it would be difficult to escape.

'They arrested my older brother, Bautista, as a traitor.' He spat towards the prison, and a glutinous gob of impotent hatred fell to the street below.

Mark unslung his Leica from his shoulder, unclipping its cap, and glanced at Eduardo for permission. Eduardo nodded and Mark adjusted the camera's rangefinder.

For the next three hours, Eduardo took Mark from place to place, along alleys and over rooftops, avoiding Guardia of all stripes. They spoke to several men, and while Eduardo translated each personal story, Mark took photos.

This was his reason for being here, not for press briefings nor for drinking and lunching with other journalists. Yet the sorrow and suffering were harrowing. He'd never seen such callous disregard for human life, but as he looked through the camera lens, a barrier rose between him and grief. It brought a distance that diffused the horror and instead filled him with a euphoric sense of purpose. All afternoon he took photos of men who had been executed and left lying-in back alleys, their blood drying into black pools.

The lucky ones, those who had people who cared, had been carried home and laid out in front rooms. Those, like Eduardo's younger brother, had grieving widows and bewildered children, who stared into his camera lens or explained, that this dead man was a member of the anarchist CNT union, or its political wing the FAI, or the POUM workers' party. That one, just an old man minding his own business. This one, a youth, merely out to get a coffee and play chess with his friend.

With each new encounter and each story, Mark wanted someone to blame, to vent his anger, but against whom? The Spanish people, on the same side of a civil war, were killing each other in internecine violence, instead of focusing their collective fury on the real enemy.

By the time they arrived at a semi-dismantled cobblestone barricade the sun had sunk in the west. It wouldn't be long until curfew.

Eduardo said, 'This is where my fathers died.'

Mark examined the barricade then looked at Eduardo. What did he mean, *fathers died*? Aloud he said, 'You lost your father as well as your brothers?'

Eduardo's jaw tightened. 'I lost my father here during la Setmana Tràgica. I was born in August 1909 just two weeks after my father died at this barricade, so I never knew him, but he fought for justice.' He paused, scrutinised Mark, and then said, 'You know about the Setmana Tràgica?

Mark shook his head.

Eduardo frowned. 'You have heard of the Rif wars?'

Again, Mark shook his head and shrugged in apology.

Eduardo took in a breath. 'The Spanish government wanted to colonise Morocco, but the Riffian people objected. So, the government called men, for the army you understand, even those who had already done national service.' He sighed. 'This time they wanted them for colonisation. The anarchists, like my father, had no interest in colonisation, nor did they have any anger towards the Riffian tribes. But when the State wants war, they call the poor. The rich pay for other men to go in their place, but for the poor it is always a tragedy. They must go to war and leave their families without a bread winner. This time my father, and those like him, said, no!'

Eduardo paused, his eyes glistening. Then he added, 'They stood together here. They fought and died bravely, just like my stepfather died at this barricade last July, fighting the Francoists coup. Now my brother is also dead at this barricade, and my other brother will die from torture in the Checa, once more at the hands of the state. This is why government must be abolished.'

He smashed his fist into his palm. 'Now I must live, for I am the only future on earth for my father. I must live to make his existence and death worth something, but we need to rid Spain of these bloody governments who kill us. This is the story you must tell for the world.'

Mark depressed the shutter on the camera. 'I will tell your story.' He promised.

Too Many Surprises

That night Mark did not sleep. Instead, he sketched scenes from his memory in an exercise book, writing accompanying notes so he wouldn't forget the details. With every drawing came more questions along with frustration at his own ignorance. As soon as dawn broke, Mark returned to the café hoping to find Eduardo or Ethel.

He arrived before the café opened. When it did, he went in and ordered coffee. After two hours, neither Eduardo nor Ethel had arrived. He didn't think he could remember how to get to Eduardo's mother's home, so he asked the man behind the counter if he could leave a message.

The weathered skin around the man's eyes crackled with suspicion. 'What do you want?' He said in English.

'I met here yesterday with Eduardo Cardona.'

The man tilted his head as if in acknowledgement.

'I need to talk to him again... Will he be in today?'

The man shrugged with the attitude of fatalism.

'Look, can you just tell him Mark Anders wants to talk. He can contact me here. He wrote his name and the name of his hotel in his notebook and tore out the page. 'Please. It's important.'

He left the café, unsure if the message would be passed on, but there wasn't much he could do about it. He supposed he might find Ethel at the radio station. Perhaps one of the other journalists would know how he could find it.

He headed for the Continental Hotel. Charles seemed to know everyone, and Mark might hear something that would shed light on the progress of the war in the rest of Spain. Now he had seen Barcelona he hankered to visit Madrid, a city under siege by the Nationalists, a different situation from Barcelona.

Although a trip to Madrid might have to wait. Even in a war zone he needed money, maybe more so, and his funds were dwindling rapidly. Hopefully, *L'Humanité* would buy his work. If they wanted emotion, his photographs had it by the barrow load.

The Continental Hotel's bar had reopened to the public, now the fighting had stopped, and Mark walked in and ordered coffee. He sat with his back to the wall from where he could survey most of the room. Twenty minutes passed before he spotted Charles accompanied by another man. The bloke on the bus...

Mark waved and Charles walked over to his table. 'I thought you were avoiding me, but now you're here, you can back me up. Sam here, says the Americans aren't colonials like the Australians by way of the American British Treaty. What do you say?'

Mark glanced from one man to the other. 'You were on the bus yesterday.'

Sam grinned. 'I was. Good to meet you again.'

Sam appeared some years younger than Mark and Charles, somewhere in his early twenties. Thin, and small. Brown hair, and hazel eyes windowed by thick-lensed, Bakelite-framed spectacles. His mouth formed a bow with a seemingly permanent smile. He leaned in with his hand outstretched. 'Samuel Riding, *Courier Journal*, Louisville Kentucky. As I said yesterday, Sam to my friends.'

'Mark Anders.' He stood up to shake Sam's outstretched hand.

'I remember. I thought I had heard of you before but couldn't place where. I think you met my aunt, Sylvia Boyle.'

'Your aunt? Is she here?'

'She's in Paris, but she took a real liking to you. Are you with *The Times* like Charles here?'

He settled for honesty. 'I'm freelance. What's this about Americans being colonials?'

Sam chuckled. '*Don't-call-me-Charlie-boy* here, called me a colonial and it started the argument, but it's just a bit of fun.'

Charles got up. 'Fun! I think not, but you've made your point, which, I suppose, means I'm to get in the first round again. What'll it be Mark? You can't drink coffee all day.'

'Thanks, I'll have a beer.'

Charles walked to the bar and Sam sat down opposite Mark.

Mark said, 'You seem to know your way around?'

Sam nodded. 'A little. I've been here for a few months.'

'You wouldn't happen to know how I might get to Madrid?'

Charles returned from the bar. 'Whatever for? The place has been bombed to smithereens?'

'That's why I need to go. Aren't you curious?'

'Nothing doing old chum,' Charles said. 'A scouting mission to find out what the Barcelona street-fight was all about was my mandate, nothing more.'

Mark opened his mouth to ask for his verdict, when all thoughts of Barcelona vanished.

Charles said, 'I have just received an imperious command from my Aunt Margaret to attend the Ritz for my cousin Beatrice's birthday. I understand it's to be a sort of coming out because she has refused to join the debs being presented to our new King. So, I must return home.'

Mark inhaled beer, which initiated a coughing fit.

'You all right, old man?'

He wiped his mouth with the back of his hand and nodded. That was the second time Charles managed to catch him off guard with an unexpected statement about his family.

Charles leaned back and continued. 'Besides I don't want to miss the coronation. If I don't leave by tomorrow, I won't make it back to London in time.' He turned to Sam. 'You Americans miss out on all this pomp and splendour, but I cannot understand why my cousin is so set against meeting the poor man.'

'Why poor,' Sam asked.

'Well, the chap never wanted the role did he, and then there is the speech impediment...'

Sam shook his head. 'You sure know how to flail a man's vulnerabilities... But I am with your cousin. She sounds like a sensible woman.'

Charles ignored him. 'I imagine her refusal went down like the Hindenburg with my aunt.'

Sam frowned. 'Poor taste, old chap.'

Charles raised both his eyebrows. 'Good lord. An American as the arbiter of taste!' He continued unabashed. 'I am rather surprised she has agreed to a coming out party. She's an odd sort, my cousin: a bit of a radical bluestocking. A bit like you Sam, banging on about equality, fraternity and all that hullabaloo. Her party should be an event though. My aunt doesn't do things by halves.'

Mark hunched over and stared into his glass, avoiding Charles's eye. He owed her an apology. In the American vernacular, he'd been an ass. He loved her, not her station in life. That just came with the territory. He'd always known that, so what had possessed him to become so self-righteous. He'd lost the only woman with whom he'd ever fallen in love, and she would be unlikely to speak to him again.

Later that afternoon, when Mark returned to his hotel, the concierge handed him an envelope. As he walked up the stairs, he ripped it open, stopping on the landing to read its contents.

It was an invitation to Beatrice's birthday party. On the back of the card she had written, *Please come. It will give you a chance to meet my family.*

His heart pounded and his mouth dried as he hurried down the corridor to his room. How could he navigate this challenge? Perhaps he could return and apologise to her without having to attend any family gatherings at the Ritz.

He paused to open his hotel room door, and as he fumbled with the key, he recognised his own cowardice in his desire to avoid her family. He couldn't run away again, although could anyone blame him? His previous experience with her family didn't leave any hope that the meeting would be a friendly event. Perhaps it was better to avoid placing himself in that position in the first place.

He shut the door and leaned against it. He should ignore the invitation. No, he couldn't do that to her. Perhaps he could write...

A rapid banging on the door jerked him from his ruminations.

'Damn it, Charles.' He wrenched open the door, but it wasn't Charles.

Sheena stood in the hallway. Hatless, her fair hair a mess, and breathless, she gasped, 'They're after Eduardo. You must help him!'

'Who's after him?'

She pushed past him, into his room. 'The bloody PSCU, that's who. They say he's a Trotskyist and one of the POUM ring leaders who started the fighting.

'Is he?'

'Well, he's POUM, and he believes the revolution is more important than any war, but that's beside the point. He's in danger and Ethel says you can help.'

'What can I do?'

Mark liked Eduardo but didn't know what he could do or even if it were advisable.

'He needs papers. He just needs them for about forty-eight hours, then you can report them missing and get them replaced.'

'How will my papers help?'

'What you don't know can't hurt you.'

'You think? If you want my help, you'd better tell me something.'

Sheena snapped, 'You're just wasting time. Even now they might have found him.'

'Well, you'll have to give me some idea of what I'm getting myself into, or I can't help.'

'You mean you won't.' She sighed. 'All right then. Ethel knows some merchant seamen who will help a fellow communist party member. They'll get him on board using the kind of papers seamen use and then he won't need a passport.'

'Sheena, I told you I am not a party member. In any case, how will he pass for an Australian?

Sheena shrugged. 'The ship's crew isn't English. They won't notice that Eduardo speaks English with a Spanish accent.' She glared at him. If you are truly not a communist, then your passport...'

Mark pressed his lips together. 'I'm not giving him my passport. I had the devil's own trying to get it in the first place, but I have something else that might help.'

'What?'

'A letter of introduction from an Australian communist leader. It has four names on it, one of them is my American friend Javier Cruz, a Spanish name. He is with the Republican Army in the north.'

Shit, he hoped Jack wouldn't mind but he had helped anarchists before, back in Ingham during the 1934 strike. Besides, Javier had been an anarchist before Jack persuaded him to join up, and he knew Javier would want to help Eduardo.

He went to his suitcase and pulled out an envelope, which contained the letter Jack had given him when he, Javier, and a couple of other blokes had set sail from Australia. The letter had opened doors for Mark even though he wasn't a member of the party. He still owed Jack for that. The others on the letter, including Jaiver, were all communist volunteers, fighting with the Republic.

The dogeared pages, a little worse for wear, were still in one piece. What harm could it do? He didn't want to see what would happen to Eduardo if the PSUC caught him. He and his family had suffered enough.

'What nationality are the people Ethel knows?'

'The sailors.'

'Yes.'

'Norwegian.'

'I may be able to help.'

'With that?' She pointed to the envelope in his hand.

'Yes. I also speak a bit of Norwegian, enough to get by at any rate.'

She held up her palms in question.

'My father is Norwegian, or rather my stepfather. I can explain this letter to the sailors and ask for their help. Eduardo will have to become Javier Cruz.' He handed her the letter.

Sheena scanned it and said, 'If you can make this work, you'll be a life saver, and I promise, if you save Eddy, we will return the favour.'

'I don't need your quid pro quo. I'm doing this for Eduardo.'

'You might regret being so bloody stubborn. Both Ethel and I have contacts. She said she will recommend you as a journalist to her benefactor. I could recommend you to my paper although its circulation is limited.'

'Who's Ethel's benefactor then?'

'Fenner Brockway.'

Mark shrugged and waited. He had never heard of the man.

Sheena stared at him. 'You call yourself a journalist and yet you don't know who Brockway is.'

Mark remained silent. He had always known he would be caught out in his lie.

He's the General Secretary of *the Independent Labour Party* Mr Anders, and he is why both Ethel and I are here. He is also the editor of the newspaper *The New Leader*.

She stared at him again. 'Good lord, you have never heard of *New Leader* or *The Glasgow Herald* I suppose.'

'I'm Australian.' A poor excuse, but the only one Mark could think of, other than exposing his ignorance of the press and political structures in Britain.

He didn't want it known that he had been a field labourer. He had never minded labouring. In fact, he'd been lucky to have scored the job at a time when many had nothing after the worldwide financial implosion. Before that he'd been a tin miner, working on his stepfather's dredge with the intention of becoming a mining engineer like his dad.

All that occurred before he'd taken on the mantle of newsman. People here would not understand, and if they saw him as a labourer, he would lose all credibility as a journalist. The occupations belonged to different classes, regardless of circumstances.

He'd learned that battling the establishment through strike after strike in the cane fields back home, when he'd come to realise that even though Australians denied they had a class structure, it was an all-pervasive channel flowing under the sands of society. Here, in Europe, it ran above ground, wide and deep, controlling every walk of life.

Revealing his past for public inspection remained a risk he refused to take at this early stage of his new career. Once he had made a name for himself that might change, but not just yet.

Sheena said, 'Working for a British mainstream newspaper is more socially acceptable than a communist newspaper like *L'Humanité*. If you are truly not a communist, we can help your career in exchange for what you can do to help Eddy, but you had better be good at what you do.'

Mark nodded. He hated to admit it, but Sheena was right.

She grabbed his arm. 'Come on then, we don't have much time.'

Refugee Plight

Beatrice had opened a new office in London, on Litchfield Street. She had devised a new administrative system to track and provide support for the refugees who poured out from Europe, not just from Spain, but increasingly from Germany as well.

Her office wasn't far from the International Brigade's office in Covent Garden and a little farther along from the *Centre for the Relief of Wounded British Volunteers* who had fought in Spain. Above the Centre, the dormitory where Mark had stayed when he first arrived in England, had been turned over to help the veterans' widows and children.

She still had not heard from Mark although she had written asking him to come to her birthday party. He hadn't replied. Had the letter even found him? She sighed; she should just put him out of her mind. Forget about him. He wasn't coming back for her.

She looked down at the open ledger. Often enough, her work covered both the refugees and the war veterans, and she had developed a system for keeping all aspects in separate compartments. Some of the unions, charitable or religious organisations, and political parties refused to participate if they thought they might be contaminated by the communist involvement.

It made organising a challenge, but Beatrice found the work absorbing. She didn't care about the politics or about who spoke to whom, so long as they kept the money and support flowing to enable her to get it to the people who needed it.

The British people were generally sympathetic to the plight of the Spanish refugees and had given generously. Yet they supported Britian's non-intervention policy. The horrors of the Great War had not faded from the collective memory, and no one wanted a repeat. Although as Grandfather said, sticking their heads in the sand would not prevent Germany having another crack at it.

Had anyone asked her opinion, which they hadn't, she would have told them that non-intervention only achieved support for the insurgents. By hampering the democratically elected government, the ordinary Briton remained so fearful of the Spanish conflict spreading to include British forces, they ignored Germany and Italy's flagrant disregard for the non-intervention pact.

She closed the ledger and got up to put it away. All afternoon she had sat at the rickety table that acted as her desk and listened to more stories of horror. Appalling tales of hunger, bombs, and strafing while on the road fleeing the Spanish Nationalist's terror.

The refugees described harrowing moments of bombs falling on besieged Bilbao, dropped by rebel insurgents, who knew they had time on their side, and who were in no hurry to engage the strong Basque army. At least, not until the soldiers had been worn down by lack of food and constant shelling.

She also heard heartbreaking stories of lost or missing members of families who became separated as they fled Nazi Germany, the Gestapo on their heels. Coal ships, crewed by socialist sailors, had saved them.

Each refugee had a story to tell beyond anything Beatrice could imagine. As they spoke, she visualised blacken and shapeless bodies, clothing blasted off in ultimate disrespect. They left her with nightmares of shapeless men chasing her through unfamiliar streets. Sometimes her dreams were filled with emaciated people surviving on rats when all the cats and dogs were eaten.

She maintained a neutral expression and wrote down every detail, checking on names, dates, and places. She explained how working visas were difficult to obtain for refugees, and gave them vouchers, money and addresses where they might seek food and shelter. One day this would be over, and people must be able to find each other. In the meantime, she would record and bear witness, if only vicariously. She wished she could do more.

If it were up to her she would personally drop bombs on General Franco, for all the carnage he'd caused in his lust for power, and on Herr Hitler for treating his citizens with such cruelty.

She placed the ledger in a cupboard, already filled with similar records, before glancing at her new wristwatch, an early birthday present from her grandfather. She had better hurry. Tonight, she would host another fund-raiser. A film night.

During the terrible cane cutter strikes over Weil's disease in Innisfail two years ago, she'd learned that people gave more freely when they were involved in social activities. She had tried to emulate the idea, becoming an organiser unaffiliated to any ideological or political allegiance.

Of course, she realised her grandfather's name and perhaps her money gave her the credibility to carry this out. What did it matter why they contributed? The purpose remained unsullied by her privilege, and both ordinary people and financial doners joined in with great enthusiasm.

The last event she had co organised had been a success, so much so that the other participants called upon her to speak. She had walked onto the stage at a local guild hall, and Peter Spencer, had hugged her, tears spilling from his reddened eyelids. Despite the jollity of the event, the awful situation in Spain deserved tears.

After that event the Labour Party leader, Clement Attlee, had agreed to attend the next fundraiser. Now at last, triumph-of-triumphs, the government had agreed to shelter the Spanish children. Of course, they were not going to pay for any of it. Miserly bunch.

She picked up a newspaper, *New Leader*. She had seen it on the newsstand and had bought it, for it held a two-page spread showing the everyday horror of the civil war on its civilian population. Tears filled her eyes as she gazed at the now familiar pictures.

Even *The Washington Post,* an American newspaper her grandfather subscribed to, had printed some of Mark's photos, and those in turn had been reprinted in a dozen other newspapers in both America and Britian, even reaching Australian papers.

His byline had become nectar for hovering gossip columnists, who demanded to know *from where had this dashing new photographer sprung?* She wanted to shout their friendship to the world, even though it had ended.

The door opened, and Beatrice composed her features as Gladys entered, accompanied by another woman.

'Beatrice dear, I hope I am not disturbing your work, but I have some exciting news. Oh, and I've brought someone to meet you. Miss Pye may I present Miss Beatrice Langham. Miss Pye is involved with the *International Commission for the Assistance of Child Refugees* in Spain and *The Red Cross.*'

Beatrice walked around her table towards a small elderly woman with greying hair, parted in the middle and pulled back into a bun at the back of her head.

'It's a pleasure to meet you Miss Pye, I have heard so much about your wonderful efforts in helping women and children during the Great War, and your bravery in China.'

The woman shook Beatrice's hand.

'Please call me Edith.' She looked around the small office. 'I'm interested to see what you do here.'

Gladys jiggled up and down as if impatient. 'Oh, Beatrice, what do you think? The Spanish children are being evacuated as we speak. They will be arriving any day.'

'That's wonderful news. How can I help? Where will they be housed?'

Gladys's face fell. 'North Stoneham, near Eastleigh. There's a local farmer, Mr Brown, who says the children can camp in his fields.'

'Camp. In tents?'

'It's all we have right now. We thought there would be fewer children, but it seems more are coming.'

'How many?'

'Four thousand, I heard mentioned.'

'Good grief. What about sanitation. A field is not suitable.'

Gladys frowned 'I know, but it's all we have and already families from all over the country are putting their hands up to take the children in. The camp is just a staging area... Our volunteers will make sure the children are looked after. Anyway, anything is better than where they are coming from.'

Beatrice looked doubtful. 'Will you also sleep in a tent?'

'Of course. I've been down to Eastleigh already, helping to set up. You should see the place. Rows and rows of tents like a field army, but we'll manage.'

The gentle clearing of a throat brought the two women back to the issue at hand and Gladys said, 'Oh, Miss Pye wants to talk about fundraising.'

''Edith Pye said, 'Gladys brought me along to meet with you because of our need for funds. I hear you are quite exceptional at raising money for the cause.'

'She is,' Gladys interjected. 'She manages to compel the most reluctant hands to empty the deepest pockets.'

'You do realise my friend exaggerates my abilities, don't you Miss Pye?'

The older woman ignored the banter as if her mission were too important for frivolity.

Beatrice's face sobered. 'Tell me what I can do, and I will do my best to help.'

Pye said, 'You see Miss Langham, we are evacuating women and children from Madrid. Swiss Aid has the vehicles, and I wondered...'

Beatrice said, 'Absolutely. I would be happy to do whatever I can... Beginning with the benefit tonight. Come and sit down and tell me exactly what is needed.'

Fight for Right

A few days later, Beatrice sat in the drawing room with her parents. The maid, Annie, collected the afternoon tea tray and rattled out of the room. Beatice tried to get back to her book but couldn't concentrate, still fuming about the lecture from her mother about her inappropriate behaviour.

Her mother now embroidered furiously, while her father had his face buried in *The Times*; presumably unable to speak to her since they had uncovered her place of business.

Apparently, charitable activities like her mother's, were for the deserving, not the hoi polloi. They should uplift one's reputation, not demean it through hobnobbing with the unsavories of Covent Garden.

Beatrice suspected Charles had said something, or how else had they found out?

Outside the daylight had faded and Annie returned to switch on the lights. 'Do you want a fire, my lady?'

Her accent hailed from somewhere in rural England, and Beatrice could seldom understand what she said.

Lady Margaret said, 'I think not.'

Beatrice had acclimatised to London's weather, but she would like a fire. Even though mid-May had arrived, the cold still wrapped its tentacles around her, and she needed fire to lighten the gloom. Ensconced, like this, with disapproving parents would make anyone melancholy. Although it wasn't just the result of her mother's chastisement. Her independence had been under threat since her father flew in from Australia a few weeks ago.

He had arrived in time to attend the inaugural sugar conference, hosted in London by the League of Nations. Uncle George had attended it too, and Aunt Emily had accompanied him to London to attend the Sugar Ball and the King's coronation. Now all the celebration were done, George and Emily had returned to Australia. Lucky Charles. She wished her parents would follow.

Infuriatingly, during the sugar conference, the Australian contingent had agreed to prevent Weil's Disease by burning all cane prior to harvest. When Beatrice heard that news she had wanted to cry. After all that Mark had gone through. The bitter strike to force the company to do something about the cane cutters in North Queensland dying from the disease, had been for nothing. Now her father had simply agreed to burning the cane before the harvest.

When she confronted him, he had said loftily, my dear, some principles simply cannot be compromised. You cannot let the communists win.

Beatrice had raged, arguing that not all of those striking and dying were communists. Men were human first. Although her father didn't consider humanity in business. He led a compartmentalised existence, but she laid the blame squarely at his feet. If he hadn't treated Mark so badly, her heart might not have been broken.

Arthur Langham lowered the broadsheet. 'I have booked our passage home for a week today. I would have done it earlier but...'

The 'but' was Beatrice's birthday party. Her mother seemed to be delaying her return to Australia by arranging events before her husband had even landed on English soil.

As if to confirm Beatrice's suspicion, Lady Margaret said, 'My dear, I think I will need to be here a bit longer. The renovations are not yet complete and then there is my charity, you know. Who will run it if I go back to Sydney?'

Beatrice almost felt sorry for her mother. She didn't want to go back either but at least she had a choice.

Arthur said, 'Your father can manage his own renovations, and you can deputise Charles to act on your behalf. The work is mostly administrative and there is not much you cannot do from Australia. What with airmail, the telephone, and telegraph communications between the two countries, it has become quite easy. I communicate with colleagues across the world in my field all the time. I don't see why your little charity shouldn't do the same.' He paused before saying, 'It's time we went home if for no other reason than the safety Australia provides. Your father thinks another war with Germany is coming.'

Lady Margaret said, 'Oh posh. I don't believe it. Charles told me he visited Germany last year and one would be hard pressed to find a more orderly and peaceful country.'

That is not what the refugees told her... She said aloud, 'I could run your charity, Mother, along with mine. We might even merge them.'

Her mother ignored her and addressed her husband. 'Charles is going to Nationalist Spain in a few weeks.'

'What for this time?'

'Sir Auckland suggested Charles might use his contacts to speak to the Nationalist administration about our collective investments. The dear boy will be too busy to bother with the charity. I really cannot...'

Arthur interrupted, his voice cold. 'Returning home is not up for debate. And Beatrice, there will be no more gadding about after refugees. As your mother has said, it is unseemly for a young woman of your social standing.' Her father shook open the newspaper as if the conversation had ended.

But Beatrice would no longer give in to him. 'I am not going back to Australia, Daddy.'

'You are and you will. This conversation is at an end.' He turned a page. 'Ah, I see Charles has an article in *The Times*.'

Lady Margaret rose and walked towards her husband. 'Do let me see. He's had nothing printed for so long, I planned to ring his editor and complain.'

Beatrice gazed at her parents. Her father hadn't worked out that he had no control over Beatrice's life now that grandfather had arranged for her to take over the management of her own trust fund.

It wasn't only her father's dismissal that hurt. Her mother did her best to ignore Beatrice's independence, competence, career choices, or anything else that did not contribute to Lady Margaret's view of her daughter as flighty and a little unstable. Sometimes Beatrice thought her mother would have been happier if Charles were her son and not her nephew.

Grandfather's decision to cut Daddy out as trustee had made Lady Margaret bitter. Beatrice didn't know what had brought that on or why her father had agreed to it, but Margaret made it quite clear that she blamed her daughter. Regardless, Father might book as many steamer berths as he wished. She would not be on one.

The sound of the front door opening floated through to the drawing room, and stopped her ruminations.

Symons's voice followed. 'Good evening my lord.'

Symons was her grandfather's valet and had once been his batman in the Royal Navy. His taciturn manner and rigid bearing barely hid his ongoing devotion to Grandfather.

She excused herself, arose, and hurried out the room. Lord Denton did something with the foreign office. What, she had no idea, but it must be something important and no doubt secret. But to her he simply remained a warm oasis in a waste zone of familial affection.

After Denton had given Symons his hat and coat, he kissed Beatrice and then holding her shoulders, he examined her face. 'Have you been crying, my dear?'

She smiled. 'You never miss anything do you Grandfather. I'm all right.'

'That wasn't the question I asked. Where are your parents?'

'In the drawing room.'

'Then we will go to my study. I have something I need to discuss with you, and you may confide in me if you wish. Symonds will bring in an apéritif. What will you have my dear?'

Once seated in her grandfather's cosy study with a drink in her hand, Beatrice said, 'Grandfather, will Germany start another war? Daddy says we must go home before it starts.'

'Does he, now. When does he plan to leave?'

'Next week.'

'Are you planning on leaving too?'

'No. I told him I would stay on here, although I don't think he heard, or if he did, he didn't believe me. You don't mind, do you?'

'I should miss you if you left my dear. You may stay on here for as long as you wish. This is your home.'

'Thank you... But do you think Father is right? Will Britain have another war with Germany?'

Denton sighed. 'I ask myself the same question every day.'

'What is your answer?'

'I have not arrived at one. The British Government, generally speaking, does not accept that Adolf Hitler is any real threat, at least not to the British. It's absurd when you realise, they made the same mistake about Germany before the Great War. The trouble is many in the establishment admire what they see as Germany's economic recovery and can't see what the fuss is about. They think the communists are a greater danger to the stability and continuing prosperity of Britain.'

Beatrice appreciated the way he spoke to her as an equal, responding to her question seriously, and with careful thought, rather than fobbing her off as if her delicate feminine ears should not be sullied by politics. She found it revitalising to be treated as an adult intellect, rather than a *mere-slip-of-a-girl* as her father often called her, as if he had only the capacity to see a small slither of her whole person.

Denton continued. 'The British people do not want another war and are quite happy with the government's efforts at appeasing any belligerent European sabre rattling.'

'But you don't agree.' Beatrice said.

'I and a few colleagues think a little differently.' He paused and rubbed his forehead. 'It's not that I advocate war but if we don't stand up to Herr Hitler he will continue. Bullies are deterred only through a show of strength, but a show of strength needs careful calculation so as not to trip, by accident, into war."

'People are saying the Spanish war will lead to a wider European war.'

'I might agree with that assessment. The Spanish war is in both Germany's and Italy's strategic interests and, if they didn't plan and foment it, they certainly gave it a helping hand. Both Count Galeazzo Ciano in Italy along with Germany's Admiral Canaris see a Nationalist Spain as an opportunity.'

'How?'

'Well, Germany needs Franco to remain a benign presence in the face of their increasing desire to plunder Europe. Hitler is gearing up for war, of that I am certain. Perhaps not with Britain but certainly to take Europe. As for Italy... They fear the Spanish Republic's strategic position on the Mediterranean. A democratic socialist government in Spain would aid Leon Blume's Popular Front in France to defend against any further Italian plans for the Mediterranean.'

Beatrice said, 'Is that why the Italians are helping the Nationalists? To have a friendly ally.'

Denton nodded before picking up his glass.

She said, 'Maybe the Russians will help the Spanish Republic.'

'They are providing some support already, but they will not commit entirely.'

'Why not? They struck an agreement with the French to come to each other's aid.'

'Yes, and that's backfired or at least Lloyd George has managed to make a case for his absurd claim that the Franco-Soviet pact caused the German remilitarisation of the Rhineland. He argues that we forced Germany into a corner, fearing a Russian/French two-pronged attack.'

'Aren't they simply parroting Germany's excuse?'

'Yes, but Lloyd George has now given it legitimacy. We in Britain are fearful of war and I am doing everything within my diplomatic power to prevent the Spanish war becoming a European conflagration.'

'If it is only Germany and Italy who want war, can't Britian stay out of it?'

'It's not that simple my dear. Britain's problem is that if the insurgents control Spain they may mount an attack on Gibraltar, leaving the Italians with strategic control of the Mediterranean, thus compromising British access to the Suez Canal. If Franco wins, in exchange for Germany's help now, he will be expected to provide some sort of quid pro quo in terms of coal, steel, pyrites, and food to bolster Hitler's capacity to wage war. That is, if he does not throw in his lot with Germany. My concern is that if

Hitler wages war in Europe, it is only a matter of time before his eyes turn to Britain.'

'Are you saying that it is in Britain's interest for the Republican government to win the Spanish war?'

He shrugged. 'I think so, but many of my colleagues do not agree. They think the Soviets are a bigger threat.'

'They can't possibly think it is in British interests for the Nationalist insurgents to win. That's a terrible thought. It means that any army that doesn't like its government can declare war.'

'It wouldn't be the first time but condoning or condemning the Spanish war depends on where one's focus lies. There are many in Britain who stand to lose a great deal if the Spanish Republic nationalises things like mines, factories and telecommunications.'

'They support non-intervention because it is actually supporting their own financial interests regardless of how it emboldens Hitler and Mussolini or hurts the Spanish people.'

Denton nodded. 'It's difficult to blame them I suppose. After all, for many it might be the difference between current wealth or relative poverty. Not everyone has the moral fortitude to take the right path knowing it will lead to their own impoverishment. We are caught between the precipice and hell's gates. My own Ministry's undersecretary, the Earl of Plymouth, is vehemently opposed to Britain's involvement in Spain. Although, like many others I suspect, he only understands what suits his agenda. Which is all very well, but of course it leaves the door wide open for Hitler's march through Europe.

The trouble is, there is so much smoke in the media. It occludes what is happening in Spain and makes it hard to know the truth. What I need is a clear-eyed account of issues on the ground, but I have no one there, or rather no one I trust to provide an unbiased account.'

An image of Mark leaped into Beatrice's mind. She could go to Spain and find him. 'Perhaps I could go Grandfather. I could report back to you.'

'My dear, that is brave of you but not even the British Ambassador is in Spain at the moment.

'Didn't he say he thought a Nationalist takeover would suit Britain.'

Denton nodded. 'The problem for Britain is not with Spain alone. Our new PM thinks Germany won't bother us and has adopted Baldwin's appeasement policy. Many of the Foreign Office agree. A foolish view in my opinion.'

'It strikes me that Mr Chamberlain is more interested in domestic issues, like sorting out the London bus strike, rather than getting involved in international affairs...' She gazed at Denton. 'Who do you most fear will drag us into war, Grandfather?'

'Personally—Germany. Italy is a problem, but Germany is the greater risk. Since we have done nothing about the German invasion of the Rhineland, Hitler becomes emboldened. He is not ready to mount an all-out war, but he will be in a year or two and he wants his ducks lined up nicely to accommodate his ambitions for a Europe dominated by Germany.'

'Shouldn't Britain pre-empt German and Italian aggression by showing them who's boss?'

Denton laughed and raised his glass. 'Have you been talking to Winnie again?' His face sobered. 'We are in no position to go to war. Not only do the British people object, but we are not equipped. That is one of the reason's I wished to speak to you.'

Beatrice fell silent and examined her grandfather. A frown had permanently run track marks between his eyes. To her, their discussions about politics and diplomacy had always been a game. But to him, this remained serious.

She loved the frank and sometimes brutal discussions they had, and he never made her feel as if she could not understand the significance of political ramifications. Even as a child, he would explain things in a way that she could grasp. He had once said he thought it high time women were recruited into the diplomatic services, for if they were, there would be no more wars. She wasn't so sure about that. If it were up to her, Britian would be supporting the Spanish Republican government to quash the Nationalist's insurrection.

Eventually, with caution in her voice she said, 'I can't see what help I could be, but go ahead.'

'The house in Surrey my dear. I hear the American tenants are vacating. Going back to America.'

'Yes. They too fear war is brewing.'

Denton nodded. 'Have you decided what you want to do with it?'

Beatrice hadn't, but an idea struck her. 'I thought perhaps I could use it to house the refugees. That's if you don't mind me continuing to live here.'

'I would not have it any other way.' Denton ran his hand across his mouth. 'As for the refugees, your concern is laudable, but it's a long way from any services. They might be a bit stranded out there.'

'I hadn't thought of that, but you are right.' She examined his face. 'I can see you have an idea, don't you?'

'I do and if you agree to my ministry leasing it, you would be contributing to Britain's preparations for war.'

Beatrice frowned. 'What do you mean? How?'

'Ha, now that, my dear, I cannot tell you. It's classified.'

She sighed. 'I have always thought the house more rightfully yours than mine.'

'Your grandmother left it to you along with her fortune. It is solely yours.'

'Yes, but it's your ancestral home.'

'And yours my dear, but my father almost lost it. If it hadn't been for your grandmother, it would be a ruin or belong to another family altogether.'

'Still Granddad, Grandmother was your wife. She should have left it to you.'

He shook his head vehemently. 'You know why she left it to you my dear.'

'Yes. You said, but it still doesn't feel right.'

'Do you doubt your grandmother's judgement?'

'Of course not.' Beatrice clutched her hands in her lap.

Denton continued. 'And she was proven correct...'

'What happened? I know something went wrong with money and that's why you signed my trust into my control, but what? I don't know and should like to.'

'Are you sure Beatrice?'

'Yes. Of course.'

'Will it suffice to say that neither your father nor your mother understands fiduciary duty. When I uncovered what they had done with your trust, I had no option.'

Beatrice fell silent before saying, 'But my trust is healthy. Brian Heggerty told me so.'

He sighed. 'Yes, but a few years ago, your father borrowed against it to enrich his own portfolio. When he got into a financial jam, your mother used charitable funds, she had collected for another project, to help him out. As soon as I uncovered the mess I rectified it, and I think they are both suitably chastised.'

Beatrice had her hand to her mouth in shock. 'You bailed them out.'

'Well, everything I own will, one day, go to her. She merely received some of it early.'

Beatrice took a deep breath. 'But what they did is a criminal act.'

'Yes.'

'You should not have protected them.'

'It wasn't them that concerned me. Their behaviour would have ruined us all. You and I do not deserve that. This must never leak. It would ruin the family's good name. But let us return to the subject at hand.'

Beatrice stared at her grandfather, competing thoughts clashing in her head, but she nodded. 'What is that?''

He smiled. 'The house. Will you allow the British government its use.

'They would rent it you say.'

'Yes, at a reasonable fee naturally.'

'I am sure it will be in good hands.'

'Thank you my dear. It will be an enormous contribution.' He got up and walked to the drinks tray Symonds had left. 'Another drink?'

She shook her head.

When he returned, he picked up the paper. 'I see your young man is making a name for himself. I took the liberty of looking into his background and character. I must admit what I found makes me think he is certainly a worthy suitor. I can't for the life of me work out why your parents objected so strongly. And most astonishingly, I hear he rather impressed Sir Henry Chiltern.'

'Oh Grandfather. He is not my young man. Not anymore, but you shouldn't be prying into his life. That's horrible. He wouldn't thank you if he knew and it would be so embarrassing if he found out.'

Her grandfather ignored her rebuke. 'I thought he said he would visit you next time he is in London.'

'Yes. He did but I don't think he meant it.'

'Are you sure about that Beatrice?'

'Well, given the way Daddy and Uncle George treated him, what do you think?'

'I think you should send him an invitation to dine with us both. I would like to meet him.'

'I think he is in Spain still. I had thought of going too.'

Her grandfather paused with his drink halfway to his lips. 'Tell me.'

'I met a woman, Miss Edith Pye.'

He nodded. 'I know of Miss Pye's work.'

Beatrice said, 'She is an amazing woman. She explained that Swiss Aid were transporting food and medical aid to Madrid and bringing out any of the remaining women and children who wanted to leave. She asked for my help in fund raising and I am of course happy to help, but I thought I might go, just once, to see what is needed. My friend Gladys is off to somewhere near Southampton to a camp they have set up for the Spanish children. I feel so useless sitting in a London office writing down names and stories. I could travel to Madrid with the Swiss Aid convoy to understand the needs of the refugees better. Miss Pye said she would arrange it with someone in Swiss Aid called Karl Ketterer.'

Denton scrutinised her face for a minute before saying, 'It seems, from what you are saying, that you are going to tag along with people who are already doing the work. Wouldn't you be of more use here raising funds as Miss Pye requested?'

Beatrice scowled at her grandfather. 'That's a horrible thing to say.'

He tilted his head. 'Perhaps, but I am trying to point out the obvious. It strikes me your motivation is misaligned. Are you sure you are not wanting to go there in the hope of seeing Mark again.'

She frowned. 'Sometimes Granddad, I just hate your logic.'

He smiled. 'Write to him. Ask him to visit. I would like to meet him, and I am sure you don't need to traipse all over a war zone in the hope of bumping into him again. I know people Beatrice, and I am certain that if you ask, he will come.'

She sighed. 'I did that already, and I have had no response.'

'What did you say?'

'I sent him an invitation to my party.'

Denton chuckled and placed his empty glass on an occasional table next to his chair. 'Your mother will not be pleased.'

She narrowed her eyes. 'What are you up to Granddad? This isn't about my broken heart, is it?'

He got up from his chair. 'I think we should rejoin your parents. It must be almost time for dinner.' He held out his arm.

The Turning Point

Mark stared in amazement at the cheque that had arrived from *The Washinton Post*. On his return from Spain, he had stopped in Paris, where he had called in to see Sylvia Boyle. She too had persuaded him that his first publications should not be with a communist affiliated paper. Instead, she had convinced him to contact Brockway. She also took some of his photos and sent them off to her own newspaper. To his immense surprise they had printed them alongside Silvia's report.

He had travelled on to London where he'd met Brockway, who had bought his photos along with a report he hadn't expected to publish. Brockway had also offered a commission for a report from Madrid along with accompanying photos. Mark not only had the *New Leader,* but he also had *The Washington Post* to add to his curriculum vitae.

Along with the cheque from *The Washington Post* he had also received a note from Charles saying his editor was keen to meet.

He had suggested they meet at Simpson's in the Strand today, at one o'clock.

The Times editor wanted to meet him! He couldn't quite get his head around that idea. Although he doubted either Charles, or his editor would be interested once they found out his background.

He had cautiously mentioned it to Silvia. Rather than recoiling, as he had expected, she had been fascinated. That gave him some hope. Still, Mark could not be sure Charles differed much from his father, George West.

He touched his top pocket where Beatrice's invitation knocked against his chest with its incessant demands for a decision. He couldn't risk his livelihood in the way George West and Authur Langham had done to him previously. Meeting them in a public place like the Ritz might be safer, but one could never be sure. These people moved in devious ways.

He now had money in his pocket, a fledgling reputation, and a commission from the *New Leader*. He should travel straight back to Spain, instead of wasting his time yearning after an heiress. She could have her pick of more suitable men, men of her class and wealth. He should be content with his career moving forward.

Having a legitimate commission would be enough to get a visa to return to Republican Spain, and on to Madrid, although his first port of call would need to be Barcelona. Brockway had given him a letter to deliver to Ethel. She had become a household name in British homes after smuggling food and letters to anarchist prisoners, as well as helping several escape the Republic's wrath. Despite her fame as the Scots Scarlet

Pimpernel, Brockway worried. He'd asked Mark to persuade her to come home.

Little chance of that. Beside she had a greater capacity to take care of herself than he might. He shrugged into a jacket, slung his Leica over his shoulder, picked up his hat, and set off. It was noon now. If he walked briskly, he could deposit the cheque from *The Washington Post* before he met Charles for lunch.

An hour later Mark walked through Simpson's arched entrance just as a nearby clock sounded a single chime. It took him a minute before he spotted Charles seated in a booth at the far end of the gentleman's dining room.

Charles looked up and waved. He stood as Mark arrived and shook his hand before he turned to the other man in the booth and introduced Mark.

'My boss, Geoffrey Dawson, editor of *The Times*. Mark Anders, fellow Australian, and freelance photojournalist.'

Dawson arose and shook Mark's hand. 'I've heard a lot of good reports about you from Charles and your photography is excellent.'

Charles moved along the bench seat. 'We've ordered the beef. I hope you don't mind but why else dine at Simpson's if not for the roast beef, eh?'

Mark sat down, noting Dawson didn't look pleased to see him despite his words. There remained a look of dissatisfaction in the doughy lines of the editor's face as if he had always expected to be disappointed, and this meeting held no exception.

The next words he spoke explained his expression. 'You are wasting your time on Spain, you know. Moving photography, good reporting, but the war in Spain is their own affair. It is not something Britain or the British people should focus on. There are other matters dearer to British interests, which need airing.'

Mark pressed his mouth into a line before saying, 'Such as?'

'I am interested in commissioning a piece about Britain's peaceful coexistence with Germany. I think ensuring peace between our two great nations is of paramount public interest.'

Mark looked down at the table. He wasn't about to share his point of view with someone like Dawson, and while he didn't know where the conversation led, he willingly went along for the ride. Besides, he wouldn't mind getting into Germany to see the reality on the ground, although he had barely scratched the surface of what he wanted to do in Spain. He glanced at Charles, who seemed to watch both men with a look of curiosity in his eyes.

By the time lunch ended, Mark thought he had a better understanding of Dawson. An absolutist, a monarchist, and a man who viewed himself as an expert on European issues. A claim Mark doubted, when Dawson insisted that the right articles in his paper would serve not only in shaping British views but would also influence Germany's activity in favour of British interests.

'It's a question of butter or guns, don't you see.' Dawson said.

At that moment, Mark knew Dawson remained a danger to the nation, with a grandiose assessment of his own influence on the Prime Minister. He wouldn't do well working for the man, although he would let him think he might be interested. Throughout lunch he made noises of agreement but managed to leave without committing himself to anything binding.

After lunch, he accompanied Charles along the Strand, listening to him extolling Dawson's virtues. They had reached Victoria Embankment when Charles said, 'You'd do well to consider his offer. He's well connected not only with the British establishment but also with influential people in the Anglo-German Fellowship. He wasn't exaggerating about having Neville Chamberlain's ear, and he's in tight with von Ribbentrop, Germany's ambassador to Britian.'

Mark didn't need to hear any more and changed the subject. 'Are you still going to your cousin's party tomorrow night?'

'You have a good memory.' Charles eyed Mark with a quizzical look.

'Not really, you see I also received an invitation. Just trying to work out whether I should go.'

Charles pulled up and turned to stare at Mark. 'Two things: why on earth would you not attend? But more importantly, how do you know my cousin? You have never mentioned it before.'

Charles had suspicion written into every smooth feature of his face and Mark held up his hands in surrender. 'I probably should have mentioned it, but you should know, your family and I don't see eye to eye.'

'Good God! You know my family too.'

'Not as such, no. I have never met your parents... Just had a difference of opinion back in Australia...'

'Over what?'

'Union matters mostly.' Mark wasn't going to go into the sorry events in Innisfail and changed direction. 'I also met Beatrice in Australia.'

Charles laughed, breaking the tension. 'My father abhors unionists. But you dark horse... Of course, you must attend Beatrice's party. It'll be the talk of the season, and you are bound to meet some interesting people. Her grandfather is an aristocrat, and some big wig in the diplomatic service. Cloak, and dagger stuff most likely, or at least I can never get a handle on what he does. Very influential. In any case, you can be sure everyone who is anyone will be there. All the political player at any rate. Money and diplomats... like bubbles to champagne.'

'Including Dawson?'

'Don't think he was invited, but I didn't ask. My aunt is an awful snob, doesn't go in much for people without titles, or deep pockets. Newspaper editors are probably not her cup of tea. She is more likely to invite the owners of *The Times*.' He seemed to notice Mark's blank expression for he said, 'The Astors, idiot. For a newspaper man you are an absolute ignoramus. Violet Astor and Aunt Margaret are firm friends, and the Astors have at least three sons of marriageable age although not sure if they are already taken. Certainly, my aunt will invite every noble born son of the right age. She thinks her honourable daughter needs a husband to keep her under control. I must say, I'm surprised she invited you. Even I am only tolerated while I am useful.'

Mark said, 'She didn't. Beatrice sent the invitation.'

'You are a dirty dog, keeping that a secret.'

'Why does Beatrice need to be kept under control?'

Charles laughed. 'You have been in Spain too long my friend. Beatrice has been making a spectacle of herself with all the wrong people, including the Labour Party leader, Clement Attlee. For that alone she should face treason charges, but she is also great friends with Peter Spencer, although,' Charles frowned, 'I had heard he'd gone off to Turkey for some reason.'

Once more Charles seemed to understand Mark's blank look. He added, 'the 2nd Viscount Churchill. He's the chap who helped set up the committee for medical aid for Spain. That's not all. She's been working with the Red Duchess, Trade Unionists, communist, as well as socialists and leftist politicians, along with other riff raff—authors, playwrights, and artists, etcetera. You'll possibly see most of them at the party rubbing shoulders with staunch Torys. As you were a union man, you might feel absolutely at home. The whole affair should make for interesting viewing, if not drawn swords and flung gauntlets. It is any wonder Lady Margaret is in despair and wanting her to make a suitable marriage. Not that any right thinking unmarried noble son would have her, after her current carry-on.'

Mark stared at Charles, a frown creasing his forehead. 'What carry-on...?'

'Refugees.' Charles shuddered in a theatrical way. 'Oh, and fund raising. She gets on stage and speaks, or rather harangues people for money, for God's sake. In public, if you don't mind, like some kind of working-class banshee.

'Where?'

'What?'

'Where does she speak in public?'

'Good Lord. I don't know. I went along to one she had last week, just to report back to my aunt. I didn't stay long. It was embarrassing to listen to her.'

'Where did she hold it?'

'Holborn Hall, I think. Why. You are not planning on going to one of those things, are you?'

Mark wanted to punch the man but kept his voice on the level. 'Why not. It might be interesting.'

'Well, you can go along to her office and ask her when the next one is.'

'Her office?' A pulse jumped in his throat.

'Good grief. You haven't been in touch since you came to London, have you?'

'I saw her before I went to Spain. Not since I've been back.'

'She has an office somewhere near Covent Garden. It's in a dreadfully bohemian area... Litchfield Street, I think.'

Mark looked around and hailed a taxicab. 'Mate, I'll see you tomorrow. Thanks for lunch and the introduction.' He climbed into the taxi.

'Litchfield Street,' he told the cabbie and then lifted his hand in a wave to Charles who stood gawking as though Mark had gone stark staring bonkers.

Mark walked into the office, where a sign instructed him to,

*Please take a seat. Someone will attend
to you in turn.*

Several other people sat, or stood leaning against walls, presumably refugees from the nature of the establishment. Mark took off his hat and sat down on a vacant chair.

No reception, and no receptionist, just a plain white door diagonally across from the front entrance, gave any indication that there might be more than one room to this establishment. The cream-coloured walls were covered with posters advertising helpful information in Italian, Spanish, German, English, and a language that might be Yiddish.

A family came out from the closed white door before scurrying through the waiting room and out the entrance. A moment later, Beatrice stood in the doorway. She wore a dark suit with a plain white blouse. Sensible Oxford's clad her feet. She had coiled her long, nut-brown hair at the back of her head. It made her look older, sober like a schoolmarm, rather than the sparkling young woman he knew from Australia.

She said, 'Who's next?'

The man next to Mark stood up.

Beatrice's eyes locked onto Mark's and her face paled.

He stood up. The man next to him objected. Mark ignored him.

Beatrice seemed to recover and said in a formal voice. 'Mr Anders I will see you at five o'clock.' With that she gestured to the man and turned back to the nether regions of her office.

The man glanced at Mark with a triumphant look and followed Beatrice through the door. Every face in the room lifted towards him in curiosity. He shook his head and walked out. He had two and a half hours to kill.

At five o'clock, Beatrice sat in one of the now empty waiting room chairs, her hands folded in her lap as she breathed in deeply and regularly to still her raging pulse. She would not give him the satisfaction of knowing her excitement. But she watched the minute hand on the wall clock as it ticked off one and then two minutes.

The door opened and there he stood.

She rose slowly. 'Mark. You are back. Nice of you to call although it might have been better if you had given me some warning.'

He removed his hat and stood in the doorway, the hat moving relentlessly from one hand to the other. 'I only heard you were here today.'

'You didn't write.'

'No.'

'Would you like to sit down?'

'Can we get out of here?'

'I suppose so, but I don't have much time. My family expect me home.'

He frowned.

'We can get a cup of tea if you like.'

He nodded.

Beatrice picked up her handbag and her keys and walked out. He followed and stood by while she locked the door. They walked in silence along the crowed pavement, until Beatrice couldn't stand it any longer. 'Why have you come to see me, Mark?'

He stopped and she turned towards him, ignoring the other passers-by.

'You asked me to.'

Disappointment surged in her breast, and she walked on, images of their last meeting playing across her mind.

He, standing like now in the street, saying goodbye, walking away.

She, calling for him to wait, asking if he would visit when he returned from Spain.

Him, saying yes.

And now here he was, true to his word, so why did she feel so disappointed?

'There's a tearoom around this corner.'

They sat at a table by a window steamed opaque from the fog of voices in the crowded room.

He stared at her, his face unreadable.

She avoided his gaze, fussing with the cruets on the table, the lay of her skirt, the buttoned front of her jacket, the collar of her blouse.

Eventually, she could bear the silence no longer. 'Say something Mark.'

'You look different.'

She blinked. 'You don't.'

He smiled. 'No. I am the same.'

'So am I.' Even to her own ears her voice sounded indignant.

'No, you have changed.'

'How?'

'You look so authoritative.'

She laughed. 'That's the look I intended.'

'What you are doing... It's fine work.'

She sighed. 'It's not enough. It's overwhelming Mark. So much suffering. I just can't do enough to even make a dent. The only thing that can stop it is political will to stand up to the bullies. Like you did in Innisfail.'

'No. I am a fool. I caused everyone to suffer, and they won in the end. The establishment have all the aces and always wins.'

'You did the right thing, and you'll be pleased to know the sugar company has given an undertaking to burn cane before harvest to prevent any future cases of Weil's disease. They decided it at the international sugar conference. Sometimes what you do only bears fruit afterwards.'

'Í hadn't heard about that. I'm pleased for the cutters back home, but I don't come out swinging any longer.'

She crinkled her nose. 'What do you mean?'

'I've taken up photojournalism.'

'Yes, I've seen your photos.'

He pressed his lips together but said nothing more as a woman brought their tea things and laid them out on the table.

When the waitress had gone, Beatrice poured milk into her cup and offered the jug to him.

He shook his head.

She poured tea into her own cup and held the pot over his.

'Thanks.'

'I don't like tea too strong she said. If you don't pour immediately in these cafés, it becomes stewed.'

Mark nodded agreement and took two lumps of sugar, dropping them into his tea before stirring it with a teaspoon.

She wished he would open-up and speak to her like he had in Australia. He had no reticence then. What had happened to him? But she knew. How could he trust it would not happen again?

She said, 'You didn't say if you would come to my birthday party tomorrow.'

He nodded again, and for a moment she thought he would remain silent, but he cleared his throat and said, 'I am not sure if I should.'

'Why Mark?'

'You know why, Beatrice. Your family hates me.'

'Some of my family, Mark, but this is England. You are a respectable photojournalist. You don't work for my father any longer. He has no hold over you. Ignore him and come for my sake.'

He took a deep breath. 'All right. I will then, at least for a little while. So long as I don't have to talk to your parents.'

Beatrice tried to keep the joy from bubbling over. 'Thank you. It will mean a lot to me.'

His gaze became less guarded and more curious as he said, 'I met your cousin Charles. I might turn up with him if that's all right.'

Her eyes narrowed. 'You are friendly with him, despite what his father did?

Mark shrugged and said, 'More like he has taken a shine to me and rather sees it as his duty to take a fellow Australian journalist under his wing. He knows I know you. Just not the extent. But he's been decent towards me.'

'I take back what I said. You have changed. And let me tell you that Charles never does anything for anybody without an ulterior motive. What does he want from you? That's the question you should be asking yourself.'

He smiled. 'He's not that bad. Annoying but not a bad man. I had lunch with him today, and his editor...'

'Dawson!'

'Yes, do you know him?'

'No, but I know of his reputation.'

'What is that?'

She paused. Her conversations with her grandfather about Dawson were private. She wasn't sure they should be brought up in a public place. 'Oh, nothing. He's known as a bit of a Germanophile. I understand he and Charles have become tight since Charles joined the Anglo-German Fellowship.' Beatrice drew a breath. 'Of course, there is nothing wrong with being a friend to Germany. It's just their government that is questionable.'

'Charles is a member?'

'Yes. Didn't you know?'

Mark shook his head, frowning as he stared at his tea. 'I think there are a lot of things I don't know.'

'Perhaps I can help.'

He smiled at her. 'You taught me to dance, remember.'

'I have never forgotten. Will you dance with me tomorrow night.'

She watched his face blanch and tried to keep her amusement from showing. While fearless in the face of real danger, social protocols had him quivering like a little boy.

'Will there be dancing?'

Did she detect a hint of panic in his voice? 'Of course. We have booked Joe Kaye's Dance Band. Mother wanted something more sedate, but I refused to attend if I couldn't have some things my way. Mummy thinks this is a sort of coming out party where I can be displayed as potential marriage material.' Beatrice laughed. 'She is desperate to marry me off and will do anything, even have a jazz band at a party.'

'Does she know you invited me?'

Beatrice tilted her head to one side. 'Does it matter? She can't touch you now.'

'I wouldn't be so sure.'

'I will tell her you will be there, and I will threaten her that if she makes any fuss, I will walk out with you. How's that?'

He smiled. 'You would do that for me?'

'I would.' She stretched across the table and touched his hand. 'I must go now. I promised my mother I would be home to discuss last minute preparations for the party and try on my dress, but I am so looking forward to seeing you there tomorrow night.'

'I'll walk with you.'

'I have my own car. It's parked behind my office.'

His expression barely changed at that statement. Beatrice expected he would have been impressed by her thoroughly modern independence, but he didn't comment.

He simply said, 'I'll walk you to it.'

The Party

The Ritz felt beyond anything Mark had experienced. Yet
despite the hollow sensation in his stomach, he followed
Charles through the glitz and under glittering chandeliers, until
he saw Beatrice. She stood next to a potted palm at the base of
the stairs talking to an elderly man in white tie and tails.

As they arrived she smiled. 'Hello Charles. Thank you for
coming, Mark. I was waiting for you... May I introduce my
grandfather, Lord Denton of Banville.'

'Delighted to finally meet you old chap. Beatrice has told me a
lot about you.' Denton shook Mark's hand. 'Hello Charles.' He
shook Charles' hand and then turned back to Mark. 'If you have
a moment, I would like to introduce you to some other admirers
of your photography; aside from me, that is.' He turned to
Beatrice. 'You won't mind if I steal him away, my dear? Just while
you greet your other guests.'

Alfred Denton took command of him as if he were a dog whose behaviour might be unpredictable. Although Mark's perspective soon changed as Denton squired him around the room, introducing him to one aristocrat after another. All of them admired his photography, or so they said, although he didn't believe most even knew his name or what photos he had taken. After all, he was not an unpredictable dog, merely the freak show at a fair ground.

Perhaps that was unfair to Denton. They stopped at another group of people, and all thoughts of his own status vanished as Denton said, 'My dear Jacobo. May I present Mr Mark Anders, the celebrated Australian photojournalist. Mark, may I introduce the most excellent Duke of Alba and of Berwick.'

The duke took Mark's outstretched hand; his face infused with the air of a smiling wolf. Another Franco supporter, but someone with the influence to get him into Nationalist held territory. Mark became determined to win him over.

The duke said, 'I have seen your photographs of my country.'

Mark smiled. 'The only bit of Spain I've seen is Barcelona and I am reliably informed it does not represent the whole country. I would like to see how the rest fares.'

Alba raised hooded eyes to glance at Denton. 'And what is your assessment of the Republican cause, Mr Anders?'

'They can't win.' Mark said bluntly. It was unfortunate, but he believed in the facts, so it became easy to say it with conviction. In any event, it would be what this bloke wanted to hear, and he wasn't going to shoot down a man who might be able to get him into Franco's territory, no matter the politics.

Before he had arrived here tonight, he had made a resolution to be whatever and whomever these people wanted him to be. Besides, he had finished fighting the wind. Now, he just sought access to take photos and show the world the Nationalist atrocities against a democratically elected government.

Charles sauntered over and stood next to Alba. 'Can I quote you on that?'

Denton said, 'In your assessment, why can't they win?'

'They're too disorganised. The anarchists are at the socialist's throats, and the socialists are trying to herd anarchists in a direction they think is bourgeois and anti-revolutionary. The liberals in the Republican government are focused on trying to win a war. In war, there can be no consultative democracy or collective decision-making. Winning requires tight hierarchical organisation, with everyone carrying out their role without question as if it's a personal crusade. The anarchists argue that just by arming the people they can win the war. I don't know how the Nationalists are organised but, for sure, the Republicans are divided against themselves along ideological lines.'

Alba's features became animated. 'Do you have a military background?'

'Ah, no.' Mark hesitated. Would candour wreck his chance to influence these people. To hell with it. Authenticity remained more important than toadyism. 'I was a unionist in Australia, and any union organiser will tell you the same thing. The decision to act might be an agreed process, democratic if you will, but, once action has been agreed, there must be control and discipline within a hierarchical command structure. If there is not, any militant action will fail. It is the same in war.'

'I agree entirely.' A newcomer interjected.

Denton turned. 'Ah, Captain Rudolf von Graff, may I present...'

'I have met Mr Anders before.' He made a brief bow to Mark. 'You may recall our meeting at Sir Henry Chilton's home in St. Jean de Luz. I am the Military attaché with the German embassy here in London now, at your service.'

Mark said, 'Of course. How do you do.' To his own amazement he managed to smile and shake hands with the Nazi Captain.

Von Graff said, 'I admire your Spanish photographs. So evocative, so heart-rending. I too am a student of photography and would like to discuss the subject sometime. That is supposing you are to remain in London.'

'I would like to head back. I was just explaining to the duke, all I saw of Spain was Barcelona. I assume it does not typify the whole country.'

'Indeed.'

'Have you been?' Mark asked.

'I was attached to the German embassy in Madrid, and spent many holidays at San Sebastian, but that was some years ago.'

Mark said, 'I would like to see Madrid, but I hear it's a bit difficult right now. He turned to the Duke of Alba. 'I understand you have a rather fine house there.'

The duke replied in a dry tone. 'If you manage to make the trip, you might report back on how it's standing up to the Republican occupation.'

Mark couldn't help himself. 'And the German bombing raids.'

For some reason, the men all laughed as if Mark had made a clever witticism.

Mark took the opportunity and said to the duke, 'Seriously, I would like to get into the occupied zone in the Basque country. So far, I have only managed to get as far as Hendaye. Barcelona. seems the only way to get into Spain for the moment.'

Von Graff examined Mark's face. 'Why would you wish to visit the north?'

'Wouldn't you? Look at the name George Steer has made for himself. I envy him his scoop on Guernica.'

Von Graff's face clouded, and he replied stiffly. 'I am not sure that it was an accurate portrayal, and I have heard he wasn't actually there at the time. So, his eyewitness account remains hearsay.'

Mark smiled and nodded. 'Yes, I heard that rumour.' He turned to Charles. Your newspaper published Steer's account. What do you make of it?'

'Steer was in Bilbao and only arrived after the event. Our reporter James Holburn said the town was destroyed by the Basque army who blew it up rather than have it fall into Nationalist hands. I myself saw the evidence of the Red's destruction by dynamite, but I think we've had this conversation before.'

Mark frowned, 'Ah yes, I recall. Still, I would like to see it and the rest of the Basque country. I hear it is quite beautiful.' He turned to von Graff. 'The real reason I want to go is to counter the gossip and propaganda. From a distance, it's hard to see through the fog to uncover the truth?'

The Duke of Alba looked askance. 'What do you think is the truth, Mr Anders?

'Mark, please. We Australians aren't known for our formality.' He stopped for a moment as if thinking. Then said. 'I imagine the Nationalist troops are better organised, more disciplined, better equipped. They are after all made up of experienced officers, and the Africa Army is a forbidding force, striking with lightning speed which nothing seems able to stop.'

Charles said, 'Are you so keen to rush off back to Spain? I thought you were considering Dawson's offer.'

'I am. Doesn't stop me wanting to see the Basque Country.'

Alba shrugged. 'All things are possible for the right reasons.' He handed Mark his card. 'We should take luncheon together, when you are free.' He excused himself and moved off to join another group.

Von Graff took Mark's elbow and led him a pace or two away. 'What is Geoffrey Dawson's offer, if I may be so bold as to ask?'

Mark smiled. 'Not precisely sure. Something to do with promoting Anglo-German understanding, I think. Not my bag.'

'Which is what Mr Anders? Your bag I mean.'

'War, sir. Although I must admit I would be keen to visit Germany.'

Charles joined them. 'Maybe Rudolf can get you a visa.'

Mark glanced at von Graff. 'I would like that.'

Denton interrupted. 'Excuse me gentlemen but I would like to steal Mark from you a minute.'

As they walked away Denton said, 'You know Mark, the people you meet here tonight can open many doors for you, but if I may offer some advice, be careful which doors you choose. Now, I have someone I want you to meet. He's a great friend and someone who has known Beatrice since she was a baby.

Mark glanced at Denton. Why did the bloke remain so solicitous of him? For an aristocrat and a Tory to boot, Mark quite liked the man and appreciated his support. Although, he couldn't tell him he wasted his advice. Mark played the game to use these contacts and get entry into their world so he might place all the grubby details in newspapers, or on the covers of magazines. First lull them into a sense of benign trust, then stick it to them in a way no one could turn away from.

The name Winston Churchill interrupted Mark's thoughts, and he refocussed his attention.

Denton held out his hand. 'He's waiting through here.'

Who? Not Churchill surely. He should have paid more attention. Mark frowned, recalling Jack banging on about Churchill in the Great War, sending Australian troops into the slaughter yard of the Gallipoli Peninsula, and after the war trying to strangle the new Soviet Russia by supporting the White Army. Jack hated him.

Mark decided candour should be used with Denton. 'I heard he was a fascist supporter... Thinks Mussolini is pretty clever.'

'No, no, you've got it wrong my boy. Winston did admire the way Mussolini got rid of the communists in Italy, it's true. He admires Mussolini's energy and decisive statesmanship, his audacity, and his ability to grasp and make happen what others see as impossible. But he loathes the Nazis almost more than communists. Wants Britain to bonk them on the nose, sooner rather than later. He's convinced Hitler's gearing up for another war, and no one but me, is listening. He claims the Soviets and fascists are mirror images of each other, although at some stage I imagine, we will need Russia on our side to curtail Hitler's ambitions. I think you should meet him. You might have a good debate although I must warn you, he's an economic liberal and an imperialist through and through. Believes in the Crown, Blighty, the Empire and her capitalist economy, and he's not a patient man. He hates political vacillation. He's also a decent painter. Beatrice tells me you are also an artist. You never know… You two might get along rather well.'

That seemed unlikely. Mark followed Denton from the ballroom, along a corridor and out onto a balcony where a man stood smoking a cigar.

'Mark, may I introduce you to my great friend Winston Churchill.'

Mark donned his pleasant-company mantel and stepped forward to shake Churchill's hand. 'I am pleased to meet you sir. I read *Savrola*. Our school library had a copy.'

'Good Grief. How dreadful for you.'

'On the contrary. I enjoyed it. Learned about leadership and solidarity from *Savrola*.'

'You have a military background.' Churchill puffed on his cigar.

Mark shook his head. 'Union man. Never in the army, nor have I been to war other than as a journalist. Never had a sword in my hand although I am handy with a rifle. Shooting wild boar and rabbits mostly.' He paused and said with slow, thoughtful inflection. 'Unionism and the military have some things in common, although without the guns, and with the benefit of democratic decisions… most of the time. Or that's how it works in Australia.' He grinned. 'Can't say the same thing about Spain.'

'And what brought about that observation?'

'Just recently, I witnessed a deadly union-led internecine skirmish in Barcelona. I remained stuck in a safe and luxurious hotel room and didn't get my hands dirty, nevertheless it was a salutary lesson.' He brought the subject back to Churchill's novel. 'But *Savrola* was my first foray into contemplating the fragility of democracy and how to stand against injustice.'

Denton made a half turn towards Mark his eyebrow inching up his forehead.

Mark smiled. Let him wonder.

Denton said, 'I can see you two have a lot to talk about. If you will excuse me for a minute.'

Churchill put his whisky glass into the hand holding his cigar and with his other hand took a fresh cigar from his pocket and held it out to Mark.

'No thanks. I don't.'

He replaced the cigar.

The door clicked as Denton walked back inside.

Churchill turned and looked across the street. 'Tell me about your photography. You have a good eye. I consider myself a bit of an artist, and I see that same leaning in your composition.'

Denton ambled back to the ballroom deep in thought, pleased his old friend had agreed to come into the city for the event. Not that he would have missed the opportunity to see Beatrice all grown up. Mark seemed an interesting mix of contradictions. Perfect material, but just in case his antennae had gone awry, he trusted Winston's judgement about people.

'Grandfather. Where have you been?' Beatrice stood, arms akimbo, blocking his pathway.

'Hello my dear. Enjoying your party.'

'Granddad. What are you up too? Where is Mark? I hardly managed a moment with him before you whisked him off.'

'You asked me to keep him away from your parents.'

'Yes, I know but not to lock him away in a closet or some such.'

Denton laughed. 'He's having a chat with Winston; about literature I think.'

'Literature!' A thoughtful look crossed her face. 'I know he is interested in art. He draws, and I suspect several political lampoons in the Innisfail newspaper were his, although when I asked, he became vague. I didn't know he was interested in literature, although he was always keen on philosophy. I remember seeing some of the books he read.'

'He and Winston will have a lot to talk about then.'

'What do you think of him?'

'I like him. But come my dear. I would like to introduce you to a charming diplomat.' He took his granddaughter's arm and led her back into the crush of people in the ballroom.

Mark shook Churchill's hand and returned to the ballroom. He'd been talking to the man for almost an hour before Churchill said he would retire. How had time escaped like that? It had been one of those rare conversations that become deep quickly and without effort. A true meeting of minds.

If truth be told, Mark remained a little bewildered by it, but he seemed to have more common with the man than he had anticipated. He could have listened to him all night although he recognised the rudeness of his absence from the party. Beatrice had asked him here and he'd barely spoken to her. Probably a wise move considering her parents attitude towards him. Still, he wanted to talk to her.

He found her standing next to Denton, her hand clutched in the meaty paws of a tall and imposing man who looked as if he had no intention of letting her go.

Denton said, 'Mark, just the man. My dear Grandi may I present my granddaughter's good friend, the renowned Australian photojournalist, Mr Mark Anders. Mark, His Excellency, Dino Grandi, newly elevated to Count of Modano and Italy's ambassador to Britain.'

The glowing account of his small achievements took Mark by surprise, but it didn't seem to impress the ambassador. Grandi tilted his head back and looked down his nose at Mark although he didn't let go of Beatrice's hand.

'How do you do,' Mark said and held out his own hand.

The man ignored the outstretched hand. 'You are the journalist who takes photographs of Red peasants?'

Mark smiled wryly; here stood another fascist who needed a good sock in the jaw, but Mark retained his good humour as he had vowed he would. Besides this man, like the Spanish grandee and Geoffrey Dawson, might get him into places that he'd find it difficult to get a visa.

He looked into Grandi's eyes and spoke in Italian. 'I'm honoured to meet you, Excellency. I hope Beatrice has kept you entertained.' He looked pointedly at Grandi's hands holding hers.

The initial surprise at Mark's rapid Italian disappeared from Grandi's eyes. He dropped Beatrice's hands and stroked his luxuriant beard. 'Your Italian is excellent.'

'I was born in Lucca,' Mark said.

The conversation quickly became intense with Grandi losing his arrogance, asking for details and history of his patronymic.

'I can only tell you of my mother's family.'

A sneer curled his lip. 'Why not your father? Anders is not an Italian name?'

Mark felt his fingers curl at the man's arrogance and took a breath. 'My father died. My mother remarried in Australia. I was a small child and don't remember my father.'

'What was his name?'

'Contarini. Alessandro Contarini.'

The sneer disappeared. 'Impossible. I know of the Contarini family. If this is true, you come from an old and venerable Venetian lineage, case vecchie.'

Denton said, 'I am sorry to hear of your father's death, but may I ask, why did your mother not stay in Italy? Surely your father's family would have wanted that?'

Mark shrugged and with a grin said, 'You'll have to ask her that.' He paused, imagining his mother telling these men to mind their own damned business. It wouldn't go well. 'I am pretty certain I am not related to the people of whom the ambassador speaks. My mother's father worked on a mulberry farm. I think you will find I hale from peasant stock through and through.'

Grandi ignored him and turned to Denton. 'This is not good enough. For an Italian man not to know his family and his country is for him to forget his own heritage. How can you know who you are, where you belong, if you do not know where you have come from?'

He turned back and glared at Mark. 'Now you are so close, perhaps you will consider a visit soon.'

Denton glanced at Beatrice. 'We planned a short summer holiday in Rome, didn't we my dear?' He turned to Mark. 'Perhaps you might join us, Mark.'

'Then that is settled.' Grandi said.

'It would be a pleasure, work permitting.' Mark stared at Grandi. He knew how to play their game, and what he didn't know now, he would learn. In fact, he would relish it. Although he didn't need to visit Italy to know where he had come from, nor where he belonged. He glanced across at Beatrice and smiled.

Beyond Beatrice, across the room, he caught a glimpse of Charles in earnest conversation with an older woman and a man he recognised as Arthur Langham. The icicled glances the woman shot towards him, suggested she might be Beatrice's mother. He was glad of the cavernous space between them. He turned his attention back to Grandi.

Lady Margaret's intake of breath hissed through her teeth in what Charles took to be disapproval. He blew smoke from his nostrils and followed her gaze.

There was Mark in conversation with the Italian ambassador. Ah, that must be the source of disapproval; Grandi clutching Beatrice's hands in both of his. 'You don't approve Aunt?'

Her eyes swivelled back to his face. 'I understand you know him.'

'No, actually I have not been introduced.'

'I thought you and he had arrived together?'

For a moment Charles remained mystified until he realised to whom Lady Margaret referred. 'Do you mean Anders?'

'Of course, who else? Your father will be disappointed in you.'

'May I inquire why you would think that? Mark is rather an up-and-coming chap in the news fraternity.'

'He is an imposter and a scoundrel.'

Charles's eyes lit up. 'Do tell Aunt Margaret.'

She pursed her lips and changed the subject. 'Don't you think it is high time you left this newsman frolic behind and took on a more grown-up job. Afterall, a newsman does not earn much of a salary. Neither is it a career that will help you make your way in the world. Besides what well-born daughter will want a man in trade, always galivanting off somewhere. You could do better Charles.'

Charles blinked. 'Are you trying to marry me off to someone Aunt?' He couldn't believe the path their conversation had taken. Surely, she didn't mean her own daughter, his cousin!

'Don't be obtuse. I am just looking out for your wellbeing.' She glanced at her husband. 'Arthur says we must go home which means I will have to leave you to manage the charity this end. However, no one wants to give money to a journalist. I think you must have a change of career if you are to look after our interests.'

Charles grinned, playing along out of amusement. 'What would you suggest?'

She seemed to take his query seriously. 'What can you do? Perhaps something in the city.' She turned to her husband. 'What do you think Arthur?'

Arthur, hands behind his back, rose onto the balls of his feet before lowering his heels once more to the floor. His mouth pressed into a thin line; his forehead creased in concentration. 'Finance would be useful, especially as you have dabbled in matters of our two family's investments previously.'

Lady Margaret placed her hand on Arthur's arm. 'A splendid idea. People are always willing to entrust their charitable donations to financiers.'

'You want me to become a banker!' Charles laughed. His aunt was priceless. Although the way she behaved indicated his uncle and aunt had already had this discussion without him. No doubt they had also discussed this with his father.

Arthur continued, 'You have the right education and good connections. Why not?'

He hummed and said, 'Perhaps because I don't have the money to start a bank so I would have to become a bank clerk. I might pass up that offer, thanks.'

Margaret sighed. 'Well, we will have to think of something...'

Charles interrupted. 'Aunt, what did you mean Mark Anders is an imposter?'

'Oh, for goodness' sake Charles. Can't you see he has no breeding. He is a labourer and a foreigner, and his politics are beyond the pale. Back in Australia he gave Arthur and your father no end of trouble with his union thuggery. He has completely turned Beatrice head. I don't know what father is thinking, entertaining him.'

She stalked off leaving Charles gazing at Mark, who it seemed had Grande laughing at something he had said. The bloke's breeding and politics couldn't be that bad if he had Grandi eating out of his palm.

He shrugged and turned his thoughts back to what Lady Margaret had suggested. Until now he hadn't given marriage a thought, but she was right. If he wanted to progress in life, a wealthy wife couldn't hurt. Perhaps he should consider a career change. He wasn't all that enamoured with journalism. It demanded hard work with little by way of status or personal reward.

A Proposal of Sorts

The afternoon had turned cold and grey by the time Mark presented himself at the house at Pimlico Gardens. The man who opened the door held himself upright as if on parade. He looked Mark up and down, a disdainful expression on his face.

Mark asked, 'Is Miss Langham home?' As the words passed his lips, he felt his own idiocy crawl up his neck. Of course she would be home. She had invited him to tea and to meet her parents properly. Thank fortune she hadn't wanted to present him in public. But he wished he didn't have to face them now. They were leaving in a few days and last night he had suggested he might just give the whole meet-the-parents bit a miss.

The man's face didn't change. 'Mr Anders, I presume.'

'Er. Yes.'

'You are expected.'

At that moment, another man came into view. 'That's all right, Symons.'

Symons stood back with an almost imperceptible bow. 'Very good my lord.'

'Hello Mark.' Denton held out his hand. 'I'm delighted you were able to make it.'

Mark had worn his best suit for the occasion, but Denton had on an old brown cardigan, corduroy trousers, and slippers. He felt overdressed and his nervousness, at confronting Langham again, gave him heartburn.

Mark followed Denton into the house, and along a corridor before turning in through large double doors. Bearice materialised at his side and took his arm, and they entered the drawing room together.

Arthur Langham stood up glowering, as if he would rather call the police than take tea with Mark. Lady Margaret remained seated, examining her hands as if Mark did not exist.

After what might be referred to as a perfunctory introduction, Denton asked Mark to take a seat. While all this took place Denton kept up an upbeat discourse about Mark's photography, his meeting with Churchill, his conversation with the Duke of Alba, and Alba's invitation to lunch. To Mark's dismay he explained Grandi's theory about Mark's heritage, and how Grandi had invited Mark to Italy.

Did Denton needed to paint Mark in a different light from the man he was, perhaps to impress upon the Langham's his suitability? He played along, although it made him uncomfortable as if he had walked onto a stage in the middle of a play for which he had not rehearsed.

Beatrice hovered the whole time, adding to his nervousness, to the point he almost dropped the fragile teacup he'd been handed by the maid.

Finally, once the tea things were cleared away, he suggested a walk around the block.

Outside, mist filled the streets leaving mere smudges of yellow lamplight, but it was a relief to get out of the charged atmosphere in the house. What matter a little dampness?

They crossed the road and walked into a public garden. He led Beatrice under the shelter of a large spreading tree.

She leaned against the trunk. 'That wasn't so hard, was it?'

He scowled. 'In contrast to what?'

'My parents will get over it.'

'Not sure I will.'

Her eyes seemed to search his face. 'So, now what?'

'What do you mean?'

She shrugged.

He looked away. 'I'm going back to Spain in a couple of days.' He switched back to gaze into her eyes. 'If you will allow it, I would like to come back and see you again... When I get back in a couple of weeks. Maybe we can pick up where we left off in Australia...' He took a breath.

'I'd like that.' She smiled.

He moved a strand of hair from her cheek. 'Beatrice I...'

'What?'

'I just wanted you to know that I still love you, never stopped, you know...' He looked away again. He hadn't meant to say that aloud.

The mist seemed to dampen sound as if the two of them stood in their own private world.

She took his hand. 'You don't know how relieved I am to hear you say that.'

He glanced back at her.

She was smiling. 'Will you kiss me now?'

'In public.' Mark glanced around.

'Who is there to see us?'

'I don't know. Your father probably has a sniper's rifle trained on me at this moment.'

She grabbed the front of his coat and pulled him towards her. 'Silly, they'll be fine, and Granddad likes you.'

To hell with the neighbours. He gave in to his desire and kissed her, remembering the softness, losing himself in her taste, the familiar scent of her hair, the sublime promise of the kiss.

She pulled back from his embrace and laughed. 'I am so happy you are here. I never stopped loving you either.'

Despite all his vows to take this reunion slowly he said, 'Do you remember when I asked you to marry me?'

She nodded and glanced at the ground.

The stone in his chest grew heavier. He tilted her chin, wanting to see her eyes. 'We still could, you know. My work is bringing in a bit, and I have some savings. Then there are the farm and business back home...Bert says it's going well...'

'No Mark. Please, not yet. Let's just enjoy the moment.'

'Why Beatrice? If you love me, why don't you want to marry me?'

'I do but...'

'But what? I am not of your class.' Bitterness twisted his mouth.

'How can you say that after all we have been through together?'

He looked away, ashamed, pressing his lips into a tight line as he felt her gaze on him. 'You're right. I should not have said that...'

'But you thought it, so I am glad you said it.' A frown creased her forehead. 'Mark you must understand, I do love you, but I want a career. I think I have one now, but I want more. I have discovered I have a talent for administration, and the refugees need me. They are pouring out of Germany as well as Spain and I can make a difference.'

'Why is it either or. Why can't you get married and have a career?'

'Would you agree to that?'

'Of course. It's what I want too. I know my photography takes me away a lot but if we we're married you might be able to come with me to places. Not Spain. It's too dangerous, but elsewhere.'

'You see. There you go immediately. My career is fine, so long as I drop everything to go off with you to places you deem appropriate.'

'I didn't mean... Oh hell. Beatrice... You're right, but let's not rule it out, please.'

'So long as you don't tell me what I can and cannot do, and we make decisions together as equal partners.'

'It's a deal.'

'You say that, but men do one of two things. They either think they are protective, or they take no responsibility for agreed decisions, then blame the woman for any failure.'

He contemplated contradicting her assertion. His stepfather would never get away with making decisions for the family unless his mum agreed. Beatrice had grown up with Langham, a chauvinist thug despite his wealth, little wonder she didn't want to tie herself to someone like that.

Instead, he said, 'You can teach me how to be the kind of husband you want.'

'Then I will marry you, but not right now. First, I must establish myself or everyone will attribute my success to you as my husband.'

'But it is your success. No one can say different. Besides not all men... What! You will?'

'See, you don't listen.' She laughed at him.

'I don't have a ring...'

'Now you are making excuses.' She teased. 'Doesn't matter. Marriage is just a convention along with a legal document, anyway. When you next come home, we can do the whole thing properly. You will have to ask my father's permission, but if we wait until he leaves, you can write and ask instead of facing him.'

Mark's eyes grew grave. 'He'll say no.'

'Too bad. It's just a courtesy. If he says no, it means nothing. I can do what I like, and he knows it. To save face he will have to say yes.'

'Can I kiss you again?'

She smiled. 'I don't know what's holding you back.'

Mark took her into his arms. The mist thickened into fog shielding them from prying eyes, but he no longer cared if anyone was watching.

Eventually, a cold trickle down his neck brought him back to the present and he released her. 'I'd better get you home before you are soaked through.'

He took off his jacket and held it over her head as they ran back to the house, stopping under the portico.'

'Will you come in?'

Mark shook his head. 'I'd better head back to my digs.'

'But you are soaked.'

'I'm fine. Can you meet me tomorrow?'

'I'm working.'

'We can have lunch, can't we?'

'All right.'

'I'll come to your office.' He kissed her and turned to go.

'Mark.'

'Yes.'

'Something's been bothering me.'

'What?' He stepped back under the portico.

'You have to speak to Jack.'

'What has Jack got to do with any of this?'

'I heard something from one of my refugees, and I can't get it out of my head. His name is Mykola Diduch. He is a refugee from Soviet Russia, accused of counterrevolutionary activity. His sin was hiding his creamery because he didn't want it confiscated by the state. He insisted that Stalin's NKVD engaged in massive theft of harvests, arrests, and killings.'

Mark nodded. 'I have heard similar stories from journalists in Spain. Stalin seems to have turned on his own people.'

'What do you mean?'

'I am not sure, but I have heard stories about soldiers returning from Spain to Moscow. When they get home, they are arrested and tried for the most ludicrous crimes.'

'Mykola was accused of hording during a drought. He kept a creamery to ensure his family did not starve.'

'I know Beatrice, but what do you want me to do about it?'

'Tell Jack what you know.'

Mark paused. 'He probably already knows. Look, I like and admire Jack, but I don't think he will listen. Communists believe their system is a better one, and he will come up with all sorts of excuses to justify their actions. Coercion is the only way they have to make people conform to their doctrine.'

'But that's terrible. If Jack knows...'

'Beatrice, do you think it is only Stalin who does bad things in the name of ideology?'

'No but... I thought the communists were all right.'

'And they are. Most of them simply want greater equality and to follow Marxist teachings. Not all of them are murdering bastards like Stalin. Ah sorry. But Stalin is no better than the fascists.' He caught the echo of Churchill's words in his voice and stopped.

'I thought you liked or at least supported the communists.'

Mark sighed. 'Most of the communists I know are good people. They simply want greater fairness in this world. They seek to level the playing field so everyone can have a go, not just those born of wealthy parents. They think communism is the answer. And it might have been, if Stalin hadn't corrupted Marx's words.' He looked at her sideways and hurried on. 'I admire their desire and commitment to equality, but blind adherence to any ideology makes good people do terrible things.'

'Like what?'

'Well, look at some of the things done in the name of Mussolini's Fascism, Hitler's ultra-Nationalism, the Soviet's Stalinism, or even Franco's Catholicism. They are all powerplays that use ideology to control people, elevating some over others. If you don't agree with them, you are persecuted, if not killed. It's been like that since time immemorable.'

'But Jack was so kind and just... Does it mean he would do terrible things?'

'I suppose it's possible that he would do things in the name of communism, but as far as I know he hasn't done anything particularly evil. In fact, he values inclusiveness. Remember how he supported both liberal unionists and anarchists when we were involved in the Weil's disease strikes?'

'But he also supports revolution and Stalin...'

'He justifies what he knows to avoid having his faith in communism destroyed. He's not alone. I am beginning to realise there are an awful lot of people who justify terrible things in the name of adhering to dogmatic beliefs. It's a kind of gang mentality. Hell, I'd probably do it to save liberal democracy, although I try not to do anything to hurt others.'

A Proposal of Another Kind

Two nights after the marriage proposal, and the day after he had lunched with Beatrice and slipped a ring, hastily bought that morning, onto her finger, Mark dined with Denton at his club. He could hardly believe he might say such a thing, but here he was, contemplating Denton across the occasional table that separated them.

They were seated in deep leather armchairs, satiated with the rich dinner they had just consumed along with a bottle of Côte de Beaune pinot noir. Mellowness infused his every limb. He liked Denton even though he represented everything that Mark thought wrong with the democratic world. The man had an admirable calm, a rational mind, and wasn't driven by unquestioning beliefs in the sanctity of the British Empire. Unlike Beatrice's father. Which was why Mark had decided to accept his invitation.

He gazed around at the expensive wood panelling, comfortable armchairs, high decorative ceilings, plush, and noise-deadening carpets. The lighting, used to separate groups from one another, gave the feeling each table represented a different world. Unobtrusive waiters passed silently through the dim patches of each territorial boundary.

The old but expensive and slightly shabby lavishness was enough to intimidate. He'd never imagined he'd be in a space like it, let alone sipping an after-dinner brandy from a balloon glass. He'd never before eaten foie gras, wasn't sure what it was other than knowing its literal translation was fat liver. Nor had he tasted pheasant, cooked in burgundy, before today. Denton warned he might bite into an occasional shotgun pellet.

Mark hadn't expected pellets in this fancy place although he'd shot enough game to have tasted the odd pellet in his time. It wasn't that the food was foreign for he'd grown up with his mother's cooking. But what had this dinner cost, and how much were the obsequious waiters paid?

Denton still hadn't told him why he had invited him to dinner or what he wanted to discuss. He also felt slightly ridiculous in the evening suit and bow tie he'd hired for Beatrice's party and hadn't yet returned. At this rate he'd have to buy his own.

A waiter hovered at Mark's elbow with an opened humidor. 'Cigar, sir?'

The whole charade felt like an elaborate satire.

Denton said. 'Do you smoke Mark?'

He shook his head. 'No thank you.'

'Wise man. You don't mind if I have one?'

'Not at all.' He watched Denton choose a cigar and waited while the waiter lit it.

Denton puffed, exhaled, and leaned back in his chair. 'D'you know I was in Australia before the Great War with Governor-General Munro-Ferguson. I was expected to advise on the setup of the Royal Australian Navy. I was recalled to London, what with the threat of war looming. Margaret didn't want to leave because she had met Arthur. Her mother, God rest her soul, was adamant that Arthur wasn't a suitable match, but Margaret got her way eventually.' Denton's eyes became shiny, and he pulled his handkerchief out of his pocket and blew his nose, then said, 'excuse me. It's daft, but after all this time, the memory still stirs me up. You see Lillian, my wife, died shortly after the Great War.'

Mark nodded sympathetically. It was a sad story, but he'd heard it before from Beatrice. Surely this wasn't why Denton had asked him to dinner.

Denton composed himself and chuckled. 'I can see you wondering why I'm telling you this ancient history.'

Mark shifted in his seat and stretched his neck, easing it from the tight collar.

Denton carried on. 'The thing is parents never think a prospective suitor is good enough for their offspring. My parents didn't want me to marry Lillian. Her father was in cotton, and my mother couldn't countenance an association with new money or trade. Rather ridiculous, as my father had lost everything he'd inherited, and we were as poor as the proverbial church mice. Lillian's money got the family out of an awful pickle, but that wasn't why I married her. I loved her.' His eyes became shiny again, but he went on. 'Then when it came to Margaret wanting to marry Arthur, Lillian was opposed. Now it's Margaret's turn to disapprove of her daughter's choice, but it'll pass. We never think our children's lovers are good enough.'

Mark stared at him.

Denton coughed. 'I suppose, I am asking what your intentions are towards my granddaughter.'

'Isn't that the prerogative of the father?'

Denton smiled. 'We already know his views, but I am convinced he is wrong. Besides, he and my daughter are returning to Australia, and as Beatrice will be living under my roof, I have a right to at least ask. I don't want to see my granddaughter hurt.'

'I have no intention of hurting her, but I will be returning to Spain in a few days, so you have nothing to worry about.'

'Do you love her?'

Mark felt his neck growing hot. 'I don't think that's any of your business.'

'I assume that's a yes.'

Mark stood up. 'Look, thanks for the dinner, but I should be going...'

'Sit down Mark. I haven't finished. Beatrice told me you asked her to marry you. She also asked if I thought it possible for her to be married and continue with her career. I just need to know if you are likely to join my family because I have a proposition to put to you, and it's dangerous. If you are going to marry Beatrice, it is only fair that she knows the score.'

Curiosity overcame Mark's reluctance, and he sat down, leaned forward, interlaced his hands, and cracked his knuckles.

Denton winced. 'Right, to business! You don't happen to speak German or Russian, do you? Only Beatrice says you're a bit of a linguist.'

'I only speak fluently in Italian and English. Why?'

'What about French and Spanish.'

'My French is passable as is my Spanish, but it's not fluent and I think I might speak French with an Italian accent.'

'Any other languages?'

'I know a bit of Norwegian, or enough to get by.'

'Beatrice said you learned that from your father. Is it similar to German?'

'I don't know. Look why do you ask? I'm not looking for a job as a translator. I have a job.'

'Bear with me a minute,' Denton said. 'Have another brandy.'

'No thanks. I'd appreciate it if you got to the point.'

Denton twisted his mouth in what appeared to be a self-deprecating grimace. 'Yes of course. It's a thought, not well-formed, but you might be of enormous service to the Crown with your reputation as a photojournalist and with your ability with languages.'

Mark pulled in his chin. 'Serve the British Crown?' Then he laughed. 'I think that's unlikely.' This was not satire, but downright comedy.

Denton puffed on his cigar. 'Well, I need another brandy.' He raised his hand in a small gesture and a waiter rushed to his side. He ordered and then examined Mark carefully before saying, 'Let me explain. You see, I need someone sensible to serve the Crown against growing fascism, even though some within my government don't think it's required. With patience and persuasion, they will come to see the problems as we do.'

Mark frowned. He'd gladly join any fight against fascism, even one led by the British Crown. Although he didn't believe the government all worked to that end. 'I thought the British Crown was in favour of a little fascism.'

'There are some who cannot see the danger it poses, and I mean to help them see the light.'

'And you think I may be able to help you do that?' Mark laughed. 'I think you're mistaken, but I'm willing to listen.' A vague memory floated in the back of his mind of him saying to Beatrice that he tried not to act in ways that hurt others. No. This was different. He would gladly hurt fascists. Wasn't that as bad...? He brushed the thought away and concentrated.

Denton waited until the waiter placed his brandy on the table then said to Mark, 'Everything I tell you is classified. I must trust your word as this is not official, and you are not governed by the Official Secrets Act although I hope you will consider it.'

'All right,' Mark said and wondered if it was, and whether he actually understood any of it. He raised his hand and covered his mouth with his palm as he listened.

Denton went on. 'The British government, generally speaking, does not accept that Adolf Hitler is any real threat; at least, not to the British. It's absurd when you realise, they made the same mistake about Germany before the Great War. The trouble is, many in the establishment admire Germany and can't see what the fuss is about. They think the communists are much more of a threat to the stability and continuing prosperity of Britain. Furthermore, the British people do not want another war and are quite happy with the government's efforts at appeasing any belligerent European sabre-rattling. But I, and a few of my colleagues, think differently. Certainly, the Spanish war is in Italy's strategic interests and, if they didn't plan and foment it, they are certainly helping it along.'

Mark opened his mouth to say that Sylvia Boyle had said a similar thing about Germany but closed it again remembering his decision to learn all he could without sticking his neck out.

Denton's eyes narrowed momentarily as if he read Mark's mind but then he continued. 'Any alliance between the two countries is a problem for Britain. The influence Count Galeazzo Ciano has in Italy with Mussolini, and Admiral Canaris has with Hitler, has created the problem because both see a Nationalist Spain as an opportunity. You see, Germany needs Franco, either on-side, or as a benign presence in the face of their increasing desire to plunder Europe. Furthermore, the German's need Spanish coal and pyrites in order to mount any belligerent attack on another country, and Hitler is gearing up for war. I am as certain of that as I am that our new Prime Minister's continuing policy of appeasement will not provide him with the legacy he craves.

Mark nodded, but what had any of it to do with him and how might he possibly be of any help to Denton? Clearly, the man understood the double-dealing and diplomatic intrigue, whereas Mark knew little of it. 'Why not appeal to the Soviet Union?'

Denton sighed. 'That would be a strategy, but many in the British government fear the Bolsheviks more than the Germans.'

'Who do you most fear?'

'Personally—Germany. Italy is a problem, and we may have to deal with Stalin later, but Germany is the more immediate threat since we have done nothing about their invasion of the Rhineland. Hitler becomes bolder.'

'What are you saying? Should Britain pre-empt Germany's aggression?'

To Mark's horror Denton appeared to contemplate that suggestion.

After a moment's pause, Denton shook his head. 'We are in no position to go to war. Not only do the British people object, but we are not equipped. Instead, I think we should rapidly rearm in case of urgent need, but what I am getting at is that Britain's non-intervention policy in the Spanish War plays into both Hitler's and Mussolini's expansionist agenda. Do you see? We need to get the winners of the Spanish war on Britain's side so, in the event of a European war, Spain will support the British and our allies or at least remain non-aligned.'

Mark gazed at Denton. Who did he think was going to win the Spanish war? 'The British leadership of the non-intervention pact supports the Spanish rebel's position. Surely you are not suggesting Britain recognise the insurgents!'

'I am not keen on the insurgents winning, just pragmatic. Someone will win, and for our own sake, Britain needs to play both sides without giving support to the rebels. Our future is at stake.'

Denton had summed up the situation in a way that gave international posturing a different complexion from that given by the newspaper reports. Was Denton's slant, right? It sounded plausible. 'What has all this to do with me?'

127

'Ah... With your budding reputation as a photojournalist, or more importantly a war correspondent, you might come across gossip that would help us to understand the threat better. Such intelligence would enable us to develop our strategy and determine if we should take a tougher line. Additionally, befriending certain people within the different factions, will help us create channels of influence where and when they are needed. You seem to have a natural flair for getting on with people, regardless of your opposing values.'

Denton had read him well, but Mark remained sceptical, noting the new title of war correspondent. Denton hadn't said it without intent.

He said, with an air of uncertainty, 'Me, work for you?'

'Unofficially of course and reporting only to me. The thing is, it's hard to know whom to trust. The Ministry is as leaky as a rowboat without a bung, and the Under Secretary, the Earl of Plymouth, is vehemently opposed to Britain's involvement in Spain. That's all very well, but it leaves the door wide open for Hitler's march through Europe. It also gives access to Italy to control the Mediterranean.' Denton glanced at his brandy and frowned. 'It wouldn't do to make Plymouth nervous.'

To hell with Plymouth's nerves. Mark felt a tremor at the whole concept. 'Why me?' Denton didn't need Mark. He had all the necessary tentacles buried in power, money, position, title, and a seat in the Lords, not to mention his job in the Foreign Ministry, whatever that was.

Denton said, 'Have another brandy my son, you look a little peaky.' He signalled the waiter. 'Now the people of most interest include the Duke of Alba. You met him the other night. He invited you to lunch. Have you done that yet? If not, please do. He's also a relative of Churchill's whom you also met. Alba might be enormously helpful, as he is Franco's unofficial eyes and ears in Britain. If he takes a shine to you, he may get you into Franco's Spain. Although, it seems the Nationalists are not as keen on the press as the Republicans.'

Mark rubbed his forehead. He wasn't in a satire or a comedy but a nightmare. While he was determined to make friends and influence people, it had been a ruse to disarm them so he might infiltrate their company and expose them. Now Denton seemed to have read his mind and used that knowledge to persuade Mark to use his strategy on behalf of Britain. The great and evil imperialist... Although Mark had tempered that opinion since leaving Australia.

A waiter approached with another brandy. Denton indicated he should put the brandy in front of Mark and then continued. 'They will be suspicious of you of course because of the way you showed the plight of the ordinary Spanish people. You are most likely aware that this is a propaganda war we're fighting. The Nationalists don't like the fact that you've seized the advantage through visions of human frailty. They want to show heroism and triumph, not the horrors that war inflicts on people. They want the Republicans to be demonised, not held up as martyrs.'

'I still don't know what you want of me. All you have outlined is the scenario as it stands, what role do you expect me to play?'

Denton examined Mark's face, took a deep breath, and said, 'I would be grateful if you would do two things to help us defeat the fascists.'

Mark sat forward alarm bells ringing in his head. 'And they are...?'

'Keep me informed as to what is going on behind the scenes. The reality rather than the propaganda.'

'Doesn't the Foreign Office have a whole network of diplomats not to mention spies, to do that for you?'

'It does. The trouble is many are blinded by ideology, and class solidarity, so to speak. They cannot see things clearly.'

Class solidarity, a term used for and by the working class. but Denton had turned it on its head, showing class solidarity was a real thing for the wealthy.

Denton drew a breath and Mark waited but Denton remained silent.

'You said two things.'

'Yes.' Denton paused again before saying, 'I have observed that you are particularly good at establishing rapport with people like the Duke of Alba, Dino Grande, and Rudolf von Graff, people with whose values you do not agree. My friend Winston thought you a jolly stalwart chap and a man of intelligence who has a thirst to learn.'

Mark frowned.

Denton hurried on. 'I would like you to pursue such relationships, so they feel you are one of us, so to speak.'

'With Mr Churchill.'

'Not necessarily although I know he would enjoy resuming your chat about art and perspective. It's the others I mean.'

'To what end?'

'Well, they can get you into places.'

'Couldn't you?'

Denton paused as if weighing up a dilemma. Then his voice dropped, and he said, 'If I were to help you in any official way they may suspect you of espionage. We in the diplomatic world have a kind of system that we all understand how to play. They will never point out the obvious if we don't, but it doesn't preclude them from knowing.'

'What the hell are you saying?'

'I am talking about you being seen as a rather outstanding and ambitious journalist who just happens to be a close friend of my granddaughter. A man who is going about his passion without an obvious political position.'

Mark took a long swallow of the replenished brandy. 'You want me to spy on them, inveigle my way into their circles, pretend to come around to their way of thinking.'

'Well, if you say so, yes, but unofficially.'

'Can't be done. My sympathies are no secret.'

'If your relationship with Beatrice is going to grow closer, many will see it as a natural progression from idealistic youth, to growing up as you approach your more mature years. People often change their minds after they have seen evidence with their own eyes. Converts are always a great coup for propaganda agents, especially ones with your blossoming profile. The summary of the war in Spain you gave to the Duke of Alba highlights my case. Your assessment, while most likely accurate, sounded as if you were leaning towards the Nationalist winning. Nonetheless, from what Beatrice has told me about you, nothing would be further from the truth.'

Mark said, 'I won't use Beatrice, and neither should you.'

'Absolutely. But this is just an observation of fact. If you are seen as Beatrice's intended, it will be their assumption.'

'Does Beatrice know you are talking to me about this?'

'Good grief, no. She would be furious. Although I am not asking that you convince people you are a fascist supporter. You might just persuade them that photography is your only object, and you are mercenary about pursuing that alone, regardless of politics. I am also not asking you to place yourself in any dangerous situations. Merely take your photos, write your copy, and provide me with an occasional assessment of what you have seen and how it seems to be panning out. I am serious about that last bit. You are not trained and should do nothing outside your normal behaviour, but I would value your assessment.'

Trained. What did that mean? Trained to do what? Spy... Mark sat back in his chair, silent and staring at his hands, which were resting, as if without a care, in his lap.

Nice as the bloke seemed, and as much as Mark hated fascism, he didn't think he could do as Denton asked and report back to him. If he were discovered, all his hard work getting this far would be wasted. Although, how was that any different from what he had set out to do for himself—to uncover and report the truth?

This wasn't the first time someone had tried to recruit him to spy. Jack had intimated Mark might do that for the Australian Communist Party although Mark had refused. How could he refuse his friend and accept Denton's request? No. It was a different thing entirely.

He would be helping a sovereign nation defend itself against fascism and dictatorship. Wouldn't Jack have said the same thing about spying for Soviet Russia? But Mark wasn't Russian. He was an Australian, a British subject with a passport to prove it. While he didn't approve of everything the British had done, he held on to the British belief in democracy. He valued the philosophy of liberalism and John Locke's treatise whereby the individual owns his own body and labour as a fundamental right.

Mark ran his hand across the back of his neck. Did he want to spy for the British? He had to admit the idea had an odd appeal. Imagine bringing down people like Mussolini, Molo, Franco, and Hitler. No, any role he might play would be minuscule in the big scheme of things. He became aware that Denton watched him. Shit, no wonder no one spoke of Denton's role within the Foreign Office. He was most likely some kind of spy master, who had done his background research on Mark, and now seemed able to read him like an open book.

Then another thought emerged. Mark flexed his fingers against each other and said, 'How much of my recognition as a photojournalist have you manipulated?'

Denton held up his hands. 'Mark, don't doubt your talent.'

'You have!' Mark felt hot lava erupt in his stomach, and he forced himself to breathe.

Denton said. 'All I have done is move the process on faster than it might have occurred naturally. You know the saying about silk purses and sows' ears. Well, if the material is already available to work with, all it needs is a nudge in the right direction.'

Mark stared at Denton. 'Who the hell are you?'

Denton smiled. 'Mark, the real question is, who are you? Or rather, what do you want to become. You can be anything you choose, and I can help you achieve that so long as our goals align.'

Dunkerque to Valencia

After saying goodbye to Beatrice, and with a commitment to return in a couple of weeks, Mark left England. He bought a ticket on the night ferry to Dunkerque. From there he planned to take another train to the Gare du Nord in Paris before heading to Perpignan and Barcelona.

Dunkerque was a bustling port city in northern France. He could have splashed out for a direct sleeper ticket all the way through to Paris, but he wanted to see how a city, bombed by German Lange Max guns in the Great War, might have recovered from such destruction.

After wandering around the port for a while he hired a taxicab. The cab drove him out to the Fort des Dunes. He soon discovered the Fort's cannons had been no match for the German Lange Max, which had pounded Dunkerque with 1700-pound shells shot from Koekelare in Belgium.

It seemed Dunkerque had recovered from the terror. Perhaps Spain and the Spanish people would also recover. Recovery of damage done to bricks and mortar was one thing. The scars etched into the Spanish soul may take longer.

As he travelled back to the station, the sun shone in a clear blue sky, and waves ran up sandy beaches, flanked for kilometres by grassy dunes and a long strip of forest. A memory of picnicking with Beatrice on the beach in North Queensland surfaced. But this place, despite its beauty had a different feel about it.

It wasn't simply that a cold wind blew in from the North Sea. It was more a sober reminder of the extensive history of conflict on these shores. Not only the Vikings and later Corsairs, but also battle upon battle for political supremacy, since man first conjured the notion of power protected in the hands of the few over the many.

He supposed North Queensland had experienced something similar upon colonisation, but nothing like the centuries of constant conflict over possession, dispossession, and repossession, which the Europeans and British had both perpetrated and endured. And still, it went on.

A twinge of regret at leaving Beatrice ran through him, but this was his career now. He couldn't stay in London although the image of lying with her on a warm beach under a tropical sun, drinking wine, and paddling in the sea stayed with him. No war, no refugees, no class restrictions and most of all no expectations from Denton weighing on his conscience.

Two days later, Mark arrived in Barcelona, although he didn't stay long. As soon as he had delivered the letter to Ethel, he found a ride on a supply truck to Valencia. When he arrived, he found the city crowded with refugees along with soldiers back from the front lines.

The Republican government had made Valencia its base when Madrid had been evacuated. Now men, and many women, wore uniforms. The few women not in uniform, wore pretty dresses and flirted with the soldiers. His own civilian clothing felt like a beacon of insolence.

Despite the war, the city had a carnival-like atmosphere, every venue crowded, and every building plastered with meeting notices, revolutionary slogans and the workers' symbol of hammer and sickle. Portraits of Marx, Lenin, and Stalin sat alongside union banners in communist red or the anarchist red and black. Motor vehicle horns blared, hawkers shouted themselves hoarse, and street musicians ratcheted up the cacophony; *live life now for tomorrow may never come!*

That sentiment echoed through his head on his second morning in Valencia after he awoke to the discordant clanging of church bells. For several moments he lay in bed, eyes open staring at the ceiling.

Then he heard the shout, 'Air raid!'

Mark leaped up, pulled on trousers, boots and jacket, grabbed his camera, and raced outside. He joined a stream of civilians, running towards the bomb shelter. Before he reached it, a formation of bombers rumbled overhead. He stopped in the street and raised his camera, while all around him, bells belted out warnings. Through the camera lens he witnessed those familiar slug shapes tumbling from the bombers' bellies.

His body vibrated as explosions shook the earth and drowned out the sound of pealing bells. A building, several city-blocks away, lit up from the inside, and moments later seemed to crumple in on itself in a kind of slow motion. Smoke drifted on the breeze, its scent a mix of fuel, brick dust and something else. Burnt almonds, and perhaps burning flesh.

Mark clicked and wound on film like an automaton. His entire being consumed by the dance of these flying demons. His body a mere pivot, a gyroscope tracking fighters showering the city with grenades. His ears registering the staccato tempo of spitting bullets and the rattle of white-hot casings. Through the lens, his eyes tracked tracer fire, noting the dead and dying tumbling through space. The whole spectacle felt dream-like, surreal as if he watched the action on a *Pathé* news reel.

Moments later, the diabolical chaos evaporated. The sky cleared. The bombers and fighters returned to their base. Leaving behind the flames and rubble, the screams of terrified mules and horses clattering over cobblestones, the groans and cries of the injured, the bells, and the stinking smoke. While the dead remained silent.

Mark had not made it to the bomb shelter. Throughout the massacre he had stayed in the open, his mind blank. His camera alive in his hands. Now, as the rush slowed, a vague recognition of his own recklessness knocked against the edges of his mind.

He kicked a rock and walked on, wandering through blackened and rubble-strewn streets filled with the wounded, dying and dead. Ambulances and citizens rushed to their aid. Flames climbed broken buildings and licked at eaves. He pressed on, capturing the carnage on film.

When he arrived at the harbour, he saw a soup of broken hulls. The raid had destroyed several Republican naval ships, but even ships that showed the British flag were not immune. Would that bring the British out in retaliation?

He turned towards the British consulate, walking past the hospital. It had been damaged by the raid as if the enormous Red Cross flag on the roof was a target, rather than an international symbol of humanitarian neutrality.

The British Consulate had survived, although one corner had sustained some damage. Mark asked to see the Consul.

The official looked him up and down and told him to make an appointment. 'And for God's sake man wear a proper shirt under your jacket. A tie wouldn't go amiss either.'

Two days later he returned to his appointment with Mr Sullivan.

He asked, 'How will the British government react to the Italian Airforce bombing British ships?'

Sullivan retaliated sharply. 'You have that all wrong, my man. That was the Nationalist Airforce.'

'Italian pilots in Italian Capronis.'

Sullivan ignored him, saying instead, 'They bombed Republican ships. All's fair, etcetera. Are you also reporting on the Republican Airforce atrocity?"

'What atrocity?

'The Republic destroyed fifty of the Nationalist planes parked on the ground in Soria. Tit for tat, I'd say.'

'That was in retaliation for bombing Valencia. Civilians, sir, not military targets. The raid here killed two hundred civilians as well as damaging foreign missions, your consulate included.'

'The damage to our building was accidental.' Sullivan shook his head. 'As I said, tit for tat. The Republicans did the same thing to the Nationalist.'

Mark lost his presence of mind. 'For fuck's sake. The Republican Airforce destroyed planes, not civilians. Destroying war planes, after the fact, is not the same thing as peremptorily killing innocent victims: blowing patients from hospital beds. Aren't you at all concerned about the damage the Italian Airforce inflicted on ships flying the British flag?'

Sullivan gave Mark a withering look. 'If indeed they were British and not Red ships in disguise.' He pressed an intercom and asked his assistant to show Mark out. The interview was at an end.

As Mark walked away, he cursed his reaction. He had a lot to learn about not shouting at the people he was meant to be interviewing, but what else could he do? He had chased every piece of evidence to highlight the injustice of this war. He had written articles about the fascist agenda to destroy democracy. Yet, at every turn, another version of events counteracted the truth.

No wonder Denton needed someone off the books to tell him what happened. With British attitudes like Sullivan's, he'd never get anything resembling a factual account. Perhaps the only way was to spy for Denton and hope his information would help propel Britain to act.

Madrid

A few days after his disastrous interview with the consul, Mark scored a ride to Madrid by volunteering to drive a supply vehicle. Experienced and competent drivers in the Spanish Republic were rare beasts, and too many had already died in the course of their duty. Volunteers were valuable. A contact in the British Transport and General Workers' Union had written a letter of introduction to Antonio González, a member of the UGT, or the Spanish Unión General de Trabajadores. After González read the letter he greeted Mark like a friend.

After they left behind the green coastal belt of Valencia, the countryside fanned off to the distance Sierras de Segura y Alcaraz. The road wound through olive farms cratered by bombing, and the highway itself was either rutted into long gouges or corrugated into teeth-juddering humps, interspersed by deep holes, some full of water.

Antonio drove the lead lorry with an ease borne of experience. Mark followed in the billowing dust, hauling on the heavy steering to manoeuvre the truck around yet another crater in the road. It would take about nine hours to get to Madrid, or a little longer if they stopped at Albacete, the headquarters of the International Brigades. Antonio was clearly an optimist.

The train line had been relentlessly bombed, and the roads remained the only routes available. Consequently, lorry loads of soldiers and military equipment crowded the highway. Motorcycle riders carried urgent dispatches, travelling at high speed, apparently invincible as they dodged bomb craters in the face of the oncoming traffic. If he got to Madrid at all, it would be astonishing, let alone in nine hours.

To the west, across the dusty plains and simmering heat waves of the Albacete region, lay the front line with the southern rebel headquarters at Cordoba. To the northwest, lay besieged Madrid, with Nationalists on its northern flank in the Sierra de Guadarrama.

The Republicans didn't seem to be holding the momentum with which they had begun this war. While they had the rebels bogged down south of Sergovia, less than 120 kilometres northwest of Madrid, the Nationalist had killed at least three thousand Republican fighters along with a thousand foreign volunteers, many from air strikes.

Planes, along with ammunition, tanks, and other war supplies would be the decider in this war. The imperative of logistics. Somewhere in his memory lingered a school-boy lesson about Napoleon's war on Russia. Supply lines won or lost wars, and the Republic was short on everything.

Mark had also heard, the rebels still laid siege along the Manzanera River, across from Madrid's Casa de Campo. While he had been in Valencia, a French journalist, staying in the same boarding house, had said that Colonel Moriones planned an offensive to push back the rebels from the outskirts of Madrid.

The push back would apparently alleviate the siege on Bilbao, by drawing the rebels away from the North. As far as Mark knew, the Basque Army still kept the rebels at bay in Biscay. Although Bilbao suffered under a protracted siege by General Molo's forces. How did Javier fare and had he made it this far?

The sign ahead said Albacete. They were nearly there. The main Republican airbase, for the few biplanes they had left, was located on the outskirts. The British Battalion of the International Brigades was a small detour north to Madrigueras.

When they arrived at the Albacete barracks it looked deserted, but for a group of soldiers carrying out training exercises in the distance. A lone soldier sauntered out of a building as Mark jumped down from the cab and walked over to join Antonio.

Antonio explained their mission, and Mark asked if it would be permissible to call into Madrigueras, so he might speak to the men of the British Battalion.

The soldier shook his head. 'The battalion has gone north to secure the Madrid-Valencia Road. They have joined El Campesino and Colonel Líster.'

Mark hid his disappointment and turned to help unload the supplies and mail they had brought with them. A short while later, the same soldier returned announcing they were to have two passengers on the onward journey.

A colonel came out of the building, followed by a lieutenant. Both were Russian. The colonel walked toward the convoy. He was a neatly compact man, no more than 5 feet 7 inches tall, dressed impeccably in a uniform that hadn't come out of a factory. He stopped and spoke to the soldier in Russian before walking over to Mark.

'I will ride with you my friend. I understand you volunteered to drive a vehicle in order to travel to Madrid. I am Colonel Dimitri Volof.'

He had heard of the man and his ruthless reputation. He held out his hand. 'Mark Anders. Photojournalist with *New Leader*.'

'I know who you are. Your photographs are famous even here in Albacete.' He smiled. 'Come you should eat and rest now, and we can move out once it is dark. It is better if we wait until nightfall to leave. The battle is fluid and during daylight, German planes scour the skies.'

He turned and led the small party back into a building.

It was nine o'clock before they left for Madrid. Volof sat in Mark's cab while his lieutenant accompanied Antonio. The drive gave Mark enough time to prevail upon the man to issue a pass for the front line so that he might get some photos and interview some of the men.

When Volof got down from the lorry at Alcala de Henares he said, 'You should drive with your lights off. This close to the front line there are often bandits and ambushes.'

A full moon lit the road ahead, rendering lights unnecessary, but it would also make it easier for an ambush. There wasn't much Mark could do about it other than be on the lookout and remain grateful enemy planes didn't fly at night.

They arrived in Madrid without incident and Mark let out a long breath. He pulled up behind Antonio who had stopped under a bridge. Mark got down from the cab and went over to Antonio's window to find the man speaking on a radio.

When he hung up, he said, 'You follow but watch out for snipers.'

'Snipers?'

Antonia nodded. '*La quinta columna*, on the roof tops, you comprehend?'

Mark nodded. He comprehended all right. He had heard the term *fifth columnists*. Everyone used the expression now after General Molo had said he had four columns marching on Madrid and a fifth column waiting behind the Republican lines. While he knew what the term meant, it hadn't figured in his image of Madrid.

All day he'd driven with one eye on the sky, searching for bombers. As they drove towards Madrid, he searched the landscape for signs of ambush. Now, as he followed Antonio through the streets of Madrid, a crackling sensation like electricity raced across his shoulders and back. Bricks and concrete littered the streets beneath broken buildings. The damage more widespread and harrowing than what he'd seen in Valencia after the bombing raid. Huge bomb craters required them to back up and seek alternative routes. Burst sewage and water pipes created rivers through which they navigated, and through all this he had to keep one eye on the roof tops.

Eventually, they pulled up on García de Paredes Street and stopped. They had arrived at the government shelter where they were to spend the night. It had once been a convent, commandeered at the start of the war by the Republicans, now turned into a transit point for evacuations.

The next morning Antonio shook his hand and said, 'If you want a ride back to Valencia, be here at first light the day after tomorrow. If you are not here, I leave without you.'

It took Mark half an hour to walk to the Gran Via, all the while imagining a sniper's target on his back. He found the press office in the Telefonica building and walked in to register. While he spoke to the press officer, the rat-a-tat-tat of a machine gun started up. Mark swung around expecting the building to disintegrate around him, but no one else showed the slightest dismay.

The press officer grinned and pointed skywards. 'There is a gun on top of the building. When the soldiers get bored, they fire on the enemy across the Manzanares.'

He directed Mark to a hotel, popular with the other journalists and told him not to worry about fifth columnists shooting him from the rooftops. 'It was a problem earlier in the war but now most are gone.'

'Gone?' Mark waited, but the man merely shrugged.

He checked into his hotel and, bolder now the threat of snipers had been laid to rest, Mark went out to explore the city. He cruised the streets for story opportunities, taking photos, and sitting in sandbagged cafés, talking to whomever would spare the time to speak with him. He watched with interest as trams, mule drawn carts, cars and lorries trundled past. There were more vehicles on the city roads than he would have imagined with such shortages of fuel. But his sense of safety was short lived.

A Taste of War.

The next morning heavy artillery from the Nationalist trenches shelled the city. Like a malevolent orchestra it didn't let up. The citizens mostly ignored it, so Mark decided to follow suit.

He found a café with a spare table inside, where he could still see outside through the sandbagged doorway. As he was about to sit down, a shell landed a few city blocks away. The boom caused the floor beneath Mark's feet to judder. A second later he found himself crouched next to the table.

The man at the table next to him, wiped his mouth on a napkin and said, 'Don't worry chum, you'll get used to it.'

Mark nodded, a little pale, slightly mortified, but otherwise unharmed. How many civilians had been killed in this war, and how long before one of those shells would come for him? He tugged his lapels to straighten his jacket and sat down.

A waiter took his order, apologising for the shelling as if he were somehow responsible. When he came back, he added, 'At least, now it is not the planes. That was bad, but it has been quiet until now. They start again. I don't know what these people think.' He placed Mark's coffee on the table.

Mark took the ceramic cup between thumb and finger and gazed out the door to the square. Despite the artillery shelling, men stopped to have their shoes shined or sat and read their papers with an air of fatalistic nonchalance.

A strange ripping sound caused the shoeshines to glance at the sky. Only as the projectile flew overhead did they and their customers move closer to a building as if that might provide some protection. Clearly, from the numbers of damaged buildings, piles of rubble and craters along every street, it wouldn't.

Boom, boom, boom. The explosions sounded in rapid succession landing at a south-westerly point some city blocks away. Adrenalin surged through him and it took iron will not to duck. Instead, Mark closed his eyes and tipped some of the contents of his cup into his mouth. Would the terror ever ease. He doubted it and couldn't quite fathom the fatalism around him. He valued his life, but he could put on an act until then.

He opened his eyes at the sounds of a scuffle. Two men stood in the doorway dusting debris from their coats. One of them looked familiar.

'Sam Riding!' Mark stood up as he recognised the American journalist he had met in Barcelona.

Sam waved and walked over to Mark, hand outstretched. 'Salud comrade. I see you made it. How long have you been here?' He grinned, his hair still covered in brick dust, his eyes appearing enormous behind pebble-thick glasses.

Mark said, 'Just arrived.'

'Nice timing... You've been making a name for yourself.'

Mark shrugged. 'Mostly through the kindness of your aunt.'

'Don't you believe it. My aunt is merciless, although she did say, if I ran into you, I should ask if you have any more photos for her.'

'Is she still in Paris?'

Sam nodded.

Mark asked, 'Have you been here long?'

Sam frowned and glanced around before lowering his voice. 'Just arrived five days ago. Had to get the hell out of Barcelona. It's not a good place to be at the moment. The hunt for Trotskyists has become relentless. Apparently, the police found a letter they claim was written by Andreu Nin. You know, the anarchist leader removed as the Catalonian Minister of Justice a few months back. They blame him for leading that fiasco at the beginning of the month. You should have seen the carnage...'

'I was there, remember.'

'That's right. You captured the aftermath on your famous photos. May Days they're calling it now. Anyway, the cops reckon that Nin wrote to General Franco about the potential for an uprising of fifth columnists.'

'Bullshit.'

'Indeed. The letter was a forgery, most likely penned by the NKVD, or at least that bastard Volof.'

Mark blinked but said nothing about meeting the Russian. Instead, he asked, 'So does this fifth column exist? I have been warned of it, but I have seen no sign. Just the bloody artillery barrage. Don't know how the civilians manage to stay so calm.'

'They must have heard you're in town.'

Mark laughed. 'Tell me about this fifth column.'

Sam grinned again. 'Okay. From what I can gather, in the early days of the war they were active, but now most have fled, been imprisoned, or summarily executed by out-of-control anarchist vigilantes. Some are still holed up in foreign embassies. I also heard that when the Nationalists were bombing Madrid last November, the Republicans locked any possible fifth columnists on the top floors of key buildings. They reckoned it would deter Franco's people from dropping bombs on their own.'

'Did it work?'

Sam shrugged. 'I wasn't here, but they are lobbing shells into Carabanchel right now, and not the Salamanca district, so go figure.'

Mark shook his head. 'Sorry mate, don't know what that means.'

'Okay. Carabanchel is a working-class area, and the Salamanca district houses all the toffs. Franco avoids bombing his own.' He glanced at his friend waiting by the door. 'We're off to have a look at the front line.' He pointed in the direction of the Casa de Campo. 'Come with us if you like.'

Mark gulped down the last of his coffee. 'Lead on.'

Sam introduced him to his companion, Gerrit de Vries, a newsman from Holland. The three men went in search of their Spanish driver. They found him parked in an alley, protecting his vehicle from the shelling.

He drove them to the western edge of the city, where the two armies faced off in a kind of trench warfare stalemate reminiscent of the Great War. A machine gun rattled, and they took cover in a bombed and blackened building.

Through broken windows Mark could make out the front line, where the Republicans were dug in. He took photos, wishing he could get closer, but their Spanish driver, told him he might go no farther. He had to be content with scanning the area with binoculars. It occurred to Mark that this is what he should be afraid of rather than the noise of artillery shelling. Oddly, now he had decided to ignore fear, the threat of imminent death gave him an elevated sense of living.

Another artillery whoosh and boom sounded, the explosion not so far from where they were.

Gerrit said, 'Trench mortar.'

Sam explained, 'Gerrit's an expert on the different artillery sounds.'

Mark envied him his knowledge until Gerrit said, 'I learned it as a child.'

'As a child?'

Gerrit examined Mark before he continued. 'I grew up in Poperinge.'

'Shit! That wouldn't have been much fun.'

'You might be surprised at how used to things you get as a kid.'

Mark stared at the man with renewed interest and respect.

During the Great War, the Allies garrisoned in Poperinge, West Flanders near Ypres. The British soldiers had called it the gateway to hell. It seemed extraordinary that Gerrit wanted to chase war as a correspondent after growing up at the centre of some of the worst action of that blood bath.

He glanced back at the entrenched Republican Army. It seemed the European world had learned nothing. Although in modern warfare the sky was king, even though there were no planes in evidence today. The Nationalists seemed to have settled for desultory artillery bombardment, while the Madrid citizens went about their business. Perhaps he understood some of Gerrit's nonchalance after seeing the stoicism of the people in Madrid. The man in the café might be right. You get used to it. If you didn't, you would become a gibbering wreck or he knew he would.

On the way back, the city seemed cloaked in a new light. Despite the bombardment, mothers still queued in the streets, seeking to buy scarce food for their children. Children played in the gutters, waiting for their fathers to come home for a meal after manning the trenches for hours. If they came home at all. Would he be that brave in war? He doubted it. Although the sense of euphoria he'd felt, so close to the front line, remained.

The addictive power of war. It brought journalists here from all over the world. They certainly kept the hotels busy and brought a roaring trade to the bars, while cafes remained open to feed them. Perhaps living alongside real fighting men and women gave them, and himself, he acknowledged, a sense of being counted. In war, soldiers are heroes. Perhaps some of their relevance rubbed off on the correspondents, who wrote about and photographed them.

Mark left Sam and Gerrit, promising to meet up the next day, and went in search of dinner, preferably with some form of protein. He had a vague notion that meat might become a tradable commodity if only he could find some.

That evening a message arrived at his hotel. Volof had made good on his promise. Mark was to be downstairs at 6 am. A driver would collect him and take him to an interview with the British Brigade.

One Good Turn

The next morning, Mark left Madrid in the dark. Lieutenant Timofey Laskin drove and introduced himself as an aide under Volof's command. Laskin was a thin, wet-eyed Russian, who seemed too weedy for war. He was a pleasant enough companion or perhaps a Russian secret police minder. Mark didn't care although he was hearing increasingly harrowing rumours about the NKVD operations in Madrid.

Laskin explained they were to rendezvous with an Englishman, Corporal Carmody. He would lead them to where the Brigade was encamped, apparently somewhere on the right bank of the Aulencia River.

They travelled north, leaving central Madrid, before heading northwest, by which time Mark had heard Laskin's life story. He had relatives in high places in the Red Army, missed his home in Moscow, loathed the summer heat of Madrid and didn't understand the Spanish people, either their language or their culture. If that was not enough, the Spanish food gave him diarrhoea. How the hell did the bloke survived in this place?

They stopped at a road junction on the outskirts of Madrid, dangerous territory if you didn't know your way around. Laskin parked the car next to a grove of trees.

'Now we must wait,' he said.

The sun rose above the lip of the horizon and Mark got out of the vehicle and took off his jacket before squatting in the shade. He stared across a shallow valley, more of a wide geological drainage ditch than anything else. The low ridge in the distance lay between them and the enemy.

Laskin also alighted from the vehicle. He walked along the road and back to Mark. 'If Corporal Carmody does not arrive soon we must go back.'

By the time Carmody did arrive, the sun had risen 50 degrees above the horizon, around ten o'clock by Mark's calculation. Carmody suggested they leave the car hidden and travel south on foot, keeping the ridge well to their east. Mark left his jacket on the seat of the car, slinging the straps of his camera and binoculars around his neck. Laskin hid the car deeper in the tree coppice.

They had walked for perhaps three kilometres when they heard the drone of planes. Carmody was a veteran of this war, and both Mark and Lieutenant Laskin took heed of his warning to take cover. They scrambled under a low bridge spanning a dry gully, overgrown with weeds and tufted grass.

Once the planes had passed, they continued to wait in case they circled back. Distant booms sounded from the southeast. Was Madrid the target or somewhere else?

The valley seemed unnaturally still as the sun bleached the ink from the sky and turned the grass into pale straws. Even the wind held its breath.

Unperturbed, Carmody squatted on his hunches and asked, 'Any of you fine chaps have any food?'

Mark pulled a cured sausage, wrapped in paper, from his camera bag. He'd paid a grand sum for that sausage although he suspected it contained little, if any, meat.

Carmody's face lit up, and he laid his rifle on the ground before grabbing the whole thing, grinning at Mark through a battle-blackened face.

With his mouth full, he said, 'Back home I never thought to catch me eating this garlicky shit, but gord knows it beats the hell out of beans.'

'Where's home?' Mark asked. He stood at the edge of the culvert, trying to gauge the distance to the eastern ridge across the valley, maybe five hundred metres. He scoured the ridge to the northeast for signs of movement but could find nothing worth a photograph, except perhaps the dark mountain backdrop.

Carmody swallowed and said, 'Birmingham.'

In the valley below the ridge, a glint caught Mark's eye. A lone black and white stork levered its body into the air. He watched through binoculars thinking of the Jabiru storks at home. It flew towards them, but, at this distance, the camera would capture little but shapes: dark clefts in the hills, the light wash of a meandering stream, a Japanese shodo of wings in front of fuzzy pines, rocks, and ravines, all bleached by bone-brittle sunlight. He dropped his binoculars, lifted his camera, and took the shot just as the bird veered off to the south.

He ducked back into the culvert, wound on the film, and adjusted the camera settings.

Carmody sat on the ground with his back to the curved culvert wall.

Mark squatted down opposite him and snapped off another photo. 'You don't mind, do you?'

Carmody shook his head. 'Always wanted to be a pin-up boy.'

Mark wound on the film and raised the camera again, capturing Carmody hamming it up for the camera, his big white teeth sinking into the sausage. His head slammed sideways. The sausage flew from his mouth. His skull smashed against the culvert wall.

Mark lowered the camera just as the bullet crack sounded. At the same time, a stencilling of red and grey viscose patterned the culvert wall.

The chorizo fell from Carmody's hand.

Laskin's yelled. 'Snayper!'

Mark pressed his back against the wall; his thoughts like cold molasses as he stared at the man slumped in the cramped space.

Another round splintered the bricks at almost the same place. It kickstarted Mark from his torpor. The sniper must be at a tight angle, preventing a good line of sight, or he would have got Mark and Laskin.

The second round hit almost the same place as the first, only Carmody was no longer there. His body had fallen out of range when he collapsed. Now he lay sprawled at an impossible angle at Mark's feet. There was no doubt he was dead.

Mark glanced at Laskin for direction, but the Lieutenant was also pressed against the wall of the culvert, staring vacantly at Carmody's body.

Mark found himself in a strange state of calm, as if the world had separate itself from him. He said, 'Now what?'

Tonelessly, Laskin said, 'We must go back.' He drew his pistol and began sliding his narrow back along the culvert wall.

Mark pulled him back. 'That bastard's still out there.'

Laskin stopped. 'We can go out the other side.'

'If the sniper is where I think he is, he'll have a clear shot to both sides of the culvert.'

Laskin slumped to the ground. 'How do we get away then?'

'I thought you might have an answer to that.' Mark took in the angle of the culvert, the rocks, and bushes outside, the ridge across the valley. He reached for Carmody's rifle and another bullet ricochet off the bricks.

Now Mark had a better idea of the angle, but the sniper also knew they were there, and ricocheting bullets posed almost as much danger. He sat on the ground and closed his eyes trying to recall the terrain.

The image of the stork filled his mind. Perhaps the sniper, taking up position, had disturbed it. He couldn't have been there before the bird took flight, or he would have shot them out in the open.

Mark hadn't fired a rifle for months, but he'd always had a good eye although he'd never shot at a human before. He'd shot plenty of game, rabbits for dinner, the odd wild boar and magpie geese that flew over his farm to the Eubenangee Swamp in North Queensland.

In his cane cutting days, sometimes at night the men entertained themselves shooting rats from the tree branches. The cane fields were infested, and they brought a disease that had almost killed his brother and had succeeded in killing his ganger. Mark didn't like rats and claimed champion status for blasting them off tree branches in mid-stride.

Carmody's rifle was a Mauser 1916, manufactured by Fábrica de Armas in Barcelona. It was a better weapon than his dad's old Krag–Jørgensen, which Mark had commandeered for use on his farm. With this he might be able to hit a man at three hundred metres if he had a scope, but Carmody's rifle didn't have a scope. If the rifle was properly zeroed, and so long as he could see the sniper and didn't get hunted first, he might still have a chance.

Then a thought struck him. Was it odd for a lone sniper to be in the valley? Were more men out there? He looked at Laskin and said in low voice, 'How many do you think might be out there?'

Laskin shook his head, his face registering alarm and his voice rising an octave. 'You think there are more?' He glared at Carmody's dead body. 'He led us into a trap.'

Mark didn't bother to respond and murmured more to himself than as a question for Laskin. 'Why would one sniper be in the valley away from his own army?'

Laskin's narrow face drooped. 'Maybe to watch the road intersection.'

A distant rumbling answered him, and Mark felt the earth tremble.

'Tanks!' Laskin looked up at the curved culvert ceiling. 'We must get back to the car before we are cut off.'

Before Mark could stop him, Laskin sidled away to the other end of the culvert. He dropped onto all fours and crawled toward some scrubby bushes growing on the side of the gully. Mark closed his eyes as the bullet hit and blinked them open in time to see Laskin scuttling backwards into the culvert, blood already oozing through his uniform from his upper arm.

Mark's mind formed angles, imaginary lines tracing from Carmody's deathblow, back to where he'd first seen the stork, and then from Laskin's wounding, back to intersect with the first line. He knew where the man was, but to draw a bead on him Mark would have to expose himself, and the sniper was good, very good.

'I'm wounded.' Laskin stared at the blood oozing through his uniform.

Mark said, 'It doesn't look too bad, but you'll need to staunch the bleeding.' He looked at the strap of his camera case, frowned, paused, then said, 'Here,' and reached over to unsheathed Carmody's bayonet. He used the bayonet to cut out the stud of the rifle sling and unbuckle it. He shifted closer to Laskin, and wrapped the leather rifle sling around his arm, fastening the strap above the wound. 'Just a flesh wound. Missed the bone at least.'

Mark sat back against the wall in the middle of the culvert.

Laskin said, 'How can we get out of here?'

'We might have to wait until dark.' Mark felt increasing vibrations in the ground beneath him, and he glanced up at the upper curve of the culvert. 'Tanks. But whose are they?'

Laskin shrugged. 'They have stopped.' He raised his eyes to the culvert roof and tilted his head.

The ground some distance beyond the culvert exploded into a burst of white earth and rocks.

Laskin mumbled. 'Anti-tank artillery...' His words were obliterated by the air-ripping screech of the tank responding and the subsequent boom of the tank shell exploding.

Mark leaned back against the flimsy protection of the culvert. Was the sniper the advance of an ambush? With any luck, the tanks would blow the bastard into the next realm.

The sounds of men shouting came to them faint on the breeze. How far away were the tanks and did they have infantry with them? As if in answer to his question the air shattered as another 45mm missile flew overhead. Almost simultaneously several tanks opened fire.

Laskin and Mark crouched in the culvert and waited while Armageddon raged overhead. Mark inched his way to the edge of the culvert and looked towards the sniper's position. Dust hung in the air limiting visibility.

A breeze cleared the air and where before there had been an empty valley there was now an army just visible behind a fold in the valley floor. Maybe Laskin was right and Carmody had led them wrong but only because the war front was a fast-moving beast. Carmody couldn't have known about this ambush.

He searched the landscape for a way out and then crawled to the other end of the culvert but couldn't see the opposition. Who was friend, who foe? He'd assumed the sniper was Franco's, but it seemed whoever had set up in the fold of the valley was expecting these tanks to roll along this stretch.

Perhaps they had also assumed Carmody and Co. were scouts for the opposition. Uniforms weren't obvious at this distance, and while a flag flew near the sniper's position, both sides used similar versions of the Spanish colours. Unless he got closer, he wouldn't be able to tell.

How long the fight continued, Mark had no way of knowing. He watched the shadows move across the ground until the air in the tunnel became stifling. Flies found Carmody's body, and Mark's arm tired with the effort of keeping them away. He gave up, attempting to ignore the horror and ignominy of death.

Turning to Laskin he said, 'Should we not retrieve Carmody's dog-tag so that the Republic will know he's dead and where to find him?'

Laskin looked at the body and his face paled. 'What is a dog-tag?'

'Ah, an identity disk.'

'That is the right thing to do, but why do you call it a dog-tag?' His face took on an injured expression.

'Ah, it's the name an America reporter used, and it just stuck, I suppose. Seems apt, in any case.'

'Americans! The name is an insult.' Laskin leaned forward and groped around Carmody's neck area before sitting back in triumph, holding the metal label in the air.

Another boom sounded nearby and Laskin ducked.

Mark didn't bother explaining the reporter had called the items dog-tags in support of soldiers' humanity. Instead, he said, 'The battle seems to be moving west.' The drone of a new wave of bombers came to them. 'We should make a run for it while the planes are overhead. There is a forest to the east. If we follow the gully, it will get us to the shelter of those trees.'

'You saw already, the gully won't protect us.'

'No, but the armies out there will focus on the planes, and if we stay low, we may get away unnoticed.'

Laskin shook his head. 'What if the planes see us? I'm wounded; I cannot go out there again.'

'Those planes are not looking for us. They have more important concerns. Besides, it's our only chance. I'll help you.'

'The car is to the north. There are armies in that direction.'

'We'll have to walk around them and come in from the northeast.'

The sound of a Hotchkiss heavy machine gun firing galvanised Mark. He didn't waste his breath in argument, just slid his arm around Laskin's waist and hoisted him up. 'Come on mate you can do it.'

'The guns...'

'They are firing at the planes. They won't be looking at us. Follow on my heels but keep your head down and run for those trees. Don't stop until I tell you, all right?'

Mark ran bent double, entangling in the brush, falling over rocks, scree sliding underfoot, all the while imagining his back, like a giant white-shirted bull's eye. He should have kept his jacket. It would have made better camouflage. You live and learn. Or maybe not. He ran as he'd never run before, tripping and sliding and trying to stay low.

A cry from behind brought him up halfway, and he turned. Laskin lay face down.

He raced back. 'Are you hit?'

Laskin was unharmed, but fresh blood oozed from his wound. Mark helped him up and they set off again. All the while bombs fell, artillery boomed, and machine guns rattled in the distance but none of it focussed on them.

When they reached the trees, Mark fell to the ground, gulping the pine fragrant air like it was the water of life. A stream ran through the trees, clear and babbling over sand and pebbles. He left his camera, binoculars and Carmody's rifle on the bank and crawled into the water. He drank deeply, waist-deep, unheeding of his soaked clothing and boots, letting terror sluice away with the dirt and sweat.

When his pulse had returned to normal, he climbed out of the stream and lay on his back in a patch of sunlight and closed his eyes. The horrors of the morning dissipated as he applied himself to the problem of getting back to Madrid. It looked like any chance of an interview with the troops at the front was off the table for the moment. Laskin sat down beside him.

The stream flowed from the north, which would seem reasonable as it probably arose in the mountains. The river they had been heading towards this morning, was likely a tributary of this one. Maybe this was the tributary, either way if they followed it, they might be able to find the car and drive back to Madrid. They were long odds, but they had to do something and Laskin didn't seem to have any ideas.

He stood up. 'Hey Laskin, are you all right to move on. I reckon if we follow this stream and stay in the trees we can reach the road.' He peered into Laskin's face. 'Are you all right mate?'

Laskin was crying. 'You saved my life comrade.'

Mark pulled in his chin and looked askance. 'I didn't do anything.'

'You returned to pick me up when I fell.'

'Yes, but you were all right. Gave me a scare though. For a minute I thought they'd got you. How's your arm?'

'It gives me pain, but it will be well when it is dressed by a medic.'

Mark gazed at Laskin for a moment before he said, 'Look, if you are all right, I would like to find a spot to get some photos of the action out there.'

'You can't leave me here.'

'Just for a while...'

'There are wild animals.'

'You have a pistol, and I'll leave Carmody's rifle.'

'If I shoot, it will give away my position.'

'Unlikely with that racket going on.' Mark tilted his head towards the battle.

'You will be killed, and I will not be able to get back to Madrid.'

'Sure, you will. If something happens to me just follow this stream until you find the road. Then all you need to do is follow the road east-southeast to where we parked, but I won't be caught, and I'll be quick.'

'How do you know that.' Laskin glared at Mark with suspicion written across his face.

'Know what?'

'That this stream will cross the road and the direction to take to find the car.'

'I don't know it. From my recall of the map, it is likely. That's all, but look, I will miss any chance of a shot if I don't go now.'

'If you come back, I will give you what you want. I have influence. My father...'

Mark eyed Laskin with a sardonic look on his face. 'And what do I want?'

Laskin shrugged. 'What do you ask for?'

Mark gazed at him for a moment, thinking. He would have come back anyway, but if this bloke had some influence to get him embedded with a front-line battalion, it wouldn't hurt his career. 'I'd like to ride with the troops, particularly when they head into battle.'

'To fight!' Laskin's voice went up a notch as if in disbelief.

Mark grinned. 'At least then I might know who is shooting at me. But seriously, as a war reporter, and you make sure my copy gets past the sensors.'

'The first part is easy but the sensors...' He shrugged. 'I will try.'

'Righty-ho. I'll be back soon.'

Mark looked around at the lay of the land. If he kept to the tree cover to reach higher ground, he might get some decent shots of the action.

The Spanish Child Refugees

Beatrice boarded a train heading to Eastleigh. Once seated alone in a first-class compartment, she took the Spanish phrase book from her handbag. Never a particularly gifted language student, she had persevered with Latin and French at school, but now she had forgotten most of what she had learned. She set about memorising words and phrases she thought might be most useful.

She placed the book in her lap and said, 'Hola niñas, mi nombre es Beatrice.'

Oh no. Niñas is for girls. Niños is for boys but what if they are a mixed group? She thumbed through the pages as the train rushed southwest through the late spring countryside.

Beatrice shut the phrase book and leaned her forehead against the window. Outside, white blossoms crowned the hedgerows, while yellow and white flowers dotted the grassy meadows. In the shadows beneath tree copses, she noticed faint smudges of purple. Bluebells. For some long-forgotten reason, they reminded her of Banville Hall, her childhood home.

Her ancestral home, her mother would have reminded her. It was somewhere out there, rebuilt in the fifteenth century on the crumbling bones of the family's medieval castle. Earlier it had been granted to a Norman ancestor by William I, after its former Anglo-Saxon owner had died fighting him. Although the Norman Earl's son, married the Anglo-Saxon's granddaughter, so in effect it had been in her family since Egbert of Wessex created the shires. In the late eighteen hundreds her grandmother, rescued the place again, restoring, enlarging and modernising it to the Hall it now was, the first home she had known.

Perhaps she should revisit before her grandfather leased it to the government. It would be good to see her birthplace, to remind herself of where she had spent the first years of her life before her mother had whisked her off to Australia. Would she want to live in a place like that again? The world had changed since her childhood. Maintenance and upkeep would cost a fortune, and she was not the homemaker type. Besides, ancestral homes were not much use when there was no male heir to carry on Grandfather's title.

She sighed and turned back to her phrase book, but she couldn't concentrate. Instead, she held out her left hand and gazed at the ring on her finger. Mark had given it to her before he had left. The centre peace contained an oval shaped sapphire with three small diamonds either side. Her thumb traced the platinum band. She would see him in Paris in just a couple more weeks. A summer holiday in Rome with the two people she loved most in the world. Life couldn't be more perfect.

An hour later, the train pulled into Eastleigh Station. Gladys waited on the platform.

As Beatrice alighted, Gladys said, 'You're late. I've already had two pots of tea and three scones with jam and cream.'

'Did you save any for me?'

Gladys gave a guilty eyeroll.

Beatrice glanced at the station clock. 'I suspect you may have been early, my dear Gladys. But never mind. How are you?' She put down her bag and leaned in to kiss her friend's cheek. Gladys pulled away. Beatrice smiled. She'd forgotten. There would be no antipodean public displays of affection for her English friend. She picked up her bag and followed her to a car parked at the entrance to the station.

Gladys drove to the farm at North Stoneham. As they crested a hill, Beatrice saw the tents, row after endless row fanned out across the land.

She gasped. 'Its enormous. So many tents.'

'What did you expect?' Gladys pointed. 'The building over there is the only brick and mortar building we have, and it's used for the clinic. Next door is the administration tent. We'll go there once we get you sorted out. The most marvellous thing is that this is all done on donations like the money you raise. The Government refuses to help. I can't tell you how stout the townspeople are. They bring fresh food and toys and whatever they can spare for the children, and...'

She glanced slyly at Beatrice, 'I am quite reconciled to the unions now as they send so much of the money we need. Without them I just don't know how we would cope.' She looked around as if someone might overhear them, and then said in a conspiratorial tone, 'I wouldn't say this to anyone else, but aside from the unions, the British Communist Party have been terrific at organising all this, along with the Quakers of course. They're an odd combination but everyone puts aside their differences to help the children. It's just the beastly government who won't help.'

Beatrice stared at her friend in amazement.

Gladys grimaced. 'I know, I know, I've changed my tune, but the Reds and Labour are just like us when you get to know them. Aren't they?' She glanced apologetically at Beatrice. 'Well, here we are. I hope you won't mind, but we are to share.'

'It's a tent!' Beatrice looked around the muddy field as if expecting a building to arise where there hadn't been one before.

'Yes.' Gladys arched a brow. 'I have already said, the only proper building we have is the clinic.'

Beatrice shook her head. 'Sorry, I don't know what I was thinking. I thought they were all for the children. I've never lived in a tent before. I expect it'll be fun.'

'It's not fun. It's awful but it's all we have, and after a while you get the hang of it. Or at least that's what I'm told. I haven't yet managed to get organised, and the slightest effort becomes such a chore, but you are only here for a few days. Look, put down your suitcase and I'll take you over and introduce you to the others. Doctor Mayhew is the duty doctor and I'm sure you'll love him. He's dreamy, but of course, completely beyond the pale. He's a socialist you know. They are not communists, although I am never sure about the differences.'

Beatrice shrugged. Neither was she. 'When will I meet the children?'

Gladys looked askance. 'You are on a mission, aren't you? They'll be having tea now in the refectory tent, and after that they will prepare for bed. Probably better to meet them in the morning when they're fresh. By the end of the day, they can be as crusty as a geriatric ward.'

'You say that as if they are loaves of bread.' Beatrice smiled at Gladys and placed her case on the narrow camp cot that Gladys had indicated. 'Come on then, let's meet this socialist and ask him to explain the difference.'

Opportunism

High on a ridge on the south-eastern flank of the Bizkargi Range, Charles West sat on a rock scribbling something in a notepad. From this distance, he saw little, other than the valley, hills, and the smoke from the burning forest. He couldn't see the battle on the ground, but he heard the noise; boom-boom like a weird kind of thunder.

The Africa Army had taken on the main section of the Basque army, outgunning and outmanning, while an elite corps of Carlist troops feinted towards the north. He paused from his scribbling, waiting for von Graff to give him more information, and the right terminology to include in his column.

Charles wasn't cut out for this. He wasn't a war correspondent and knew nothing about company structures, battle tactics or armaments. Von Graff said they were safe here, but what if they weren't?

The June sun beat down on his shoulders, and the air thickened with noise, smoke, and debris. Insects ratcheted up the volume to a demented level of tinnitus. A nicotine craving gnawed at his stomach. He'd left his case in the car, and exhaustion plus a healthy level of fear prevented him from returning to collect it.

The rock beneath him cut into the bones of his backside, while he dripped sweat onto his notebook, silently cursing von Graff, who had insisted, only an eyewitness report would be unassailable. Although eyewitness seemed like rather a lofty euphemism for what he did. In reality, he had no idea how the battle progressed, had witnessed little, and merely wrote down what von Graff told him.

'The red caps have broken through. See...' Von Graff pointed, the glasses planted against his face. 'Through that unburnt section...' He breathed a heavy sigh. 'They've taken it my friend.' He handed Charles the binoculars. 'They have planted the flag.'

Charles stood up and adjusted the field glasses. 'It's just a hill.'

'Not just a hill. They have breached the Iron Ring—taken the high ground. We will be in Bilbao within days and have those Reds running with their tails between their legs.'

Von Graff turned and walked down the stoney pathway to the vehicle. 'Come now, El Caudillo will be in a magnanimous mood especially as you helped with identifying the placement of the defences.'

Charles noted von Graff's sarcastic tone for General Franco's self-assumed title as leader. But then von Graff acknowledged only one leader of Europe, and he wasn't Spanish. A little more circumspect, Charles said nothing, merely followed von Graff back to the vehicle.

A few days later, Charles entertained the Burgos establishment in the Rio Tinto executive guest quarters: his home for the time being. He gazed around the room at the military uniforms, and the gowned and bejewelled women. The large, and airy first-floor apartment had French doors leading out onto a spacious patio, now bathed in moonlight.

It had taken Charles no time at all to shake off his newsman persona in favour of the guise of an independent financial advisor and investment consultant. His first contract, working with his family's extensive mining investments in Spain. His next job, his aunt's idea, would be to take over the management of his little cousin's portfolio and for that he needed Mark.

His chest expanded. Everyone of importance was here, except General Franco and the supreme brother-in-law Ramón Serrano Suñer, the latter, the brains behind the throne. He hadn't managed to meet either man, although Don Frederick told him, his mission meant promoting Franco's sacred cause to the British people. Only then might he collect the dividends.

Tall, patrician featured and white-haired, Don Frederick Ramón de Bertodano y Wilson, eighth Marquis del Moral spoke Spanish poorly for he'd been born in Australia. He and Charles's father, George West, had been classmates at Sydney University. Later they had both served in army intelligence. During the

Second Boar war, Moral had brought about Breaker Morant's court-martial, an interesting connection in itself.

Lady Margaret had suggested he introduce himself to Moral, and the man had immediately discussed a project he had brewing. Like the Germans, he planned to set up a Friends of National Spain, and he knew Charles would be willing to help.

Charles wasn't naïve and knew Moral's embrace arose from the propaganda perspective he had provided through his job with *The Times*. In exchange, Moral had given his, and Lady Margaret's, families an undertaking to do his utmost to protect their investments in a Franco led Spain.

But he'd left the newsman career behind. Charles stubbed out his cigarette and gazed around the room, noting Luis Bolín in deep conversation with von Graff. What were they plotting? He glanced across to see his companion's reaction to Bolín, but he wasn't looking in that direction.

Moral had brought about Bolín demise as chief press officer, although Bolín had no one to blame for his abrupt career end, but himself. The Republicans looked after the press well. Nationalist Spain might learn from them.

Charles touched the older man's elbow. 'Another glass of something Don Frederick?'

Moral shook his head.

It was Moral's influence, along with von Graff's friendship, that had originally helped Charles get into Nationalist Spain. Prior to that, a paranoid Bolín had made it difficult for a journalist to enter the territory at all. He had little sympathy for the man's removal from the position.

Moral remained the source of Charles's belief that the bombing of Guernica was the work of the Basque Army—Reds to the man, and he'd had carried that line through all his news reports, despite contrary accounts from eyewitnesses.

The battle for Bilbao had been his last report. When he'd resigned, he had recommended Mark Anders to both Moral and Dawson as his successor in Franco territory. If Mark married Beatrice, he would become extremely wealthy, and Charles had plans for that wealth. He needed the man where he might influence him.

Moral interrupted his thoughts. 'Do you think this Australian photojournalist might be amenable.'

Charles pursed his lips. 'You saw his coverage in *The Times* where the battle clearly showed our troops cutting off Republican supply lines into Madrid. I think he can be trusted and led to the right conclusion, but it will need to be subtle. He's not political, just hell-bent on getting the best photos to show what he calls the truth.' Charles laughed. 'I suppose he might be called naïve. God save me from the worthy. I recommended him to Dawson because of his connection to Denton, but I also thought the offer should be at arm's length from the Nationalist. To you, he'll appear to be just another war correspondent, sent to cover the war in the north.'

Sheer curtains billowed as Don Jacobo came in from the patio. Tall and debonair in his uniform he gazed around. The chatter quietened for a moment before glasses were raised to a chorus of, 'Arriba España.' He smiled and waved.

Don Jacobo or Jacobo Fitz-James Stuart y Falcó not only held the titles of the 17th Duke of Alba, 10th Duke of Berwick, but rumour elevated him as the legitimate heir to the throne of Scotland. In any event, he was related to half of the aristocracy in Britain and Spain. Charles had first met him at his cousin's birthday party. Both Don Jacobo and Moral had been in Salamanca for the past few weeks persuading General Franco that Jacobo should be appointed to an official Nationalist ambassadorial role in London.

Jacobo walked over to Moral and said, 'I have just heard General Dávila has Ulíbarri on the run. We have secured Bilbao. The Republic is finished.'

Charles said, 'Aren't you forgetting Madrid, great swathes of Castilla La Mancha, Valencia and Catalonia, not to mention half of Aragon.'

Fitz-James Stuart shrugged. 'What can they do? They have few men left, hardly any planes and even less by way of armaments. It's merely a matter of time, my dear Charles.' He gave Moral a wolfish grin, winked, and turned back to Charles. 'Have you heard from Lord Denton recently? I understand he may contemplate persuading his colleagues to grant belligerent rights to General Franco...'

Charles grinned. 'Nice try old boy. Although I am told, all good things come to those who wait.'

Charles had already written a long letter on behalf of Geddes Auckland the chairman of Rio and sent it off to Denton. Although he had not heard back, he contemplated whether his little cousin's grandfather might be influenced further. Mark may be more useful than he originally anticipated as he seemed to have Denton's ear.

It was a pity Sir Henry Chiltern had retired. He would have been useful. Charles didn't know the new chap. An error that must be rectified as soon as possible. Charles rather liked mixing in this rarefied air. Why had it taken him so long to realise his calling, wheeling and dealing in political diplomacy?

The Spanish war wouldn't last forever, but this job might lead to finding a more lasting, and lucrative spot in the British foreign ministry. Of course, Denton could make all that happen and more. Charles would simply need to make the right connections and elicit the right amount of indebtedness from significant players in the game. Yes, Mark would prove a useful ally, indeed.

Lack of funds appeared the trickier part of his diplomatic efforts. While his father and Uncle Arthur gave him a decent stipend, and Rio Tinto paid him a fee and his expenses here in Burgos, the shortfall remained ever present. He still owed a horrible amount of money for the Jaguar SS. And some of the gambling debts, he'd left behind in London, were in the habit of catching him unawares.

The last time he'd sent those to the accountant, his uncle Arthur had said it would be the last of the payments they would make. Charles was a little afraid of Arthur and swore off gambling. He'd meant it at the time, but how else might he keep up his end, socialising with people for whom money was no object.

He'd just have to find an additional source of income. Usually, von Graff obliged. That last payment he'd received for persuading a contact to transfer Goicoechea's blueprints of Bilbao's Iron Ring defences to an aerial map, had seemed enormous at the time. But like water in a dessert, it had evaporated.

What with the Jaguar, a few tailor-made suits, and his new watch—he pressed his hand onto the gold and steel Jaeger-Le Coultre reverso on his wrist—the payment had gone along with his last month's stipend from his directorship on the board of Lady Margaret's charity.

He scanned the room, ensuring his guests enjoyed themselves. Von Graff's companion looked bored, and Charles excused himself from Moral and Don Jacobo to saunter across the room.

He smoothed his blond hair, supremely aware of his good looks, slim hips, Grecian features, chiselled lips, and straight nose. As usual, his clothing was impeccable although rather dashing and he knew the effect of his lithe but graceful body movements on women. This one was no exception.

She smiled as he drew up. Her pink skin glowed. Thick blonde eyelashes drooped over cornflower blue eyes as she brushed an imagined lock of hair from her neck, drawing attention to the plump half-moons rising above a tightly laced bodice.

'Fräulein, may I replenish your drink?'

Her cheeks dimpled and her eye lashes fluttered. 'Please call me Clara, Herr Vest.'

He narrowed his eyes, unhappy with the pronunciation of his surname. 'And you must call me Charles.'

He deftly swapped her empty champagne glass for a full one off the tray of a passing waiter. As he handed it to her, his fingers lingered on hers for a moment more than necessary, giving him an opportunity to gaze at her enticing cleavage.

It had been a while since fashion, with its peepholes and glimpses, had favoured such expanses of naked chest and Charles decided it was time for a return. 'If I may say, your dress is exquisite. Paris?'

'Nein, Berlin. The design is based on Bavarian tradition. It is where my family come from.'

She placed her small hands on her nipped-in waist, drawing attention to her hourglass figure and did a slow twirl, lace petticoats showing briefly as her skirt lifted above her calves.

'What are you doing with my young cousin?' Rudolf von Graff placed a heavy hand on Charles's shoulder. 'You must be careful of these Englishmen, Clara. They are dangerous.'

'Your cousin!' Charles tried to cover his surprise. He had assumed Clara was von Graff's mistress. 'Please introduce me.'

'My dear Charles I am not so sure that is wise. I promised my uncle I would take care of her.' He smiled.

Clara thrust out her hand. 'How do you do Mr Vest, Charles, it is a pleasure to meet you.'

She stuck her tongue out at Rudolf as Charles took her tiny hand in his. It felt like a soft and quivering bird, so easily crushable.

'The pleasure is all mine, but I also must correct your cousin. I am Australian not British.'

With a toss of her fine mane, she said, 'Now Rudolf, my caring cousin, we are formally introduced.'

Rudolf said sotto voce, 'But does he know who your Papi is Clara, and if you tell him, will he run away?'

Her eyes widened, the innocent little girl look, and really, she looked like a drawing in a nursery rhyme book.

She glanced at Charles still holding her hand in his. 'My father wouldn't scare you, would he, Charles?'

'I don't know your father, or at least I don't think I know him, but why on earth would anyone be afraid.' He smiled at Clara.

Von Graff bowed to his cousin. 'No more teasing my little Sonnenschein. This man is my friend and a good friend to Germany, but as you already know he is Charles West, Australian British of the best kind. Charles, may I introduce my cousin Fräulein Clara Hauser. You have heard of Deutsche Waffen und Munitionsfabrike, the German munitions manufacturers?'

Charles almost whistled. That Hauser. He glanced at Clara with renewed interest.

'Now it is getting late. We must leave your fine soiree, Charles, for we have a long drive to Salamanca in the morning. Perhaps we may return your hospitality soon.'

Clara made a moue of disappointment and fluttered her lashes at Charles. She laid her hand on von Graff's arm and turned to leave, hips swaying. Before reaching the door, she glanced back and twinkled her fingers in farewell.

He would have to find a reason to visit von Graff soon. Clara's industrialist family was worth more than a small kingdom.

A Taste of Real Horror

The Brigade waited for orders to move. They were strung out in an untidy train of donkeys, mule carts, men, lorries, and armoured vehicles, interspersed by the odd gun carriage. Mark stalked back and forth along the hot, dusty road, as distant gunfire echoed off the embankment.

While he was grateful to Laskin for arranging this stint with the British Brigade, the incessant waiting drove him crazy. For the past few days, he'd done little other than pacing and kicking stones. There were only so many photos a person could take of soldiers digging trenches.

The summer sun beat down on his shoulders from a cloudless sky, desiccating the landscape and sucking the colour from the Iberian oaks dotting the grass and gorse plains. He almost imagined himself back home in the dry country, beyond the Great Dividing Range, where a similar ceramic-blue dome arced across the chalky, stone-filled earth. Hills rolled away to the mountains in the north, interspersed with forests and streams like the one he and Laskin had followed back to their car, just a few weeks ago.

The Brigade's orders were to take Villanueva de la Cañada. Although, of the men Mark had asked, none seemed to know why they had stopped at this point on the map. Even the Lieutenant didn't seem to know anything more than they did.

Lieutenant Bricknall had taught at a school in Shaftesbury, Dorset, he'd told Mark, before he gave it all up to help the Spanish Republic fight the insurgents. When he'd arrived in Spain, he'd known nothing about fighting. Now, as one of the few survivors of the battle for the Jarama, he claimed veteran status.

Mark found him to be a man of reason, yet he held fast to the communist cause. Misguided in Mark's view given Stalin's corruption of Marxism, but Bricknall, like most of the communists Mark knew, just wanted justice and a fair go for all. He too, saw Spain's fight as a stand against global fascism.

Bricknall, a thin, wiry man, light on his feet, slid down from his seat in the lorry and called out, 'Take a spell, lads. I'll find out what's happening.'

The men sat where they could and relaxed, smoked, or hunkered on their haunches while they waited. The old hands scanned the sky for the tell-tale black dots marking an approach of Condor Legion Junkers.

Yesterday, one of the new recruits had asked Bricknall. 'What will it be like?'

'Like a bloody picnic,' he'd replied. 'Flies and all.'

The Brigade was still referred to as the British Brigade although more than half their numbers had been left rotting in bloody fields. It now included Spanish soldiers from other battalions. New recruits, with no combat experience and minimal training, had replaced the British or English-speaking dead. Most did not speak English and many of the British men didn't speak Spanish.

Mark had taken on the unofficial role of translator for Bricknall. It gave him access the insider knowledge. Yesterday, he'd overheard some of the officers speaking about the brigade's chances in the coming offensive. It wasn't looking good.

Rumours, blame, recriminations and leadership clashes reached the ears of the new recruits, and it took all Bricknall's leadership skills to keep his men focused. Mark counted himself lucky that he'd been assigned to the Anti-tank battery, where the old hands seemed not to engage in too much gossip and the new men didn't say much at all.

He snapped another photo of the waiting men, their uniforms assorted and ill fitting, some threadbare, some with feet clad only in espadrilles. Guilt at his relative prosperity tugged at his conscience and he constantly had to remind himself that he was a reporter not a soldier.

He stopped pacing and squatted in the shade of an Iberian oak, patting, as if by habit, his breast pocket where he'd folded the letter from Beatrice. She wanted him to join her and her grandfather on a trip to Rome. He recalled the invitation at her party but hadn't thought much more about it. Now he had a date to meet them in Paris one week from today. He hoped he might make it back in time. Missing her felt like an empty space in his chest, but leaving right now wasn't an option.

With any luck the Brigade would take the town within the next couple of days, and then he could leave with his photos and an article in the bag. He would dispatch from Paris and join Beatrice and Denton on the next leg of the journey to Rome.

As if by magic, the column ahead began to move, and a prickle of anticipation ran across his shoulders. He climbed back into the Lieutenant's lorry, and they headed west, northwest to their destination. A few kilometres on, the convoy turned off the road and bumped along a rutted track before stopping once more.

Bricknall alighted from the truck and said, 'Headquarters for the moment.'

He moved to a flat area of dirt and spread a map on the ground. Soldiers clustered around, and Mark followed, opening his camera to capture the scene.

Bricknall said, 'Can you translate.' He turned back to the men. 'You can all hear the shelling up ahead. The enemy is over that ridge. Our orders are to wait here until nightfall before we make a move to this high ground. He pointed at the map and then looked up, his eyes creased against the glare. 'Over there.' He pointed towards a low hill a fair distance away. 'Get some rest and food into you but do it quietly. We will get under way as soon as darkness falls.'

Mark translated, and the men went about their duties in silence, setting up a temporary camp, digging shallow trenches in case they came under fire.

The sun beat down, while the distant shelling continued. The men found cover beneath the oaks or in the shade of rocky outcrops. Mark tilted his canteen to his lips and then stopped and replaced the lid. He would have to save water or run out. Who knew how long they would have to wait.

That night they took their places, in preparation for orders to attack. Mark stayed with the anti-tank unit as they took up positions on the high ground. Then they waited, staring into the darkness until a false dawn lightened the horizon.

The attack on the village took place at dawn.

Mark watched through field glasses from the safety of a high ridge. Eventually the Brigade seemed to gain the advantage, and he saw fleeing Nationalist soldiers, who appeared to use civilians to shield their retreat.

Once the Republican soldiers had cleared out the village, Mark took photos of the carnage before he visited the mobile casualty station in a large tent on the outskirts of the village. The noise of men screaming, sobbing, calling for mothers. The cicada-scritch of the saw on bone. The smell of vomit, faeces, and blood as nurses hurried past with bed pans and buckets made Mark's gorge rise. Without raising his camera, he stumbled outside gulping air to dilute the horror.

The next morning Soviet-made tanks rolled into the village along with reinforcements for the Brigade. They were ordered to secure the heights overlooking the Guadarrama River, and the distant village of Boadilla del Monte.

Mark had just enough light and the time to begin a photo shoot of the men. He arranged them in front of the tanks and fiddled with his lens.

The familiar drone of planes came with the sun rise. A shout and men scattered.

Mark stood transfixed as he watched the Condor Legion arrive. The next moment he ran for his life as grenades rained down followed by bombs. Shrapnel, dirt and stones flailed the smoke-filled air. Fire sucked oxygen from his lungs. He found cover behind an outcrop of rocks and crouched into as small a target as possible with hands over his ears as the inferno raged.

Finally, the bombardment stopped, and the Brigade regrouped, stumbling out from whatever cover they had found. Mark remained with the anti-tank unit, while the tanks and infantry men move uphill.

They hadn't gone half a mile when an artillery attack opened up from the very ground to which they marched. It seemed that under cover of the bombing raid Nationalist reinforcements had moved into the position the Republic coveted.

Undeterred the Republicans pressed on, the men seeking cover behind a tank as they struggled up hill. At the crest, the tank reared and overturned, leaving the infantry exposed. Heavy artillery pounded their position. Fighter planes swooped, and machine guns cut a swathe through human bodies. The battle became a bloody killing field.

The anti-tank unit received orders to fall back. As they retreated, the ground nearby erupted. Lieutenant Bricknall spun around, knocking into Mark. Both men tumbled into a rocky gully. An avalanche of earth and stones hammered down on them.

Dazed, Mark lay still for a minute before he tried and failed to push Bricknall off. Another foreign soldier lost to a family who would never know what had happened or where he lay buried. Did he even have a family? Mark had never asked.

He lay on his back staring at the heat glazed sky, the weight of a man he'd considered a friend keeping him pinned to the ground. The world around him felt heavy with its silence. He watched a dog fight between a Republican biplane and a German Messerschmitt in the sky above. The biplane spun into a nosedive, black plumes trailing before it ploughed into the ground and exploded.

Even with the distance between him and the crash site he felt the earth shake. Still, there came no sound, just the rocky ground around him dotted with yellow Broom. Bees foraged silently in the blossoms seemingly oblivious to the human folly going on around them.

Then a noise like no other. Air splitting mortars, artillery thumps, machine guns rattling, and the screaming of mules and men. Mark had lost his camera. Panic set in and he heaved Bricknall off, scrambling out of the layer of dirt, only to find the camera still hung around his neck.

He pulled himself to the top of the gully, dusted the dirt of the camera and clicked. It worked. He took shot after shot until he heard Bricknall groan. With a last glance at another uneven dogfight, he slid down the incline.

'Mate, I thought you were dead.' Mark brushed his hand across his neck and felt something sticky. He patted the area but could find no broken skin. Yet, blood continued to seep from somewhere.

Bricknall said, 'Not that easy to get rid of me and if you are looking for the source of bleeding, it's your ear.

'Fuck, why?'

'The blast, no doubt.'

Mark shrugged. 'Can you stand?'

'I think so.' Bricknall tried to sit up and fell back. 'Shit. Give me a hand will you.'

'Maybe I should check you over first.'

'What the fuck do you know about battle injuries?'

Mark shook his head. 'I can see the obvious. Do you have any pain?'

'Not a skerrick.' His face blanched to a pale gesso.

Mark said nothing, just helped him into a sitting position leaning against the bank.

Blood oozed through Bricknall's trousers. Mark raised the ripped khaki and forced down his gag reflex. 'It looks like a bone's snapped. I'll help you get to the casualty station.'

'My rifle. Find my rifle.'

'What rifle?'

'My rifle. Find it.'

Mark didn't recall Bricknall carrying a rifle, but he hunted around and found a pistol, an Astra 400, a few metres away. He dusted off the dirt and handed it to Bricknall. 'Soon as we move out of this ditch we are exposed. I reckon we follow the depression along that way before doubling back to casualty.'

'Where's the rifle. I can't leave my men.'

'Sorry mate, that's all I found, but there not much you can do with a broken leg either.'

'Fuck.'

'I'll take you on my back until we are away a bit. You keep the pistol ready in case, but don't shoot me by mistake.'

Bricknall sniggered.

Mark wedged his shoulder beneath Bricknall's arm and hauled him across his back. Bricknall screamed. Mark almost dropped him, thanking his lucky stars for Bricknall's wiry frame. Bent double, he ran or rather staggered away from the fighting, following the curve of the depression.

Once certain they were out of the enemy's line of sight and hidden from fighters in the air, he stopped and lowered Bricknall to the ground. The Lieutenant tried to gain balance on one leg, but it was clear he couldn't go far.

Mark tried to speak but his throat choked. He'd lost his canteen, so he saved his breath, and hoisted Bricknall over his shoulder in a fireman's lift. Bricknall's scream cut off abruptly and he flopped with the weight of an unconscious man. Mark hoped he had just fainted and wasn't dead. He stumbled towards a distant mirage beyond which lay the village and the casualty station.

When he arrived, he was almost blinded by exhaustion, heat, thirst, and pain. Two orderlies helped him get the unconscious Bricknall onto a stretcher before he staggered away. There was no time to rest. He had to get back to witness the rest of the battle.

A nurse blocked his path. 'Where do you think you're going?' Her face swam into focus, grey and pinched, her uniform apron drenched in blood. She was another mirage, just wavy lines of heat, and he didn't have the spit to make words. Mark shook his head and winced as knives sliced through his brain. He sidestepped and staggered out of the tent. He had gone less than ten yards before he pitched forward into oblivion.

Arrest

Mark recovered quickly from what they told him was exposure, severe dehydration, and heat exhaustion, along with a burst ear drum. At least he still had all his limbs and, aside from his ear drum, no other puncture holes. He accompanied the wounded, including Bricknall, back to Madrid.

They were taken to *The Palace Hotel*. A place of contradictions, of glamour and gore. Graceful old furnishings side by side with bloody stretchers. The odour of ether rising to meet crystal chandeliers. Walls with framed posters advertising glorious holiday destinations.

Mark stayed overnight among the recovering injured. Glad to listen to them talk, even though most was gossip, blame, and conspiracies. Who could blame them? These were men who, in one day, had won and then lost.

From what he learned, the battle to save Madrid's supply routes had gone from triumph to farse. Russian advisors to the

Republican army didn't help either. Instead, they blamed the men for their command's tactical errors, and shot any who tried to challenge their decisions, claiming they were traitors or deserters.

In this sorry war the Nationalist forces, with German and Italian air superiority, were winning and Mark didn't want to die watching it take place above him. Tanks were the past. Air power was the future and the poor Republicans, with their curtailed resources and outdated weaponry didn't have a chance, despite their bravery.

Mark had had enough. He would file his report and meet Beatrice in Paris. He said goodbye to Bricknall whose time at the front was over. Once recovered and able to travel he would be repatriated. His wife would be pleased to see him alive. Mark promised to stay in touch.

After leaving the hospital he went straight to the Telefónica building in the Gran Via. He submitted a report, a sanitised version that would pass the press censor's scrutiny and not drop Laskin into any deep pit of trouble. A deeper level of analysis, brewing in his head along with photos, could wait until he saw Denton again.

A familiar figure hailed him and hurried closer with a broad grin on his face. His thick lensed spectacles were held together at the bridge with sticking plaster.

'Sam,' Mark said. 'Good to see you again mate.' He shook Sam's outstretched hand.

'Lucky devil, I heard you got to travel to the front line. How did you wrangle that?'

'As you said, luck.' Mark grinned. 'What happened to your glasses?'

'Bloke knocked them off and stepped on them. Can't get a new pair until I get home, so this will have to do.'

Mark gazed at Sam for a minute. 'That was unfriendly.'

'Yeah. Bit of paranoia in some quarters but it worked out fine. Another bloke stepped in and saved me. Now he's my best friend.'

'You don't say.'

Sam tilted his head toward the main doors. 'He's been following me around like a puppy dog—waiting outside at the moment, in fact.'

'Let me just lodge this copy and make a call to London, then maybe we can take him for a nice walk while we find somewhere to have a drink and something edible other than white beans or lentils.'

'Good luck with that.'

An hour later, after lodging his copy, and then telephoning to reassure Beatrice he would be in Paris on time to meet her for their trip to Rome, Mark and Sam left the press office, passing by the man waiting outside. He immediately fell in behind them.

They walked to a bar, a place frequented by the press, entered, and found a table near the sandbagged window. The man following them waited in the doorway.

'What do you suppose he wants?' Mark nodded in the direction of their shadow.

'No idea but when he helped me up off my backside earlier, I think he had mistaken me for someone else. Kept calling me Sénior.'

'Shit that's bad.'

'That's what I thought. I am going back to Barcelona tomorrow and then home. I think I may have done my dash here, especially if the Republicans believe I'm a fascist sympathiser.'

'Why would they think that?'

'Ha! You haven't heard. I wrote an article about the disappearance of Andreu Nin, the POUM leader.'

'What happened?'

'Where have you been?'

Mark grinned. 'I was a bit too busy to read the news.'

'Oh yeah. Well, he was arrested and disappeared. I reckon the NKVD have him, and if he's not dead already, he soon will be.'

'No wonder the bloke called you Sénior, rather than comrade. Shit mate you're in a world of trouble.'

'I know. You too.'

'Me.'

'Yeah, contaminated by my proximity.'

'Na, I'll be all right. I know the head man.'

'Who?'

'Volof.' Mark grinned.

'How the hell...?'

'Gave him a lift from Albacete. He liked me.'

'Is that how you got to accompany the Brigade.'

Mark moved his head from side to side. 'Sort of. It's a long story, but yeah. The bloke seemed quite charming.'

'Don't kid yourself. He's Stalin's devil.'

'I'll keep that in mind. But hey, tell me what you know about Bilbao. I heard the insurgents have the Basque Army on the run.'

Sam's mouth turned down. 'It was a bloody mess. Seems someone sold them out, got a copy of the iron ring fortifications from the architect and translated them to an aerial map. The Condor Legion knocked them out from the air. Franco just marched into Bilboa while the Republican army fled.'

'Shit!' Mark stared across the hub of journalists drinking at the bar, an image of Javier blocking his vision.

'Are you okay?'

Mark shook his head. 'Fine. That's bad about the Basque army though. Wish I could get into the north to see what is happening up there.'

An hour later the two men left the bar in search of something to eat. Their shadow waited outside, leaning one foot against the wall, and picking his teeth. When he saw them, he pushed himself away and fell into step behind them.

The crack and echo of rifle fire brought Mark up short. A scan of the buildings opposite showed a fleeing figure bent double behind a balustrade. Mark fumbled for his camera, unclipping the catches to get a shot. Too late. The figure had vanished. He turned around and saw their shadow sprawled on the ground, a pool gathering beneath his head.

Sam knelt by the man's side; hands wrapped around his neck. It took a moment before Mark realised his friend's actions were to staunch the blood, not throttle the man. He strode over to help but as he bent down, he saw the man was dead.

Sam's face, pale in the dim light, his hands black and slippery, looked up at Mark. 'Help me.'

Mark shook his head. 'No use now mate. The bloke's gone. Come on we'd better get off the streets and clean you up or we'll be the next target.'

A crowd had gathered. He heard a shout and running footfalls. He hauled Sam up. The volume increased, but Mark wasn't paying attention to the crowds, only to their own survival. Sam swayed and he steadied him. 'You alright mate?'

'He's dead.'

'Yes. Come on.'

A car screeched to a stop. Another followed. Doors opened. Several men got out. The shouting dropped to a murmur. The next moment they were surrounded, three rifles and a revolver pointing at them.

Mark slowly raised his hands and pointed to the top of the building. 'Un hombre con un rifle le disparó a este hombre.' He pointed at the dead man. 'A man with a rifle shot this man,' he said again, and added, 'quinta columna—fifth columnists.'

The bloke with the pistol gave two men an order and they raced across the road.

They would find nothing. The shooter had bolted as soon as he'd fired the shot.

While they waited Mark kept his hands in the air. Sam did likewise. The men who arrested them, were not military, at least not in uniform. Maybe they were Cuerpo de Seguridad, the new police force that had swallowed all the previous outfits. From what Mark knew, it had two branches, one uniformed police and one a plain clothes investigation service called Sección de Investigaciones Especiales, but what the hell did they want with him and Sam?

He tried again. 'We are press. Journalists—periodistas. Australiano,' he pointed to his chest. 'Americano,' he pointed at Sam.

The man with the pistol narrowed his eyes and said, 'Pasaportes.' He held out his hand.

Mark pointed at his inside jacket pocket and the man nodded. He took out his passport and press pass and handed them to the man.

At that moment, the two men, who had been sent off to scout for potential fifth columnists, appeared on the roof top across the road. One of the men shouted and made a gesture which indicated they had found nothing.

The revolver holder gave a command, and Mark and Sam were hustled into the waiting Hispano-Suiza. As the vehicle moved forward, Mark looked out the rear window at the gawking bystanders. The slain shadow lay unattended as if invisible. It seemed, in this war the dead no longer mattered, other than to their relatives.

Sam sat white faced, on the other side of one of the captors, using a handkerchief to scrub the blood from his hands. His thick lensed spectacles sat askew on the bridge of his nose, as if in shock the tape holding them together had given up. Both he and Sam were sitting next to the car doors with only one captor between. If they coordinated, they could open the doors and escape when the car slowed to turn a corner. He glanced behind. A second car followed. Besides the man in the front seat still held on to his passport and press credentials. He wouldn't get far without them.

The cars pulled up outside what looked like an erstwhile church annex, turned security headquarters. Hopefully not one of the notorious Checas. At the start of the insurgency, different Republican factions, mostly the unions, had commandeered buildings as their headquarters, most with improvised prisons attached. The Republican government had since managed to close many of them, but some survived. Mark just hoped this was a legitimate facility, and not a factional kangaroo court where assassinations were swift and merciless.

They were escorted inside and hustled into a windowless room filled with the sour odour of its former inhabitants. A bucket simmered in the corner and a naked light hung from a fraying cord. The heavy door slammed, punctuated by the crash of a bolt shooting home.

Mark glanced at Sam who peered through his lopsided lenses at the heavy door. 'Are you all right mate?'

Sam took off his glasses, fiddled for a moment, then looked up. 'I think so... You?'

Mark nodded and squatted on his haunches, his back against the wall. He scanned the room. High ceilinged, measuring approximately three by two yards with walls that had once been whitewashed. They were now covered with scratched names, dates, symbols, and brown stains that may or may not have been blood. The concrete floor had a gutter along one side. The light hanging from the ceiling, along with the bucket in the corner, were the only furnishing.

'I think I may have got you into this mess.' Sam stood with his back to the opposite wall.

'You mean, the article about Nin.'

Sam nodded and hesitated. 'I also may have bagged the Russian interference in the Republic's democracy.'

'What did you say?'

'I simply indicated that Nin's disappearance had the hallmarks of Stalin's purges, removing all opposition since he condemned Trotsky last year. Trotsky's leftist form of communism is the one that appeals internationally, but it's a threat to Stalin's hyper-nationalist view, which, if you dissect it, is actually a form of fascism in itself.'

'So, you're a Trotskyist.'

'No, I'm a reporter who presents what is happening with objective care.'

'And a liberal eye.'

Sam frowned. 'I'm a Republican.'

'I meant liberal as in the philosophy not a political party.'

'Okay sorry, but now I am persona non grata at least I hope that's all I am.'

'The bloke killed, your shadow, who do you reckon he was? Why was he following you?'

Sam shrugged. 'Your guess is as good as mine.'

Mark stared into the middle of the room. What the hell had he got himself mixed up in? He sighed and sank to the floor. 'I guess we will be here for a while. Best get some sleep while we wait.' He lay down on the hard dirty floor and shut his eyes against the light.

Sam said, 'How can you sleep now?'

Mark opened one eye. 'What else is there to do?' He shut his eyes again and retreated into his mind, trying to figure a way out of the quagmire. The men who had arrested them were not

Russians but Spaniards. Maybe they had been arrested on behalf of the NKVD because of Sam's article. Alternatively, it might be nothing to do with the Russians.

He could beg another favour from Colonel Dimitri Volof, although that was bound to create a debt he wasn't sure he wanted to owe. Still, after he had delivered Laskin alive back to the NKVD headquarters in Alcala de Henares, the colonel and his lieutenant said he should call on them for any help he needed.

A noise outside their door had Mark back on his feet in a second. The heavy wooden edifice swung open. Four guards entered and ushered Mark and Sam out into a corridor. From there they were led to a reception room. At one end of the room a guard manned a counter. Their escorts made them sit on two chairs, pushed up against the wall, while they sat across the room; rifles held across their laps.

Mark decided to wait before he used Volof's name as his trump card. If he miscalculated, they could be in more trouble. He mulled over what he knew about policing in Madrid. The Guardia Civil had been replaced by Guardia Nacional Republicana. The Guardia de Asalto was mostly deployed to the front line and didn't operate in Madrid.

The police, and especially its investigative branch Cuerpo de Investigación y Vigilancia had been taken over by Dirección General de Seguridad or DSG. The DSG ran the Comité Provincial de Investigación Pública or CPIP, the main policing body in Madrid, but Mark thought that had been dissolved. These were only a few of the policing units he'd read about in the papers, but all of them were supposed to have been collapsed under the banner of Cuerpo de Seguridad (CS) with its two branches, uniformed and investigations.

The guards sitting across the room wore uniforms. Presumably the CS uniform indicated a professional outfit rather than one of the militias, but in the fast-paced policing structure and restructuring in Madrid, rivalries escalated in the vacuums created by change. Who knew what hangovers from past bids for power might still exist.

He decided to ask.

The two guards glanced at each other before one laughed. 'You are out of date my friend. We are Departamento Especial de Información de Estado.'

Sam came out of his torpor. 'I demand you call the American embassy.'

'You wait for the captain.'

Mark tried again. 'What does your department do?'

The two guards leaped to their feet as a deep voice said, 'Counterintelligence, seeking out reactionaries and spies. Which are you?'

The words came from a newcomer. A man with a moustache, an officer's cap, and Sam Browne belt, who walked in and stood in front of them.

Mark stood up. 'In that case, can you get a message to Colonel Dimitri Volof. Let him know I am here.'

The officer's gaze flickered across Mark before he pointed at Sam. 'You, come with me.'

Mark followed, but one of the guards stopped him. 'You wait,' he said.

Mark returned to his seat.

It seemed like an hour or more had passed although he had no way of telling the time.

Another man came into the room and spoke to the guard who got up, pointed at Mark, and said, 'You come.'

The guard hustled Mark back to the cell.

'Hey,' he said. 'What's happened to Sam... to Mr Riding?'

The door shut with a thunk, and a bolt shot home. For a moment Mark stared before he turned to pace the room. This place would not get to him.

The Prisoner

Mark remained locked in the room alone for what seemed like an eternity, but for exactly how long he had no way of telling. Each time a guard brought him food, usually lentils and watery coffee, sometime a chunk of bread, he asked where Sam was. After receiving no reply, he began asking for a message to be sent to Colonel Volof.

On one occasion the guard opened the door and Mark remained lying on the floor. He hadn't been asleep, but he couldn't be bothered getting up. Automatically he repeated the same refrain.

The guard surprised him by answering. 'Colonel Volof has gone back to Russia.'

He sat up. 'How long have I been here?

'Three days.'

Mark blinked. It seemed like a lifetime. 'How much longer...'

'Until your trial.'

'Trial for what?'

'Espionage.'

'Bullshit!' He muttered. If they believed he was a spy he would have been interrogated a lot more violently.

'You want we call the British embassy for you? The guard smirked.

He neutralised his own features. 'Why would they care. I am an Australian. You can call the Australian embassy. Oh no, we don't have one.'

The guard's face took on a sour note, and he began pulling the door closed.

Mark leaped up. 'Wait. Can you send a message to Lieutenant Laskin? He works for Volof.'

He hadn't asked to see Laskin before because he didn't think the man had the clout to get him out, but with Volof out of the country, Laskin was all he had left.

The guard said, 'He knows, and doesn't care.'

The door shut and Mark leaned back against the wall. Denton's warning that if he pulled any strings, Mark would be suspected of spying, left him cautious. It had not become too awful, and it had only been three days. Perhaps the demand for consular assistance would seem more usual in a journalist, but that would not help get him out. Embassy officials would follow the process and that meant a trial. More likely a kangaroo court.

The absence of daylight in a cell with constant electric light felt worse than the indolence. He didn't know what day it was, let alone the hour, and he couldn't be sure how many times a day the guard came in to bring food.

He slid to his haunches. Sometimes it seemed like days had passed, and at other times, like he had just been given a meal. In the interim, exploring his mind and exercising his body seemed the only occupations.

Was it possible to be alone and silent in a place where clanging doors, unearthly screaming, and the tromping of boots was all he heard, and still keep his thoughts from going into dark places? He had not found a way to do that.

Time passed. Food came and buckets went. No one spoke to him, and the abyss crept closer. One day he came out of a fitful and restless sleep with his face wet with what he supposed were tears.

He got to his feet and took stock of the filthy-stinking specimen he had become. Somewhere another scream rang out. A minute later he found himself crouched in a corner holding his head as if it would fly off if he let it go.

His voice echoed in the empty room as he repeated lines of a poem. 'What passing-bells for these who die as cattle? Only the monstrous anger of the guns.' Although he concentrated, he could not remember the rest, only that the words were written by Wilfred Owens about the Great War.

The narrow focus helped, and sanity prevailed. He unfurled his limbs and stood to exercise in the small space. Finally, exhaustion reglued his head to his shoulders, and he slid down on his haunches again.

Instead of poetry he'd forgotten, he thought of Plato's cave. He tried creating images in his head, which he then imagined were projected onto the wall of his cell. One by one images of people he knew formed and marched by as if in a police line-up.

Jack Henry materialised and turned face on, accusing Mark of failure. 'You sit on the fence of democracy, while humanity flounders in poverty.' His voice sounded stern. 'You do nothing but record it in black and white images.'

'I'm trying!' Mark shouted.

Jack shook his head. 'The only thing these bastards understand is violence. Revolution is all we have left between us and death. Photography does nothing to change injustice.'

Mark stood up and took two steps to where Jack had been moments before, but his face had melted away. He threw his fist at the blank wall, and bloody prints joined all the others who had gone before. He stared at his mashed knuckles as if they did not belong to him.

Had he gone mad? He fell forward onto his hands, straightened his torso and began counting each press up. At some point he collapsed in exhaustion and fell into a deep sleep.

Javier came to him in his dreams, holding his head in his hands. 'Never trust a liberal democrat.' Javier sneered. 'One stroke of kindness from the head table, and you turn your back on your mates. Mates that had your back in the cane fields.'

Mark sat up. 'No, you are wrong. He is not like them. He fights fascism and I work for him, and only for that reason.

'And for the sake of his granddaughter's pretty face.'

'Leave her out of it.'

'Admit you are a traitor.'

'No. I am with the Republicans. They fight for a liberal democracy, but Stalin wants the country communist. Stalin is an evil bastard, and the NKVD are destroying any chance the

Republic might win this war. They shoot the volunteers for no reason.'

'Only the cowards who run.'

'They say, but they accuse soldiers unjustly of sabotaging victory.'

'Bullshit. They are Trotskyites and you helped them. You are a traitor to the cause.'

'You know I never believed in the cause the way you do. Besides I didn't help them. At least I didn't help their revolution. I don't believe revolution will bring about justice and equality. It will create a political vacuum where the strong man seizes power, making all within his grasp his vassals. It is another form of Feudalism. Stalin's form of communism was never what Marx meant.

Javier's face quivered. 'You've turned your back on your mates.'

The head morphed into his own head and Mark found himself staring into his own eyes. 'Are you dead mate. Is that why you have come here?'

'If I were dead, you would no longer have any responsibility for me, and you could rid yourself of guilt.'

'Guilt!' Mark shouted. 'I am not fucking responsible for you, or your choice to fight in this damned war.'

'No, your guilt lies in not joining me and it's eating away your soul.'

Mark awoke with a yell, his body slick with sweat, although the temperature in the cell remained cool. He sat up and found his face wet again, as if he'd been walking in the rain. Had he been crying?. He ran his hands down his face and around his neckline. Checking. A lingering feeling remained that his head might part company from his body.

Rome

Alessandro Contarini leaned with both hands on a gold topped cane. Elderly, late sixties early seventies, he dressed in a tailored morning suit. His strong jawline was clean-shaven, and he wore his silver hair brushed back from a high forehead. Large, dark eyes remained watchful and hooded above an aquiline nose.

Beatrice felt a shiver run across her shoulders. The man appeared formidable. She and her grandfather stood together in the Grand Hotel's vaulted and multi-pillared lobby, while Dino Grandi the Conte di Mordano, made the introductions.

She was delighted to return to Rome although sad Mark had not made the rendezvous in Paris. She hadn't heard from him, and worried, despite her grandfather's reassurances that his tardiness was most likely due to train delays.

He had said reassuringly, that if anything had happened to Mark the embassy would have heard and Denton would be the first to know.

Contarini's face remained aloof as he said in English, 'So Grandi claims I have a grandson.'

Beatrice glanced at Denton, who with a mild smile in his eyes shrugged lightly. 'It is Dino's fixation, which is why he insisted we meet. We merely holiday in Rome at Grandi's invitation, and he suggested we have lunch.'

Contarini interrupted. 'Where is this person?'

Beatrice interjected. 'My fiancé is on assignment, a journalist. I had hoped he'd be here, but he's been delayed. He claims nothing in relation to... but that is not why we are here.' Her cheeks became pink with her attempt to protect Mark, so she busied herself with opening her reticule to find a photograph, which she held out to the old man.

He took it with long parchment-covered fingers, stared at it stoney-faced for a moment before handing it back. 'Felicitations He looks like a fine young man.'

'Look,' Her grandfather stepped in. 'We are only here because Grandi thought it was a good idea to meet. It is unlikely the man is related to you. He is Australian although of Italian heritage. Nonetheless, I am glad to make your acquaintance. We have a mutual friend. Sir Bernie Rathbone, with the Bank of England. I understand your bank has had some dealings with him.'

Grandi looked put out at Grandfather's comment and said, 'I understood the meeting was your idea, but I recall you heard him say his father's name was Contarini, and you agreed that he spoke the truth. This means there is a relationship. Contarini is a venerable name in Italy. Besides,' he turned to Contarini, 'if he is related, you would want to know, is that not so?'

'I do not think Mark is looking for any lost relations in Italy,' Grandfather said.

Contarini glanced at Grandi but spoke to Grandfather. 'I know Bernie Rathbone. He is the rogue who over dinner and brandy in his club, convinced me to invest in the Zeppelin Company.'

Grandfather's face became solemn. 'The Hindenburg fire was a dreadful accident.

Contarini said, 'My wife and I had complimentary tickets, but circumstances prevented us. My wife insists it is because God has other plans for me.'

'Bernie would have had no knowledge...'

'I thought bankers in England knew everything.' Contarini's shoulders straightened, but a glint in his eyes told Beatrice he was joking.

'They merely think they do.' Grandi joined in the British baiting. 'Although it is not God who has plans for you my dear Don Alessandro, but Il Duce.'

Contarini fingered his lapel pin and said nothing, but Beatrice noticed a dark shadow passing across his face.

Grandfather tried to lighten the gloom. 'Or perhaps the British merely control most of the financial world.'

'I thought that was Switzerland.' Grandi said.

Grandfather merely smiled, that same smile she knew well, which told one nothing of what he thought.

He turned back to Contarini. 'Your bank has a branch in London does it not?'

Contarini nodded and in a more conciliatory tone said, 'I spent several years in your country before the Great War and learned much from the British.'

The maître d'hôtel approached and spoke to Contarini. 'Don Alessandro, your table is ready.'

Contarini nodded and held out his arm to Beatrice. They walked slowly towards the dining room with Denton and Grandi following.

'Are you enjoying the sights of Rome, my dear.' Contarini asked.

'The city is magnificent.'

'What have you visited so far?'

'Gosh. The Trevi Fountain, the Pantheon, the Colosseum, the Vittoriano.'

'Ah, our monument to celebration of Italian unification.'

'Yes. It is a grand edifice.'

It seemed fathers rather than mothers were revered in fascist states, a problem with a culture of machismo perhaps. But she had seen so much more than mere monuments. Yesterday, Grandfather had made an obligatory visit to the British Embassy, while she had walked along streets baked by the sun, and lined with earth-toned buildings.

On a detour through a cobbled alleyway, she had stopped to watch a marching band. They were young fascist Balilla with their tasselled Fez headwear. A police officer stopped the honking traffic and waved them on. The policeman turned the job into a performance, dressed in white from his pith helmet to his gloves as he twirled his baton to conduct the traffic.

This morning, while Grandfather went off to meet with an old friend, she had found the Via del Portico d'Ottavia, turning aside to wander through the narrow lanes of the old Jewish quarter. A place made up of ancient ruins, cosy plazas, crumbling red brick, flaking travertine stone, and air saturated with history.

Children's voices floated out from a window above, singing to a piano accompaniment. After several wrong-turns and backtracks, she had reached the Ponte Fabricio, where the Tiber River rolled ceaselessly, metres below. The glow of newly built flood containment walls glowed like a sunset along its banks. Overhead, young plane trees cast welcome shade, while birds squabbled in their branches. It felt peaceful in the midst of so much chaos, the background din of the city muted so close to the river.

If only Mark had been with her, it would have been perfect, but they could come back. Wouldn't it be a turn-up to find he was related to this charming old man. A modern fairy tale, although, under the current circumstances, she didn't think Mark would be pleased. As Contarini pulled out her chair, she smiled her thanks and the fascist pin in his lapel winked back at her.

Once they were all seated and the waiter had poured the wine, Grandfather engaged Contarini. 'How is the Swiss banking business?'

Beatrice fiddled with her fork. Her grandfather never did anything for no reason, and she had never known him to go off idly on holidays. But what he had to do with banking, she had no idea.

Contarini shook his head, a frown lodged between his immaculately trimmed, silver eyebrows. 'You plan a career change at this stage of your life... I have use for a man with your connections.'

Grandfather laughed. 'I must be out of practice. I was merely making conversation.'

'I imagine anyone who works for the British Foreign Office is aware of the gold fluctuations, thanks to American chicanery. Their decision to sterilise gold inflows has the Swiss sector awash with the stuff. Now Europe becomes protectionist in order to defend against another 1930s financial fiasco caused by the United States of America's protection tariffs. Here in Italy, devaluation creates a problem for Il Duce's policy of self-sufficiency. The country struggles to sell its manufactured goods in a protectionist world.

Grandi said dryly. 'Sanctions, imposed by the League of Nations, didn't help.'

Grandfather raised a brow. 'I understood they had little impact, which is why they called them off.'

Contarini, his voice sharp, said something in Italian and Grandi shrugged before saying to Grandfather, 'He is angry over Il Duce's recall of foreign investments, but it is nothing.'

Grandfather leaned forward. 'How so?'

Contarini's mouth tightened, and his fingers once again found their way to the Roman Fasces pin in his lapel. 'Sanctions take a long time to have an effect, and your sanctions did not apply to oil.'

Grandi took a sip of his wine. 'It is just as well. An oil embargo might have curtailed our leaders' ambitions.'

Grandfather said, 'You would have bought oil from the U.S.'

'Perhaps, but it would have been expensive.'

Grandfather changed the subject. 'Your bank's head office is in Geneva. Is that not so?'

Contarini nodded. 'My father had wanted the bank to become international. He sent me to England to learn what I could before I moved to Geneva in 1905 to set up what is now our banking headquarters. Of course, the original bank is still here in Rome. While Geneva is nominated as headquarters and my family's home, my wife likes to live here. I travel between the two cities.'

Beatrice watched the men in silence. This was why they were here. Money and who was doing what with global trade and finance although she didn't pretend to understand what. Perhaps this was why Denton wanted to meet Contarini, and it had nothing to do with Mark. Or did it? She could never tell with her grandfather.

The three men were circling each other like Sumos. Perhaps she should focus on the moment instead of second guessing their motivation, but people were always more interesting than finance. She leaned forward. 'I would have liked to have met your wife.'

'My wife does not go out much these days.' His eyes softened as he looked at Beatrice. 'She is not well.'

He ran his palm down his face as if wiping away telltale signs of emotion and Beatrice inhaled. The gesture was so familiar.

She said, 'I am sorry to hear that.'

The waiter arrived with an entrée, and the conversation moved to matters of trade.

During a lull, and in an attempt to move the subject to more interesting territory, Beatrice asked, 'Do you and your wife have children Don Alessandro?'

He looked at her for what seemed like a long time before he said, 'We had a son. He died in the Great War.'

'Oh gosh! I am so sorry.' Beatrice took a long drink of her wine. She should stay away from intimate discussions. No wonder men spoke of trade and banking. It was less dangerous territory than people and relationships.

The waiter cleared their plates and brought coffee.

'You could not have known.' He waved her apologies aside. 'We are... were, proud of our son. His mother has not been well since he died.' Contarini paused and then as if deciding to expose more of his pain he said, 'he was Alessandro like me, but he did not want to enter the family banking business. Instead, he went to Florence to study art. When the war broke out, he volunteered for the Corpo Aeronautico Militare.'

Contarini's eyes misted, and he remained silent for a moment staring at his glass of wine, then he said, 'My son was born in Geneva, and our residence was listed as such, so he had no obligation to enlist, but he did anyway.'

He pulled himself together and looked at Beatrice. 'He was young, barely twenty-five-years old when he joined the war, and certainly never married, did not even have a girlfriend that we knew of.' He paused as if remembering something, shook his head and said, 'So your young man is unlikely to be related to us.'

Beatrice's eyes filled with tears and without thinking she said, 'Mark's middle name is also Alessandro.'

Grandi clapped. 'That settles it. This can be no coincidence.'

Contarini leaned toward Beatrice. 'Your fiancé, Mark, is it? He was born in Australia, yes?'

'He was born in Lucca, but he travelled to Australia when he was very young.'

'In what year, do you know?'

'1908.'

'At that time Alessandro was too young to have fathered a child. He was not eighteen years old, just out of school and enrolled in Accademia di Belle Arti di Firenze. You will see why I am certain.' He paused again as if remembering something, shook his head and said, 'So your young man is unlikely to be related to us.'

Beatrice said, 'Of course. I am so sorry for your loss.'

Contarini nodded and his face saddened. 'Sandro was sent on a bombing raid to Lubljana in 1916 and never returned. Your young man would have been eight or nine years old by that time, and living in Australia, a world away. How could my son have sired a child on the other side of the world and gone to his death not knowing. It is unthinkable.'

Grandi sat back and sighed.

Grandfather said. 'It does seem unlikely.'

Grandi slapped his hand on the table causing the forks to jump. 'So, it seems unlikely, but how unusual to have the same name, and there is a certain look. I have not given up.' He drank the last of the coffee, turned to Denton and said, 'I am afraid I must leave you. Please do not hurry for my sake. Let your lunch digest. I am a servant of his excellency Il Duce Supremo, and I have duties to perform. I will see you for the opera tomorrow evening. I will send a car.'

Contarini didn't move and the three of them watched Grandi walk across the room. A galleon in full sail as the eyes of the room followed him.

Contarini sighed a soft sound of relief. 'He was a socialist first you know.'

'Who?' Beatrice asked.

'Benito Mussolini.'

'That's astonishing. Grandfather did you know that?'

Denton did not reply but remained looking at Contarini who continued. 'Benito found the ideology didn't give him the power he desired so he created his own form of ultra-nationalism to combat socialism. That is the trouble with ideology. It has no flexibility. Allows no dissent. The socialists, the communists, and the fascists all want to overthrow the world order, take power by force if necessary, and wrest it from the clutches of the aristocracy. But what they don't understand is that ideology is a blind lunatic, without the ability to see the future, to adapt and change slowly and at a measured pace that does not create chaos. Ideology will eventually crush all in its clutches, using the hate of those who believe to carry out its work. Revolution and counter revolution will leave a vacuum that can be filled only by retribution and corruption.'

Beatrice interjected. 'But neither should the world be ruled exclusively by wealth and status. Ordinary people must have the power of their own representation.'

Contarini looked taken aback but responded calmly. 'Power cannot survive under ideology for it will be constantly under pressure from its competing forms of economics. This is your Karl Marx's own thesis and antithesis. My view is that power must exist in tradition and pragmatism, where policies are flexible, and above all benefit the majority.'

Before Beatrice could argue further, Grandfather said, 'I am glad we have had the opportunity to talk. Perhaps I might call on you when I am next in Geneva.'

Contarini sighed and looked at Denton. 'I understand your need, but I am an old man. I seek to go slowly and hesitating to my grave, in a dignified and uneventful way, you understand. I no longer enjoy the rush and hustle of politics and power. I only desire peace and tranquillity.'

'You are not much older than I am, sir. Besides, I am sure we can accommodate your desires.'

A man approached the table and Grandfather excused himself. He walked a little way away and they spoke quietly for a moment before the man handed him an envelope and turned to leave.

Denton returned, placing the envelope in the inner breast pocket of his jacket. He sat down at the table. 'I beg your pardon. Embassy business... You were saying Don Alessandro?'

Contarini continued. 'Not even you, my friend, as influential as you may be, can offer peace. This world is destined for war. It is something we can all see like the red smudge of dawn on the eastern horizon. The question is, on whose side will Italy fight this time around? I fear we will abandon our former allegiances.'

'Which is why you and I should talk.'

Contarini smiled and shook his head. 'Now I must go. My wife is expecting me. It has been a pleasure.' He turned to Beatrice. 'I am sorry I could not give you better news for your young man, but I wish you every happiness for your future together. He looks like a fine person.'

Beatrice watched him walk away. It would seem, after all, he wasn't related to Mark. Had Contarini thought there might be a shred of possibility, he would have been keener to delve deeper.

A sudden longing seized her. She wanted to see Mark. Where could he be, and why hadn't he joined them as he said he would? Grandfather said she shouldn't worry, but she couldn't help it.

As his chauffeur drove him north, through the city, to his villa, Contarini sat brooding in the back of the Lancia Aprilia. He would have to tell Adriana; it was too cruel not to let her know. She had never recovered from Sandro's death. That photo had shocked him, like looking at a ghost. He needed time to think about the consequences as well as the impact on Adriana's health. Her heart wasn't strong.

He had loved Sandro, but the boy had been a budding philanderer. Although he had told the young woman that his son had never had a girlfriend, it was a lie. The trouble was the amount of girlfriends Sandro had.

He'd been sent home from school early after having been caught in flagrante delicto with a married woman, the wife of a master, but it hadn't stopped there. He was arrogant too—thought banking was a trade and gentlemen did not work in trade. In his view, gentlemen did not work, period. The product of four years in the British schooling system. He expected to be kept in grand style as he wasted his time in the study of art. As far as Contarini understood, most of his expenses involved drinking and cavorting with loose women.

Adriana kept his drawings and paintings in a room set up like a gallery; a shrine to her son who had done no wrong in her eyes. Contarini knew otherwise and couldn't bear to enter it. The box with Alessandro's personal effects, sent home after his death, remained in that room.

The box held a photo of a pretty girl along with a letter of farewell. She was sailing to Australia with her family, but the letter said nothing about pregnancy. Nothing to indicate love although a wistful sense of loss in her phrasing made it clear she left with regret.

The photo showed her clutching an older woman, who held a baby wrapped in a shawl. They were surrounded by a labouring family and standing in front of a peasant's cottage. In the letter she had apologised, saying it was all she had to give him. Had the baby been this young man?

Surely the girl was too young to have had the child, and although beautiful, he doubted Alessandro would have wanted to marry her. Surely, he knew Contarini would have forbidden it, paid her family off. After all his son would inherit the bank and all its financial subsidiaries. Studying art was one thing, but marrying a peasant girl, even a beautiful one, could not be countenanced. Despite the boy's youth, he would not have contemplated bringing such shame to the family.

Notwithstanding his low birth, the baby, the boy—the man in the photo had Sandro's blood running through his veins. He saw that in the face. Those familiar features, perhaps not arrogant like Sandro, but clearly ambitious for he was about to marry into a noble English family. Unheard of, although the world was changing. These things mattered less than they had before the Great War.

Why had his son kept the woman's letter for all those years? For the first time in his adult life, Contarini didn't know what to do. He also feared Dino Grandi's intentions. The man would not let his curiosity rest, especially now they had Contarini where they wanted him.

Did they also seek to compromise this young man or perhaps to interfere in Alfred Denton's business. A member of the British government and its Foreign Office, whose granddaughter would soon marry the possible—no certain—grandson of a newly minted, if coerced, member of the National Directorate of the Italian Socialist Party.

He ripped the pin from his lapel and dropped it into his pocket. For his own safety and theirs, he would not recognise the young man even if he wished to do so. Although he knew that argument would not wash with Adriana.

She would have to listen to him and return to the house in Geneva. Rome became too dangerous. Mussolini's influence, an invisible but oppressive fog, had recalibrated the axis of Europe to feed his desires. Contarini wasn't even sure he would be safe in Geneva. The OVRA, Mussolini's secret police, knew no boundaries.

Persona Non Grata

On what Mark thought might be the twentieth day, or maybe the sixtieth, they came to get him. After a shower and clean clothes—his own surprisingly—a guard escorted him to an office.

A Russian officer, whom he had not met before, sat at a desk and invited Mark to sit opposite him.

'Mr Anders, I apologise for the length of time you have been incarcerated.'

The man's English held only a trace of an accent.

Mark waited, longing to ask how long, but he wasn't prepared to give the man the satisfaction.

'Can I get you anything? Cigarettes, coffee, food...'

Mark shook his head. It seemed loose, stuffed with cotton. He touched his neck as if the fitting might not be as solid as he thought, but his voice came out strong. 'You can tell me who you are and why I am here.'

'Who I am is of no consequence, and as to why you are here, it seems the result of a series of unfortunate coincidences.'

'What's happened to Sam, Mr Riding?'

'He has gone back to America, his visa revoked. You are prone to making friends in the wrong places, Mr Anders, which has led to your stay in this facility. However, we have determined it is a measure of naivety rather that treachery on your part. You have high recommendations from several sectors. Comrades who vouch for your courage, and steadfastness to the cause. Our only concern is some of the company you keep. It has been explained in some measure, but there are still some outlying matters we need to clear up.'

Mark leaned back and cracked his fingers. How should he to play this game? He used delaying tactics while trying to activate his antennae, ramp up his sluggish brain, which screeched through its gears as he tried to piece together what the bloke knew. 'My life is an open book.'

The man laughed. 'Now that is not quite true, is it Mr Anders?'

Mark stared at him. What did he know?

'You have done some strange things, which would seem to go against your espoused unionism and commitment to the communist cause.'

'Like what?'

'You refuse to join the party.'

He remained silent.

'Why is that Mr Anders?'

'I believe in democracy.'

'As do we Mr Anders.'

Mark let that statement go. Democracy in a one-party state was not truly democratic. 'If I had joined, I would have found it harder to operate as a journalist.'

'Au contraire,' the man said loftily. 'Communist journalists are given unprecedented access.'

'To your propaganda but not to establishing the truth.' A muscle jumped in Mark's jaw. Damn and blast his big mouth. He blamed the fuzziness in his head.

'The truth!' The man's laughter this time came from deep in his chest. Real amusement, it seemed to Mark. 'Is that why you were seen dining at Simpsons with Geoffrey Dawson, the editor of *The Times*, and later with Jacobo Fitz-James Stuart y Falcó, an aristocrat, who the British accept as Franco's ambassador to London. Do you think these men represent the truth?'

Mark pressed his lips together, but the officer continued. 'If the Australian Queensland Secretary hadn't vouched for your allegiance and explained your relationship to Lord Denton's daughter, one might be given cause to wonder at your real sympathies. Yet Captain Laskin also swears you are a loyal person, who saved his life. General Laskin requests I pass on his gratitude for saving his son.'

'Captain Laskin...' Mark frowned.

'Yes, he was promoted after you returned from the front. He has a posting to London. You should remake your acquaintance when you return.'

Mark's head cleared. They were planning to let him go.

The man continued. 'We also have a personal recommendation from Lieutenant Bricknall, whose life you apparently saved despite your own being in danger. Perhaps a medal is more appropriate than incarceration. Although there is still the matter of a man dead in the street. A reformist of little consequence, but nevertheless a dead man.' He paused, eyeing Mark before he said, 'and then we are faced with the work you do. Your articles express great sympathy for the Spanish people but resist either praise for the Republic or condemnation of the insurgent enemy. Furthermore, you take commissions from newspapers run by the sworn enemies of the third international.'

The wooliness returned, and Mark shook his head. 'Sworn enemies. Who are they?'

'The newspaper run by the British Independent Labour Party for one.'

'Sorry, I am lost here.'

The man stared at him.

Mark tried again. 'You will have to explain to me why a freelance journalist, accepting a commission from *New Leader,* is dealing with sworn enemies of the Comintern.'

The man sighed. 'You display your naivety or is it mere play acting. Are you a good actor, Mr Anders?'

Mark said nothing.

'They are Trotskyists who support the fascists through their actions in Barcelona against the Republic.'

The man's words were emphatic, and Mark searched for signs of anger in his face but found nothing but exasperation. It renewed his optimism.

'I know nothing about that.' He held his breath hoping they did not know about the help he had given Eduardo Cardona.'

'Are you aware of the article your friend Mr Riding wrote?'

Mark nodded. 'He told me about it, but I didn't read it. He did mention he had become persona non grata because of it.'

'Why did you not read it?'

'I was busy.'

'Yes, we have heard. Why do you think he wrote such an article, Mr Anders?'

'I don't know his motivation, but he told me he saw it as the truth of the situation. I understood he wrote purely from journalistic professionalism rather than from support for an ideological point of view.'

Another sigh. 'Again, you present as naive Mr Anders. There is no such point of view. Everything is political. Yes, even you, when you lay out your photographic reports as if attempting to avoid politics. It is there.'

Mark nodded. 'I understand. Perhaps Mr Riding was unaware of his liberal bias, only attempting to write in a spirit of objectivity.'

'At last, we can agree on something even if the polish is laid on unevenly.'

'You think I have an unconscious ideology.'

'I do not think this. I know this. It is good you understand it for I have a deal to make with you Mr Anders. One you must carry out to earn your freedom.' He leaned to one side and dragged a canvas kitbag up from the floor. 'Your possessions.' He took a folder from the top of the bag. 'We took the liberty of processing your rolls of film, which were remarkably interesting. But I note you have not run these through the censor's office.'

Mark shook his head. 'I ran the ones I used through the censor when I submitted my copy. I didn't run these through because I wasn't planning on using them.' His eyes didn't flicker at the lie.

'Still, you know the rules. But might I ask why you did not seek to use them? They are excellent as far as my untrained eye can assess?' The man scrutinised him carefully.

'They are mostly of the enemy in battle.'

'Yes. Alas a battle we seem to have lost, I suspect through betrayal or a lack of commitment from the troops.'

'Perhaps a lack of equipment and strategic objectivity.'

'Careful Mr Anders you fly close to the sun when you criticise our strategic command. Do you think the rebels have better leadership, better weapons?'

'I have nothing good to say about Franco's army.'

'Then my deal will be easy for you to carry out.'

'What do you want me to do?'

'I want you to write up an account of the battle, one which will show the atrocities Franco carries out in the name of his god, using these photos. When you have done that, we will send you home.'

'You will revoke my visa?'

'Yes Mr Anders. Despite assurances, I do not trust you. Unless however you chose to join us. As a committed communist comrade, you will have unfettered access to the Republican controlled areas.'

Mark looked down at the hands folded in his lap. It seemed an innocuous request, but his career would be ruined and any chance he might have had of getting into the north would be gone—unless... 'I have a better idea.'

'You are not in a bargaining position, Mr Anders. You may have powerful friends but...' he shrugged.

Powerful friends. Mark had overlooked the fact that Laskin's father was a general in the Red Army and would have given Laskin some clout in protecting Mark. So long as the father stayed out of Stalin's sight. No wonder he had got off lightly. The NKVD wasn't known for their compassion. Still, he could not agree to the terms. The consequences would be on-going.

'I'm not bargaining. I am offering you a better deal; one the Republic would find more useful than canning my career.'

'Go on.'

'I will publish a light account of Franco's victory, so you can accuse me of siding with the insurgents. Kick me out—make me persona non grata, publicly. If they think I am on their side, I might get a visa into the North. While I am there, I can see how they are set up and then provide the Republic with information.'

'You are volunteering to spy on Franco for us.'

'For the Republic.'

'It is the same.'

Mark let that go although he would not be doing it for Stalin's Russia but for Republican democracy.

The man sat back in his chair and gazed at Mark in silence. A muscle twitched in his cheek, which told Mark he contemplated the offer.

Eventually he said. 'Why would you do this? It is dangerous. Besides, we have our own people...'

Interesting. The Republic, or rather the Russians, had infiltrated Franco held territory, perhaps even his command. He decided the truth here would do the job better than a lie. 'I have been wondering how to get into the north for a while because you see my friend is in the Basque Army and, given their situation, I want to see if I can help him. If he is not dead already.'

'What is your friend's name?'

'Javier Cruz. He's an Australian like me. Or rather an American. We worked together in the cane fields in North Queensland, along with the man you mentioned, the Queensland Secretary for the Australian Communist Party. Javier's family are all from the Basque country.

'This man, Javier, is he a communist?'

Mark nodded. 'Yes. He joined up in 1935 when we were fighting the sugar company.'

'Yet you did not.'

'No.'

'Why not join up now? We can keep your membership a secret.'

'Nothing remains secret for long. There is always a leak, and if I got into Franco's territory and it came out, I would be dead.'

'We do not leak secrets.'

'Not unless it suits you, or they too have their people here.'

The man said nothing to that, but he wrote something on a piece of paper. Then he said, 'Mr Anders I am afraid I will have to detain you a while longer, although perhaps we can give you more comfort. Is there anything you require?'

Mark's shoulders sagged and his head felt wobbly as if it might fall off. 'I thought you were going to kick me out.'

'I need to take your proposal to my superiors. If they like it, we may do as you suggest.'

The man rang a bell on the desk, and a guard came back. 'The guard will take you to your room, where you will be served lunch. Please let him know if you have any other needs. He handed Mark's kitbag to the guard. I will see you again as soon as is practical, Mr Anders.'

The room to which the guard led Mark was an improvement, with a made-up bed alongside a desk and chair, some writing implements and paper, a table lamp and an armchair with an occasional table and an ashtray. The room even had a window which looked out on a back laneway with a blank wall opposite. Despite the dismal view, daylight flooded through the glass. Most importantly, a switch for the overhead light dangled down next to the doorway. Another door led into a bathroom.

He looked at the guard. 'Whose room?'

'It is the duty-officer's quarters. I will bring a tray of food. You would like a little wine, a cigarette?'

Another Life.

Mark stared out the car window at rolling parklands interspersed with formal gardens, and a tree-lined avenue. A gate house stood sentry. Over to the right, several horses grazed within a large paddock contained by a white paling fence. Only a part of the main house was visible from the road, but that was more than enough to realise *house* was the wrong word. Although he had no idea what term might be used instead.

When she said it was rented out, he'd imagined an ordinary country farmhouse, perhaps a little larger than most but nothing like this. How the hell could anyone afford to rent something this size, let alone own it? It was bigger than most hotels he'd seen and could probably accommodate all the homeless people in Britain. He glanced across at her scowling face.

'You're horrified,' she said.

'A bit shocked is all.' He grimaced.

The modern hairstyle she had adopted while she had been in Italy was enough of a surprise without this.

She glanced at the long driveway. 'You hate it.'

'Hate is a strong word. I hate fascism. I hate injustice, but a house is bricks and mortar. Why on earth did you agree to marry me, Beatrice? You could have anyone.'

She glanced down at the engagement ring on her finger. 'Aren't you glad I did?'

His eyes remained serious as he said, 'It doesn't mean I understand why.'

'Sometimes I wonder myself.' She laughed.

He picked up her hand and kissed the inside of her wrist. 'Let's go back to London.'

'Don't you want to look around?'

'What about the tenants?'

What a bizarre description for the people living here.

'They know we're coming. Besides, they are packing to *scoot off back to America*. Their words because they think another war is coming and they want out.'

Mark nodded. 'Let's hope they're wrong.'

Her brow furrowed. 'But I... we need to decide if I... we will live here when we marry.'

'I've seen all I need to, but Beatrice, you'll need to give me time to adjust. I can't live in that place. I'd be terrified someone would arrest me for trespassing.'

'Mark, this style of living is your birthright. You were robbed.'

Mark frowned. 'It's not true, Beatrice. The man didn't even acknowledge it might be true, and besides the last thing I need is a fascist banker in my family.'

What must the old bloke have thought, being confronted by a phantom grandson? Mark had never bothered much about his biological father. Besides, he didn't think his mother would thank him for scratching in that particular quarry. She had always discouraged such natural curiosity.

He saw the mulish look settle in the line of Beatrice's mouth and altered his tone. 'Look, if he wanted to know me, he would have said. Relationships are what people make of them; not what biology destines. I don't care who my biological father was. Eric Anders is my father. He has always been there for me and that is all a father can be. Biology is irrelevant. Contarini is right not to get involved with a past that cannot be undone.'

Beatrice sighed in defeat. 'Well, if you don't want to live here, where will we live?'

'We can rent a house in London. You will be close to your work, and I will still be able to...'

She finished his sentence. 'Hop on a train to the next continental war...Where will you go next? China.'

'I wasn't going to say that but well... I suppose you are right. It's my career Beatrice, just like the refugees are yours.'

'I imagined it would make a great refugee centre.' She said changing the subject and gazing wistfully at the house.

'Its miles away from anywhere.'

The explosion of air that came up from her chest and out of her mouth, told him she was fed-up with him.

'That's exactly what Granddad said. She sighed more gently this time. 'It doesn't matter anyway. The government wants to lease it. I wanted to ask your advice. Do you think I should let them?'

'For what.'

'Who knows. Secret wombat stuff.'

'Are they offering a decent rent.'

She nodded.

'You should take it.' He felt the weight lift off his shoulders.

'Fine. That's done. Now to the next thing.'

'What's that?'

'Grandfather thinks you should go through my trust. If you are going to be my husband, you should know what you are getting into. You won't like it, at all.'

'Beatrice, it's your trust, your money. I don't need to know anything about it. Would rather not, frankly.'

'You will have to. Once we are married you will take on a fiduciary responsibility.'

He shook his head. 'We can set up some sort of legal barrier.'

'Mark, you don't get it do you? If we get married, we are together in everything or we are nothing?'

His mouth twisted into a wry smile. 'I don't suppose you'll ever want to go back to Queensland and live on the farm.'

'Do you?' She arched a brow at him.

'When we've finished what we set out to do here. That's more important for the moment, isn't it?' Mark put the car into gear and turned around to go back the way they had come.

Beatrice glanced at him slyly. 'You know all the land around here, and most of the village, belong to me also.'

He slammed his foot on the brake and turned to examine her face for evidence of a practical joke. 'That's not funny.'

She shook her head, her short nut-brown bob flicking across her glee filled face. 'It's true though, so you better get used to it.

You are marrying into that echelon of society you have always despised, but it's not too late to change your mind.'

'How—what?'

'Farms and tenancies mostly.' She patted his arm to take the sting out of her words, knowing full well how much the details would upset him.

'Beatrice, I can't...'

She shrugged. 'I knew you would hate it, but it's not all bad. When my grandmother rescued the place, she built an iron foundry and glass factory for the village. To provide employment. You might have approved of my granny. She was a progressive American for her time.'

Mark exhaled. 'Who looks after it all.'

'Various people. The land agent lives in the village. A company manages the businesses, along with an accountancy firm and a legal firm and...'

'Right. Maybe that's enough for now.'

This was too much to deal with. The best thing would be to pretend none of it had happened. Javier's spectre in his dream had been right. He was the supplicant at the head-table although he didn't need this kind of moral responsibility.

It was bad enough that fascist relatives may have wormed their way out of his family woodwork, even if, as Denton speculated, they were coerced into joining the party. He had thought communist friends would be a problem in this job although they had got him out of more than one jamb. Now, he had joined the blasted British aristocracy along with all the social trappings he'd despised for so long. Being confronted by the extent of Beatrice's wealth gave him heartburn.

He felt a pleading expression infusing his face. 'Maybe we can pretend none of it exists.'

Beatrice laughed. 'Said like a true Australian. Never mind you'll get used to it.'

He released the brake and drove on down the road, trying to comprehend the enormity of change in his new life. After a minute he resolved to stop thinking about it. Instead, he would go back to London and act as if everything remained as before.

Beatrice interrupted his musing. 'I am not staying in that awful boarding house.'

'It's a residential hotel, not a boarding house, but alright, you stay on with your granddad, until we are married and then we can find a place together.'

'You too. Stay with us.'

'Not a clever idea, Beatrice. It will create scandal.'

'And you are determined to go back to Spain.'

'I have to finish what I started.'

'But they arrested you.'

'It was a mistake, and they let me go.'

'I fear for your safety, that's all. They branded you persona non grata and called you Franco's flunkey, and a traitor to the cause. Doesn't that bother you, Mark? You were such a passionate supporter of the Republic, and they have rejected you. I don't understand what happened. Was it your report from the front line? What did you see that made you report on Franco's triumph?'

Mark pressed his lips together and concentrated on the road. 'It's complicate Beatrice. I am just a reporter, not an agitator. I only want to report on the truth, not propaganda.'

'Is it true that Franco's winning then?'

'I think so.'

He felt guilty not telling her, but he'd discussed it with Denton, and for her own safety as well as for her role with the refugees, they thought it better she didn't know. He also knew that decision would make her spit fire, but he had become trapped between wanting to respect her independence and wanting to protect her. Or maybe himself...

Denton had already sent out the gossip hares, and Mark was now known as a liberal reformist, horrified by the way Stalin had encroached on Spain's liberal politics, which in a way was true. He had also introduced Mark to the Reform Club in Pall Mall.

Ordinarily, Mark would never have contemplated joining such an establishment, nor would he have been accepted. As it was, the membership gazed at him speculatively, knowing there was some mystery behind the colonial, who had infiltrated their sanctum. Although as Denton's soon to be grandson by marriage, he must be all right, and by all accounts, he was a good photojournalist. His odd ways might be put down to his colonial upbringing, and wasn't there some mention of Italian blood, possibly related to an old family?

The Reform club had other colonial members but most of the ones he'd met were of British stock and had risen through the ranks of the Oxbridge system. Mark had one champion among the club members. Charles West soon to become cousin-in-law.

One couldn't help one's relatives, although that was probably meanspirited. Charles had remained a steadfast friend despite Mark's attempts to avoid him, and, truth be told, he was a little jealous. That scoop Charles had scored with his eyewitness account of the fall of Bilbao, had Mark frothing with envy.

📷

A few days after their return to London, and at Beatrice's insistence, Mark went to see her accountant, Brian Heggerty, at his office in London. Heggerty left Mark in a private room where he hunched over a ledger, trying to grasp the meaning of what he found.

Beatrice's trust contained a mishmash of shares, cash, business investments and British, Australian, and American property, but that wasn't it. A large chunk of her financial portfolio had, in recent years, been invested in Rio Tinto's Spanish mines, British and German arms manufacturing, shipping, automobiles, banks, and the Italian aero industry. Was that her father's doing?

He put down the pen and gazed at a portrait of the accountancy's founder, Sir Roland Heggerty. He couldn't deal with this by himself. It was bad enough that she made money off the backs of tenants and their labour. He'd railed against that anachronism since he'd learned about his own mother's ancestors, slaving on mulberry farms, producing silk for the Italian nobility.

Now, forced to understand the accounts, he became honour bound by forthcoming fiduciary duty to ensure that he put aside his own views in matters of investments, to act only in the interest of protecting the trust. To have money invested in German, Italian and Franco controlled territory was not only fraught with instability but also morally destroying. How much did she know about her investments, and did he have the right to ask her to move it? Would it be safer in Australia or America?

His small experience with investments included owning a few tin shares. He'd chosen tin because it he knew something about it from his short-lived dredging career in Australia with his mining engineer stepfather. But now he needed advice. How could he explain his concerns to Beatrice?

After he finished talking to Heggerty, he went to the newspaper offices where he met with Geoffrey Dawson. The man had sent him an offer for a short stint in Franco held territory to replace one of *The Times* correspondents who had taken leave.

The job offer could not have come at a better time and Mark accepted it gratefully, guilt ridden, but overjoyed to leave without having to confront any more surprises about what his future might hold.

Dawson recommended Mark purchase a book on Spanish history, something he would need to learn before going into Franco controlled Spain. They called into the book section in Simpson's department store, after which they headed to the dining room for what Dawson called a spot of lunch.

As they walked through the door, Fitz-James Stuart hailed them. It seemed suspiciously like an ambush. Had the meeting been set up? He followed Dawson and Fitz-James Stuart to a table at which a man sat alone. The man arose when they arrived and Fitz-James Stuart introduced Mark to Frederick Ramón de Bertodano y Wilson, eighth Marquis del Moral.

'A fellow Australian,' the duke explained as if it might be mandatory for Australians to meet their own species when they were so far from home.

How on earth had an Australian became a Spanish grandee? He thought of his own situation. Anything seemed possible no matter how unlikely.

Fitz-James Stuart invited Dawson and Mark to join them, and Mark had the distinct impression Dawson was in on some scheme that they all tried to present as coincidence. He didn't like being manipulated but sat down and acted as if this was all quite normal, which, he conceded, it might be for these men.

Throughout lunch he remained affable, answering questions about the Duke of Windsor 's marriage to Wallis Simpson to the best of his knowledge. He hadn't particularly taken note of the scandal other than listening to Beatrice's obsession with the gossip. These men must think he had insider knowledge.

He changed the subject, asking Moral about his life growing up in Australia, sharing stories about his own childhood and schooling at a Catholic school in North Queensland.

Moral said, 'I am delighted to hear of your Catholic faith.'

Mark almost dissuaded him but then thought, it wouldn't hurt if these men thought he was a practicing Catholic. 'With my heritage, what else would I be?'

'Of course. We have heard...' Fitz-James Stuart and Moral exchanged a glance.

What had they heard? Surely not about Contarini... Unless, Grande had said something. Mark changed the subject again, by pulling out the Spanish history book he had bought. He asked the two men if they might sign the front page. He had a vague notion their signatures might come in handy. Even if not, the request served as a distraction.

241

Dawson waited until the signatures were done and then spoke about the possibility of Mark obtaining a visa to visit Nationalist territory.

So that was his game. Mark played along. At least he knew why he had been brought to meet these Spanish grandees. 'I am looking forward to this assignment. I hear Northern Spain is quite beautiful. I must admit I have had a hankering to see it for myself for quite a while. Besides, my fiancée has rather a lot of money invested in the region, and it will be good to see that her investments remain in safe hands.'

Moral raised his eyebrows at Fitz-James Stuart and said, 'I understand your fiancée is Alfred Denton's granddaughter.'

That's right, but don't hold that against her.

Fitz-James Stuart looked from one man to the other a crease between his eyebrows.

Moral laughed and said, 'An Australianism my dear Jacobo. I must admit it is a delight to hear a fellow countryman again. Although I am Spanish to my soul, I do miss Australia.'

'I can understand that. I get homesick all the time, but life here is a little more interesting for a war correspondent.' Mark glanced at Dawson to see if he would balk at Mark's new title.

He'd had enough of simply taking photos for other people to put words to. He wanted to craft both messages the way he'd done with the copy he'd sent after his release from the NKVD Checa. Even if that copy included propaganda, it was a message over which he had control.

No one flinched and the conversation continued.

Mark learned that Moral had persuaded Franco to enter the propaganda war although he did not call it that. He explained that Nicolás Franco, General Franco's brother, had turned the media in the Nationalist territory into a benighted mess. His chief press officer Luis Bolín had been sidelined and Franco's brother-in-law, Ramón Serrano Suñer, had taken over. The Nationalist press office now welcomed friendly journalists from certain newspapers. They were delighted that Dawson had offered Mark a commission.

Lunch ended on the promise of a visa and a pass to visit any of his fiancée's investments that would be safe to travel to.

After lunch, Mark called on Denton at his office in Broadway where he gave him a rundown of the encounter.

Denton listened and nodded. 'Not to detract from your ability Mark, but there is a deeper agenda here.'

Mark laughed. 'I expected nothing less.'

Denton smiled. 'They are still angling to have us grant belligerent rights. They'll be trying to get you to represent that need, I imagine.'

'Is there any chance of that happening?'

Denton ran his palm over his mouth. 'There have been suggestions that belligerent rights might be granted to both sides, if the war is just between the Spanish people, and all other nations withdraw their so-called volunteers.'

'They are targeting the International Brigade.'

Denton nodded. 'Fraid so, but it means the Germans and the Italians will have to pull out too.'

'But they won't, will they?'

Denton shrugged. 'We must hope they will keep their word. The British government has decided a presence is needed in

Burgos to represent our interests, but that last bit is not finalised so keep it under your hat.'

Mark sat forward. 'Seriously? That's a turnaround. Does that mean Britain thinks the Republic will lose the war?'

'I fear so.'

'Look, sir... I know it would be useful for me to do more snooping than I have done to date. Initially, I was in two minds about the whole spying agenda but, while I was locked up, I had time to think more about it.' Mark paused and glanced at Denton, who watched him without comment. He continued. 'You know I made a deal with the NKVD to report back from Franco territory. At the time I didn't know how I was going to get into nationalist held county, but now I have, so I will have to give them something to honour the deal.'

Denton didn't move.

'I don't mind giving information to the Republic but giving it to Russia will not necessarily help the Republican cause. In any case, what I am trying to say is that I am prepared to carry out your request.'

'My request?'

'Yes. You asked me before to spy for you.'

'Well, that's rather a blunt way of putting it. '

Mark ignored the interruption. 'You see sir, I think I need to take a stronger line for my own sanity.'

'Pardon.'

'Long story, but while I was in the Checa I had time to think, and I need to act rather than merely record evidence.'

'Good Lord, you are not suggesting you enlist with the volunteers, are you?'

'No. I thought about it, but I fear the cause is lost. I am suggesting that I might take on more of a role in providing you with the information you need. To be blunt, I am prepared to spy on Britain's behalf, if that might be useful in stopping the fascist takeover of Europe.'

Denton exhaled. 'I'm pleased to hear it but...'

'I have not spoken to Beatrice about it because I think it would just worry her for no good reason.'

Denton pulled at his lip.

'You do still want me to?'

'Yes and no. You see there is more to it than you imagine. Firstly, as a journalist you were doing your job, bringing back information to inform the British public about the real events on the ground. Up until now your reporting, along with the private analysis you have provided to me, gave a more colourful picture of the situation which I found valuable. However, to purposely gather intelligence in a foreign country on behalf of Britain is dangerous, especially as you do not have diplomatic immunity. The Nationalists are ruthless. They will think nothing of putting a bullet through your head if they think you are spying.' He tilted his head and smiled. 'If anything happened to you my granddaughter would not speak to me again.' He paused becoming more serious. 'Nonetheless, I would value any evidence you might stumble upon, but I could not ask you to collect anything specifically, at least not without training. Perhaps, if you are still keen when you return from this job, we might formalise our arrangement and make sure you have all the required skills at your command. It is the least one might expect before being sent off into the field on His Majesty's service.

Mark squinted. 'Not sure I understand.'

Denton took a breath. 'There are processes and bureaucracy to deal with, but in the interim, go to Spain. Do your job as foreign correspondent. Come back safely and we will talk. Do nothing more than that. Unfortunately, Franco has no reason to love the British, although he's playing a careful game in order to gain support for recognition as a belligerent from The Non-Intervention Committee. Not that his lack of status in this regard has deterred his behaviour so far. He has acted outside international law all along and has not suffered any consequences. Now, I fear Britain must prepare to defend itself from several nations, who think they are above international law and order. Our job is to ensure Franco doesn't side with any of them, in the event of further aggression. But in the short-term, his people know you will become part of my family, and that will keep you relatively safe, so long as they think you might be useful in persuading me to support belligerent rights. Let them think that but give them nothing to say you are a British spy. Does that make it clear?'

Mark remained thoughtful for a minute then said, 'I think so. But if I were to see something useful, what would that be?'

Denton waved his hand vaguely. 'You'll come to dinner at the house tonight, will you, my boy. We can talk further over a whisky or two and I can regale you with tales of Chartwell House. It is not far from Banville Hall, which you and Beatrice visited recently, I understand. Anyway, last weekend I had business down that way and popped in to have a tipple with Winston, see how his pond building was coming along. He made some interesting observations, which might help.'

Nationalist Spain

Lieutenant José Maria Fernández y Anchorena introduced himself as Mark's assigned guide, driver, and translator. Mark guessed his primary role was minder and spy for Franco's regime. At first the officer's attitude seemed faintly aloof and dismissive as he asked Mark if he was the English photojournalist. When Mark explained that he was here at the direct request of Ramón Serrano Suñer, El Caudillo's brother-in-law, José puffed out his chest and lifted his clean-shaven chin a little higher. Mark half expected him to snap off a salute.

Now they had sorted out the pecking order, José became obsequious. 'Mr Anders it is a pleasure to welcome you to Spain although I understand this is not your first trip. You have been in Barcelona already. You must tell me how you found it.'

Mark hid a wry smile at this unsubtle dig. He placed his new leather suitcase and matching holdall at his feet before adjusting the strap of his camera bag on his shoulder, and said, 'A quarrelsome nuisance. Thank you for meeting me. I am grateful for this opportunity to see your beautiful country, and please call me Mark.'

José blinked rapidly.

The blunt appraisal of the anarchist rebellion, with its vicious and deadly street fighting in Barcelona, Mark had calculated, would send a message of political indifference. A statement indicating his interest in photography, rather than in Republican infighting. The Nationalists had received the news of the Barcelona uprising gleefully, but no one would describe it as merely quarrelsome.

He remained mindful of Churchill's comments, passed on by Denton. *War is not simply about the visible impacts, but also about that which is hidden,* or words to that effect. Denton had reminded Mark that a foreign correspondent's job was not only reporting on significant events but also in promoting cross-cultural understanding. He should attend as many functions as possible, looking for opportunities to build relationships, not only with the Spanish, but also with German and Italian officials. Denton had added, do not simply observe the obvious but look for that which lies beneath.

How the hell he was supposed to do that was a mystery Denton had left him to solve.

José asked, 'Do you have a steamer trunk to collect?'

Mark shook his head. 'I like to travel light.'

'I have a car waiting. If you are ready, we can leave now for Pamplona.'

Mark glanced at the officer. 'I thought we were going to Burgos.'

'Pamplona is on the way. It is safer than travelling directly to Burgos because that requires driving close to the front line and there are many bandits. We can spend the night in Pamplona and if you like, you may take photos of the beautiful city.'

'I'm keen to get to Burgos and register with the media censor's office.' Mark said.

José assumed an authoritative tone. 'I have business to attend to first in Pamplona.'

Mark raised his eyebrows but followed José out of the station. The lieutenant stopped to unlock a four-door Citroën sedan before placing Mark's gear on the back seat.

They set off, José driving slowly in second gear, carefully steering through the bomb scarred streets of Irún, his face set in grim determination. He was not an experienced driver and to put him at ease Mark asked where he'd learned to speak such excellent English.

Between tedious stops and starts, Mark heard that José's father had worked in London in the diplomatic service of King Alfonso XIII's government under President Miguel Primo de Rivera. José had attended Stonyhurst in Lancashire, a Jesuit boarding school.

'You know Stonyhurst?' He said without looking at Mark but didn't wait for a reply before asking. 'Where did you go to school?'

Mark said, 'Mount St. Bernard. You wouldn't know it.'

José took his eyes off the road for a second to glance at Mark and the car veered to the right as if tracking his gaze, but he quickly corrected his direction.

'It's a Catholic college in northern Australia.' Mark said.

'Ah, you are Australian?'

'Yes. Would you like me to drive?'

'Why?' José frowned at the offer. 'Is there a problem?'

Mark said. 'It's going to take a while to get to Pamplona in second gear.'

'Ah, I forgot.' José tried to change gear without engaging the clutch and the car objected with a loud grating screech. He glanced at Mark apologetically. 'I am new to this.'

'I'd be happy to drive, and you can navigate.'

'No thank you. I must practice, but if you have tips, I will be grateful.'

'Sure.'

'I have not heard of any schools in Australia, but Stonyhurst is an exceptionally good British school. Perhaps you know it?' He asked the question again as if seeking endorsement for the quality of his education.

'The great British public school system.'

'You don't approve.'

'On the contrary. A good education is important. That's why my mother insisted I attend the school I did. It was a good school for the region where I grew up, but it's a bit different in Australia.' He sighed and his tone changed. 'The country here reminds me a bit of my home. He craned his neck to see the sky through the windscreen. 'Same grey clouds threatening rain.' As if Mark had conjured it, fog swirled around them, and it began to drizzle.

'You sound nostalgic.' José turned his whole body to look at Mark.

'Better watch the road, mate. But you're right I am a bit. It's nice to see the world but I miss home. Spain and Australia have a lot in common.'

José smiled for the first time. 'How is that?'

'Topography I mean. This mountain range particularly. I have a farm at the foothills of a mountain range that separates the coast from the interior although they are not so high.'

'Ah, the sea and the mountains.'

'Exactly.'

The rain began falling in earnest as they climbed higher, and Mark suggested José might like to turn on the windscreen wiper and the headlights.

He stared at the dashboard for a minute. 'My apologies. How do I do that?'

Mark pointed to the switches on the dashboard. 'How did you draw the short straw to have to escort me around?'

José shook his head. 'Short straw?'

Mark grinned. 'What was your crime?'

José took his eyes completely off the winding road. 'My crime... I don't understand.' The car veered onto the other side of the road.

Mark put his hands on the dashboard and said, 'Mate, watch the road!'

José tried to correct his course, but he reacted too slowly, and the car bounced off the road and into a ditch where it promptly stalled. He sat with his hands on the steering wheel, pale with fright. 'I'm very sorry for this.' He reached towards the ignition. 'I will drive out.'

'Wait a sec.' Mark got out of the car and walked around. Then he opened José's door. 'Let me do it. If you spin the wheels, you'll bog it.'

José got out of the car, carefully avoiding the mud. Once Mark had manoeuvred the vehicle back onto the road, he remained in the driver's seat and José shrugged, getting into the passenger's side looking wet and miserable. 'You may drive the rest of the way.'

Mark put the car into gear.

'What did you mean, my crime?'

'Sorry?' Mark frowned and eased the car forward.

'Why are you sorry?'

The car accelerated. 'I mean, I beg your pardon—what crime?'

'The crime you said I made.' José face filled with indignation.

Mark glanced across at him. 'I said?' He changed gears. 'Oh!' He laughed. 'I meant you must have done something to earn the misfortune of having to escort me. Forget it. It loses something in the translation.'

José looked mollified. 'I have a girlfriend, Pillar, who has threatened to break it off with me if I do not get to her birthday celebrations in Pamplona tonight.'

'Ah-ha. Good reason to volunteer as my driver.'

'It's the war. I am never able to see her.' José shrugged. 'You are a good driver.'

'I've been doing it for a while.' Mark changed the subject. 'What type of trees are these growing along the road?'

José shrugged again. 'Are you a botanist?'

Mark laughed. 'Just interested.'

'You ask a lot of questions.'

'Isn't that what journalists do?'

'But the questions are unrelated.'

'I'm not a very good journalist.' He said grinning at José.

After that, they travelled in silence and José's head began to nod. By the time he awoke, they had crossed over the mountain pass. It had stopped raining, and the sun hung mid-way down the western sky. As they reached the outskirts of Pamplona, a sign said, Plaza de Toros.

Is that the bull ring Hemmingway wrote about in *The Sun Also Rises?*' Mark asked.

'It might be, but I do not have any interest in Ernest Hemmingway. He is sympathetic to the Republicans and therefore a traitor to the holy cause of restoring Catholicism to its rightful place in Spain.'

'Did you read the book?'

José shook his head and sighed. 'He is not all bad because he lives like a man, hunting, drinking and bullfights but he writes propaganda for the Republic.'

'I just wondered how accurate his account of the bullfight might be.'

José shrugged. 'You will be able to see a bullfight while you are here. If you wish you may run with the bulls in the San Fermin fiesta.'

'Have you ever done it?'

'No. I am not athletic enough.' He pointed to a turning and directed Mark to the hotel. The streets were full of people out for an afternoon paseo or huddled in group conferences at corners. Military vehicles tracked back and forth along the road and military personnel hurried along the pavements.

Mark would have been happy to drive on, agitated at the delay caused by the planned overnight in Pamplona given it was only a couple of hours from Irún. They still had plenty of daylight, for the sun only set at about 9.30 pm and they could have made it all the way to Burgos in one trip. In fact, according to Mark's rough map of the place, they could have driven to Burgos via Vitoria and cut miles off the trip. Either José wasn't into risk-taking, or the girlfriend must be special.

José must have read something in Mark's silence because he said, 'Tomorrow, I will show you the place General Molo's plane crashed. This would be interesting for a journalist, yes? He was a great hero of this war.'

General Mola, one of the key leaders of the failed 1936 coup d'état, had help start this civil war. There had originally been nine leaders of the rebels' coup, but one by one they'd fallen, some exiled by Franco, at least one shot by the Republicans. Mola was the latest to die in eerily similar circumstances to the original leader of the coup, José Sanjurjo y Sacanell, who also died in a plane crash a year ago. Now Franco, the last of the original plotters, remained unchallenged. Mark remembered the conversation he'd overheard some weeks ago when he'd eavesdropped on Charles and Captain von Graff talking about getting Molo out of the way. Coincidence or something more?

He said, 'Can you tell me a bit about General Mola, the man not the leader?'

José shook his head. 'I know little. He was born in Cuba and was said to be a person of discipline.' He paused and then added, 'But one without compassion.'

'How so,' Mark asked?

José shrugged. 'Perhaps because of his military father, who fought for Spain in the Cuban War of Independence. There is a story that his men repeat that I think describes his nature. When he heard the Republicans had imprisoned his brother in Barcelona, Mola said *My brother knows how to die as an officer*.'

'What happened to his brother?'

'He died, but by his own hand.'

'Brutal.'

'It is a mortal sin. But the General is... was brutal and even worse to his enemies. He wanted to make a terror so great, the Reds would quake at his name. His methods were calculated to erase those who opposed him. So, he was also a good general and has made the northern campaign a success.'

'His plane hit the side of a mountain in fog. Is that right?'

José pursed his lips. 'Molo died carrying out a final reconnaissance before the battle for Bilbao. Now the north is vanquished and soon the whole of Spain will be in our hands.' He fell silent and although he hadn't answered Mark's question his eyes had filled with tears.

'You liked him then?'

'Like! I did not know him. My superior officer Major Doval was the General's aide de camp. He told me Mola was impatient of incompetence. He did not always make the right decisions himself and was often said to be slow to act.' José sniffed, wiped his hand across his eyes and said, 'I feel guilt for his death.'

'How so?'

'I was supposed to be on that plane, but I had stomach trouble. Major Doval was terribly angry, but now I am alive, and my superior and the General are dead. Tomorrow we will pay our respects.'

The next day, Mark again drove with José navigating. They arrived at the Vitoria airbase, and José told Mark to wait in the car while he ascertained the exact location of the crash site. As soon as he went inside Mark got out of the car and sauntered over to a broad field on which were parked numerous aircraft.

He spoke in Spanish to a man in overalls. 'You have your work cut out for you.'

The man just shook his head. Mark examined the man's overalls. He could not tell if they were those of a Spanish Nationalist, but he wore a badge with the Italian fascist bound rod and axe on a black background. He switched to Italian. 'Are you from Italy?'

The man's face lit up, and he hurried towards Mark, wiping his hands on a rag. 'You are from Italy?' He shook Mark's hand and introduced himself. 'Caporale Ugo Vecoli.'

They talked for a few minutes about people Vecoli knew who had emigrated to Australia, with Mark clarifying that Australia was a big country and he hadn't met Vecoli's friends.

He pointed to his camera. 'Let me get a picture of you and you can send it home to your girlfriend.'

'I don't have a girlfriend. Do you have someone in Australia?'

'In London.' Mark pulled out his wallet, and flicked it open to a small portrait he'd taken of Grandi and Beatrice at the party. 'My fiancée, Beatrice with Conte di Mordano.'

Vecoli looked impressed. 'You know Dino Grandi?'

'Yes... quite well.' He lied.

Vecoli examined the photo. 'You're a lucky man. When I go home, I will marry also.'

Mark said, 'I thought you didn't have a girlfriend. Do you have someone in mind?'

'Yes, a beautiful girl, Maria after the Virgin, my neighbour, but when I left, she was too young. When I get back, she will be the right age.'

'I can take a photo for you to send to her. She can see you as an Italian hero helping Spain and the Catholic church.'

Vecoli liked that idea and posed awkwardly as Mark took several photos of him from different angles, all with aircraft in the background.

Three planes took off, circled the airfield, and flew north. Mark checked their markings. All had the Nationalist crosses. 'Where do you reckon, they're going?' He asked.

Vecoli shrugged. 'Maybe on their way to the front.'

Mark wished he knew more about how to recognise aircraft. 'Were those German?' Mark nodded in the direction the planes had gone.

Vecoli looked at Mark with incredulity in his features. 'Of course.'

'Sorry, I can't tell one plane from another. They might be Italian or Spanish aircraft for all I know.'

Vecoli frowned. 'No Spanish. Why do you say that—see, I show you.' He turned to point. 'The first row are Fiat bombers and next to those the Savoia-Marchetti fighters, Italy both. Then eighty German planes—Heinkel and Junkers. In front, is the new Messerschmitt and over there, the Dornier, also German.'

'What's that one?' Mark pointed to a lone fighter on the fringe.

'Pah, Hispano-Nieuport.' Vecoli grimaced.

'What's wrong with it?'

'Too slow.'

'You know your stuff,' Mark said admiringly as he opened his camera. 'Are the men over there Italian or Spanish?'

'Italians.' He pointed at a group of men working on a Fiat bomber. 'And Germans.' He pointed to a group at one of the Heinkel bombers.

'But the planes have Nationalist markings.'

'Of course.' Vecoli said, 'That's how we are ordered.'

'I am surprised, with the sanctions on trade, that any planes can get it to the country.'

With a tone of pride, Vecoli said, 'That's easy. New German planes are brought by submarine to Vigo, on the Atlantic side, then taken by train to León where they are assembled. One of my compatriots volunteered to work on the assembly of the German planes at Herrera de Pisuerga near Leon.'

'Is that where the Italian planes come in also?'

'No, these are flown in from the Balearic Islands and Ceuta where our ships unload them.'

Mark nodded as if suitably impressed. 'So, the Italian navy controls the Mediterranean and Germany controls the Cantabrian Sea to the Atlantic. Who says Britain rules the waves—eh?'

Vecoli laughed. 'Maybe once but no longer. Now, Italy rules the Mediterranean and when the war is over the Balearic Islands will be payment, and we will control some parts of Morocco. Then the Mediterranean will belong once again to Italy.'

'The return of the great Roman Empire.' Mark said, hoping his feigned admiration hadn't gone too far for credibility.

Vecoli merely nodded.

Two men in overalls brought up a fuel tanker to the plane Vecoli had been working on, and he called out that it was ready. They busied themselves with refuelling but otherwise took no notice of Mark.

Mark raised his camera and shot off some quick snaps.

Vecoli glanced at him with a worried frown. 'I'm not sure photos of the aircraft are allowed, even for uno di noi.'

Mark smiled at the reference to *one of us*. If only he knew. 'Mate, I'm a photojournalist, what else would I do?' He grinned at Vecoli, noting his sudden nervousness. 'Don't worry I have an official permit. I am just waiting for my escort. He works for, or rather, did work for General Mola. Do you know what happened to his plane?'

Vecoli shook his head, his face infused with a shifty look. 'A terrible accident, bad weather they say.'

'You don't buy that?'

Another shrug of the shoulders and Vecoli glanced about furtively.

Mark changed the subject. 'How long have you been here?'

'Six months, but before I was in Abyssinia.'

'You volunteered for this mission?'

'Certainly.'

'Why?'.

Vecoli shrugged. 'My brother is an officer with the Corpo Truppe Volontarie, and he said it's better here.'

'Better—how?'

'There is no mustard gas. In Abyssinia, I didn't have a gas mask. They said we didn't need them because only the enemy got the gas, but sometimes the pilots are confused and drop the canisters in the wrong place. I didn't want to get gassed by accident.'

Mark smiled. 'Good reason.' He'd heard the Italians used gas in their attacks on Ethiopia, but Mussolini had denied it. 'Chucking gas out of planes is pretty barbaric.'

'Not barbaric—is war. War is always bad, but we are not as bad as the Germans.'

'How's that?'

'They have found a new evil they call the Devil's Egg. They mix gasoline and old engine oil in a drum and then tie bombs on each side. When the drum hits the ground, it burst, and the bomb ignites the fuel. The destruction is diabolical. Fire shoots in all directions sticking to everything, even human flesh.'

Mark stared at Vecoli in horror. He recalled José's assessment of General Mola's aim to terrorise his opponents. That kind of bomb would surely succeed. Although the Italians had razed whole Spanish cities with their bombing raids. Was one form of bomb worse than another or worse than gas?

Mark had no idea. They were all intended to kill and all created terror, particularly in the civilian populations. How had humans resorted to this form of waging war? Although could any form of war, other than in defence, be justified? He didn't have those answers.

Mark saw José come out of the building and said, 'Ah, my escort is back. Nice talking to you Caporale Vecoli. Where is your brother stationed?'

'He is Captain at the barracks at Maranda de Ebro.'

'I'll call in. Do you have a message?'

'Just say I am well.'

'I'll leave the photo with him.'

Vecoli nodded then spoke rapidly in a low voice. 'General Mola was in Franco's way. That's why his plane crashed.'

'Who did it?' Mark asked.

Vecoli had walked away but he said something indistinct that might have been. 'Guarda alla Legione Condor—*look to the Condor Legion.*'

José bore down, his eyes popping as if they would burst from their sockets. Mark waved to the corporal and walked to meet José.

'You must stay in the car. Did you take pictures?'

Mark shook his head. 'I just spoke to Corporal Vecoli over there, and I took a photo of him for his girlfriend.'

The puff went out of José as the explanation seemed to placate him. Girlfriends were an understandable necessity.

Mark asked, 'What did you find out about the General's plane?'

'I have the coordinates. The site is northeast of Burgos. We will drive that way. But we must be careful of bandits.'

They found the spot about eighty kilometres southwest of Vitoria, just off the road to Burgos near the tiny village of Alcocero. There wasn't much to look at now the crash site had been cleared.

'It's pretty amazing that anyone found them.' Mark said looking around at the isolated spot.

'A shepherd saw the plane come out of the fog and explode. He reported it at Briviesca.'

'The plane exploded?'

'That is what he said, but I think he meant the plane crashed into the mountain.'

José showed Mark where the General's body had been found some meters from the crashed plane. 'The only way they identified Mola was the sash around the waist. Also, because he had no shoes on.'

'What is the significance of shoes?' Mark asked.

'A gitano, ah-um a fortune teller, told Mola he would die with his boots on, so he always took them off when he flew.'

While Mark took photos, José droned on about Mola's funeral in Burgos, for which he had played a small part acting as an altar server for the requiem Mass. 'Generalissimo Franco himself led the funeral procession. The band played *Sueño Eterno*. You know it...?' Mark shook his head. José continued. 'I will find you a recording. It is beautiful. People cried and threw rose petals from the balconies.' He sighed. 'Now he rests in Pamplona cemetery, and his soul is rewarded in heaven. He is a fallen hero for God and Spain.'

'You believe that?'

'Why not? You are a Catholic. Can you tell me different?'

'No mate.' Mark thought he should change the subject. 'How is the war going now General Mola is no longer running it?'

'General Fidel Dávila has replaced Mola. He is an accomplished general and took 90,000 troops under his command.'

'That's a lot of men. All Spanish.'

'Twenty-five thousand were from Italian divisions.'

'Does he also command the airfield we were just at?'

'Of course. He has 220 aircraft including those of the German *Condor Legion*, and the Italian *Aviazione Legionaria*, the ones you have seen in Vitoria. In three days Bilboa was finished. Soon the rest of the country will follow.'

'I thought Bilboa had been under siege for months?' Javier's face flashed across Mark's mind. He hoped he'd got away.

'Of course. I told you, Mola was slow to act, but Dávila soon had the Basque Army on the run.'

'Any prisoners taken?'

'I heard more than ten thousand.'

'That's a lot of prisoners. What will happen to them?'

José shrugged. 'I do not know. If General Mola was still here, all would be shot.'

Mark remained silent thinking about Javier. He hoped he was not among the prisoners. The Republicans didn't treat prisoners of war well, but the Nationalists were another level of brutality altogether.

Burgos

The streets of Burgos were busy and the day mild with that crystalline brilliance Mark had come to expect from Spanish sunshine. A fresh breeze blew in from a northerly direction, ruffling the leaves on a line of trees marshalling the street outside his hotel.

For the past couple of days, Mark had played by the rules for journalists in rebel territory, registering with the office of the press censor, listening to the other journalists, before deciding most were pro-Franco.

He spent his mornings reading the newspapers, took clippings for his file, discussed the war's progress over a beer or coffee. Two days ago, he'd called on Charles, who insisted he move out of the hotel and into his apartment.

This morning, he roamed the streets, photographing civilians living the ordinary humdrum lives in a city at war, but one far away from the front lines. Burgos was the administrative capital of Franco's northern conquests; its buildings covered in poster art and nationalist flags. They reminded him a little of the Republican cities. Except the posters here heralded *Franco, Franco, Franco* stamped across heroically stylised farmers bearing the land's bounty, or sometimes soldiers crushing Republicans underfoot.

Yesterday, he could have taken off unofficially to the front line with some of the other journalists who had hired guides. Instead, he decided to conform for the sake of future favours and had requested permission and an escort from the censor's office. In the interim, Charles had suggested they go and inspect a Rio Tinto quarry close by at a village called Trespuentes. Mark had indicated interested because Beatrice had several investments in Rio Tinto's Spanish mines.

Charles nodded. 'Yes, I am aware of my cousin's investments. I managed them for my Uncle when he was still trustee of Beatrice's fund. Being in London while he lived in Australian made it convenient. Now, of course, many of those same investments are in disputed territory. But you will be happy to know, I have Franco's assurances that once the Nationalist clear the land of the Reds, our family's assets will be returned to us.'

Mark pursed his mouth and nodded in a feigned expression of admiration. 'How did you manage to extract that commitment?'

'Natural charm my dear chap, natural charm and a modicum of skill in negotiation.' Charles grinned.

Mark recalled the half-heard conversation between Charles and Captain von Graff. What had the transaction entailed?

Trespuentes wasn't far from Maranda de Ebro and Mark figured he might achieve two goals with one journey. First inspect the quarry and then call in on Caporale Ugo Vecoli's brother, Captain Luigi Vecoli. It would give him a chance to inspect one of the rebel barracks.

They set off in Charles's Jaguar; a vehicle Mark had admired earlier and itched to drive. They passed a few farmers with mule drawn carts, a bus, and sporadic military vehicles along the Burgos-Vittoria Road before they turned off, to drive along a gravelled road leading to the quarry.

Charles pulled up outside the quarry's administration building.

Supervisor Gonzalo Vázquez, tall, thin, and stooped with the aesthetic countenance of temperance, hurried out to greet them.

Once inside the building, Charles took Vázquez to an adjoining room leaving Mark alone. He gazed about the room. Just an ordinary office. A grimy window overlooking the driveway. Shelves containing files and ledgers. A coat stand, with hat and coat hanging on it. A desk, on which sat a pile of ledgers on a large blotter. Two chairs, one behind the desk the other against the wall next to a tallboy with multiple drawers.

Charles returned alone, and said, 'Supervisor Vázquez will find someone to take you for a tour of the quarry while I check the books.

A few minutes later Vázquez came back with a man he introduced as Esteban Díaz, a short powerfully built man wearing a black beret.

Díaz led Mark outside and in halting English asked, 'What you want to see?'

'I'd like to get a few photos of the quarry and the men,' Mark replied in Spanish.

Díaz grinned, his crooked teeth stained from tobacco.

Mark asked, 'How is working for the British?'

'Not too bad. They only steal a little.' Díaz replied with a shrug.

Mark frowned but decide against commenting. He took a few photos, setting Díaz to pose in the foreground of two company lorries parked next to the administrative buildings.

Fifteen minutes later, they arrived at a workshop where the men mixed potassium nitrate, charcoal, and sulphur, into black powder for blasting.

Mark asked, 'Why use black power, isn't dynamite better?'

Díaz said, 'You know about black powder?'

'I used to be a miner. Tin dredging mostly but I've also done a bit of copper prospecting.'

'Mi compañero trabajo. *My work colleague...*' He stopped speaking as if he'd said something he shouldn't and mopped his face with a rag. 'Sometimes black powder is better. We can use it underwater. Dynamite is expensive, mostly kept for the war.'

Mark found the process fascinating. He knew a little about it from his stepfather, who had taught Mark and his brother about prospecting and the explosives used to expose the copper ore.

'I have only ever used ammonium nitrate and fuel oil to blast apart rock, never black powder.'

Diaz nodded. 'You want to see it in action?'

'Sure.'

The men stopped work and escorted Mark to a spot where holes had been drilled in the quarry wall. Díaz packed a charge into one of the holes along with a twist of what looked like brown paper filled with black powder. Mark assumed it acted as a fuse. It wouldn't give them long to take cover.

He searched for a safe vantage point while Diaz completed the blast set up. While he waited, he recalled his younger brother Finn landing himself in hospital after attempting to get a closer view of the blast. He'd only suffered minor abrasions and a burst eardrum. Mark touched his own ear, still slightly deaf from the concussion of the bomb blast and moved further away.

The explosion broke a great slab of rock wall from the side of the quarry. It crumbled, as if in slow motion, before falling into a pile of rubble at the base of the quarry.

Mark took photos as fast as he could wind on the film.

On the way back to the quarry office Mark asked Díaz if he knew the whereabouts of the Italian's camp. 'I'm told it is not too far from here.'

Díaz frowned and said, 'Which one—the Airforce or the so-called volunteer corps near Maranda de Ebro.'

Mark looked at him speculatively. 'You don't like the Italians being here,' he asked?

Díaz spat and said, 'I have no opinion on war, politics, or people. Only mining.'

His denial brought Mark hope. Not everyone here supported Franco.

He handed Mark a twist of paper filled with the black powder, and smiled, 'A souvenir. Your friend takes money; you take the black powder.'

He turned away abruptly and walked off, leaving Mark puzzled by the comment about Charles taking money.

When they were again in the car he asked.

Charles replied, 'The man doesn't speak English well. I check the accounts when I can for the firm. It's a type of quality insurance. Now, you wanted to visit the volunteer camp on our way back.'

The Vittoria to Burgos Road was busier than it had been earlier, mostly comprising military vehicles although there were also mules, horses, pedestrians and several farm carts. Once they turned off to Miranda de Ebro, they didn't have far to go before they found the villa which served as the officers' quarters for the Italian volunteers.

Over dinner in the officer's quarters that night, the wine ran freely, and the food tasted delicious. This land not only sheltered lucrative mining ventures but also harboured rich farming land. Whereas the Republican controlled territory barely produced enough to feed their army.

Captain Luigi Vecoli stood to raise a toast to Il Duce and victory. Vecoli was as tall as Mark, but his shoulders were narrow, and where Mark had dark hair in need of a barber, Luigi's was fair and cut short to little more than golden stubble.

Earlier in the day as the two men had shaken hands Mark experienced a curious sense of déjà vu, for Luigi looked a lot like his brother. Vecoli had explained that Mark was lucky to have found him as the next day they were once more leaving for the front. He had invited Mark and Charles to stay the night. Charles declined, and suggested Mark might stay if he found his own way back to Burgos.

Vecoli explained he was a member of the Milizia Volontaria per la Sicurezza Nazionale, the fascist military wing of the Italian army, which made up the majority of the Corpo di Truppe Volontarie. In 1935 he had joined the Blackshirts Battalion as part of the 28 Ottobre division, which went on to win the second battle of Tembien in Italo-Ethiopian War. His division had been disbanded, and he had volunteered for Franco's crusade against the Bolsheviks where he joined the Division XXIII di Marzo.

Now, Mark discovered that Italian hospitality outdid itself for friends of the captain, especially considering the shortages in the rest of the country. As part of an after-dinner toast, Vecoli recounted the Italian soldiers' heroic march into Bermeo. He likened it to action he had seen in Ethiopia as his division helped to expand the empire.

When he finished, he raised a glass to Mark. 'I drink to friends, my country men, my Catholic brothers in arms, and to fellow fascist."

The men around the table raised their glasses.

Vecoli took a breath and sang. 'Youth, youth, Spring of beauty.'

The other officers joined him. 'In fascism is the salvation of our freedom.'

Then he turned to Mark. 'We welcome our comrade. Mr Anders is an Australian, but not by choice. By birth he is our brother, born in Lucca.'

The men raised their glasses.

After dinner the officers milled around Mark asking, if he knew their cousins, who had made a business in Sydney, or a brother who had moved to Melbourne. If he'd met the Colombo family living in Adelaide, or Uncle Pietro Pagani in Brisbane.

Mark shook his head. Australia is a big country, and I have a farm a thousand miles north of Brisbane and 1,500 miles north of Sydney. Unless your relatives live in Innisfail or in Herberton, I am unlikely to have met them.

Luigi spoke over the volley of questions. 'Once we have cleaned out the Reds in Spain, I too will own a farm here in the Basque country.'

'Is that so?' Mark said.

'Si, General Franco has promised land to those who risk their life to cleanse Spain of the Bolshevik filth. But we do more than that. One day the world will see this war as part of our crusade to create the New Roman Empire, when Italy will once again rule the entire Mediterranean region.'

The conversation swirled around the room without filter or reticence as men bragged about how many Spanish Reds they had individually killed, and the brutality they inflicted on the enemy.

The contrived façade of admiration and support for the men made Mark's face hurt. He was relieved to retire to the guest quarters for the night.

The next morning, he said goodbye to Luigi and climbed aboard a truck heading for Burgos. The driver was from the Army Support Corp and introduced himself as Cobo Hernández.

After Mark had introduced himself, Hernández said, 'You speak Spanish. Few English journalists who come here do. This is good. You will understand better why it is our duty to God and Spain to wage this war.'

271

Hernández invited Mark to sit in the cab with him. 'We leave the back for the prisoners and their guards.'

'What prisoners are those?'

'Red scum. Should be shot, but I am ordered to transfer them to San Pedro de Cardeña.'

Mark frowned. 'Is San Pedro on the way to Burgos?'

'A little south. The camp is at the old monastery. It is where the Reds must go after classification. They make labour gangs for the farms. We need to get in the harvest quickly to make sure we have food for the army.'

'Where are they held now?'

'Here at Campo de Miranda. We must carry out a small detour to fetch them before we go.'

Mark raised his eyebrows. 'Do you think I might interview them... Maybe get some photos?'

'The Reds! Why would you want to talk to such animals. They reject God.' He blessed himself in a haphazard manner.

Mark followed suit and shrugged. 'If they are animals, perhaps God has rejected them.'

Hernández pursed his lips as if thinking about the possibility. 'This may be true. I had not thought like that, but if they are animals, they have no soul. 'You are right my friend. God would not want them. But El Degollao runs the camp, and he will not let you speak to the prisoners.'

'El Degollao, doesn't that mean...' Mark mimed cutting his throat.

'Sí, it is the name the prisoners have for Captain Juárez. He is a hard man. There are also Germans at the camp supervising the building works.' He spat out of the window.

'You don't like the Germans.'

'I do not trust those men. They spy for the Gestapo attaché, Winzer.'

'Winzer? I don't think I know of him.'

'He is from the German Embassy in Salamanca. When we get to the camp you must stay in the truck. The Gestapo enforce the rules.'

They crossed a river and drove along next to a railway line before they arrived at a desperate looking walled compound of baked clay. A broken-down pyrites storage shed scented the air with its sulphurous fumes. A newly constructed administration building sat next to the gate and opposite stood a civil guard post. More buildings, possibly barracks under construction, showed working prisoners under guard.

German uniforms stood out among the guards and Mark realised he had entered the mouth of the dragon. After Hernández had alighted the truck and walked towards the administration building Mark glanced around before lifting his camera lens to the vehicle's window ledge. Although he could not see what he captured he depressed the shutter and wound on the film to repeat the action. With luck, one of the shots might be useable.

A German soldier walked towards the truck, slowly as if curious, and Mark pushed his camera under the seat. The soldier spoke in execrable Spanish.

Mark smiled, nodded, and pulled out his press pass and passport before he tried speaking some of the limited German he had been attempting to learn. The German glanced briefly at the papers, and said in English, 'Your German is worse than my

Spanish. So, what is an English journalist doing in a prison camp?'

'Just catching a lift back to Burgos. I spent the night at the Italian officers villa in town with my friend, Captain Vecoli. Do you know him?'

'How does an Englishman know an Italian officer?'

Mark chuckled. 'I'm Italian through and through, but like the Marquis del Moral I was born in Australia.'

'You know Moral.'

'I had lunch with him and the Duke of Alba only a week ago at Simpson's in London.'

The German looked impressed, then frowned as if a thought struck him. 'I see you are well connected, but how do you know an Italian officer who does not live in London.'

Mark glanced past the German to where Hernández walked back towards the truck. He searched for an answer, hoping a hackneyed stereotype might satisfy. 'I'm Italian, mate. Didn't you know, we are all related.'

Behind Hernández a small group of prisoners shuffled ahead of two civil guards. As they came closer, Mark spotted a familiar figure. It looked like Javier, thin, limping, unkempt with his leg encased in blood-soaked bandages, but unmistakably Javier.

He caught sight of Mark, and his mouth fell open with a stupefied expression on his face. Mark ran his palm over his own face willing Javier to say nothing.

The German glanced towards the prisoners, but Javier had taken the hint and moved forward with his head bowed.

To distract the German officer, Mark said the first thing that popped into his head. 'I would like to visit Germany to improve my German. Is obtaining a visa possible?'

A Republican Spy?

Mark received permission to travel to the front-line, but now he knew Javier was a prisoner, he became intent on finding a way to have him released. Charles was well connected and might be able to help. Yet he didn't trust Charles with the truth and spun him a line about obtaining permission to do a story on POWs.

Charles said, 'What on earth for?'

Mark shrugged. 'Human interest.'

'Good grief, don't tell me Dawson is getting soft in his old age.'

'It's more self-interest. Sentiment makes for more advertising revenue. More advertising revenue may increase my earnings.'

'Marry my cousin and you will have pots of money.'

Mark pulled a wry face. 'I want to earn my own keep, and besides, I need something other than being a glorified bookkeeper for my wife's trust.'

Charles shrugged. 'I guess managing money is not everyone's cup of tea.' He gazed at Mark for a moment with what looked like speculation in his expression before he said, 'You do realise, I manage my family's and Uncle Arthur's investment portfolios. I rather enjoy the work. So, if I can be of help... I am a bit whizz at the job. Been doing it all my life, and I still managed the accounting and investments for Lady Margaret's charity. Just say the word if you need advice... Although I don't plan to be here long. I have a hankering to have a go at the diplomatic lifestyle. Think it would rather suit, don't you know.'

'That's new.'

'Not really, I have been thinking about it for a while. I spoke to some old college chums in the service, and they are happy to put in a good word. One of them has a father in high places, but I also hope to recruit Denton to my cause. But come along now, get dressed, best bib and black tie.'

'Where are we going?'

'There's a reception at the military headquarters. If you insist on interviewing Reds you might ask for some advice tonight. Although I warn you, they won't look on it favourably.'

An hour later, Mark and Charles arrived at Burgos military headquarters. They entered the main reception hall, where chamber music played in the background. Dress uniforms blazed with medals. Silk dresses swished through air saturated with tobacco smoke, and perfume. A chandelier threw refracted light across a room so full of certainty, authority, righteousness, and the ringing *Arriba España* salutes, it made the religious scenes in the stained glass seem vulgar.

Mark's heart raced. How on earth could the Republic counter the international support, and Catholic zealotry, of Franco's Spain?

Charles quietly pointed out a British Baron, a Spanish Princess, an American tycoon among the multitude of uniforms from Spain, Germany, and Italy. 'Ah, and there is von Graff back in town with Clara.'

The man seemed to be everywhere. Mark followed Charles over to the German couple.

'You know von Graff but let me introduce you to his beautiful cousin, Fräulein Clara Hauser.'

Mark took the woman's hand in his and asked, 'Any relation to Hauser munitions?'

'You know about Papi's company.'

'Doesn't everyone? I saw the prototype of the car his firm is building. Very impressive.'

Charles gazed at Mark for a minute before saying, 'You are a surprise. How is it you know about Hauser munitions?'

Mark saw an opportunity. 'Beatrice holds quite a large chunk of shares in your father's firm.'

Clara asked, 'Who is Beatrice?'

Charles interjected, 'My cousin.'

Mark smiled. 'My fiancée.' From his inside pocket he took out a folded leather wallet, opened it and extracted the photo of Beatrice at her party, posing with the Italian ambassador. He held it out to Clara.

Clara turned fully to Mark, her shoulder excluding Charles, and fluttering her blonde eyelashes said, 'I thought you were a journalist, Mr Anders.'

Von Graff chimed in. 'He is and a very good one, my dear.'

Clara said, 'And you have a beautiful fiancée. I would like to meet her. Why do you not invite her to visit?'

'She is a busy woman with her own enterprises to manage.'

Clara, mouth formed a moue, whether of disappointment or disapproval he didn't know.

Von Graff took Mark's arm. 'Mr Anders... Mark you must join our friends of Germany community, but tell me, what assignment are you working on at the moment?'

'Ah, I'm hoping to witness the fall of the Santander province. I spoke to Captain Luigi Vecoli, you may know him... He is heading up that way. My permissions came through and I'm off to the front tomorrow. He suggested I join the Corpo di Truppe Volontarie.' He paused then added. 'There is also another matter I thought worthy of a story...'

Charles smiled and said helpfully, 'The human-interest angle for those disinterested in war.'

Mark nodded.

Clara tilted her head. 'What is that?'

'Prisoners of war. I would like to do a story on their incarceration and treatment. I understand they are treated well and given farming jobs, which will help the nation.'

Von Graff gazed at Mark for several seconds of silence, an unnerving stare until he smiled. 'Yes. I heard you had visited. I can put in a word for you with Attaché Wizer, but you will have to go to Salamanca for access papers.'

Mark tried to read von Graff's expression. 'Word travels quickly in these parts.'

'I know the architect at the camp. He and I did officer training together, many years ago. He has been given charge of the prisoner camps. But he also said you wished to visit Germany to learn German.'

Relief rushed through Mark's veins, and he laughed. 'He told me my German was worse than his Spanish. I thought I should do something about it.'

'We will have to ensure you do, my dear Mark. Now, what can I get you to drink. I can see you are not drinking the manzanilla. You are more a beer man, am I correct?'

Mark put on a sheepish look and nodded. 'Fraid so.'

'Do not apologise. Drinking beer is a good German quality.' Von Graff beckoned a waiter.

While von Graff spoke to the waiter, another man joined them.

'Mr Anders, I have been looking forward to meeting you. Charles, my good man, will you do the honours.'

Charles said, 'Oh hello Bolín. My cousin-to-be by marriage, Mark Anders. Mark, may I present Luis Bolín, former Chief Press officer. What are you up to now Luis?'

'I have a new project, very hush-hush for now, but Mr Anders, I would be obliged if you will call on me in the morning. We can be of mutual benefit.' He handed Mark his card.

Mark took it, frowning at how entangled he had become with this regime. He had also noted that now Clara was interested in him, presumably because of Beatrice's investments, Charles claimed him as a cousin. How easy it had been, and all because he knew the right people and mixed in the right circles, thanks to Denton. What would happen if they came to suspect him? He took a glass of beer, offered to him by the waiter, and took a large gulp.

📷

After the reception, von Graff dropped Clara back at his apartment before rejoining Charles and Mark as they entered the El Campeador café. Dim-lighting, and scantily dressed women serving tables, gave a clue to the calibre of the joint. A woman in a sequined dress crooned into a microphone. Charles observed quietly that her décolletage would give Fräulein Clara's a run for her money.

Mark sent an inquiring glance towards von Graff, but the man appeared not to have heard. Instead, he explained that the café was named for a hero of the Spanish Reconquista, the long-running revolutionary battles that had reclaimed the county from Moorish invaders. Oh, the irony, Mark almost laughed aloud. Now they were using those same Moors to wrest the country from the Spanish Republic. Did Franco see it?

A woman sauntered over to their table, and von Graff placed his arm around her waist. Although she smiled, no humour reached her kohl blackened eyes beneath their heavy brows. Mark examined her face; certain he'd met her before. Unlikely, he knew, but she looked so familiar.

Von Graff pulled her onto his lap and kissed her neck. She pouted ruby lips and adjusted the traditional Basque costume as it rode up to expose her thighs.

Mark glanced at Charles, who blew out a lungful of cigarette smoke and grinned back. 'Mate, it's the equivalent of a local whore house. Not officially but most of the waitresses are happy to oblige. This is Carmen, von Graff's particular favourite.'

The name struck Mark with the blow of recognition. Javier's cousin, Carmen Rodoreda, whom he had met briefly at an appeal for relief of the Spanish Republic in Brisbane. She not only persuaded Javier to fight for the Republic, but her photos of the Madrid bombing had contributed to Mark being here.

He recalled his first reaction towards her, dark eyes full of fire and passion as she pleaded for Australia's help. Heavy work boots, trousers, and shirt had swamped her petite form as she had given a speech begging for Australia's help. An image materialised: the small child flung dead on a Madrid street like a rag doll. He'd never got that photograph out of his head.

How could he to sit still and let von Graff maul her? In Brisbane, they'd barely spoken before she was engulfed in the crush of well-wishers. There was a good chance she wouldn't remember who he was. But he'd have to speak with her, if only to tell her Javier was alive and where to find him. Although what good that would do, he had no idea.

He excused himself, stood up and looking sheepish said, 'Too much beer. Is there a lavatory?'

She looked at him with a blank face.

Von Graff said, 'She doesn't speak English, but you will have to go outside, down the alley behind the café.'

Mark watched her face, knowing she spoke English. He said in halting Spanish with a broad Australian accent, 'No matter, she will find me.'

Von Graff laughed and corrected Mark's grammar, '*You will find it*, you mean. 'Seems like your Spanish is as bad as your German, my friend.'

Mark smiled and in English, said, 'I had a friend in Australia... A Spanish bloke called Javier Cruz. He tried to teach me a few words, but they were mostly not for use in polite company.'

He walked out, not knowing if she had recognised him, or understood his message. He followed the side of the building until it turned into an alley at the back of the café. The smell of piss and spew rose in waves.

He leaned against the wall, waiting. A few minutes later she came out a door at the other end of the alley and hurried towards him, seemingly oblivious to the lavatory horrors she might encounter along the way.

'You recognised me?' Mark said it in English and with relief.

She shook her head and said in Spanish, 'I do not understand.'

Mark spoke in Spanish. 'I know you speak English but never mind. Do you know who I am?'

She shrugged. 'I have been expecting someone to contact me, but not here.' She scrutinised his features. 'But I don't think I know you.'

'We met in Brisbane, Australia. I am Javier's friend.'

She gripped his arm. 'Where is he? Is he alive?'

He nodded. 'He's a prisoner at Miranda de Ebro. What did you mean you were expecting someone?'

'It is nothing. Just a new customer...'

'From the Republic?'

She shushed him and glanced around. 'You must not mention such filth.' She spat and then winked at him.

He didn't know what to make of her. Was she a Republican spy or merely trying to survive in enemy territory? He paused and then said, 'I'm sorry I can't stop that man pawing you.'

He gazed at her, remembering her vow in Brisbane that she was going back to Bilbao to take up arms with her father and brothers. Where were they now? Working in this place wasn't something many Spanish men, or any other man for that matter, would tolerate, not even for a spy. Although it was also possible, she had little choice in the matter.

She seemed to read his mind as she said abruptly. 'I can look after myself.'

He nodded. 'I'm going north tomorrow, but I'll come back here when I can.'

A look of resignation took over her features, and she brushed hair away from her eyes. 'I can see you somewhere else then, and we can talk.'

She turned and hurried back to the café.

A little while later, Carmen brought their order to the table and smiled at von Graff, leaning close to whisper in his ear. Von Graff didn't look pleased. Carmen sat on his lap and stroked his face. Then turned to look at Charles and in Spanish said, 'I like you. Maybe you want to join me after Mister Germany goes away.'

Charles looked taken aback, licked his lips, glanced at von Graff, and said in Spanish, 'Sorry darling, I am rather smitten with someone else...'

Carmen frowned. 'Love—pah!' She glanced at Mark, pulled a face, and said unenthusiastically, 'Maybe you then?'

Charles stepped in. 'He's engaged, and what is this? Touting for more business. A bit blatant, isn't it?'

Carmen shrugged. 'I must eat, and I like to choose my meal tickets, especially rich foreigners.'

Mark, watching the exchange, realised Carmen had given him an excuse to come back to the café.

Von Graff slapped Carmen's thigh. 'I am your only meal ticket for the moment and don't you forget it.'

'You'd better stay in España then.' She patted his cheek, got up and swished away, hips undulating from side to side.

Later that evening, when Charles and Mark returned to Charles flat, minus von Graff, Mark asked Charles if he meant what he'd said to the waitress about being smitten. 'Who is the unlucky girl? Not von Graff's cousin by any chance?'

'You understood that?' Charles sighed. 'I don't think I have a chance in hell.'

'Why not?'

'Not in her financial class, my boy. Her father's wealth... you know...'

'Don't let that stop you.'

'Oh, that's right. You swept Beatrice off her feet when you were merely a labourer on my father's farm.'

'I worked for the sugar mill, but yeah something like that.'

Charles sat forward in his chair, 'Look, mate, you could do both of us a favour.'

Mark felt dread rising in his chest. 'Such as?'

'Well, Clara knows your fiancée has shares in her father's firm and that appeared enough for her to fawn over you.'

'I noticed that.'

'If you persuade Beatrice to give me a role as her investment manager or financial advisor, I could do some of the tasks you hate, and she probably ignores.'

'What, like visiting any assets she has in Germany?' Mark laughed.

'Yes, possibly, but at the same time, you can tell Clara what a whiz I am as her investments or financial advisor or some such title. That should impress her no end.'

Mark shook his head. 'I don't have any say in Beatrice's investments,' he lied. Nor do I have any idea how financial markets work. Clara would see through me in a heartbeat.'

He thought of the paltry shares he had collected throughout his working career. Bert Manzone, Mark's friend, and business partner, who still managed the farm, the shop, and all Mark's business affairs in Australia, might be called his investment manager. In his last letter he had urged Mark to buy shares in an iron and steel company at Port Kembla in New South Wales. Bert also remained convinced another war was coming.

He turned his attention back to Charles who pursued his argument with some passion or perhaps desperation. 'With a small deposit, I could begin your portfolio. Wolframite is going to skyrocket if this war extends to the rest of Europe. I would make you rich, quickly, and you wouldn't even have to pay me.' He added with a wry smile, 'or maybe just a retainer for expenses.'

Mark remembered the wolframite his father had discarded when dredging up the cassiterite to extract tin. Australia had huge supplies of the stuff, used for hardening steel, but he had never thought to buy shares in it. It had always seemed like a waste product to him. 'Wolframite you say?' He pursed his mouth.

Charles nodded. 'The Germans are stockpiling the stuff. For just a few thousand I can get you a good deal. What do you think? It would help lift my status in Clara's eyes enormously and it would only be for a while unless you wanted the arrangement to continue. You know I have the experience as I already manage Uncle Arthur's and my father's investments, and it wouldn't be difficult to take on another portfolio. You are unfamiliar with the markets, and I enjoy the involvement. It gives me the air of being a pair of safe hands, financially. Win-win all round, I should think.'

Mark smiled. 'You imagine I have that kind of money to play with.' He wouldn't trust Charles with his money, and he certainly would not persuade Beatrice to entrust her cousin with her trust fund. Besides, 1937 was proving a volatile year for the markets.

'I happen to know the going rate for your articles. You'll be doing well out of it.'

Mark shook his head. 'Too many travel expenses.'

'Surely you recoup those from the papers.'

'Sure, I tender my expenses.'

'Clearly not enough. There are common tricks. I will have to explain them sometimes. All the newspaper men do it. The editors expect it.'

'That so?' Mark said.

'Just think about it.'

'Right. Well, I'm off to bed. Good night, mate.'

The next morning, Mark agitated to get away before he would be forced to answer Charles on the matter of investments. He didn't think, for the sake of familial relationships, he could tell Charles he didn't trust him, especially not after accepting the man's hospitality. Still, he couldn't leave for the front until he'd seen Bolín and had an assigned minder. To avoid Charles, he left the apartment early to wait in a café opposite Bolín's office until the man arrived.

An hour later, Mark sat in Bolín's office stunned by his offer. 'Let me make sure I understand you Sénior Bolín... Instead of just a day trip to the front line, you will extend my visa and have my guide take me through all the Basque battle sites so that I may do a photo montage that might titillate. Have I understood correctly?'

'Yes, you have a blunt Australian way of putting it, but in essence that is correct.'

'May I ask, why?'

'I am afraid not. That is a secret, but the scenes must be uplifting, just a hint of brutality and force but nothing to put people off.'

'Propaganda?'

If you like but not for that purpose.

'Romanising war and heroism.' Mark gazed at Bolín with slowly dawning suspicion. 'Battlefield tours...'

Bolín looked alarmed. 'Did you hear something... You must say nothing of this. It is not formulated.'

'All right.' Mark sat back in his chair. 'I'll make you a deal.'

Half an hour later Mark took off on his journey with a new minder and spy, Lieutenant Santiago García. The officer drove well and spoke passable English.

Mark sat in the passenger seat and kept his ability to speak Spanish to himself. In his pocket he held a letter of introduction to the commander of the San Pedro de Cardeña prison camp. It granted permission to speak with prisoners and photograph their quarters for the western press. The deal he'd made with Bolín in exchange for a battlefield photo montage.

He had asked to visit the prison camp at Miranda de Ebro, but for that he would need Winzer's permission. That would be his next task, but at least this visit would show Winzer a pattern to demonstrate he had a newsworthy interest in POWS. It wasn't too far out of his way and if would make a good story even if it meant waiting to contact Javier.

Of course, he could also take photos for his newspaper, but they, and any written articles, about either POWS or battle fields would have to be properly vetted before Mark left Spain. Mark felt he would hand Bolín a huge propaganda coup for Franco. A pact with the devil. Would the ends justify the means? While it gave Mark unfettered access to photograph key installations for the Republic, and a chance to figure out how he might help Javier, the notion of battlefield tours left a shadow over what he hoped to gain.

Javier

The midday sun beat down on the prisoner's back as he dumped the rocks next to the road before straightening and flexing his shoulders. Gruelling work for anyone and reminiscent of cutting cane in North Queensland. At least that's what Javier told himself.

At night he sometimes dreamed of being back in the cane fields, salivating over one of Bert's breakfasts of steak and eggs, food to sustain a man for a day in the fields. Not here. Only watery and tasteless lentils day after day. He placed his tongue against a wobbly molar. It wouldn't remain in his gums for much longer. Not that teeth were required in this place.

The guard sauntered toward him, and Javier scratched at his cargo of body lice before picking up the empty basket. The road should be finished by now but there had been sabotage. By whom, he had no idea, and although it meant redoing the section, the thought that someone still resisted the bastards filled him with hope.

He'd been filled with hope before when he thought he'd seen Mark. He was feverish from the wound he received on their flight from Bilbao, before they were caught. Seeing Mark sitting in a truck talking to a German officer was clearly a delusion.

He'd only been in the camp a few days then. After he had been captured along with his unit, he had tried to blend into the background. Simply another foot soldier. Although he had been born in America, his family were from the Biscay province, and he spoke Bizkaian like a native. It had kept him alive as other foreign fighters along with the officers were lined up in the bullring and shot.

After the bullring massacre, the surviving prisoners were taken to the camp at Miranda de Ebro. Throughout his interrogation he had played the role of a vacillating Catholic foot soldier, conscripted into his country's army, unsure about the Nationalist claim to legitimacy. So far it had kept him alive because if they thought a man could be rehabilitated, he would be useful as cannon fodder or put to work on infrastructure rebuilding or farming.

They treated his leg, and gave him the category, *reaprovechables,* or a redeemable person. After that he had been put to work on road building. Rehabilitation through work and sacrifice. The great justification of the Nationalist Catholics for their atrocities. Franco had the effrontery to invoke the Geneva convention when using prisoners as forced labour as if the Nationalists were a legitimate state rather than the rebel insurgents they were.

The world seemed to take for granted that Franco would win. Perhaps they were right all along, especially now Franco proclaimed he was justified in staging the failed coup in '36 to prevent a communist takeover. That is what had led to this war. The revisionist history of the victors beginning before they had even won.

A truck rolled up and stopped. An officer stepped out, spoke to their guard. The guard summoned the prisoners to stop work and gather around.

The prisoners slowly moved closer.

The officer said, 'I need skilled tradesmen. Those of you who seek to make amendments for the destruction you have 'helped create. This is your penance, but it will be rewarded by rebuilding Spain for the glory of God and Generalissimo Franco, who even as I speak, marches in God's glory to take back the Santander province from the Reds.

Javier paused, fighting a surge of new hope. Skilled workers might have better treatment if Franco's bastards thought they were worth something. Did bricklaying count? He had once worked as a hod carrier in New York.

One of the men in their group dropped his basket and took off, scrambling across the freshly laid rocks. He had almost reached the other side before a bullet toppled him. Like a silent movie, the impact stopped him, and then, in slow motion, he fell over the embankment.

In the resulting confusion, Javier took the opportunity and walked towards the truck with the other artisans. No one objected so he kept going. He didn't know why he chose to volunteer. Perhaps he had a death wish but the urge to relieve the monotony of carrying rocks to rebuild the road drove him on. As he pulled himself up onto the lorry's tray, he felt a sense of exhilaration only freedom might bring. Even freedom through death might be preferable to slow starvation and slave labour.

The truck did not return to Mirada de Ebro but carried the men to San Pedro de Cardeña. Armed guards led the prisoners into a building and hustled them into a room with benches and sinks lining the walls. A copper vat boiled on a stove. The guards told them to strip and chuck their clothes into the boiling water. They then lined up for a kerosene wash down to kill off any remaining lice before being led naked to the river.

Javier reasoned they weren't being cleaned up to die. Something else was happening. After scrubbing his body with sand, he climbed out of the river and followed his naked comrades back to a building. They entered another room where second-hand, but clean, civilian clothes had been laid out. They dressed and followed a guard who led them to another building.

It was an infirmary, although there were no patients. A line of empty cots, with folded blankets on straw mattresses, filled the room. The guard indicated they should each make a bed.

When they were done, they filed out into a courtyard where they were told to sit and wait. Three guards were now in attendance.

A little while later, a friar in a brown robe arrived and gave them a sermon about their duty to Spain, to God and to Franco. He proceeded to glorify General Franco's victories and gave an account of the Nationalist victory in securing the Madrid-to-Extremadura Road. Now, he said, they must pray for the glorious army, who would soon take the Palencia and Santander provinces.

After the homily and a few prayers, guards brought in a vat of weak coffee and some stale bread. A last supper? Javier kept his head down and said nothing, not willing to draw attention by speaking.

Car tires sounded in the driveway, and a bell rang, its melody now flattened and tuneless. Past artillery fire had taken a bite from its brass leaving a sound like the clattering of tin cans. The prisoners looked up expecting further orders, but all three guards were staring out the windows.

The men resumed sucking on hard crusts dipped into lukewarm coffee. It tasted of old dregs but was an unexpected luxury all the same. A few minutes went by and then another disturbance at the door caused the guards to leap to attention.

The warden walked in, followed by a lieutenant in the uniform of Franco's army. One of the guards shouted an order. The prisoners stood to present the fascist salute as they had been taught. Flat hands only. Clenched fists punishable by restricted rations.

Javier had his hand out level with the row of extended hands, when he saw Mark. He actually existed, or at least someone who looked a great deal like him. Although this man gave off the air of a journalist, one who wore his mantel with confidence; a poise that came with success and the expectation borne of accomplishment. A camera bag hung over his shoulder, and he held a notebook and pencil in hand.

Javier's hand remained a fraction too long in horizontal fascist salute. He dropped it, standing to attention with the other prisoners, eyes fixed on the warden who spoke too quietly for Javier to hear. He tried to focus, rather than merely stare open mouthed at Mark.

The group of men moved closer, and the warden indicated the prisoners, saying in English, 'These are some of the men captured after the fall of Bilboa. You understand, there are few here now. This is merely a transit camp. These men are recovering from battle wounds, but all are artisans, very valuable skills. When they are fully recovered, they are keen to begin rebuilding Spain for the glory of God and Franco.

Of course, other prisoners have already passed through here, but they were selected for military duty, labouring, farming or factory work depending on their abilities. Many have already returned to the front, keen to fight for El Caudillo and our beloved Spain. Arriba España.'

On cue the prisoners dutifully chanted, 'Una España, Grande España, Libre España. Franco, Franco, Franco!'

Mark gazed at the men, his eyes brushing past Javier as if he did not recognise him. He spoke to the warden. 'I would like to interview them individually. Do any of them speak English?'

The Lieutenant stepped forward. 'I can translate.'

Mark shook his head. 'Things get lost in translation and I don't want to misrepresent anything. Captain Bolín would not be happy.'

The Lieutenant's shoulders snapped back with the implied criticism.

Mark placed a hand on his shoulder. 'This work, translating for these Red fiends, is beneath you. One of the prisoners can do this job and if I uncover anything useful for you, I will let you know. Besides, you have not had lunch or a siesta. Perhaps the warden can arrange something for you now.' He glanced at the warden and winked. 'You would not offer to translate Sénior.'

The warden looked shocked, and the Lieutenant's eyes narrowed as if attempting to read Mark's motives. Then he glanced at the line of prisoners. 'You are right. They are peasants.'

'But perhaps one here can speak English.'

Javier watched the exchange, recognising Mark gave him an opportunity, but also aware that if he said he spoke English there would be questions asked.

How could a conscripted Basque Army Private, a peasant from the land, know another language. He might be expected to know Castilian, and perhaps one or two of the dialects of the Basque language. Some may even speak French. But to speak English would require a plausible story and at that moment he could not think of one. It occurred to him that as a peasant he was also unlikely to be a skilled artisan. But he couldn't think about that. There were just too many contradictions to deal with right now.

To his relief another man stepped forward. 'I speak English,' he said.

Javier held his breath. How would the warden react?

The warden merely nodded.

Javier exhaled. Perhaps he should have spoken up. Too late now.

The warden said, 'I do not think individual interviews are necessary. Besides there is little time left. You can talk as a group, and now you have your translator, Sénior Anders. When you have finished here,' he summoned one of the guards, 'this man will show you around their quarters for your photographs. 'He held out a hand to the Lieutenant and the two of them walked out, leaving Mark under the protection of the guards.

Mark tightened his jaw unsure how he might have a private conversation with Javier. Nevertheless, he introduced himself to his translator as if he were relying on him to organise the interview.

The man said his name was Pedro Pérez.

Mark said, 'Can you ask the men to gather around the table?'

Pedro turned to the men and spoke in Castilian. 'You will sit here at the table, but you will only tell this reporter the things Friar Ortega talked about earlier. Your duty to God and Spain, your respect for General Franco and the glorious Nationalist victories.'

Mark found it difficult to maintain a straight face at the translation. A spy in the prisoners' midst. He assumed the prisoners had also made the connection, so he didn't have much hope for the man's continuing breath, neither did he feel an ounce of sympathy for his inevitable fate.

While the men arranged the seats around the table, Javier manoeuvred towards him. Mark made sure he sat beside Javier. So far so good. There was a guard at each door and one who stood behind Mark. How to get rid of him?

He placed his camera and notebook on the table in front of him and asked the group. 'Do any of you play a musical instrument? I would like to get some shots of the group singing.'

Pedro translated. No one said anything but one of the guards standing at the exit stepped forward and spoke to the translator.

Pedro turned to Mark. 'He will play the guitar.'

'Great,' Mark nodded. 'Can he bring it in here?'

The guard looked at the other two guards and then nodded.

As he walked away the guard behind Mark took his place at the exit.

Mark asked each of the men around the table their name, where they were from, and how they were being treated.

As each man spoke, Mark wrote in pencil on his note pad, angling it so that Javier might see his words, *Hang in there, mate. Will get you out of here.*

Mark wrote down a prisoner's name followed by the words, *Three weeks. Be ready next time you see me and the next night after that.*

He wrote down another name, followed by, *Carmen is fine.*

He added another name, followed by *Black powder in brown paper, use as distraction to get away.*

From the corner of his eye, he saw Javier frown. Never mind. He'd work it out. He wrote on the pad. *Will have transport waiting.*

Javier's turn to speak arrived, and he spoke in Castilian, the language Franco demanded, 'I am Alvaro Ruiz a mechanical engineer from Reinosa. Tomorrow, I go north to do my duty, to resupply the brave soldiers, who will die for the liberation of Palencia. For the glory of God and Spain. Viva Franco. Libre Santana. ¡Arriba España!'

Pedro translated the first bit, left off naming Reinosa and changed Palencia to Biscay.

Mark understood the words, although he wasn't sure what Javier tried to communicate. Did he mean the Nationalists were planning to take Palencia next? That would make sense, but the bit about Reinosa remained a mystery. Perhaps that would be the road travelled by Franco's troops.

Reinosa was a town in the Santander province, between Burgos and the city of Santander. If harboured an armaments centre for the Republic. Were the Nationalists planning to wrest it from Republican control? And what did Javier mean with his claim to be a mechanical engineer? It was an odd choice although if the Nationalists took Reinosa, that is where the skills of a mechanical engineer might be useful.

He merely nodded and moved on to the next man. Once all the prisoners had spoken, Mark tidied up his notes asking further questions, rubbing out the incriminating words, and writing notes over the top of the smudges.

The guard entered and held out the guitar.

Mark picked up his camera and asked the translator if he would sing.

Asking Pedro to sing was a childish double entendre, which he hoped Javier would understand. Although he had spoken English all his life and would surely recognise how Pedro had skewed his words. If he didn't know Pedro was a snitch before, he would know now. Besides, Red prisoners and the fascist guards singing together would make a sentimental portrait, appealing to Bolín's nationalistic sentiment.

Mark directed the two men to sit on a grassy slope outside. They all trooped into the sunshine. He took photos of the men, standing in small huddles, watching the singers.

When the song ended, he asked he could see their sleeping quarters. While the guards chivvied the prisoners, Mark slipped Javier the brown paper parcel of black powder.

Inside the dormitory, the beds were laid out in rows along the room with an aisle between each row. The beds were of the hospital variety. This was an infirmary, rather than a dormitory. More propaganda. But none of this was about truth or reality. It was merely a claimed position that had not been, nor could it be, disputed.

He fiddled with his camera while the prisoners each peeled off to stand by a bed. The camera flash brightened the dim interior, and at the same time, drew attention away from Javier, whom he hoped would take the opportunity to hide the black powder.

After leaving San Pedro de Cardeña, Mark spent the next seven days traipsing around some of the Biscay battle fields, carrying out Bolin's assignment. The tour took him from Durango to Guernica to Bilbao. Destruction of towns, cities and people was commonplace in this new kind of total warfare, which targeted civilians, but nothing had prepared him for the horror of Guernica.

Mark's triumph, at finally reaching his destination, collapsed as he witnessed the distressed, and hollow-eyed, civilians mostly women and children, eking out an existence among the blackened corpses of their homes. He managed to speak to a group of women before Lieutenant García chased them away. Accounts of a deluge of fire, three hours of bombing, three quarters of the town's inhabitants burned to death or machined gun while they fled. The deliberate killing of women and children sheltering in churches from the fire storm. Now only ash and ruins were left, and Nationalist troops took any available food.

He hid his emotion behind the shelter of his camera lens as his guide and minder, boasted of the Nationalist's conquests and reiterated the Nationalist position that the Reds had devasted the town before they had fled.

'You know Basques are all miners. They carry black power and dynamite in their packs. They left fuel and set blasts so that when our troops arrived nothing was left. This is what these savages do to their own people.'

It took all of Mark's self-control not to throttle the man.

They moved on to Bilbao where García showed him some of the fortifications the nationalists had overcome. He recruited a local group of soldiers to reenact glorious scenes, for Mark to photograph. In comparison to Guernica, Bilbao had not been annihilated. Still its citizens had endured famine and relentless bombing campaigns for months before Franco's troops had marched into the subdued city.

Division XXIII di Marzo were in Bilbao, and Luigi Vecoli greeted Mark like an old friend. Once again, he invited Mark to stay at the Italian Officer's quarters. Mark was relieved to shed García's company for an evening.

After dinner was over, and Mark and his convenient friend, the newly minted Major Vecoli, had consumed two bottles of wine between them, Luigi suggested they retire for the night.

He raised his glass. 'To the end of Biscay's resistance. You print that in your newspaper.' He took a long drink of what remained in his glass, and his eyes misted. 'They are brave soldiers.'

'Your men?'

'Eusko Gudarostea '

'The Basque Army?' Mark's brow creased.

'Si.' Vecoli nodded. 'They fought well, and when they retreated they left Bilbao intact for their people to live. They demolished only one bridge. Even the telephone exchange was not destroyed. Now we can connect to the rest of the world. This is a moral thing to do, although foolish.'

'Isn't killing the prisoners the wrong thing to do then?'

'Why wrong? This is war, and those Red devils kill too many of my soldiers. Now, they must all die.' He slammed his empty glass down on the table. 'I must sleep. There is still work to do. We have superior air and manpower, more than twice their numbers, but the terrain advantages the Reds.'

Mark inhaled and, with thudding pulse, said, 'Maybe Franco will give you a medal for capturing Reinosa.

Vecoli frowned. 'That is not my men. I have not heard of its fall.' He paused his mouth pursed. 'I have heard the Navarrese brigades have Reinosa surrounded, but not of their victory. Where did you hear such news?

Mark drank the last of the wine in his glass and said with as much nonchalance as he could muster, 'Gossip, mate. You know how journalists are. Always looking for a story. Whoever takes Reinosa will be heroes. Frano will hand out medals for the victors.'

'Medals, pah! He talks of monuments to the dead.' Vecoli smiled. 'Promotion is more useful for the living. I will be a colonel by the time I get home.' He chuckled. 'Good night my friend. Sleep well, for tomorrow we have more work to do. You will travel with us?'

Mark sighed. 'Tomorrow I must go back to Burgos. Then, back to London. I am not sure how long it will be before I am back in Spain.'

What he didn't say was that he had to warn the Republic about the imminent assault, and the plan to capture the armaments factory at Reinosa. Now that Vecoli had confirmed Reinosa was a target, he was certain that was what Javier had been trying to tell him.

Paris to London

Mark submitted the photomontage of the Biscay war sites to Bolín before returning to Charles's apartment to pack and say goodbye. He suggested they have a farewell dinner at El Campeador café.

Charles arched his brow at Mark. 'While the cat's away, eh? But I wouldn't if I were you. You are heading back to London, and Beatrice, I presume. Surely, you don't want to contract the pox before seeing your fiancée.'

'I said dinner!' Mark grinned. 'I am not about to muscle in on von Graff's woman. She was pretty keen on you though.'

Charles held up his hands in mock protest. 'Quelle horreur! Von Graff would skin me alive. But no harm in dinner. The food was rather good and the atmosphere amenable. All right then, but I have a meeting at seven. I might have a role to play here, for British interests, but that's not for public consumption. Keep it under your hat, old chap. I'll meet you at the café at 9 o'clock. A celebration perhaps.'

'I'll see you then.'

That evening Mark made his way to the café, arriving at 8.30 pm. He spoke quietly and rapidly to Carmen when she brought a jug of wine, explaining what he knew about the imminent assault on Reinosa. He suggested the Republic might consider bombing the Burgos aerodrome, while all its planes were on the ground.

'The time to do it is when Franco holds the Mass in Salamanca to give thanks for the Vatican recognition. All eyes will be on the event and planes will be on the tarmac with little concentrated oversight. The distraction will give them a chance.'

She nodded and walked off. Mark stared moodily into the wine. Had she understood? Should he call her back? She had managed to stay alive this long; she must be good at what she did.

Still, disabling a military aerodrome so far behind enemy lines was no easy task. Planes would be spotted long before they were in range. If not bombs from the air, Burgos was certainly out of range for Republican artillery, so that left sabotage. Even so, many things could go wrong.

Charles arrived ten minutes after nine, brimming with good news, which he said he would only share if Mark swore to keep it between the two of them.

'I am to be appointed to support Sir Robert Hodgson, when he takes up his role here representing the British government in Burgos later in the year. It hasn't been announced, but it will be soon.'

'Congratulations mate. Who is this bloke?'

'A retired British diplomat, the British government has appointed to represent their interest here.'

'They must be convinced the Nationalists will win.'

'Aren't you?'

Mark nodded. 'I have been for a while now, but not everyone shared my sentiment.'

'Well, you were right my friend, and I will be in on the action from the ground floor. Ambassadorship, here I come.'

'That calls for another jug of wine.'

This is what Denton had mentioned previously, and it seemed Charles had wrangled his way into the fringes of the diplomatic service, as he said he would. Mark didn't doubt he'd rise rapidly through its ranks.

'Of course, this will not interfere with my financial advisory role to you and Cousin Beatrice. But you will understand, assuming a diplomatic persona will make me more acceptable to Clara's family. After all, that is what her Uncle is.'

Mark merely nodded. Von Graff was a lot more than a diplomat, but he wasn't going to burst Charles's bubble.

Carmen avoided their table for the rest of the evening. Smart woman, maintaining professionalism, while he remained a jittery novice in this game of espionage.

The next day, Lieutenant Garcia drove Mark to the border at Irún. Mark was glad to see the last of him. He crossed into Hendaye and boarded the first of several trains that would take him to Paris.

He arrived at Gare Montparnasse the following day, gritty eyed, and tired, but he had no time to rest. Not far from the station, he found a reasonable hotel. He booked a room for the night, promising to return within the hour with his passport, although he had no intention of returning.

He then found a large department store and bought himself a plain stainless-steel wristwatch with a leather wrist band. Jewellery and personal possessions held little appeal, until he had been locked up in that Madrid cell, unable to distinguish night from day. Now, like his camera, a watch had become a necessity. After strapping it on, he exited the store, from a different door, onto a different street, and boarded a bus heading for the Louvre Museum.

Once the bus had crossed the Seine, he alighted and walked along the river embankment towards Pont Neuf. Once more he crossed the river and tracked towards the Pont de l'Archevêch. When he reached the bridge he crossed the river again, this time heading back to the Notre-Dame Cathedral. No one followed him. Still, one test remained. A visit to the Cathedral.

Once inside, he remembered to genuflect and cross himself. If he had missed a tail, they might think he was merely a good Catholic paying his respects to an iconic symbol of power.

After fifteen minutes of contemplation beneath the gothic arches and chandeliers, he had not seen anyone who might be interested in him. He arose and walked toward another exit, his footfalls assertive across the chequered floor.

He crossed the Pont au Double and meandered along several roads until he found a café on the Saint-Germain boulevard, filled with the lunch time crush. The air, warm and still with a bold sun high in a cloudless sky, enhanced the river odour. He lost his appetite and ordered Pastice.

If anyone followed him, they were good at their job, but he wouldn't get sloppy. When he finished the Pastice he paid and left the restaurant, climbing aboard the next bus that trundled down the Rue du Sommerard. He jumped off two blocks later, stopped to gaze into the window of a bookshop, and checked the reflections on the street behind him.

After a few minutes, he crossed the road and walked along the Rue de la Sorbonne until he found the Chapelle Saint-Ursule. Inside, he took off his hat, genuflected and crossed himself again before finding a pew near Richelieu's Tomb. He sat down placing his hat on the bench. Then he waited.

After thirty minutes he picked up his hat, and was about to rise, when a man genuflected in the aisle adjacent to his pew and took the seat behind him.

'Do not turn around,' he said in a low voice, the inflection eastern European. Probably Russian. Certainly not Spanish.

Mark remained as he was, staring at the tomb.

'You have the film?'

Mark said, 'I was told a man from the Spanish embassy would meet me.'

'I am he.'

'You are not Spanish.'

'Nevertheless, I am your man.'

'I need to talk to someone from the Republic.'

'I am with the Republic. I will pass on your message.'

'Not possible.'

'This was the deal.'

Mark turned around and faced the man. 'It was not the deal. You are not from the Republic.'

'Do not look at me. Someone might be watching.'

'No one is watching—unless you were followed.'

The man shrugged. 'I act for the Republic.'

'You act for Stalin. I want to talk to someone from the Spanish Embassy.'

Mark rose and stalked out of the church, forgetting on the way to genuflect. But then no one watched. Of that he was certain.

The Russian followed him, catching up as Mark reached the street. 'If you go to the Embassy, your cover is blown. Franco's people watch.'

'Shit!' Mark sat on a nearby bench.

'What is the problem?' The Russian dusted the surface of the bench with a handkerchief before he lowered himself to it. He straightened the creases on immaculately tailored and pressed trousers and adjusted his suit jacket before tucking the hanky back in his pocket. 'You know I act for the Republic.' His face expressed a sense of hurt at Mark's unfriendliness.

'How do I know that?'

'I understood you were the one who designed and agreed to this deal. A true comrade, one we are advised to keep in the shadows.'

'They told you that.' He paused. 'I agreed to carry out some surveillance for the Spanish Republic not Russia.'

'Yes, but the terms of the agreement were made with my comrades in the NKVD in Madrid. They sent me because it is sometimes hard for them to trust others to do the job right.'

'If I give you the photos you will send them to the Republican Ministry for War?'

'Of course.'

'Not Russia.'

'Certainly, they will go to Russia also.'

Mark sighed. It didn't seem like he had much choice. He wished he knew how to navigate this issue. He had formulated a plan, hoping to inveigle the Republic's help, but now, with only the NKVD as intermediaries, that plan seemed fantastic. He couldn't ask the Russians. Even if they agreed, they would demand too high a price. Javier's extraction would require a rethink.

He stuck his hand into his coat pocket and pulled out a roll of film. 'These are the installations around Burgos, or those I managed to access anyway.'

'What else can you tell me.'

'The Nationalists are planning to take the Santander province and after that, Asturias. They have 90,000 men. The Republicans have less than half that. Franco took more than Ten thousand of our men prisoner when they took Bilbao. The battle for the Palencia and Santander provinces will begin soon, if it hasn't begun already.'

The man nodded. 'The terrain will be difficult.'

'Not for the Condor Legion. They will simply bomb the Republican forces into submission.' Mark continued. 'From what I can make out they still have more than two hundred aircraft, mostly German and Italian planes, with an airfield outside of Burgos. Unless Russia sends more planes and pilots, the Nationalists will have free access to the skies above Northern Spain.

I have marked the aerodromes on a map in one of the photos on the film.' He paused. 'I also understand there is to be a requiem mass in Salamanca to give thanks for Vatican recognition and welcome the newly appointed Vatican charge d'affaires. It is planned to coincide with a renewed assault on Madrid. All the details are on the map. This will be the time to attack the airbase and wipe out most of their planes. It will take the Nationalists time to replace the planes, which are smuggled in from Germany via the port at Vigo.'

The man nodded, his narrow face bland. Mark had no idea whether he had absorbed the information.

'You have done well.' He slid an envelope from his pocket and pushed it along the bench toward Mark.

'What's this?'

'A small reward.'

Mark stood up. 'I don't want it.'

'You are going back. You will need expenses, and we must make a time for the next meeting.'

'No mate, I have kept my end of the bargain. There won't be a next time.'

Mark walked off and did not look back.

The clandestine nature of the meeting and handing over the roll of film to the Russian, and then the man trying to pay him, left a bad taste in his mouth. He found a bar and ordered another Pastice. The aniseed cooled his mouth and washed the sense of distaste away. He'd paid his debt, that was all.

By the time he left the bar, and found a cheap pensione near the Gare du Nord, the sun had sunk in the west. He handed over his passport and paid in advance for a room with a window. He never again wanted to sleep in a windowless room.

The room at the back of the building, overlooking a courtyard, wasn't as bad as he had expected although not worth the price. It had a basin in one corner, a chair and a narrow bed under a small window through which he saw the scaffolding of a fire escape. Not much of a view but at least it let in light.

That night he found a café where he ate dinner and then returned to his lodgings. Traffic and people slowed his pace, so he shortened his stride to ambled along the pavement under streetlights flickering in the muggy air.

When he entered his room, he stopped short. The place was a mess. The drawers had been pulled out, the mattress overturned, the wardrobe doors stood open. His suitcase had vanished along with its matching travel bag. Worst yet, his camera case, long distance lens, and the flash attachment, were gone. Burglary or something else?

If something else, who? NKVD or Francoists? There was no one else. But surely the bloke he'd met today wouldn't have done this. Mark had kept his part of the bargain. Had he been followed despite his careful counter surveillance efforts? Although, once the job was done, he had relaxed his vigilance. Damn. He was no good at this cloak and dagger stuff.

Of course, this might be a regular burglary. Should he report the theft? Not to the police. That would hold him up, but perhaps the receptionist might have seen something, although it would have to wait until morning. The reception was now closed.

He should be outraged but all he felt was despair at the realisation that the bag with his rolls of film was gone. He straightened the chair and sat down. The rest of the stuff could be replaced but not the film. That was his livelihood. He unhitched his camera from his shoulder. There was an almost a full roll of film still in it. What did it have on it. Was it enough? It would have to be. He sighed and got up to straighten the mattress.

A clattering noise sounded outside, like a dustbin had fallen over in the courtyard. Mark looked out the window and saw a man with his suitcase turn the corner. He must have just missed the intruder. He tried to lift the window, but it held fast.

He ran from the room and leaped down the stairs to the ground floor. He raced out the front door and pelted down the street, dodging pedestrians, heading in the direction he had last seen the man. When he arrived at the corner the man had gone. Presumably, the bloke would try to move as far from the scene of his crime as quickly as possible.

Mark ran a city block before he saw him ahead, turning another corner. He sprinted after him, before slowing. Mark wanted his stuff back, but he also wanted to know who had sent him. He followed leaving a short distance between them.

The thief maintained his focus on the road ahead, walking towards the Canal Saint-Martin. He reached a pedestrian bridge spanning the canal, but instead of crossing it, he ducked beneath and disappeared into the gloom.

Mark sprinted to the bridge. He found the thief kneeling on the ground, rummaging through the open suitcase. The camera bag and the holdall lay on the ground next to him.

Mark stood over him. 'You looking for something, mate? That's my stuff you've got there.'

The thief glanced around then leaped to his feet, the open suitcase swinging from his hand. It collected Mark on the left side of his head. The suitcase clattered to the ground.

Mark staggered back, partly blinded by the swipe.

The thief turned to scoop up Mark's suit jacket.

Mark's vision cleared and he threw himself forward, tackling the man around his legs.

The man staggered and fell, before he rolled onto his back and drove his boot heel into Mark's shoulder. It gave him a moment to wriggle free.

Mark staggered to his feet.

The thief ran and tripped over the camera case.

Mark was on him again.

They struggled until Mark grabbed him around his neck in a choke hold. The man bucked and heaved but Mark was bigger and stronger from a lifetime of labour and growing up defending himself and his mates in pubs and street brawls.

The thief sagged, and Mark slackened his grip.

After a minute, the thief said in French, 'Take it. It's worthless rubbish anyway. Leave me and take it.' His pronunciation was accented like he wasn't from these parts although it was hard to tell as his voice was muffled against Mark's arm.

'I'm a bit insulted by that.' Mark said. 'Where are you from, mate?'

'What is this?'

'Just tell me where you are from. I'm interested. I am from Australia, and I can tell by your accent you are not French. So out of politeness, humour me.'

'I am Kazakh from Sozak.'

'Never heard of it, but it sounds like somewhere in Soviet Russia.'

The man squirmed, and Mark tightened his hold.

The thief sagged and held up a hand in surrender.

Mark let up the pressure again. 'You don't like the Soviets?'

The man coughed, and said, 'That Stalin is the devil. Those Soviets killed my family and drove me from our village.'

Mark gambled. 'Why work for them now?'

The man's body softened and seemed to lose the will to fight. 'He offered money if I brought him your stuff. He only wanted film or papers, but I have found none. He promised I could keep the rest.'

'How much did he offer.'

'Fifty francs.'

Mark's mind flicked to the contents of his wallet. 'I tell you what, I have a one hundred franc note in my wallet. Mark figured that would be about as much as an unskilled labourer would earn in a week. 'You can have it, if you tell me who the man is, or what he looks like.'

The thief twisted his neck. 'You can let me go now. I will tell you what you want to know.'

'Tell me first and then I will let you go.'

'He works for the Russian Embassy here in Paris. He makes me work for him or he will tell the French I am a criminal, in this country illegally.'

'What's his name.'

'I only know him as Oshurkov, but that is not his real name.'

'What does he look like?'

The man shrugged. 'He is average in everything, but he likes young men, boys. Ten years is best for him.'

It took a moment for this information to penetrate Mark's brain. He dropped his hands and stepped away, as if he had to distance himself from the messenger. He knew blokes who fancied men all right. There were a few of them in the cane, but so long as they didn't bother him, he reckoned live and let live. But kids! That was something he could not countenance.

The thief turned and held out his hand. 'My money.'

Mark handed over a hundred franc note, and the thief turned away as if to leave. Then, quick as a London pickpocket, he grabbed a bundle of clothing lying on the ground and took off.

Mark watched him go. That was his best suit, but clothes were replaceable. A least he had his film back. He picked up his hold-all, weighed it in his hand and guessed they were all there.

He would check when he got back to the hotel. This place was too public. The thief had simply not known where to look. He picked up a few stray articles of clothing and placed them back in the case before collecting the camera case from where the thief had kicked it.

When he got back to his room, he emptied the holdall of underwear, socks, handkerchiefs, and toiletries. He slid his fingers across the lining, until he found the two levers. He pressed them, one up and one down, until he heard the click. Mark lifted out the false floor.

With a sigh of relief, he replaced the floor before replacing the clothing and other articles he had taken out. Then he placed a chair under the locked door handle before straightening the mattress. He fell onto the unmade bed, fully clothed. The holdall and camera, now back in its bulky case, lay within reach.

The next afternoon, he caught an overnight train to London, arriving at Victoria station in the rain. Not the usual London drizzle, but something akin to the tropical deluges Mark had been used to in North Queensland, except here the rain was cold.

The tube station looked crowded and not a place for a man carrying what Mark's holdall held. He opted for a cab although usually he would walk to Denton's office.

When he eventually managed to hail one, the Cabbie said cheerfully, 'Hope you aren't going far mate. Half of Knightsbridge is underwater, and Gord knows where else.'

'Has it been like this long?' Mark tracked the water running down the window with his finger.

'Just started again... Chucked it down last night, but before that it was as dry as my sainted mother's Sunday roasts.'

Mark smiled.

'Where to mate.'

'Ah... Broadway.'

'Number?'

Mark didn't know the number and frowned.

'St James Park station or Victoria Road end?' The Cabbie said turning fully to look at Mark.

'St James Park will do fine.'

'Righty ho.

Mark got out at St James Park Tube station and crossed the road. Denton expected him and took him along several corridors, to a small conference room.

He put his suitcase down and placed the holdall, now minus his underwear and toiletries, onto a table.

'You got them?'

Mark nodded.

'No problems.'

He shook his head.

'Excellent job. Sit down. Do you want a cup of tea? Better yet, let me just clear the deck here and we'll get a spot of lunch at the club.' Denton peered at Mark. 'That's a nasty shiner blooming along your jaw.'

Mark ran his fingers along the tender spot. 'Is it that obvious?'

'Not terribly, but I can see the swelling and a purple bruise beginning to deepen in colour. Who was the knave who did that?'

'It's a long story. Look sir, do you mind if I find somewhere to bathe and change. I can fill you in on the details later. I would like to call in on Beatrice as soon as I can make myself presentable.'

'I'll ring the club, and you can stay there if you would like. I know you have not received your membership but that will be a formality I can assure you. These things take time.'

Mark shook his head. 'I would feel more comfortable at the place I usually stay.'

'It goes without saying you are always welcome to stay with us.'

'Thanks sir, but that might not be wise given the circumstances.'

'You are right of course, but I don't think Beatrice understands.'

Mark smiled. 'I'll see you later. I have a bit to explain, and I need your advice.'

'Come to dinner. I too have a bit to tell you, and another mission for your role as journalist, if you are interested. We can talk tonight.'

Mark walked down the stairs and stopped in the foyer. It was still raining but not so heavily now. He opened the door and stepped onto the pavement, turned up his collar and tilted his hat to shield his face.

There was an empty cab rank across the road, and he waited for a car to pass before racing across to shelter under the building's awning. He wiped the rain from his eyes and found a familiar figure walking towards him.

'Lieutenant Laskin! You're in London.'

Laskin joined Mark under the awning, lowered his umbrella and said, 'Captain now, my dear Mark, and you must call me Timofey or Tim if you like. Most British people prefer Tim.'

'Ah yes, I forgot. Congratulations.' Mark's mind reeled. Was Laskin following him? 'Mate, I didn't thank you for getting me out of that jam in Madrid.'

Laskin waved his hand. 'A misunderstanding: I am assured.'

'Still... I wouldn't have got out if it hadn't been for you and perhaps your father's intervention, but what are you doing in London?'

'I am a hero now, thanks to you for saving me. We are, as the British say, even-Steven. And I have finally achieved my desire to have a post at the London embassy. A junior post, you understand.' He shrugged 'Nonetheless, I am here.'

Mark took in Laskin's three-piece suit, the fob and old-fashioned high collar, the black umbrella and the Homberg and smiled. 'The quintessential gentleman about town.'

Laskin preened. 'You think I look all right?'

'You look like a toff, mate. Tip top.'

Laskin's face gleamed. 'But you have also been of service to matushka Rossiia and we are grateful. Perhaps if you have time now, you will let me buy you lunch. We can renew our friendship.'

'Mate, I am sorry, but I am in a hurry. I have my copy to get to the newspaper and then I am going to see my fiancée.'

'Ah yes, the beautiful Beatrice. I recall our conversation. You have been to see her grandfather.' He glanced across at the building across the road.

Cold stole through Mark's veins, and he became still as his brain searched for a rejoinder. A cab arrived and he waved it down before turning to Laskin. 'Great to see you again Tim. I'll be in touch. I can find you at the embassy, right?'

Laskin nodded. 'Yes. Call me on the telephone and I will meet you.'

A Plan of Sorts

That night, after dinner, Beatrice sat next to Mark on the sofa, and across from her grandfather. Earlier, she had asked if Mark wanted to speak with Grandfather alone, but he asked her to stay, and Grandfather had nodded. She stayed, hearing about his time in the north, and his short journey home via Paris.

When he'd finished his account Grandfather said, 'I had the photos developed this afternoon. They and the maps and inventories you brought back are invaluable. Well done.'

She could barely take it all in. Then Mark explained the theft in Paris and his meeting this morning with Laskin.

Denton leaned forward. 'I am not surprised they know where I work. They wouldn't be much good at their jobs if they didn't. They obviously think you might be working for the British, which is why they had your room searched. They would have known you only gave them what you had agreed to give them and were looking for the rest of it. It wouldn't surprise me if Laskin tries to recruit you.'

Grandfather thought that the Russians were having Mark followed and wanted to recruit him. Her internal voice went up an octave in the Australian way. But why would they be interested? Neither of them explained that part and she was hesitant to interrupt with questions.

The whole tale seemed a tad unbelievable or perhaps, as she expected, Mark left out all the salient parts that made sense of the story. She had known Mark would be carrying out some tasks for her grandfather, but this was more than that. He was beginning to sound like grandfather's spy.

She put her hand to her mouth. Of course, that is exactly what he was.

A surge of anger ran through her that her family were again using him for their own ends, but she stopped. He wouldn't do anything with which he didn't agree. He never did.

Mark stopped speaking for a moment and took a sip of his brandy, placing it back on the occasional table, before glancing at her. 'Are you all right listening to this? All this talk of work and war must be boring. You might like to do something else.'

Boring! Who was this man? Beatrice shook her head. 'I'm fine. Can I get anyone another drink?'

The two men shook their heads, but she got up and walked over to the drinks trolley to pour herself a stiff brandy. She hadn't been going to have a drink, but this was too much to absorb while sober.

She stopped as Mark's words cut through her thoughts. Javier, a prisoner of war! She hadn't known Javier well, but she had liked him immensely when they had met at a dance hall in Mourilyan and he'd asked her to dance. She recalled he'd been a bit gruff, with his slow drawl, but his American manners were endearing.

That had been during the strike in 1935. The strikers' wives had arranged dances to take their minds off the difficulties and deprivations they were suffering, all thanks to her own father.

At least, Javier was still alive. So many foreign fighters had died in Spain. She read about it in the papers almost daily, wanting to weep at the waste of life, and for what? She didn't understand war.

She sat back down on the sofa as Mark said, 'I have a plan to get him out, but I will need your help.'

Grandfather nodded encouragement as Mark explained his plan.

When he had finished Mark said, 'I will need a passport and maybe press credentials to get him out. He's American so the American embassy...'

Grandfather leaned forward. 'I can help with that. Leave it to me son. But it's a dangerous mission to carry out by yourself.'

Beatrice said, 'Can't Charles help?'

Denton shook his head. 'It's not common knowledge but Charles has got himself a job with the British mission to Burgos.'

'What mission?'

'The government is sending a consular agent to Nationalist Spain.'

Beatrice frowned. 'That's extraordinary. I thought working for the diplomatic service required exams and all sorts of bureaucratic processes, not to mention working one's way up the chain of command before getting a foreign posting.'

'Usually it does, but there are exceptions. Besides Charles sailed through the exams, some months ago. This is rather an unusual situation, but expedient. Charles not only has connections within the service from his time at Cambridge but is known and friendly with a number of the players in Franco's administration. He will smooth the way for the appointed agent.'

'Who is that?'

Denton said, 'Hodgson. But again, I must reinforce this is not public knowledge.'

Beatrice pursed her mouth. 'I thought he had retired.'

'He had but he's agreed to take on this post.'

'Did you know this Mark?'

Mark shook his head, not willing to expose Charles's confidence when he had promised he would say nothing. His mouth compressed into a thin line.

'There's something you are not saying.'

He took her hand. 'It's nothing, just that our values don't align. Even if he wasn't going to become a diplomat, I couldn't trust him to help me get Javier out. He is in favour of Franco winning this war and doesn't have much time for the Republicans, mostly because he thinks they are all communists. Won't agree they are a democratic nation fighting for their survival. He is also friendly with the Nazi regime, including wanting to marry the daughter of one Germany's biggest arms manufacturers. None of which is a crime, but it doesn't sit well with me.' He sighed. 'Oh, another thing... He also asked me to mention his credentials in relation to managing your investment portfolio, said it would give him credibility with Clara Hauser, the woman with whom he claims to be in love. But I wouldn't advise it.'

Grandfather watched Mark keenly, and Beatrice said, 'What scheme are you dreaming up now Granddad?'

Denton glanced across at her. 'Scheme!' He shook his head. 'But Mark is right not to trust the man, especially not with money.'

'What do you know, Grandfather?'

'Ah, nothing. It is just that Mark's caution aligns with my view of the man in his role in your mother's charity. Like Mark says, it is not something concrete. I find it merely advisable to remain cautious.'

'But won't you place Charles in a terrible position if you are caught, or even if they work out it is you who broke Javier out of prison?'

Mark frowned. 'Yes. I have been racking my brain to think of a way to get him out of Spain while I arrange things.'

'Can't you recall him on some pretext to do with the service Granddad?'

'He will not be working under my jurisdiction, but even so he has not yet taken up the position so it might incur too many questions if I were to intercede.'

Beatrice stared at the intervening coffee table as if it might provide an answer. Eventually, she said, 'Isn't there a diplomatic means to free Javier rather than risking Mark's life on a mission that may turn into a disaster?'

Denton nodded. 'There have been a few exchanges, but Mark's friend has cast himself as a Basque national and not one of the

International Brigade. That makes it tricky, if not dangerous, for him to now admit he is American.'

Mark grimaced. 'Franco's people shot the foreign fighters they captured when Javier's battalion surrendered. If he admitted to being an American they would shoot him as a spy.'

Beatrice covered her mouth. 'This is terrible. It seems so dangerous, Mark. I wish you would rethink going back again.'

'I must go back but I'll be fine. They think I am a Franco admirer, and I have made friends with some of the Italians fighting in Franco's forces. They all think I am one of them. But Javier is in danger. Any day he might be sent to the front to fight against his own side or worse. Even if he's just placed in a labour gang, he's in peril. Some gangs are worked to death. Even in the best scenarios the conditions for POWs are not good. I am not worried about my safety, but Javier might not survive.'

'Why now? You were not worried when Javier fought as a soldier.'

Mark frowned. 'I know it's odd, but that was his choice. This isn't.'

'I don't pretend to know what it's like, but I hear horror stories from my refugees. I'm afraid for you... If you return...'

Mark interjected, 'I will be perfectly safe, I promise. All I will do is orchestrating things in the background. There are a few Basque loyalists waging a silent war of resistance in Burgos right now. They will undertake the dangerous stuff. You must remember, Javier is not the only prisoner. Many other families have relatives in Franco's prisons, and they are just as keen to get them out.'

'But you will be safe.'

'Absolutely.'

'Then I will come with you.'

'No!' Both Mark and Denton chorused.

'Hear me out.' Even to her own ears her voice sounded sharp. She modified her tone. 'I have been thinking about this for some time. It is not a whim. It seems like Franco is winning, right.'

Both men nodded.

'Well then, if Franco wants the world to recognise him, he had better show his humanitarian side.'

'Not sure he has one,' Mark said.

Beatrice ignored him. 'The Red Cross has a delegation in Salamanca. Edith Pye said they are short of funding. I will go to talk to whomever I need to, to find out what humanitarian assistance I can provide to the refugees and displaced people through my fund-raising work in London.'

Denton sat back smiling, and she knew he would support her, but Mark shook his head.

'It's dangerous Beatrice. Franco and his people don't see the other side as human beings. They slaughter indiscriminately, women, children, old and young, innocent, or guilty, doesn't matter to Franco. If they oppose him, they are dead.'

'You think I don't know this. You think I don't hear the stories. But he's a devout Catholic. I will appeal to his religious superstitions. Besides, he wants belligerent recognition, and he knows who my grandfather is. Or if he doesn't now, he soon will. I know that will change nothing from the British perspective, but he doesn't know that. As I said before, you will not dictate terms in relation to my job or where I chose to go. You promised; remember.' She glanced at him sideways. 'And you need my help.

327

While I am there, I will find a means to get Charles out of Spain, while you put in place your rescue. They will not suspect you if I am there.'

Denton added. 'At least, they will hesitate to harm my granddaughter. I think it's a fine idea Mark.'

Mark sighed and turned to Denton. 'You said you had something you wanted to discuss with me.'

'I did.' Denton said. 'I had hoped you might travel to Switzerland in a few weeks, but perhaps you won't have time, given this mission to rescue your friend.'

'I hope it won't take more than two weeks. If the stories on the wire are true, there have been running battles across Palencia where the Nationalist 1st and 4th Navarrese brigades have the Republicans in a pincer movement. They have trapped them in a valley near Reinosa.'

'I heard the same thing. From what I can gather, the Republic's armaments factory in Reinosa has fallen into Nationalists hands. That will leave the Republicans critically short of weapons.'

Mark nodded. 'They are also short of air power and if they do what they did in Brunete, the Republic will open a new campaign to draw Franco away from the north. Not sure that worked well for Brunete, but they might try it to give the remnants of the Basque Army a chance to shore up Asturias. Even so, I reckon it won't be long before Franco takes the whole of the north. Then he will turn his forces towards the south. If I can't get in and out quickly, I may be too late.'

'In that case we should hire an aeroplane.' Mark's mention of air power had given Beatrice an idea.

'What?' Mark swung around to face her.

Denton laughed.

In a voice bordering on sullen she said, 'It is the fastest route and surely, if we have permission, no one will mind if we land at Burgos. You said there is an aerodrome nearby.'

'It is a military aerodrome. Besides, who do you think you might find foolish enough to fly a plane into Spain?'

'Foolish! I think not. It wouldn't be the first time. You told me yourself that Deutsche Luft Hansa fly in and out at will.'

'That's true.' He paused, but they fly from Berlin to Salamanca, not London to Burgos.'

Beatrice wasn't going to let him get away with dismissing her suggestions. She appealed to her grandfather to back her up.

Denton said, 'It is possible, but I have heard of a British pilot being shot at when he tried to land his passengers at Burgos, even though he had permission.'

Undaunted, Beatrice straightened her skirt. 'I shall call on Baron Geddes, Rio Tinto's chairman, for his support. Mother has always been a good friend to the man, and the family have a large holding of shares in his company. He must have some influence with Franco's people. I am sure he will be of assistance.' She turned to Denton. 'Perhaps you might prevail upon the Duke of Alba.'

Denton shook his head. 'I am afraid I cannot be involved in this. My position... The non-intervention pact...' He had the decency to give her an apologetic shrug.

She swung around to face Mark. 'You know the man. We could meet him together. I think he will expect some formality, otherwise I would be happy to approach him...'

'Hang on Beatrice. We need to think this through. It'll cost a fortune...' Mark face folded with worry.

Beatrice got up and paced the floor between the drinks trolley and the two men. Her blood pumped in her throat to the point she thought she might choke, but she kept her voice even and cheerful. 'I have thought this through. You are simply not keeping up. Granddad, if you can arrange the passport and papers for Javier, I will make the travel arrangement. Mark, you can arrange our visas and spend tomorrow sorting out your job requirements. I suggest we leave as soon as possible. Gosh this is thrilling. I've always wanted to see Spain. By the way, how are you planning to get Javier out?'

His face smoothed and he grinned, breaking the tension in the room. 'It would help if we had one or two of Rio Tinto's trucks...

She frowned. 'Geddes can't be compromised...'

'Of course not.' Mark grinned again. 'I planned to steal them from a quarry near Burgos. I confess, I appropriated some blank forms with Rio Tinto letterhead from Charles desk before I left, with this in mind.'

Over the next couple of days, Beatrice worked at lightning speed. Mark watched in awe of her organisational skills and single-minded determination. She had arranged an appointment with the head of the red cross delegation in Salamanca, had secured a letter of support from Fitz-James Stuart, along with permission to enter rebel-held Spain. Fitz-James Stuart assured her she would be quite safe on her travels throughout Franco held territory. He would personally make sure of that.

Mark convinced Dawson to commission another piece on Franco's advances in Northern Spain.

Earlier, when he and Beatrice had met with the Duke of Alba, he'd explained that while Beatrice was in Salamanca, he wanted to visit Asturias.

Fitz-James Stuart suggested he speak to Marquis del Moral, also currently in Salamanca.

And so, three days later, Mark found himself boarding a privately chartered de Havilland DH.90 Dragonfly, a biplane with a plywood monocoque shell and strengthened fuselage. It didn't sound at all safe and he felt his stomach seething as they arrived at Croydon airport south of London.

Beatrice scoffed at his concerns. After all, she had flown from Brisbane to London last year and claimed everyone flew now, rather than taking ship.

Mark didn't say, not everyone. Flying remained expensive. When Beatrice had done that trip with her father in 1936, it would have cost him a years' worth of wages to fly the Imperial Airways round trip from Brisbane to London and back again.

While he had more assets now, with his farm, business and a small share portfolio as well as his photography income, he could still not afford this kind of travel. Beatrice hadn't insisted on paying all the costs, she had just done it without consulting him. He didn't ask how much she had spent. He didn't want to know.

He lined her up, next to their pilot at the steps of the aircraft and took a photo before following her into the cabin. Their seats were behind the pilot with two more empty seats to their rear as the plane could accommodate four passengers.

They taxied along the tarmac, and he felt the lurch as their wheels left the ground. He glanced at Beatrice who gazed serenely ahead, while he barely managed to control his panic. He forced himself to look out of the porthole.

Outside the weather had cleared and, with bated breath, he gazed down at sunlit pastures of emerald and gold rushing beneath them. Dread turned into captivation. He breathed out. 'I can fly.'

Beatice leaned closer to him. 'What did you say. I can't hear you above the noise.'

He shook his head and grinned. A delirious surge of energy engulfing him, like the kid he'd been at eight when his dad taught him to shoot. He imagined flying the plane would be like that, an immense sense of power and control. He squeezed Beatrice's hand.

They flew on over the White Cliffs, and across the undulating steel-blue sea. Grey clouds gathered in the east, and a chill ran across his shoulders as they flew into northern France. The pilot would not enter Spanish air space but had agreed to fly them to Bordeaux. From there they would take a train to Hendaye, a route with which Mark was now familiar.

Charles had promised to meet them at Hendaye station and drive them across the border and on to Salamanca, where Beatrice had an appointment with the Red Cross. Mark felt his plan just might work.

Rescue

Beatrice awoke to the Salamanca sunshine streaming through her window. She stretched and sat up. Outside a skylark chirruped and trilled. She arose and walked to the window of the hotel in which they were staying.

Between the upright branches of a stand of trees, she spotted the cathedral, and across the road, people were seated at a café. Aside from the military uniforms and the occasional vehicle it hardly felt like a bloody and treacherous civil war raged in the country.

She dressed and put on her shoes just as someone knocked on her door.

Mark, camera slung over his shoulder said, 'I promised to meet Charles in the Plaza for breakfast. It's a lovely day.'

'Don't you have an appointment at the press office?'

'Later. We have plenty of time.'

When they arrived at the café, Charles stood up to greet them, saying, 'I must say I prefer Burgos to Salamanca.'

Beatrice gazed around the Plaza. 'They are not keen on flora, but the sandstone buildings are beautiful. Although, I do think more trees might soften the edges.'

'Monuments to Empire—no room for softened edges.' Mark said quietly as he pulled out a chair for her.

Charles laughed. 'Careful, you could get shot for less, but you are right. The grandeur is all about power.'

The waiter arrived and Mark ordered coffee and rolls.

Charles sat back down. 'So how did your meeting go with Dr Junod yesterday, Cousin?'

'Very moving. They simply do not have enough funding to carry out all the work they need to do here.' She gazed at Mark. 'I know I can make a difference.' She placed her reticule on her lap. 'Charles, how much influence do you have with the authorities? I understand you are friends with a few people in high places.'

Charles raised one eyebrow and looked at her sideways. 'What devious plans do you have brewing beneath that rather fetching head piece?'

Beatrice touched her straw hat. 'Is it awful?'

'Now, why would you think it awful when I have just called it fetching?'

'I know you, Cousin. You are usually at your most charming when you are being sarcastic.'

'Dear me. Am I that transparent? I will have to work on my technique. But you are right. The hat is a little dull.'

'It's appropriate, I think, for my mission.'

'Mission! My goodness.'

'Yes Charles, my mission. I want to help and for that I need you.'

'Good grief, what can I do?'

'You helped my mother with her charity, and Mark says you are friendly with all sorts of influential people, both in Spain and Germany. I am thinking of selling some of my shares.'

'To the Spanish and Germans?

'Don't be obtuse.'

Charles glanced at Mark as if to ask what on earth she was talking about, but at that moment the waiter returned with their coffee and breakfast rolls.

After the waiter had gone, she saw Charles wink at Mark as if in thanks. Her blood boiled. As if her fiancé would turn to treachery to influence her decisions on behalf of a cousin. She covered her rising colour behind her coffee cup.

Charles leaned toward her. 'You know I will help in any way I can, but I am not sure what you want me to do.'

'Thank you. Now, Mark assures me you know a lot about investments.' There was that smirk again. The man was insufferable. 'I have a large amount of money invested in Deutsche Munitionsfabrike. I understand you know the company owners or at least their daughter, and I need your advice.'

'Hmm.' Charles hummed.

'She patted her hair into place beneath her hat. 'Given views about Hitler's regime in Britain, I am not sure if I should sell my shares. I need rather a lot of cash to help the Red Cross, and those shares are the most obvious ones to go. What do you think?'

Charles sat back in his chair and contemplated her for a moment before he said, 'Firstly, if I am to give you any financial advice it is that you do not use your own money to fund charitable causes. That is what fund raising is for. And secondly, you are listening to the wrong views in Britain. Too much of your time spent with Major Attlee and Co. I imagine.'

'Clement says Hitler is hell bent on expanding the Spanish war to the whole of Europe.' She crossed her fingers under the table, hoping the man would forgive her for placing words into his mouth. She had no idea if he thought Hitler wanted to expand the war although it was a common enough cry from the left, and she knew Mark remained convinced of it. But her ploy had worked. She had her cousin's full attention. She added, 'If that is the case, I should get my holdings out of Germany don't you think?'

'I am certain Clement Attlee is wrong. Since Herr Hitler took over the reins, Germany has achieved a remarkable recovery. They follow Mussolini's example with a policy of autarky and fund private industry to carry out work on behalf of the government. Hitler's astute financial knowledge has helped the country to shrug off the financial misery inflicted by the Treaty of Versailles. I can assure you that Germany is now stable and prosperous with full employment... more than I can say for Britain.' He gave her another long look.

She smiled at Mark. 'You were right. I do need good financial advice. Thank you.'

Mark nodded and looked away.

Poor man. Beatrice noticed the colour rising in his neck. She continued speaking to Charles. 'I had no idea that you were a financial wizard, my dear cousin.'

Charles cleared his throat. 'Well, I have been across our two families' holdings for a while now. In fact, I recall your father buying your shares in Herr Hauser's company in 1933, back when Adolf Hitler became chancellor. Even then, we saw the potential. I would say those shares have increased significantly in value and will continue to do so. You would be well advised to hold on to them.'

Beatrice pressed her lips together and hummed agreement.

'You sound as if you might doubt me, Cousin.'

She sighed. 'I like to know my money is in good hands, and I am not sure armaments fit the bill.'

'I think if you met Herr Hauser, you would see his company is more than weapons manufacture. I understand he has a new prototype for a motor car, something everyone will be able to afford. That is of course if their design is chosen. It's a fierce competition because Hitler wants a vehicle for the common man, something along the lines of what Henry Ford did for America.'

'How wonderful. Now that is something I would like to invest in. Do you think, if I went to Germany, I would be able to see what they do at the factory?'

A flash of excitement crossed Charles' face. 'I am sure they would be delighted. I can provide a letter of recommendation.'

'Oh, but you must accompany me.'

'My dear Cousin, I have a job to do here, and not everyone has money to burn as you do.'

'Dear Charles, as my financial advisor your expenses would be paid, along with a fee of course.'

Charles tried to hide his glee, but he wasn't much good at it. Were all men that transparent? Perhaps they saw only what they wanted to, ignoring women's emotions while they focussed on their own. Although, she admitted, Mark did try to understand her needs, but Charles had no such concerns.

Charles turned to Mark. 'What about you, my friend? Will you accompany us to Germany? I know you told von Graff you were keen on visiting the country.'

'I am.'

'What about your work here?' Beatrice looked down at her feet.

'Well, it depends on when you are planning to go.'

'I thought straight away.' She said quickly. 'I have finished what I came to do here. If you are going off to film some war front or another, I will be left on my own. I thought, a quick trip while you are away, and back before we return to London. Either that or I will stay in Germany for a little longer and you might join us when you are done. Please Mark, I don't want to hang around a hotel while you are away working. I would be so bored, not to mention lonely. I don't know anyone in Salamanca.'

Mark wiped his hand down his face and looked at Charles. 'I don't know old man. Do you have the time to accompany Beatrice?'

'It would be a pleasure.'

'All right. I will get my work done here then join you in a week. If that's not too long away.' He turned to Charles. 'How are you planning to get to Germany?'

'We can take my car.'

'Isn't it rather a long drive.' Beatrice asked.

Mark smiled. 'Beatrice is mad keen on flying everywhere.'

'Hmm.' Charles said, 'If not the car, I think perhaps we should take the train. Flying in and out of Spain is not as safe as elsewhere. It wasn't long ago some poor English pilot was shot at as he came into land at Burgos airport.'

'A Luft Hansa flight to Berlin will be safe enough I think.' Beatrice smiled. 'I will make the arrangements if you can arrange our visas, dear Charles.'

'You're the boss.' Charles said.

'Thank you, Charles. I can always count on you.' Beatrice cringed inwardly at her toadying. Perhaps she had taken a step too far, but he didn't seem to notice.

Mark got up. 'I have to get to my appointment with Merry del Val.'

Charles raised a brow. The new chief of propaganda and press. What are you seeing him about?'

'Just making connections. Although I hope to get his perspective on the war. He is more forthcoming than Bolín and easier to get an interview with than Franco.'

Two mornings later, Beatrice and Charles left Salamanca for Germany aboard a Deutsche Luft Hansa Junkers G.38. Charles had left his Jaguar for Mark to drive back to Burgos.

As soon as Beatrice and Charles had taken off, Mark began the journey. Everything now would be about timing. He had a week, no more, to make his plan work. If he failed it would be the end of his career and maybe his life. For Javier, it would certainly be a death sentence.

Once he reached the outskirts of Salamanca, he opened the throttle enjoying the power of the Jaguar. He arrived in Burgos before nightfall and let himself into Charles's flat.

At 10 pm, he took out the Jaguar again and drove to the El Campeador café. Carmen looked up as he entered but quickly looked away. Another waitress led him to a table and took his order

After he had eaten, Carmen made eye contact.

He waited for her in the alleyway, the stench more robust than previously. It made his eyes water, and he sighed with relief when he saw her step out the back door of the restaurant.

He gave her his address and returned to the Jaguar to drive back to Charles's apartment.

It was 3 a.m. before he heard the soft knock. Carmen slid inside the moment he opened the door.

'Don't put on the lights.' She whispered.

Mark led her through to the sitting room where a small lamp burned.

She gazed around. 'You have a nice place.'

He took in her clean face, plain black dress, cardigan and felt hat. Before him stood the woman he remembered from Brisbane. 'It's Charles West's place, not mine.'

Alarm crept across her face.

'It's all right. He's not here.'

She relaxed.

'Have you arranged the drivers? He asked.

'Yes. Two. They are ready but say they must have the paperwork in case they are stopped.'

'No problems. I have it.' He picked up an envelope in which he had placed the Rio Tinto headed consignment notes he'd stolen from Charles's desk. 'You will have to fill in the details.'

She nodded. 'Do you know where Javier is now?'

'Not sure. When I saw him two weeks ago, he said he would be in the Santander province. I assumed the prisoners would be with Franco's troops as they try to take the province.'

'Tell me your conversation.'

Mark grimaced. 'There was no conversation. I gave him some black powder and told him to use it as a distraction the night after he next saw me. Other than that, I told him you were well and that I would get him out.'

'That is not a plan. How will he know what he must do?'

Mark ran his hand across the back of his neck. 'I don't know, but how am I to get a message to him.'

Carmen stared at him. 'This is not good.'

'Did you manage to pass my message to the Republic?

'How can I do that?'

He stared, dumbfounded. 'I thought that's what you did.'

Hell, he should have trusted his instincts. Instead of voicing his thoughts aloud, he sighed. 'I was hoping the Republic might send a bombing raid, but I was not able to discuss plans with them.'

'Why not?'

'The Russians got in the way.'

Her mouth turned down with disapproval. Whether for the Russians or for his own ineptitude, he wasn't sure.

It seemed that, if Carmen was a Republican spy, she could not get word to the war ministry in Valencia. On the other hand, she might be covering up. Maybe she had passed it on, and they had not acted on it. Either that, or the Republicans were fighting a defensive war rather than an offensive one. Perhaps that was why they were losing. No. They were losing because of bad advice and interference by the Russians along with a lack of supplies. But he couldn't say any of that to Carmen.

She said, 'So, what is your plan now?'

'I will find Javier, break him out and we will make a run for the Irún border.'

'That is not a plan. Do you have a car, or are you planning to take the mining truck?'

He gazed at her. 'I will take Charles West's car. It is parked here.'

With sarcasm lacing her tone she said. 'What will Javier do? Hide in the boot.'

Mark grinned. 'I have a passport and press credentials as well as clothing for him. When we break Javier out, we can also help the rest of the prisoners, like I promised. You can use the trucks to take them close to the Pyrenees and across into France.

'You are mad.' She shook her head and sighed. 'We tried to arrange a ship to get them out through Santander, but that is impossible now. It has a blocked.'

'A blocked?'

'Si, a blocked.'

'Ah, a blockade.'

'Is what I said.' Carmen placed her hands on her hips. 'But first we must find them and get them out. Have you money?'

'What for?'

'You can bribe the guards.'

343

'That's too risky. Some of them are fanatics and the prisoners have at least one spy in their midst.'

Carmen blew out through her lips. 'I will talk to my comrades, but they will want the prisoners to remain in España. We need them at the front.'

'At the front! The war is all but lost Carmen. They need to get out before they are all killed. So should you. Maybe I should come with you and talk to your comrades.'

'They will not see you. You cannot know who they are. If you are caught, the fascist will torture you, and you will give my comrades away.'

'But you must see that things are going badly for the Republic.'

'No. There is a plan. The Republic already moves to take back Zaragosa. Franco will send troops and split his army. It will give the Basque army time to recover, and they will then push back.'

'The Republicans tried that before Bilbao was taken, and it didn't work.'

She shook her head. 'I should not have told you. Now you go. Find out where is Javier but come back and speak to me before you do anything more. I make the arrangements.'

The next day Mark found Luigi Vecoli at Soncillo, north of Burgos. The major had grey smudges under his eyes, and his cheeks were drawn as if he had aged ten years. He told Mark they had been involved in a massive battle at La Virga twenty kilometres to the west, and south of the Rio Ebro, he said pointing at the map.

'The Reds had French armoured vehicles and soviet tanks. Many of my men died, but we have them on the run now. And you were right my friend. The 1st Navarrese Brigade have taken Reinosa, and we have captured many prisoners and supplies. Already we have put the prisoners to work making ammunition for us. Without armaments they are finished. It is not long now.'

A tremor of excitement ran through Mark. He'd guessed right about what Javier tried to tell him. 'What about you? Will you head to Reinosa now?'

'No. Tomorrow we go north to the El Escudo Pass. Then those Red devils have nowhere to go. They will be trapped.'

'How can I get to Reinosa?'

'You don't want to come with us to El Escudo?'

'I would like to see the armaments factory.'

'For your photographs?' Vecoli pursed his mouth. 'You should come with us to the El Escudo Pass. There you will get better pictures of real battle.'

Mark grinned. 'Hard to get good photos of heavy artillery in battle when the enemy is miles away, unless you are planning to use tanks at the Pass, but the mountains will be too steep, I think.'

'I see what you mean. We take the Pass and hold it, trap the Reds in the valley below.'

Mark nodded. 'The camera lens doesn't have the distance guns do. I will get nothing other than your men manning the field guns.'

'What is wrong with that?'

'What does it show the world? That you have artillery. The Red prisoners working in their own factory, forced to make weapons for the Nationalists tells a better story. One of great irony.'

Vecoli frowned as if contemplating this point, then he nodded. 'Irony is good, and you are right my friend. I arrange for Corporal Bianchi to take you. He makes a supply run between Burgos and Reinosa, but you will have to meet him at Burgos. It is too dangerous for you to travel by yourself through Palencia. There are Red bandits everywhere.'

Mark left Soncillo and drove to Bilbao. He checked into a hotel, paying a week in advance for the room. He didn't intend to use the room for at least a few days, but he needed the alibi while he effected Javier's escape.

Then he drove back to Burgos.

When he arrived at the barracks, he'd planned to present himself as an Italian journalist, but it wasn't necessary as the place was wide open. After an enquiry at the gate, he found Corporal Bianchi leaning over a truck's engine.

Bianchi spoke a little English and told Mark he had been expecting him earlier. He'd received orders from Major Vecoli and was ready to leave early the next morning.

'Six o'clock, no later,' Bianchi added.

It didn't give Mark much time.

He headed for the El Campeador café for a late dinner. He had much to arrange and for that he needed Carmen's comrades.

She served him and he asked her when Captain von Graff would return before he dropped his voice to a low murmur.

When she returned with his beer she placed it before him, and leaning in close she said, 'But you don't even know Javier is in Reinosa.'

Mark muttered. 'I think he tried to tell me that when I saw him. Besides, we won't get another chance. Even if we don't find Javier, there are other prisoners and arms. Don't you want to get your hands on them.'

She nodded. 'I will see what I can do. For the men and the weapons my comrades will do much to help you.'

With that he had to trust her, but that night he didn't sleep. Instead, he tossed and turned, imagining everything that could go wrong, and trying to find alternative solutions.

Next morning, he arose, bathed, and dressed before leaving his suitcase, camera and papers in Charles's car. Then he took a bus to the barracks.

Leaving at 6 am, to Corporal Bianchi, meant they didn't get on the road until 7 am, by which time Mark had consumed three cups of strong Italian espresso. He wasn't sure if fear, impatience, or the coffee drove him, but as he climbed into the cab next to Bianchi his hands shook.

Four soldiers climbed into the back of the truck, and they set off. They took the road to Aguilar de Campoo. Mist hung above the road, leaving sprays of glistening droplets across the windscreen. There were no wipers on the passenger side, and the mist obscured his view. Luckily, there were few other vehicles on the road, and they made good time to Aguilar.

As they left the town, they came to a roadblock just outside the town's northern boundaries. A Navarrese private approached and spoke to Bianchi.

He took a wad of folded papers from his top pocket. The soldier waved the papers away and Bianchi placed them into a jockey box next to his seat.

The private walked around to the back of the truck and spoke to the soldiers in Castilian. The soldiers were Italian and clearly didn't speak Spanish. Bianchi called out in bad Spanish, and the soldier spat on the ground. He cleared the back of the truck and arrived at Mark's window. 'Papers.' He held out his hand.

Mark handed him his passport, along with his press credentials and the pass Vecoli had given him.

The soldier turned the passport, the pass, and the press credentials over one by one, then called his sergeant.

Whether he couldn't read or was merely suspicious Mark couldn't tell. Blood rose and a pulse thumped in his throat.

The sergeant barely glanced at the papers before waving them through.

Mark let out his breath and fixed his gaze on the horizon.

They drove on through bomb damaged fields, now fallow and overgrown, until they passed a small village and a ruined church, blackened by fire and age. Half a mile past the village, the road dipped and ran alongside an oak forest growing close to the side of the road.

They had only travelled a quarter mile farther, when a bend obscured the road ahead. As they rounded the bend they came to a bridge over a gully.

Bianchi swore. Beyond the gully, a large tree lay across the road blocking their way. Bianchi alighted from the cab and shouted to the soldiers in the back of the truck.

It took a moment for the tree's significance to dawn on Mark. Rather than getting out to help as he normally would have done, he stayed where he was, pressed against the seat as if it might absorb him.

The four soldiers, rifles in hand, took their places next to the leafy branches of the tree and heaved. The tree didn't move. Bianchi ordered them to the other end where they placed their weapons on the ground before all four soldiers put shoulders to the trunk and heaved. The tree moved a few feet.

Bianchi stood in the middle of the road with his rifle held across his chest and shouted orders. The soldiers stood back and flexed before readying themselves for a new attempt.

Perhaps this was not the place after all. Mark opened the truck door to alight the cab.

The air cracked and Bianchi fell backwards, blood spurting from his jugular, his rifle clattering to the road.

A moment of precious time passed, while Mark along with the Italian soldiers processed the corporal's collapse. By the time they realised what had happened they were surrounded by armed men.

Mark counted eight although one of them was a boy of about sixteen, and another an old man who looked like the boy's grandfather. None wore military uniforms but dressed in an assortment of labourers clothing, along with the ubiquitous black Basque beret. All but the boy carried rifles.

Oddly, the boy seemed to be in charge, waving a pistol to indicate his intentions.

With a glance at their rifles laying where they had left them, the Italian soldiers raised their hands.

Mark jumped down from the cab and stood silently. No words were exchanged but two of the newcomers tied ropes around the tree. The boy waved his pistol and the other men along with the Italian soldiers hauled it off the road.

The boy turned toward Mark.

'Carmen! I didn't realise it was you.'

She stalked over to him wearing men's clothing with her hair tucked into the black beret. 'You're late.'

'We didn't leave on time.'

She spoke to the old man, pointing to Bianchi's corpse. Strip him. She turned back to Mark. 'You wear the uniform. She walked off to supervise the other men while the old man deftly took the boots, jacket, and trousers off Bianchi's corpse.

Bianchi lay in his underwear as the old man walked towards Mark. 'Saludo camarada. Eres Marcos Andrés?'

Mark nodded. 'Saludo. Si, I am Mark Anders.'

He handed the corporal's rifle and uniform to Mark. 'You do a good thing for my nephew, comrade.'

Mark said, 'Your nephew?'

'Si. Javier. My sister's son. She is on my back all the time.' He grinned. 'Now I can give her good news.'

'Javier's mother is here?'

'She is in America.'

'So, Carmen is your daughter.'

'Si.' He turned fond eyes towards her. 'She is a warrior.'

'She is indeed.' Mark took the uniform and placed the rifle against the truck. The Corpo Truppe Volontarie wore their distinct Italian military uniforms rather than those of Franco's army.

He stripped off and donned the corporal's uniform. There was wet blood on the collar of the black shirt, and on the jacket. The trousers were a bit short, the puttees tight, but the Bianchi's boots were too small. His own ankle boots were not too dissimilar so they would have to do. In any case, uniforms in Franco's army had become an eclectic assortment of traditional khaki summer gear accessorised by German military supply and divisional, or country of origin, allegiances.

Carmen's father said, 'I look after your clothes. Now you help.'

'Sure.'

He returned to the corpse and Mark followed. Together they picked up the dead corporal, dressed only in his undergarments, and deposited him a little way into the forest.

Mark stared at Bianchi's corpse lying on the ground. He didn't look human any longer. The angle of the limbs was all wrong. For a fleeting moment, Mark felt a twinge of remorse over the man's death. Not the grisly nature of it, but its futility.

This was war! The death of the enemy, a necessity. Mark returned to the truck with a dawning realisation that he'd gone beyond reporting to become a player, taking sides, rationalising murder. Yet hadn't he always taken a side and fooled himself into believing otherwise?

Carmen called to him. 'You speak Italian?

Mark nodded.

'Good. Tell the soldiers to take off their uniforms.'

When they had stripped, four of Carmen's men donned the uniforms over their own clothes, leaving the Italian soldiers in their undergarments. The Basques handed their own rifles to Carmen's father and picked up the Italians' rifles.

Four of the Basques, now in Italian army uniforms, leaped on to the back of the truck, while one climbed into the passenger seat of the cab.

Mark held up a hand to Carmen in thanks, pulled himself into the driver's seat, put the truck into gear and released the clutch.

Ahead, Carmen ordered the Italian prisoners forward with a wave of her pistol. They walked towards the trees where Bianchi lay. The forest closed behind the men, but before Carmen followed them she glanced back towards Mark, held up a clenched fist, and then ducked under a branch and disappeared.

Mark drove onto the bridge. Aside from scattered leaves across the road, and a tree lying off to one side, no one would know what had taken place moments ago. The whole exercise had taken less than fifteen minutes. It was carried off with such precision it was as though they had practiced it. Perhaps they had.

He held out his hand to his passenger. 'Saludo camarada. He added, 'I'm Mark Anders.'

The man grinned and spoke erasable Italian. 'You are corporal...' He stretched out his hand and plucked an ID booklet from Mark's top pocket. 'Ha. Si. Caporal Maggiore Tommaso Bianchi.'

Mark nodded. 'And you?'

The man pulled out the ID from his own top pocket and examined it. 'Soldato Aldo Ajello.'

'What will you do with the Italians?'

The fake Aldo ran his thumb across his throat and placed his finger to his mouth. 'Guns too much noise.' He said in English.

Mark stifled his conscience and asked, 'Where did you learn to speak English and Italian?'

'Before these bastards,' he spat out the window, 'my father was with the Spanish embassy. We lived in many countries. I learn little of each language. Carmen says you are Australian.'

'Yes.'

'How do you know Javier?'

'I worked in the cane fields with him in Australia.'

'Ahh.' He glanced ahead and placed his finger against his lips again. 'We come to Reinosa. Now, we speak only Italian.'

Mark said in Italian. 'You know where the armament's factory is in Reinosa?'

'Si. Before now, this is where I worked. But you must first go to the barracks and report. What is your reason?'

'Reason?'

The man nodded.

Mark shrugged. 'I don't understand.'

Aldo leaned towards Mark and scabbled in the Jockey box, pulling out the consignment note that Bianchi had stowed earlier.

'Here is your reason.' He read out the list of ammunition required, and as he read his voice became excited. 'Ha. These are supplies for the front.'

'Maybe supplies for the Italian artillery troops. They were heading for El Escudo.'

Aldo grinned and in his mangled Italian he said, 'We deliver.' He laughed, delighted with himself. 'How many prisoners do you escape?'

Mark shrugged. 'I don't know. We'll have to work out a plan when we get there. But I am most concerned with Javier. By the way, the Francoists know him as Alvaro Ruiz.'

Aldo nodded. 'But only Javier can go with you. His Madre is sick. Carmen says he must go to her. The rest we take with us. Soldiers and ammunition for the Republic.'

Mark glanced across at Aldo. 'How are we going to get all the prisoners out?'

'You look to Javier. We do the rest.'

When they arrived in Reinosa, he directed Mark to the garrison entry.

Mark pulled up at the gate and handed over Bianchi's booklet, speaking first in Italian before switching to Spanish, and emphasising his Italian accent.

The Carlists at the gate nodded and checked the truck. He spoke to the men in the back.

Mark got down and said, 'They don't speak Spanish.'

For a moment, the soldier paused. Mark's heart jumped into his throat. Then the Carlist soldier shrugged and moved on to Aldo.

Aldo spoke in Italian.

Luckily the soldier didn't know the language, or he would soon realise Aldo wasn't much good at it.

Eventually, the soldier waved them through, telling Mark to head towards an administration building to check in.

They had to cross a forecourt through milling Nationalist soldiers, and Mark's heart pounded in his chest. Having Aldo at his side gave him some reassurance. A bit like contracting a cold and hoping it would prevent catching the plague, the reassurance remained irrational, but nice to have a more benign companion at your side.

The registration went off without much difficulty. Mark, in keeping with his cover, spoke first in Italian before switching to Spanish.

Aldo ostensibly spoke no Spanish or only a few words, but he remained attentive, delivering the odd prompt quietly to Mark in his execrable Italian.

They were then shown to the guest quarters and told to be at the armaments factory at 9 am the next morning.

A portion of a Navarrese Brigade managed the garrison, made up of the administrators, those too young, and those in charge of logistics, or at least those not required on the front line. There were no German or Italian units in sight.

The Navarrese soldiers seemed relaxed and almost in a holiday mood, friendly and chatty until they found communication with the Italians too difficult. Mark and Aldo wandered around the garrison until they had become familiar with the barracks area and were recognisable enough to the Navarrese soldiers.

When they left the compound to look around the town no one stopped them. The Rio Izarilla ran along side of them, and Aldo explained the Rio Ebro lay to their east and the Rio Hijah to their west. Aldo added they would find the armaments factory in the latter direction, but first they would go east.

They walked until they came to a Catholic church. The Angelus rang out in commemoration of the Incarnation and the Passion of Christ.

Mark said, '12 o'clock,' and glanced at Aldo.

'You know the Angelus, my friend.'

'I was brought up a Catholic,' Mark said, 'but I don't know why we are here.'

Aldo grinned. 'This is my brother's church.'

'He is a priest.'

Aldo nodded. 'Si, and he will help us.'

'I thought the Catholic church supported Franco.'

'Bishop Mateo Mugica Urrestarazu in Vittoria refused to sign the Catholic bishops' letter supporting Franco, and my brother reveres his bishop.' Aldo shrugged. 'But he is also a priest who loves the God of the New Testament, but not the Spanish church and not Franco.' He paused then said, 'My family had a farm near Urbasa, on the Ebro. It is where we were born. You know it?'

Mark shook his head.

'Now it is the graveyard for my family. General Molo's men killed them. Only my brother and I escaped. He was at the seminary in Burgos when the coup happened, and I worked here in the factory at Reinosa. The circle of fate and retribution has good symmetry, yes?'

A half hour later, Aldo walked out of the sacristy, dressed as a priest, and with his brother in tow. He introduced his brother to Mark.

The brother gave them directions to where the prisoners were kept in their barracks and handed over a brown paper bundle with Aldo's Italian uniform including his boots.

Aldo and Mark walked back the way they had come. Before they had gone halfway, they turned off and crossed a bridge.

'If Javier is there, I should warn you that there was a traidor with his group,' Mark said, using the Spanish word for traitor. 'He calls himself Pedro Pérez.'

Ahead they saw the stone walls of the munitions factory compound. Mark hunkered down in a tree thicket a short distance from the gate and watched Aldo as he walked towards the guard house.

From his hideout, Mark noted the top of what he presumed were the prisoners' quarters at the back of the factory. They looked like hastily erected sandstone walls, roofed in canvas.

A guard came out wearing a red beret and Mark sighed with relief. The Carlists were Catholic fanatics unlike the less devout Falangists. A Carlist would be more receptive to Aldo's claim to be bringing the word of God to the fallen heathens.

Nevertheless, Mark breathed shallowly until the guard opened the barrier to let Aldo through. Now all he had to do was wait, although he wasn't sure the ruse would work, or even if they would find Javier.

An hour later the guard changed, and Mark waited for another hour. Eventually he saw movement. The priest returned.

He raised his hand in blessing as he spoke to the guard. The soldier knelt and crossed himself. He then stood and raised the barrier for the priest to leave.

The priest walked with a slight limp along the road looking neither left nor right. Once Mark was sure no one had followed he revealed himself and fell into step.

'Javier.'

Javier turned, saw Mark, and grinned. 'Fuck. That was bold.'

'Did it go all right?'

'Yeah, but I don't know for how long. That bastard Pérez will figure it out, soon as he sees him. It's good to see you again, comrade.'

'Will the others be all right?'

'Yes, they are loyal. It's just Pérez.'

'Aldo knows about Pérez.'

'Aldo?'

Mark shrugged. 'The priest... oh hell, I don't know his name. It's a long story. Come on we'd better hurry. We must be back at the compound before dark, but first, there is a culvert along here where you can change your robes for an Italian private's uniform. You are the new Aldo, and you do not speak Spanish.'

'I can't speak Italian, mate.'

'No one else around here can either. It seems to be exclusively under Navarrese control. The Italians are over to the east. They have the loyalist Republicans trapped in the valley between here and the Sierra del Escudo.'

'I heard. The guards brag a lot. So, what happens next?'

'I'm in the dark about most of it, but the deal I made with your cousin Carmen...'

'Carmen!'

'Yes mate. She is amazing. From what I have seen she oversees a small band of behind the line fighters.'

'Los guerrilleros.'

'I guess.'

Javier's eyes opened as he stared at Mark. 'She has done this.'

'And a lot more, I think.'

'So, what happens next?'

'We go ahead and pick up the Italian's armaments consignment tomorrow morning. It was destined for El Escudo and the Italian forces, who I understand were heading to Lanchares. We drive the truck with the armaments back towards Burgos. Aldo said they would meet us on the way then take the truck south to the Aragon Front. With any luck, by the time anyone realises it's gone astray they will be in Republican territory. Or that is the plan as far as I know it. Carmen keeps her business close to her chest. My job is to get you out of Spain. We will travel as reporters. I have clothes, an American passport, and papers for you in Burgos. It's pretty easy to travel around Franco controlled areas if you have the right papers and keep out of the main army's way. They tend to congregate in the towns and ignore the bush roads. Also, they don't have an extensive network of patrols or surveillance. So, getting out of the country is relatively easy if you have an exit visa, which you have. Getting in is the harder part.'

'I should join Carmen.'

'Javier mate. The war's lost. It would be better if you persuaded Carmen to come with us, rather than to stay here with her. Besides, you don't look like you are capable of rejoining the fight.'

Javier nodded. 'I am not strong. They don't feed us, but you think the war is lost.'

'I'm fairly sure. The Republic has nothing left to fight with. They'll be chucking rocks at Franco's army before long, but Franco has all the resources he needs from the Germans and Italians.'

'Russia will send more weapons for the Republic.'

'Maybe. Although to date they have been pretty stingy about supplying enough weapons, fighters, fuel or anything other than advisors. There are always plenty of those.'

Escape

At 9am the next morning, Mark drove to the armaments factory and pulled up at the gate. A sentry took his papers into the guard house before returning them with an approved stamp. Mark put the truck into gear and followed the signs to the loading zone.

He pulled up and alighted the vehicle, with Javier following. They walked to the back of the truck, and Mark told the men to disembark. He spoke in Italian. None of them understood him, but his gestures were enough for them to get the meaning.

They stood about waiting until a Navarrese sergeant arrived, checked the paperwork, and called another guard, who rounded up prisoners to load the truck alongside Carmen's men.

Mark noticed Aldo stood with the prisoner contingent, but he could not see the traitor Pérez.

Loading the crates seemed to go on forever and Mark could scarcely breath with the tension. It would not take much for their ruse to be uncovered. He let out an inaudible breath as the final crates were loaded.

He signed some papers with an illegible squiggle and waited for the official to stamp them. But the man wanted to chat.

'How were things on the drive from Burgos?'

Mark replied in a mix of broken Spanish and a stream of Italian, nodding like a fool along the way.

The official looked puzzled and scratched his chin. Was he suspicious. The cords in Mark's neck ached. Finally, the man stamped the consignment note.

Then he said, 'Wait here.'

Fuck! They couldn't wait. What the hell was the matter? He cast a glance towards Aldo, who was standing with the prisoners Where was Pérez?

Mark wasn't going to hang around to find out and climbed back into the cab. Javier and the rest of Carmen's guerrillas followed suit. Once in the cab, Mark saw the official speaking to a soldier.

He muttered, 'Mate, hang on to your hat. We are getting out of here.'

Just as Mark put the truck into gear, an explosion came from the direction of the prisoners' quarters.

Javier ducked, then glanced at Mark sheepishly. 'Bad habit. That will be your black powder. I gave it to Aldo when we swopped clothing.'

The soldier, speaking to the official, swung around and with an expression of puzzlement on his face, he raced toward the exit.

Aldo and the other prisoners began to mill about randomly. Guards shouted orders, trying to reestablish control.

Mark pressed down gently on the accelerator. The official waved and ran towards him, but Mark pretended he hadn't seen him. He wanted to be as far away as possible, although without unseemly haste.

They exited the factory area as soldiers began to stream in through the gates. No one stopped them. The sound of another explosion reached them. This time it sounded like a mortar, quickly followed by another. Again, the sound came from the other side of the complex.

Soldiers poured out of buildings, running into the quadrangle, leaping aboard vehicles, or racing on foot toward the other side of the factory. The rattle of a machine gun started up along with rifle fire. Mark didn't know who was shooting but it sounded like the beginning of a full-blown battle on the other side of the compound. He hoped the explosions would help Aldo, and the rest of the prisoners, escape.

No one stopped Mark's crew. They left the garrison and passed the town limits, before hurtling along the open road. Mark's foot pressed flat against the floor of the cab, trying to get every ounce of power from the truck, while his shoulders and neck burned with anticipation of attack.

Two miles down the road he rounded a bend. Two trucks were parked at angles across the road. Shit, could he get through? Then he saw Charles's Jaguar on the roadside. Carmen sat in the driver's seat. He stomped on the breaks, screeching to a halt just metres away from one of the parked trucks.

Carmen called out, 'Follow me.'

363

The parked trucks moved out of his way, and he followed her as she turned off down a side road. In his rear mirror he noted the mining trucks were following behind him.

After they had driven a few hundred yards, Carmen stopped and got out. She ran to the passenger's side of the truck.

Javier opened the door and climbed down to hug his cousin. His uncle joined them, and they clasped each other's arms. Javier began to move among the men shaking hands and embracing those he knew.

Carmen became impatient at the chatter. At her command the men immediately left off greetings and began unloading the supplies from the Italian's truck. They reloaded the armament boxes into the mining vehicles.

She turned to Mark and Javier. 'Go now!' She thrust the car key, his civilian clothing, and a map at Mark. 'I have marked the farm roads, circumventing major towns. It will be slower, but you can avoid Franco's roadblocks.'

Mark strode to the car and opened the boot. He took out the changes of clothes he'd packed for Javier and began stripping off the Italian corporal's uniform. When both men had changed into civilian clothing suitable for a journalist, press bands and all, Mark gave Carmen the Italian uniforms and shook her hand. 'Make good use of them.'

She said, 'They will be returned to their owners along with the truck.' She pointed, and Mark saw the bodies laid out on the side of the road.

Brutal but clever.

He frowned, shook his head and said, 'I wish you would come with us.'

She stared at Mark. 'This is my country. I must fight to save it.' She embraced and kissed Javier. 'Go now before they come looking. We will make this look like a bandido ambush for the Italians. They will not find evidence Mark Anders came this way.'

The driver of one of the mining trucks watched them before averting his face.

Mark asked, 'Is that Esteban Díaz?

'Is better not to ask questions.' She turned her back and walked towards her men.

Mark called after her. 'What about Aldo, will he be all right?'

She turned with a frown. 'Who is Aldo?'

'The man who did the prison swap with Javier.'

She smiled. 'He will be fine. We go now to find him and the others at our rendezvous.'

Mark got into the car, and with Javier in the passenger seat, they took off along a farm track, barely a rut. He handed the map to Javier. 'You navigate mate.'

'I should stay with my uncle and Carmen.' He turned to look back at his cousin with a strained look on his face.

'No, you should not. We didn't do all this so you could get yourself killed. Besides, I understand your mother is ill and needs you back home.'

'My Madre...'

'Yes.'

'How do you know?'

Mark shrugged. 'Your uncle told me. That guerilla group made the decision that you must go home. Besides mate, you have done enough. When you recover your health, you can do a tour of the States to raise awareness. Raise money. Get the Americans to intervene. Only the intervention of Britain and America can save the Republic, and at present, they don't look like they are about to lift an eyebrow let alone a finger.'

'I don't understand why.'

Javier's eyes glinted with what to Mark looked like guilt or tears. He didn't know which, but he pressed down on the accelerator. Saving Javier was the only thing about this whole bloody war that seemed within his control, and he wasn't going to stop until it was done. Javier wasn't going to sabotage his survival through some misguided sense of martyrdom. To hell with that, but he couldn't say any of that to Javier. So, he said, 'Me neither mate, me neither.'

They drove all day through back roads and tracks, now and again pulling into tree corpses to hide from overhead planes or convoys of military vehicles. It was late when they reached Irún.

This was the decisive moment. Denton had arranged a forged exit stamp on Javier's papers, but whether it would work was yet to be tested. Their next move rested in the lap of fortune.

Mark watched Javier as he walked towards the border post. Before returning to Burgos to request his own exit visa, he would need to complete the earlier preparations he'd made for establishing his alibi.

He turned away. Javier would be in good hands. Denton had arranged for a British embassy official to meet him on the French side of the border. He'd see him again in a few days, as soon as he returned to London himself.

Mark left Irún and drove until the sun had gone and darkness shrouded the road ahead. When he found a secluded spot he pulled over to catch an hour's sleep. Folding his limbs in the cramped and cold car to lie down seemed impossible, but now the adrenalin had worn off, it was either stop and sleep or fall asleep while driving, which was never a good idea.

When he awoke, he continued his journey along back roads until he arrived in Bilbao. It was 7 am when he let himself into the hotel room he'd previously booked for the week. He bathed, changed, and went out to find coffee and breakfast, speaking to anyone who crossed his path, hoping if they were later asked, they would remember he was here.

After he'd eaten, he walked to the press censor's office. Other journalists already occupied most of the desks and chairs. The Franco government now had access to international telephone communications, thanks to the Basque Army who had chosen not to destroy Bilbao before they retreated.

While in the press office he learned that 15 battalions of Basque soldiers had surrendered to the Italians. The Pact of Santoña they called it. The remains of the Army fled west. Santander city was now just days away from falling to the Nationalists, and the Santander province was all but lost.

Speculation swirled around the office that Franco's focus would turn to Asturias, the last stronghold of the Republic in the north of the country. Mark found an unoccupied space and sat down to read a pile of papers from the past few days.

Only one day had passed, and none of the articles mentioned trouble in Reinosa, a missing truck load of weapons, an ambush, nor any escaped prisoners. Instead, the papers were full of stories about the surrender of the Republicans, Franco glorious advances, and three German diplomats who had been expelled from London ostensibly on spying charges.

The Times quoted Herr Woermann, the German Charge d'Affaires in London, as saying, Mr. Norman Ebbutt must remove himself from Germany within the fortnight because of activity outside his professional duties.

Norman Ebbutt was the chief correspondent of *The Times* in Germany. A bit of tit for tat. Poor old Ebbutt. Mark had only met him once, but he was a straight shooter who didn't much like the Nazis. He had been warning Geoffrey Dawson for years about them, but Dawson was too intent on playing down the Nazi threat and moderated all Ebbutt's copy to keep the Germans on side. At least Ebbutt's expulsion might change Dawson's mind about being a friend of Germany's.

Mark joined a group of journalists for dinner before he returned to the hotel for a night's sleep. Much to his relief, there were still no rumours circulating about the breakout yesterday. The next morning, he checked out and drove back to Burgos via Vittoria.

All the way, he debated with himself whether he should follow the war west to Asturias or get out of Franco territory before his luck ran out. He was tempted to see it out, bluff his way through. Maintain his innocence, arguing, if they asked, that he had decided not to go with Bianche, but had instead headed for Burgos.

After all, he had established he had been in Burgos all week so why would anyone think differently? The only people who might dispute his account were the soldiers at the roadblock outside Aguilar de Campoo. They had seen his passport, but with any luck they were illiterate and would not recall his name.

But Beatrice waited for him in Germany. Dawson expected Mark to travel to Switzerland next, to cover the conference in Nyon. Besides, how hard would it be to put two and two together when they discovered that Corporal Bianche's delivery had been hijacked.

It seemed strange the press had not got hold of it. Although Franco's people were not keen on publishing losses, only victories. In reality, he had one option. He needed to obtain an exit visa from the Burgos press office, and leave the country before the trail of evidence, showing that he had accompanied Bianche on his trip to Reinosa, coalesced into his obvious guilt. It wouldn't take much for a good detective to figure out his role in the Reinosa escape.

A sadness came over him. He would be unlikely to return to Spain. Personna non grata in both the north and the south, when all he had wanted was tell the truth to the world. Although, he had discovered, the truth was as slippery as the Wild River Sooty Grunter he'd tried, as a kid, to catch with his bare hands.

Berlin

Mark arrived on the train in one piece, thank goodness, and after settling into the hotel, Beatrice took him for a walk in the Tiergarten. While they strolled along the park's pathways he relayed what had happened, from the time she and Charles had left Salamanca until he had left Spain.

Javier had travelled to England, where her grandfather had taken him in. Disappointingly, Mark had no idea how Carmen and her men had got along after he had left them outside Reinosa.

Beatrice felt a flair of jealousy as he talked about Carmen. How fearless the woman sounded. Carmen had risked everything to rescue her cousin, more than she could see herself doing for Charles. In any case, Mark had survived and got away, seemingly without suspicion.

They walked back, arm in arm, to the hotel for lunch. Every few yards red and black banners, emblazoned with swastika, hung from buildings. Surely, with all this festive bunting, the

German people must believe in their own government. For unlike Britain, there were no anti-fascist street protests here.

After lunch, Beatrice needed a bath and a rest. Mark left her, saying he would explore the city further. He was so late back she began to worry.

When he returned several hours later he said, 'We should make plans to go home.'

'Why? You only just arrived.'

'I have to get back to work.'

'Is that all?'

'Yes. What else would it be? You have done what you came for. What is the point of remaining?'

'Don't you want to see Berlin.'

'I have seen enough.'

She frowned. 'You don't seem quite yourself.'

'Sorry. The last couple of weeks have been stressful, and I am expected to cover the conference at Nyon. I think I need a holiday. Perhaps, before I go, we could spend a few days in Paris, just to reset my equilibrium.'

'Why not take a break here.'

'Beatrice, you must know there will be no rest here. The invitations you have received would keep us busy for a year. Perhaps we can come back another time, when I am not trying to squeeze in a holiday between assignments.'

'I see.' Although she didn't and glanced at him sideways. 'I cannot leave until we have said goodbye to everyone properly.'

'We will see the Hauser's this evening. You can say goodbye then.'

'I mean to make my farewell properly. They have been incredibly hospitable, and I need to at least repay them in a small way. Perhaps I can prevail on the hotel to arrange a cocktail party. That would be the easiest as I can return all the hospitality Charles and I have received with one event.'

He grimaced. 'Can't we just say goodbye.'

'Mark, the people I have met here have been wonderful to Charles and me. I wouldn't dream of leaving without thanking them properly, but a nice cocktail party can achieve that quite simply.'

'How long would you need to arrange a party.'

'I will ask the hotel, but we will need to give our guests adequate notice.'

He tightened his lips but did not argue further.

That night Mark took his camera and all his film with him in his camera bag, so as not to have a repeat of Paris. He could not let the film fall into the hands of the Gestapo or they would be done for. He shouldn't have taken such a risk with Beatrice at his side, but Denton thought it important, although he had warned Mark to leave immediately afterwards.

They dined with the Hauser's and Beatrice broached the subject of leaving and invited them to her cocktail party. As Mark had missed most of the tours she and Charles had done together, he prevailed on Mr Hauser to escort him on a tour of the factory the next day.

She suggested Charles accompany her to the zoo. Clara and Mrs Hauser immediately insisted on escorting her.

Elke Hauser said, 'The driver can pick you up at the hotel.'

The next morning, after breakfast, and before they dashed off on their various excursions, Mark walked with Beatrice to the lift but then stopped. 'I need to visit the embassy. Do you mind if I leave you alone for an hour. I will be back before the Hausers call for us.'

'An hour! It's only next door.'

'Yes. Perhaps less. I won't be long.'

'Why do you need to go to the embassy?'

'I need to sort out some visa issues, for the Nyon trip.'

'Why can't you telephone from the suite.'

His face creased into a worried frown.

'Mark what is going on?'

He took her in an embrace, as though to say goodbye, and placed his mouth against her ear. 'I need to give them my film to send to your granddad.'

She narrowed her eyes and said in a low voice, 'Why?'

He kissed her cheek murmuring against her skin, 'I don't think it's safe to take photos without going through the Berlin press office.'

She whispered back. 'That doesn't make sense.'

He let her go and placed his finger against her lips before tucking a stray curl behind her ear. His face had that please-understand look.

She pulled a disbelieving grimace. Really, this took things too far, but she said as softly as she could, 'Surely, they will expect a tourist to take photos.'

'I won't be long.'

She smiled and tucked her arm through his. 'Then I am coming with you.'

He sighed.

Once they were out in the street, Beatrice said, 'You are hiding something from me Mark. I can tell. What is it?'

He glanced around before saying softly, 'Beatrice not everything is as it seems on the surface here. You have only seen what they want you to see.'

'What do you mean?'

'Let's not talk of it. You never know who might be listening.'

Beatrice opened her mouth to insist he explain but thought better of it. Mark wasn't one to dramatize without cause. Besides, he might be right. She'd been shown a prosperous and harmonious Germany. With all the wonderful hospitality she had received since arriving, she had fleetingly forgotten the awful stories she had heard from the Jewish refugees.

Once inside the embassy, Mark disappeared with an official leaving her in a waiting room, accompanied by a fashion magazine. A woman brought her tea in a service, monogramed with the stamp of the British government, and left her alone with a women's magazine.

Mark seemed to take forever, but she supposed it was her own fault for insisting on accompanying him. After all, he had said an hour, but how handing over rolls of film took that long, was anyone's guess. She sighed and returned to flicking through the magazine. This was her grandfather's doing, of that she was certain.

A British Connection

Mark followed the embassy official down a corridor and into a windowless room. A large table, surrounded by chairs, took up most of the space and gave the impression of a meeting or conference room. A telephone sat on the table.

The official turned to Mark, 'Have a seat, You will be connected to London shortly. When you are finished just hang up. I will return to escort you out.'

Mark nodded. 'Thanks.'

The bloke left and the door clicked shut. Left alone Mark tried to put aside his abhorrence of windowless rooms and sat down to stare at the phone. Would it actually ring? If not, how would he know when to pick it up?

Dust motes hung in the still air, and silence pressed against his damaged eardrum, making a sound like the cicadas back home. He glanced at the door. Had he been locked in? What was to stop him leaving to wander about the embassy? An urge to get up and test the door almost overwhelmed him. Nonsense! Surely, they wouldn't lock him in. He arose and strode towards the door. The phone rang. He returned and snatched the receiver from its hook.

Other world noises whistled and whined and then he heard a man's voice. 'Please hold.'

A click and Denton's voice came down the phone, tinny and far away. 'Mark are you there?'

Mark nodded and then remembered to speak. 'Yes sir. I'm here.'

'Good, good. Have any trouble getting in?'

'Not at all. Everything went as planned.' How's Javier.

'His ship leaves for New York in the morning. He said to thank you and that he'd write.'

'Damn I was hoping to see him when we get back. Is he well?'

'He needs to get home to his mother as soon as he can. Doctor gave him a clean bill of health to sail, and he gave us a great deal of information, so thank you from me too. He asked me to tell you he'd write and perhaps you could visit America at some time in the future.'

'That would be interesting.'

'The issue in Berlin. Did you manage to find it?'

'Yes, I have photos. They are compromising so I will need to leave them with someone here to send through to you.'

'The man who showed you the room. You can give him anything you have for me. Other rolls of film too if you like. I can let you have them when you are home.'

Home. Mark smiled. Was London his home now?

Denton said, 'Did you see anything of interest.'

'Not sure what you might find of interest, sir. Gatow is certainly a fully operational air base and training facility. It's quite large, and located about 10 miles west southwest of Berlin, 2 ½ miles southwest of Gatow and 1 ½ miles northwest of Kladow. I marked the coordinates on a map in one of the photos, but they are 52 28 25 north and 13 07 45 east. The runways are grass, and a perimeter road runs along the Eastern and Southern boundaries to the hangar area. There are two large barracks in the woods, one behind the main group of hangars, and the other in a wood off the northwest of the airfield. Oh, and there is a rail line that runs into the complex.'

'Anyone see you?'

'No sir.'

'How did you get all this?'

'I borrowed a delivery bicycle in Kladow. Afterwards, I left it in a field in the other direction from Gadow and then rode a freight train back into Berlin. I don't think anyone saw me. For all they know I was in the hotel, with Beatrice, resting.'

'You've done well Mark, but don't take any more risks. You and Beatrice need to leave Germany as soon as you possibly can. If there is the slightest suspicion... well you know how it is.'

'I spoke to Beatrice already, but my biggest fear were the rolls of film. Once I have got rid of them, we'll be fine.'

'Right. They will send them through to me in a diplomatic bag. That will allow you a breather, so you won't have to make your departure look too hasty. That screams guilt as much as wandering about where you are not supposed to be.'

'If that's all you need from me, we will see you back in London in a week. We plan to stop in Paris for a few days on the way back and before I head off to Nyon.'

'I have something else I wanted to discuss. Well two things. The first is personal, the second business. I planned to wait until you returned to break the personal news, but I shouldn't keep this information from you any longer.'

'That sounds ominous.'

'I hope it is not. I think you are already aware that Dino Grandi attempted to connect you to the banker we met in Rome, Alessandro Contarini.'

'Yes.' Mark felt a shiver run across his shoulders.

'Well, the thing is, I have not been completely honest with you about this...'

He paused but Mark remained silent. He didn't want to hear this. Should he hang up now before Denton forced him to confront something he had avoided all his life?

'You see, I received confirmation in Rome, but I shelved it hoping Contarini himself would say something. When he didn't, I let sleeping dogs lie, so to speak. But now he has. He flew to London last week on banking business and had hoped to meet with you. He was disappointed you were not here and asked me to extend an invitation for you to meet him in Geneva, after you have covered the Nyon conference.

'Why does he want to meet me?'

'I didn't ask, but I assume he seeks to recognise your relationship.'

'There is no relationship. So, it's a waste of time.'

'This is where you are wrong, Mark. As I said, when Beatrice and I went to Rome, I asked the embassy to look into it. They provided me with enough evidence to indicate you are related. I didn't take it further, but Contarini did. He contacted your mother in Australia. She confirmed it.

Oh fuck! She would be furious with him. If it wasn't bad enough that the man was a fascist, he was also an aristocrat, something his Nonno and his stepfather had railed against all Mark's life. He hadn't even told them about Beatrice, well he had, just not her family's status. He'd have to phone... maybe a letter would be safer...

'Mark, are you still there?'

'I'm here. You said, two things. What was the other?'

Denton gave a brief chuckle before he said, 'I expect you would like me to stay out of your family business... So, to work related matters. There is a German chap, a Wehrmacht colonel, with whom I'm acquainted. He's about fifty, tall, slim frame, thinning and greying hair. He will make himself known to you in the next day or two. It will be a brief introduction, where he indicates he has met me and wishes to convey his respects. This meeting is just so you recognise him in future. He and a few likeminded people in Germany's strategic command have ethical and pragmatic issues with the direction the country takes and are keen to work with us in an attempt to change the course. I won't say more now, but you will know when he makes contact. Do nothing. It is only a meeting to establish a connection and perhaps a future corridor.'

Farewell

On their final night in Berlin, Beatrice walked into her party holding Mark's arm. She had to hand it to the hotel. They knew how to do things in style. She gazed about the already crowded room. Bejewelled and furred women in shimmering gowns glided beneath the glittering chandeliers. Many she had met since arriving here. Some she didn't recognise, but then she had left the invitations to the Hausers'.

Frau Hauser had suggested the Black Forest theme, explaining she felt nostalgic for her birthplace. Beatrice had been glad to oblige. Now, attentive waiters looking uncomfortable and faintly disdainful dressed in lederhosen, crisscrossed the room offering champagne, canapes, and cigarettes.

Across the room, a jungle of flowers and foliage banked a painted, moonlit, forest backdrop. A string quartet played in the background, their music a little sombre for both her taste and for a cocktail party. Despite that, the colour, movement, and light, created a sense of by-gone romance, and she loved it. Or perhaps it evoked a tragic romance.

Mark, like Cousin Charles, wore an evening suit or as the Americans called it, a tuxedo, but many of the male guests had come in uniform. Everyone seemed to have a role in some military organisation or another, almost as if they were at war. In a way she supposed they were—In Spain.

She touched the flowing orange silk organza of the new Schiaparelli dinner dress she'd bought in Paris. A little risqué, perhaps, with one shoulder left bare, especially among these conservatively dressed German women. She ignored the scandalised looks she received from the older matrons. With the dress, kitten-heels, and short, bobbed hair, she felt like one of those glamourous American film stars. Acerbic looks down long noses would not spoil her party.

A passing waiter offered a tray of champagne and Mark took two glasses, handing one to her. He raised his glass and smiled at her before his gaze swept across the crowed room. She followed his direction to where Charles stood with Fräulein Hauser.

Before Mark had arrived, Clara and her mother, had accompanied her and Charles on most of the jaunts, dinners, picnics, receptions, and parties, even on a tour of a factory. Elke had also hosted a welcome party when they had first arrived.

She had spared no expense, beginning with a rather vulgar display with fountain of champagne, surrounded by bowls of beluga caviar. A centrepiece her mother would have put down to the ostentation of the nouveau riche. A full orchestra had played in a ballroom, which, Clara had confided, had been inspired by the Galerie des Glaces at the Palace of Versailles.

Beatrice had paused at that and had asked her if she had ever seen the Hall of Mirrors.

Clara blushed and admitted she hadn't.

Even so, the opulence of Clara's home, this lifestyle, and the cocktail party tonight, compared starkly to the accounts of the refugees she had recorded. Mark's concern about being overheard, reminded Beatrice that her experience had been vastly different from that of the refugees who had suffered dreadful treatment. Berlin began to feel murky as if putrefaction hid beneath the pünktlichkeit, the ordnung, the brotkultur and the volkstümliche musik.

Aside from efficiency, order, and food, the omniscient military presence, the street parades and spectacle, were intended to intimidate. Although, in this hotel, one would never know a different world existed in the streets outside.

What did that say about her that she had so easily forgotten? Perhaps not forgotten but put aside the harrowing tales she had heard. As if like a play, life acted out on a glittering stage where the only signs of reality were brief glimpses of truth through shadowy wings.

She had seen some of those on the journey from the airport. Broken-heeled civilians, scurrying through streets, sporting star-patched armbands and holding the hands of thin, downcast children.

Nevertheless, she could not deny the joyful street parades, with the population screaming their support. It made it hard to find fault despite her disapproval of the Nazi regime. Had she been blinded by flattery?

Since that first drive from the airport, hadn't she been driven everywhere in the Hauser's chauffeured Rolls Royce. Other than parades, she had seen little street life through the closed window blinds. Now that she thought about it, it seemed quite strange.

Elke had explained she didn't like the glare. Beatrice had accepted that at face value, but perhaps Mark was right. She had only seen what they had wanted her to see. Up until Mark's arrival, all their outings had been planned by others. Although she had suggested the zoo outing, the arrangements were immediately picked up by Elke Hauser, and once again they had travelled in the Hauser family car.

Beatrice had concluded the flattery was merely because they were after her investment potential. She had been introduced as Lord Denton's granddaughter, an heiress and an investor with significant assets. Like syrup to flies she had told herself as she endured the overly fawning solicitude shown towards her, or more likely towards her money. Cultural differences she had reasoned, but perhaps she had been mistaken. It might, instead, have been the means by which they controlled her movements around the city.

Still, the only reason she had come to Germany was to keep Charles away from Spain, while Mark found Javier. In a way she had also saved her cousin. Perhaps not as dramatically as Carmen's rescue had been, but nevertheless, she had given Charles an ironclad alibi, even if he remained unaware he needed one.

She left off her musing as she saw Herr Hauser and Elke approach with Clara. What had become of Charles? Until tonight, he had hardly left Clara's side, and she expected an announcement any day.

Herr Hauser took her hand and said, 'I am so sad you both must leave us tomorrow. Are you certain you cannot stay longer?'

She glanced at Mark, who in a more assertive voice than the pleasantry warranted said, 'Work calls Herr Hauser. Our flight is booked.'

Elke narrowed her eyes. 'It is such a pity your stay has been so short Mr Anders. You have been able to see little of Germany, I think.'

'I will return, I am sure, but right now my editor wants to see me as soon as I can get back. Beatrice must also get back to work. She has been away too long, and her business cannot survive without her.'

He smiled and Beatrice nodded in agreement. 'I must return to London. Mark is right, I have been away too long.'

Clara said, 'A charity, I understand.'

'For refugees.' Beatrice smiled at Clara. She seemed so sweet, like a pretty porcelain doll with her wide blue eyes and white-blonde hair.

Elke said, 'You mean Jews.'

Beatrice inhaled sharply and held Elke's gaze until the older woman looked away.

The silence lengthened until Clara excused herself. 'I will be back in a minute. I have just seen a friend.' She smiled an apologetic smile and skipped off.

A man in his late twenties with white gold hair, and sapphire-coloured eyes, approached the group and the awkward moment evaporated.

Hauser said a little too heartily, 'Ah, Bernhard my boy. You are back. I am glad to see you.'

The two men shook hands and Berhard kissed Elke.

By his familial resemblance, Beatrice realised this must be the prodigal son, returned from a business trip to Portugal.

After he had been introduced, he bowed and said to Beatrice, 'You are leaving tomorrow. Germany's loss but I also hear you will travel on an aeroplane to Paris. This is adventurous for a woman, is it not?'

He glanced at Mark who placed a hand on her lower back. 'Beatrice is a seasoned traveller.'

Beatrice smiled at Bernhard, but her eyes were drawn to his companion, attired in the dress uniform of the SS.

Bernhard turned to his companion and introduced Dr. Werner Best, police chief and SS-Obergruppenführer.

Best took her hand and held it while he surveyed her with eyes the colour of granite but said nothing.

Beatrice felt a chill run across her shoulders and turned quickly to include Mark. 'Do you know Mr Anders?'

'I have not had the pleasure, but I have heard much about his talents. How do you do Mr Anders. I understand you have recently returned from Spain.'

Mark shook Best's hand. 'Indeed, and I hope to return there soon. I understand General Franco's troops have taken Llanes in northern Asturias and they have the Basque Army surrounded at the Sierra de Cuera.'

'I do not follow the Spanish war closely. My remit is preventing crime on the home front. Did I hear correctly, you are leaving tomorrow?'

'Yes. My editor wants me back in London before I attend the conference in Nyon.'

'That is a pity, as you will miss der Führer's meeting with Mussolini. I have heard you have Italian heritage, and Il Duce is arriving here on a state visit to show friendship and solidarity between our two countries. Your editor may wish for you to cover such an auspicious event for your newspaper.'

Mark smiled, 'If he does, I am sure he will send me back again, for I understand our last correspondent in Berlin was given his marching orders. A touch of quid pro quo, perhaps.'

Best's eyes narrowed. 'An unfortunate event, but it seems Herr Ebbutt is not what he appears. I hope this is not the case for all *The Time's* correspondents.'

Beatrice watched Mark in conversation, with a growing realisation that he had changed. When she had first met him his looks had attracted her, but it was his strong, moral compass that drew her in, particularly as he defended others against injustice or exclusion. His intelligence, level temper, and wisdom beyond his years, cemented the deal. She knew she would have him when he'd confronted her powerful father, the first man she'd known to do so. Selfless courage in the face of power, even after the state imprisoned him for a fabricated crime, set him apart from most of the men she'd met.

Then she had discovered his unwavering sense of justice. It made him a trusted and respected figure among the workers in the region. He stood as a symbol of decency and honour in the face of adversity. That principled behaviour was what she loved most about him. And that characteristic remained, so she could not pinpoint what had changed, exactly.

Certainly, back in Australia he would not have tolerated this company with such aplomb. Perhaps it wasn't him that had changed but something more superficial. The expensive clothing, for example. He wore the evening jacket, she had ordered, with an elegance that was a far cry from the one cheap suit he'd owned when he first arrived in London.

No. It was not just his clothing. Neither had his attitude changed. Although, as he spoke to Best, he had the look of relaxed sophistication, which had not been there in the past.

But even that wasn't it...

Best was looking at her expectantly. She said the first thing that came into her head. 'Will you attend the conference in Nyon, Dr Best?'

Best's lips twitched into a secretive smile. 'My dear Fräulein Langham, Germany is not a member of the League.'

Mark interjected. 'The Nyon conference is not exactly a League conference though, is it? I imagine your government might attend to discuss the issue of submarine attacks in the Mediterranean.'

'And why would we do that?' Best asked. 'The Non-Intervention Committee should rightly handle these issues. Why do the British set up another conference?'

'Isn't shipping safety an important concern for all shipping nations, not just those concerned with the Spanish war?'

'Foreign politics is not my forte.' Best's face greyed and his eyes became no more than slits as if to prevent his thoughts from spilling over.

Beatrice took a small step away, but Best's expression cleared and his voice took on a syrupy edge she didn't trust.

'Perhaps you will both return for a visit at a later date.' He looked at Hauser. 'I am sure you would be welcome.'

Hauser joined in. 'Of course. We would be delighted to extend such an invitation.'

Clara re-joined the group and took her brother's arm. 'Bernhard, welcome home.' She kissed his cheek. 'But you have not introduced me to your charming companion.'

'Ah, you must have met Werner before now.'

'I don't think so.' She fluttered her bunny-rabbit lashes at him.

Best turned and bowed over Clara's hand.

Beatrice took a breath, relieved the man's attention was fully focused on Clara. He seemed dangerous although she could not put her finger on why.

Clara turned to Beatrice, 'Have you seen Charles?'

Beatrice shook her head. 'No, I was wondering where he had got to myself.'

Best said, 'Ahh, I prevailed upon him to show me an investment option he spoke about. He has gone up to his room to collect it for me.'

Clara tossed her head. 'I shall endeavour to find him. He cannot disappear at your farewell party.'

Beatrice smiled, and Clara skipped away.

A sudden longing for England engulfed her. She no longer felt safe in this country. Perhaps she had picked up on Mark's mistrust. People had been nothing but kind to her, but now she was certain she had been prevented from seeing the real Germany. The Hauser's made sure she only saw the affluence. How could she have let herself be so easily beguiled after hearing such harrowing tales from the refugees in London.

Another German officer sauntered over to join Best. 'Please introduce me to our lovely hostess, Dr Best.

Best looked uncomfortable as he introduced Colonel Hans Oster.

Oster took her hand. 'I am delighted to meet you Fräulein, and you must forgive me for attending your party uninvited. But you see I once had the good fortune to meet your grandfather, and I wished to convey my warmest regards.'

Beatrice warmed to the man. There was something easily likable about Oster. Perhaps he reminded her of Grandfather for he had a similar look about him. 'I will certainly pass on your regards, Colonel. How did you and my grandfather meet?'

'I had business a few years ago in Britain, and we dined at your grandfather's club.'

Best excused himself. Bernhard took Herr Hauser's arm and led him a little distance away. Beatrice introduced Oster to Mark.

Mark asked, 'Do you often have occasion to visit Britain, Colonel?'

'Please call me Hans. But to your question, the answer is no Mr Anders. I would like it to be different but alas, no. Which is why I have taken the opportunity to introduce myself to your beautiful fiancée. I perhaps will not get another opportunity.'

Mark said, 'If we are to be on first name terms, my name is Mark. Can I get you a drink Hans?'

'Thank you, but I cannot stay. I understand you will attend the Nyon conference. Perhaps we will meet again soon.'

'I'll look forward to it.'

Oster bowed, clicked his heels so softly the movement went almost unnoticed. Then he bent over Beatrice's hand again. 'Auf Wiedersehen, meine liebe Miss Langham.'

At that moment Charles arrived. 'Cousin. You have outdone yourself. This is truly a wonderful send off.'

Oster nodded, turned and left.

Beatrice said, 'Thank you Charles. I wondered where you had got to and Clara is looking for you.'

'Last minute business to attend to, you know how it is.'

'Yes of course. But wouldn't you like to stay a while longer?'

'If you are leaving, my job here is done. After all, I only travelled here at your request.'

'But I thought you and Clara were getting on so well.'

'And we were..., are. I hope she will visit Spain again soon, but I too have a job to get back to. My plane leaves the day after yours'. He turned to Mark. 'I sincerely hope you have left my Jaguar in good order, old chap. How did you find the drive back from Salamanca?'

Mark grinned. 'That beast flies like the wind. I am envious...'

Beatrice left the two men talking about cars and walked towards another group of guests.

Later that night, as she and Mark entered their suite, she caught a faint whiff of tobacco. Neither she nor Mark smoked but perhaps it lingered from the party on their clothes.

'I need a bath. I reek of tobacco.'

Mark wrinkled his nose and glanced around the room. 'Not sure it is you.'

He walked over to his camera bag. The unused film in the bag was gone as was the spool in the camera.

She was about to say something about Mark having had the forethought to deliver the rest of the film via the embassy, but he once again placed a finger to his mouth.

She stared at him, fury rising in her chest. 'In our suite!' She mouthed.

He nodded and came in close to whisper in her ear. 'They will certainly be listening.'

A cold shudder ran through the length of her body. Leaving this country couldn't come soon enough.

Going Home.

Charles, along with Elke and Clara, saw Mark and Beatrice off at the Tempelhof airport. As usual they travelled in the Hauser's Rolls and saw little of the world they passed through. Charles had arranged to leave the following day, travelling directly to Burgos.

As he embraced Beatrice he said quietly, 'My dear Cousin, thank you for this opportunity and please don't hesitate to write to me if you need any further financial services. I would be only too happy to help in whatever small way I can.'

'You have been invaluable Charles.' Beatrice had almost forgotten the ruse they had used to extract Charles from Spain. Since arriving in Germany, she had barely discussed financial affairs with him at all. He must think her very odd.

He said modestly. 'I have arranged several possible options for your investments and the sale of some of your holdings. I can write up a report and send it to you if that would suit.'

'Absolutely. Thank you Charles.' She blushed with sudden shame. The poor man had gone to so much trouble and it would be for no purpose. She had no intention of buying more shares in Germany, and she would instruct Brian Heggerty to divest any German holdings as soon as possible.

Once seated, she learned the Deutsche Luft Hansa flight would take approximately three hours to reach Le Bourget Airport. She picked up a magazine and relaxed with anticipation of their stay in Paris, a city without fear of eavesdroppers.

Mark had requested the window seat. Now he gazed out the porthole, his face in profile, vulnerable as a young boy in a toy shop. At that instance it dawned on her how Mark had changed. That moment of vulnerability reminded her of the man she had first met in Innisfail. Back then he had not tried to hide his allegiances or his beliefs. He was a man who simply appeared as he was.

Since going to Spain, he had grown into a debonair and sophisticated news reporter. Yet, despite his affability, he now hid more than he revealed behind a complex urbanity that hadn't existed in Australia. Now, it was hard to know who he was, what he believed, or what he stood for. Worse than that, she now found it difficult to read his emotions most of the time.

How had that happened...?

The plane taxied along the runway and Beatrice opened the magazine, but she could not focus. Instead, barely aware of the lurch as the wheels left the tarmac. her thoughts turned over the ramifications of Mark's new façade. It was only when Mark's hand fumbled for hers that she glanced at him again.

'What is it?'

'Magic.' He grinned. 'Just magic.'

The tension left her, and she leaned towards him, trying to see what he saw as he turned to gaze once more out of the porthole.

A few minutes later, when they were fully airborne he turned back to her. 'This is the view the Condor Legion pilots have. They fly over the limestone walls of the Sierra de Cuera, eagle eyes in the sky looking down at the Basque army, mere rats in a maze.'

'That's truly awful, Mark.' She pulled back; her eyes darkened with distress.

'Yes. But don't you see Beatrice... This is the future. Tanks were the advantage in the last war, now it's the aeroplane's turn. Birds of prey rather than slogging it out on the ground.'

'They had aeroplanes in the last war, you know.'

'Those were donkey carts to the racing cars they are developing now.'

He glanced out of the porthole. 'When I get back from Geneva, I want to learn to fly.'

She stared at him for a moment, her mouth pursed. 'You think there will be a war.'

His face when he turned it to her again was grave. 'Perhaps we should return to Australia.'

She closed the magazine. 'Do you mean that?'

He shrugged. 'I don't know Beatrice. I don't know what the best thing is... What do you want to do?'

'A few days in Paris will bring clarity, and then we can decide.'

Mark sighed and sank into the seat before turning his thoughts to the conference ahead. He had to attend that, at least. He'd given his word. Anything else would have to wait. The chosen venue at Nyon separated the meeting from the League's conference in Geneva immediately afterwards. Why the conference at Nyon would proceed without the Spanish Republican government was a mystery. Especially as the issue for discussion remained Republican ships and supplies being sunk.

Admittedly some had been British ships delivering food to the Republic. The British public objected to the Italians playing pirates with their ships. They demanded the government do something. This conference gave Chamberlain an opportunity to pandered to an audience at home, for despite their obvious culpability, none of the politicians wanted to accuse the Italians of piracy directly. He agreed with Denton. Diplomacy in the face of fascism would not work.

Chamberlain had gone further stating that he didn't want the Spanish dispute to get in the way of stopping the piracy. The Russians had no such qualms and took it upon themselves to make a direct accusation. Mind you, they had lost numerous ships to the attacks, so they had good reason. Despite this, the British hadn't wanted to include Russia at the conference.

It wasn't until the French had insisted they were invited. Now Russia had aired the accusation, Italy used it as an excuse to boycott the talks. So, he supposed Chamberlain had a point. Although Denton didn't agree with Chamberlain's solution. He was worried that the conference would give both the Soviets and the Italians far too much information about Britain's strategic interests.

Mark doubted that many in the British leadership even knew where its strategic interests lay. It seemed as if Chamberlain played a wait-and-see game rather than attempting to formulate any kind of strategy. Do nothing and hope for the best. Although for once Eden and Chamberlain seemed to agree about having the conference. Presumably Eden wanted to show that Britain would act if pushed. Chamberlain just needed the problem to go away without upsetting Italy.

As if seizing an opportunity, the Irish delegate had taken the issue into completely different murky waters. He accused Britain of bringing the whole thing on themselves by their punitive actions toward Germany after the Great War. His argument suggested that the only rational outcome was for concessions to be made, including giving Germany back some territories lost in 1919.

What that had to do with Italians sinking British ships, Mark had no idea. It seemed Germany and Italy were winning the propaganda war. Indeed, rather than punitive retaliation against Italy for piracy, some of the League members were calling for their sanctions, imposed after the invasion of Abyssinia, to be lifted. The whole divisive debacle had ignored Italy's piracy, seemingly more concerned with the threat of communism nationalising their wealth.

He knew that wars could not be won or lost on propaganda alone, although winning the propaganda war would help. Mark would have been in despair had he not talked to Denton over the embassy's secure telephone line. At least someone in Britain had a strategic plan and took steps to protect the democratic world. And, as Denton had explained, it seemed they were to have a friendly link into the German spy agency through Colonel Hans Oster.

He closed his eyes. In the beginning, at least for him, journalism had been a means to combat propaganda and expose the truth, but he had failed. Journalism itself was rife with propaganda, depending on who you worked for, and what you believed. Perhaps the truth wasn't as simple a proposition as he had anticipated. For any idea or action to be widely acclaimed as truth, required broad agreement, and in the world right now, such agreement seemed as unlikely as Britain intervening in the Spanish conflict.

It also seemed he had learned nothing but to repeat his own folly. In 1934 he had tried to avoid union politics in the cane fields. Yet he had gone on to almost drown himself in it. If Jack hadn't saved him, he might still be in prison. Earlier this year, he'd left Australia seeking to find and expose the truth of the Spanish war. Instead, he had learned to swim in deception; to become a liar and a thief for the British Crown.

He had wanted his reports on Spain to bring British sympathy to the Spanish Republic's plight, although he'd achieved nothing more than a reputation for himself. Now, for the thrill of the adventure, he had dropped the desire to expose the truth in favour of direct action, by spying on the enemy.

Those first days on the job mocked him. At least then he'd believed in an honest mission no matter how naïve that might seem. Now, he wasn't sure what he chased, and worse, his elusive goals might place Beatrice in danger?

How had he come to this point in his life? There seemed little he could do to change anything. And on top of everything else he had to contend with his mother's ire before he confronted his fascist grandfather! It might be easier to take up Republican arms against Franco.

He hadn't mentioned Denton's conversation with Contarini to Beatrice, hoping he would find some way to free himself from any obligation to the man. Free himself! That was another joke played by fortune on humanity. Like truth, freedom was a subjective value with little agreement to its meaning. But what options were left to him?

Flying! At least that was honest work, which might give one the feeling of freedom. He glanced at Beatrice, in the seat next to him, absorbed in a magazine. Maybe if he learned to fly they could take off together, leaving war and horror behind them. Travel the world and stop where they wanted.

She remained committed to her job saving refugees. An irony, as his career was reporting on the wars that made those same people refugees, all the while, ferrying secrets to and from Denton. His fanciful desire to learn to fly was probably just that, a flight of fantasy. He closed his eyes, needing a break from politics, skulduggery and death. A few days with Beatrice in Paris might be the perfect remedy. After that he'd be fighting fit to once more rejoin the fray, whatever that might bring.

About the Author

Gillian Long has a PhD in creative writing, and a background in publishing, psychology, politics, and executive leadership in both civil service and the not-for-profit sector. She has lived and worked in Africa, and Europe and now lives on a farm in the Australian Wet Tropics of Far North Queensland. Her previous novels, short stories, forthcoming titles, and other writing can be seen athttps://gillianlong.wordpress.com/

A Wilderness of Mirrors
Gillian Long
978-0-9945598-7-6

When Harvey Kashton, a billionaire investor in a bauxite mine, is found dead in the gentlemen's withdrawing room of Bancroft House, the housekeeper Susan Ainsworth acts swiftly to prevent a scandal. Yet within days, his death will bring police, spies, and gangsters all traipsing through the gracious old hotel, but they underestimate Susan's ability to deceive and misdirect. That is, until the unassuming intelligence officer, Chris Davis arrives in this wilderness of mirrors.

The 9th District.

Book 1 in the Mark Anders Series

Gillian Long

ISBN 978-0-9945598-3-8

This historical novel is based on real events set in North Queensland during the great depression, when men's lives are cheap, immigrants are expendable, and a mysterious disease is sweeping through the cane fields.

Mark Anders has had enough. He challenges the powerful sugar industry, and the fight becomes brutal. But Mark's weakness is Beatrice, the daughter of his nemeses who will stop at nothing to discredit a godless Bolshevik.

Disgraced and driven from his home Mark discovers his real heart's desire. It's not his farm or the woman he loves, but does he have the courage to leave everything he built behind to bear witness to the truth?

Greenwash
Gillian Long
ISBN 978-0-6455760-5-4

Set in Queensland this global conspiracy acts out through a local crime, and an environmental disaster as Dr Jack Fallon races against time to expose the truth before catastrophe destroys all he loves.

Jack is often accused of being a loner, but that suits his role as a mining engineer, who spends most of his time in the outback. His mother disappeared under strange circumstances when he was a child, and he took solace in the riches of the earth. But its geological structures are notoriously unstable and may yet take everything he now holds dear including Sophia, the woman he loves.

Becoming Helen
Gillian Long
ISBN 978-0-6455760-0-9

Becoming Helen is a 1930s tale of deceit, disillusionment, and retribution after a British Intelligence Officer compromises a young German girl into spying on her own country, expecting her to lie, cheat and bed chosen German military targets for the Allied cause.

Magdalena von Herff barely knows what name to use before men begin to exploit her beauty, intelligence, and talents, but she soon realises that none are there to help her, except perhaps one—her enemy. Set in Europe, Britain, and America.

Dying Days
Gillian Long
ISBN 978-0-9942671-1-5

Matt Reid, an ex-British Special Forces soldier, arrives in Australia in search of his biological father.

He meets Alan Fletcher, a retired war correspondent, whose story about the disappearance of a Rhodesian SAS soldier in 1980, sends Matt off to Zimbabwe on a mission to find the truth.

What he doesn't plan is to become a person of interest to paranoid secret police or to uncover plots of treachery and revenge and a half century old family feud.

This is a story about discovering family, falling in love and finding redemption.

The Trouble with Maggie
Gillian Long
ISBN 978-0-9942671-8-4

Maggie had everything she wanted; a wonderful husband and
two gorgeous kids. Her life was perfect, until the fateful
moment she ignored her dead grandmother's warning, and her
life changed forever.

Set in rural Australia, this story is about the trials of marriage;
secrets, guilt, love, and temptation, but most of all, it is a story
about Maggie's journey to redemption, while filled with heroism,
hedonism, hanky-panky, and hocus-pocus.

Watershed
Gillian Long
ISBN 978-0-9942671-4-6

It's the end of the 2020s and Australia struggles under tyranny. The economy has collapsed as terrorism escalates. Conscript Blake Lincoln returns from an endless Middle East war, wounded and a national hero. When he meets Charlotte, all he wants is to have his old life back. Instead, he uncovers secrets that will blow the government apart.

Watershed is set in Brisbane, Sydney, and Canberra, and takes in the vast wilderness of Cape York, and the raw beauty of the Kimberly region.

It is a story about the insidiousness of political corruption, the dangers of social injustice, the fragility of democracy and the power of family, as one man prepares to abandon all he believes in to save the woman he loves.